NIGHTINGALE

NINE JACK NIGHTINGALE
SUPERNATURAL SHORT STORIES

By

STEPHEN LEATHER

CONTENTS

STILL BLEEDING... 1

CURSED 51

BLOOD BATH 93

I KNOW WHO DID IT 133

MY NAME IS LYDIA 179

THE CREEPER 211

CHILDREN OF THE DARK 255

TRACKS... 289

THE UNDEAD 325

STILL BLEEDING

Jack Nightingale had never been a fan of Fridays. They always seemed to get in the way of a perfectly good weekend. Friday was always a bad day to start a case and finishing one on a Friday meant the bill wouldn't go out until the following week. All in all, he found it hard to drum up any enthusiasm for Fridays. There were the odd exceptions. Bank Holiday Fridays were always a pleasant surprise, and every now and again New Years Eve and Christmas Day fell on a Friday. This particular Friday was different, though. As soon as he stepped into his office, his assistant Jenny McLean told him that he had a client waiting for him.

'There was nothing in the diary,' said Nightingale, hanging his raincoat by the door.

'I never put anything in the diary because you never open it,' said Jenny. 'He's a priest from the Vatican.' She was wearing a blue dress that looked expensive and had tied her blonde hair back into a ponytail.

'The Vatican?'

'Yes, where the Pope lives.'

'Italy?'

'Well, strictly speaking it's a separate independent city-state, but yes, that's the one.' She pointed at the door to the office. 'He's waiting for you in there.'

'What does a priest want with a private eye?'

'I don't know. Maybe you could ask him.' She shrugged. 'Just a thought.'

'You're in a sarcastic mood today. Coffee?'

'I'd love one.'

Nightingale grinned and shook his head. 'I meant would you bring me one in. And one for the client.'

'I hear and obey,' she said.

'How are we off for chocolate biscuits?'

'Did you buy any?'

'No.'

She smiled sweetly and turned back to her computer monitor. 'Then we haven't got any,' she said.

She went over to their coffee maker as Nightingale headed into his office. A tall dark-haired man with piercing blue eyes was sitting on the chair opposite Nightingale's desk. He was wearing a clerical collar and a floor-length black cassock. He stood up and offered his hand. 'Jonah Connolly,' he said. His accent was difficult to place but it certainly wasn't Italian.

Nightingale shook hands. 'You're from the Vatican, my assistant tells me.'

Connolly smiled. 'I am indeed.' His hand disappeared inside his cassock and reappeared holding a slim black leather wallet.

'But you don't sound Italian.'

The priest gave him a business card and slid the wallet back inside his cassock. 'Not everyone who works at the Vatican is Italian, Mr Nightingale.'

Nightingale studied the card. The name on it read 'Jonah Connolly' and underneath it was a Post Office Box number in Vatican City. And a phone number. A mobile.

'Connolly? So you're Irish?'

'Do I sound Irish?' asked the priest.

'No,' said Nightingale. There was a flatness about the man's accent, not Irish and not English but not American either, somewhere in between. Nightingale walked around his desk and sat down.

'There you go then,' said Connolly as he sat and smoothed the cassock around his legs.

Nightingale tapped the card on the desk. 'And what do you do for the Holy See?'

The priest smiled amiably. 'I'm sort of a middle man.'

'But you are a priest?'

Connolly gestured at the white collar around his neck. 'I'm not wearing this as a fashion statement,' he said.

Nightingale held up the card. 'It doesn't say priest on this.'

'No, that's true. Would it help if I recited the Lord's Prayer? Would that convince you?'

Nightingale smiled thinly. 'How about you tell me what's in Luke Chapter Eleven, Verse Nine.'

The priest raised one eyebrow. 'Are you serious? You want to test me?'

Nightingale said nothing.

Connolly sighed. 'Fine. And I tell you, ask, and it will be given to you; seek, and you will find; knock, and it will be opened to you.'

'Close enough.'

'Perhaps you should also consider Deuteronomy Chapter Six Verse Sixteen. You shall not put the Lord your God to the test, as you tested him at Massah.'

'Yeah, well I'm not testing God, am I? I'm testing his representative, which seems fair enough. Isn't that what John said?'

Connolly frowned. 'John?'

'John Chapter Four, Verse One.'

Connolly's frown deepened, then he nodded slowly. 'Beloved, do not believe every spirit, but test the spirits to see whether they are from God, for many false prophets have gone out into the world.' The priest smiled. 'You know your Bible, Mr Nightingale. Are you by any chance a Catholic?'

'I'm afraid not.'

'But clearly a believer?'

'I read the Bible every now and again. Do I need to be a believer to get the job?' He put the card down on his desk.

'It wouldn't make any difference either way,' said Connolly. 'I came to you because your website makes it clear that you have some expertise in supernatural matters.'

'I've had my moments,' said Nightingale. 'What is it you want doing?'

The priest bent down and Nightingale realized there was a battered leather briefcase at his feet. Connolly picked it up, opened it, and took out a newspaper. He passed it over to Nightingale. 'Page three,' he said.

The paper was the Bromley Times, and the story was headlined 'MIRACLE GIRL HEALS CANCER SCHOOLBOY'. Nightingale quickly read through the story. A twelve-year-old girl had begun to bleed from her hands and feet and from a wound in her side. Stigmata. The wounds corresponded to the wounds of Christ on the cross. The girl's name was Tracey Spradbery and according to the newspaper the Virgin Mary had appeared to her in a vision. Living next door to Tracey and her family was a ten-year-old boy who had Leukaemia. According to the boy's parents, the disease had gone into remission the day after he had gone around to play with Tracey and after a week doctors had pronounced him fully cured.

'Interesting,' said Nightingale. He looked at the date of the cutting. It had been published a month earlier. 'This is a big story, why haven't I seen this in the nationals? Or on TV?'

'Because as soon as that appeared in the local paper the family shut the doors. The girl hasn't been seen since and they don't allow visitors. You'll see in the article that no one from the Spradbery family spoke to the journalist and there's no photograph of Tracey.'

'So she hasn't healed anyone else?'

'There's no evidence that she healed anyone,' said Connolly. 'The entire story is based on an interview with the next door family.'

Jenny knocked on the door and brought in a tray with two mugs of coffee. She put it on Nightingale's desk. 'There's creamer and sugar on the tray,' she said to the priest and he thanked her.

Nightingale looked back at the newspaper. There was one photograph of Ben Miller, the boy who had beaten Leukaemia, standing with his parents 'So how did they know the little girl has stigmata?'

'Good question,' said the priest. 'The little boy saw the bandages on the girl's hands. And he said she told him about seeing the Virgin Mary. But we've made our own enquiries and from what we have discovered, the wounds are genuine and she is still bleeding from her hands and feet and from a wound in the side. The stigmata sites.'

'And what's your interest? Why is the Vatican so concerned?'

'Because it could well be a miracle,' said the priest. 'And we investigate all miracles. Especially those that involve the appearance of the Virgin Mary.' He stood up, took one of the coffee mugs, and sat down again.

'And for that you hire a private detective?'

The priest smiled. 'Generally we do the research ourselves. But this case is unusual in that the family are refusing to speak with us.'

'Sounds as if they don't want any publicity,' said Nightingale. 'Who can blame them?'

The priest held up his hands. 'Absolutely, it's perfectly understandable. But we would still like to know if this is a genuine miracle, or something else. In a case like this it's sometimes more advantageous if we use outside help.'

Nightingale nodded. 'You said you'd made enquiries?'

'We've managed to get a look at her medical report. She sees a doctor on a daily basis. The doctor changes her dressings and takes a blood sample. We've managed to get a look at her blood tests and everything is fine. Liver function, cholesterol, blood sugar. She's a fit and healthy twelve-year-old girl. Except for the fact that she's bleeding.'

'So it's a miracle?'

The priest chuckled. 'It's not as simple as that.'

Nightingale pulled a pack of Marlboro from his pocket. 'Do you mind if I smoke?'

'Not at all,' said the priest. 'It's one of the few vices we're allowed.'

'You smoke?'

The priest grinned. 'Like a chimney.'

Nightingale took a cigarette for himself and offered the pack to the priest. The priest took one and Nightingale walked around the desk to light it for him.

'She has the stigmata,' Nightingale said as he dropped back down into his seat. 'That's a sign of Christ, right? The marks left from the nails when Jesus was crucified and the wound in the side where he was stabbed with a spear.'

'Do you have any idea how many cases of stigmata the Vatican investigates every year, Mr Nightingale?'

Nightingale shook his head.

'Well over a hundred. All around the world. And then we have sightings of the Virgin Mary, angels appearing, vegetables that look like Christ, the face of Jesus in damp patches on ceilings. Do you know how many of them turn out to be miracles?'

'I'm going to guess that the answer is none.'

The priest smiled tightly. 'And your guess would be right. None. There are no miracles, Mr Nightingale, at least not involving civilians. That is not how the Lord God demonstrates his presence in the world. In every case we have ever investigated, the stigmata has had another explanation.'

'So you think she's faking it?'

The priest shook his head. 'Not necessarily. It could be psychosomatic. The brain is a very powerful organ and can affect the body in ways that we barely understand. Or it could be the parents doing something to her while she is asleep. Or forcing her to wound herself.'

'Why would they do that?'

'In the past we've had parents who want money, or fame, or just to be noticed. But usually in these cases the parents are keen to get as much publicity as possible. These parents won't let journalists near the little girl.'

'Which means what?'

The priest shrugged. 'Maybe they're in for the long haul. They live in a council house, maybe they could spin this into them getting a better house. Or a book deal. A reality TV show. Who knows? There are lots of ways of benefiting from a kid who can perform miracles.'

'You'd think that if this was a genuine stigmata they'd want someone from the church involved.'

'The family's not religious,' said the priest. 'The father's a confirmed atheist, that's what I've heard. The mum is a very lapsed Catholic, which might be what's behind this.'

'How come?' asked Nightingale.

'Maybe the mother has suppressed her belief to be with her husband. And the stigmata is her way of getting it out in the open.'

'So you think the mother is deliberately harming the child?'

'It's a possibility, yes.'

Nightingale took a long drag on his cigarette. 'You believe in God, right?'

'Of course. There'd be no point of being a priest if I didn't.'

'And Jesus?'

The priest nodded. 'Yes.'

'So why can't you consider the possibility that this is a genuine stigmata, that this is Jesus proving his existence?'

The priest shrugged carelessly. 'It might be,' he said. 'But the simple fact is that stigmata events like this always turn out to be something else. Jesus Christ does not make his presence felt in this way. Why would he?'

'I've no idea. But then I'm not a priest.'

The priest flicked ash into an ashtray. 'It wouldn't make any sense. God makes his presence felt in countless ways, he doesn't need cheap parlour tricks.'

'That's what you think this is, a trick?'

'Any of the TV magicians like Derren Brown or David Blain could put together a very convincing stigmata show. It's not difficult.'

'But suppose it was real? Suppose this really was Jesus showing the world that he exists.'

'Jesus doesn't work that way,' said the priest. 'Neither does God. We have no right to ask them to prove their existence. We need to have faith. We are the ones who need to prove that we are worthy of his love, not vice versa.'

Nightingale nodded thoughtfully. 'So specifically what is it you want me to do?'

'Visit the family. Meet the girl. Find out what's going on there.'

'And if I find out that it's a real miracle. What then?'

The priest's eyes narrowed. 'What do you mean?'

'Suppose it's genuine. Suppose Jesus has given this girl a real stigmata. What does that do to your Church? Aren't people going to wonder why Jesus is talking to the people and not to the Pope?'

'God talks to us all,' said the priest. 'The question is whether we are prepared to listen.'

'So you wouldn't want to suppress the fact that there had been a genuine miracle?'

'The church welcomes true miracles. That is how we choose our saints. But occurrences like these are without exception not miracles. I am confident that will be what your investigation shows.' He reached into his cassock and brought out his wallet again. 'Can I pay in advance, with a credit card?'

'The church has a credit card?'

'We use Visa,' said the priest, holding out the card.

Nightingale took it. 'That'll do nicely,' he said.

* * *

'So he's never had sex?' asked Jenny, as the priest headed downstairs.

'What?'

'Catholic priests are celibate.'

'It didn't come up,' said Nightingale. 'No pun intended.'

'So did you confess?' asked Jenny.

Nightingale tossed her the newspaper that the priest had given him. 'Stigmata in Beckenham,' he said.

Jenny quickly scanned the story. 'And they want you to do what?'

'Check it out. See if she's genuine.'

'Because you're a world authority on stigmata? I sort of thought the Catholic Church would be the experts.'

'The family aren't talking.' He grinned. 'Fancy a drive?'

'You mean the MGB's playing up again?'

'You know me so well.'

* * *

'So what do you know about stigmata?' Jenny asked Nightingale as they drove south over the River Thames towards Beckenham.

'Probably not much more than you,' he said. 'Marks or wounds on the body in places that correspond to the crucifixion wounds of Christ. The nails in his hands and feet and the wound in the side.'

'Did you know that eight per cent of stigmatics are women?'

'I didn't know that.'

'Well they are. Quite a few are nuns. But the most famous was a man – St Francis of Assisi. These days they almost always turn out to be fakes.'

Nightingale turned to look at her, surprised. 'How come you know so much about it?'

'I Googled it while you were in the loo,' she said, braking to avoid a black cab that had suddenly decided to do a U-turn in front of them. 'They're usually in poor Catholic countries and it's usually a way that the families can make money. They start selling souvenirs or charging for interviews.'

'That's not what's happening here,' said Nightingale. 'They won't speak to the priest, or to the Press.'

She grinned over at him. 'But they will talk to Jack Nightingale, private eye?'

'I was hoping they'd be more open to his pretty young assistant.'

Jenny sighed. 'So I'm not just the designated driver, I'm actually doing the legwork, too.'

'Just knock on the door, play it by ear,' said Nightingale.

'And what to I tell them exactly?'

'Tell them you've got a kid that's dying from Leukaemia. You heard that their daughter can help.'

Jenny's nose wrinkled in disgust. 'Are you serious? You want me to lie to them?'

'Jenny, honey, they're hardly likely to talk to you if you tell them your client is the Vatican.'

'I'm not comfortable about inventing a fictional sick child,' she said.

Nightingale sighed. 'Okay, tell them you work for a charity and that you have kids who need help.'

'So now I'm inventing multiple fictional sick kids. Explain to me how that's better?'

'It's less personal,' said Nightingale. 'Look, tell them anything you want, just see if you can get in and have a chat with Tracey. I'd do it myself but I know they'll be more likely to talk to a pretty face.'

'Yeah, flattery'll do the trick every time,' said Jenny. 'I tell you, Jack, this is part of our job that I really don't like; lying to people.'

'If you can think of a way of telling the truth and getting the info we want, you go right ahead,' said Nightingale.

* * *

They pulled up outside the Spradbery house just after mid-day. It was a semi-detached house on a council estate, the paint on the doors and windows cracked and peeling. Moss was growing between the paving stones that led up to the front door. There was a white van in the driveway of the Spradbery house and a five-year-old blue Nissan next door. There was a rusting metal swing set and a BMX bike leaning against the garage door of the neighbouring house.

Jenny climbed out of the Audi. Three hoodie-wearing teenagers standing outside an off-licence were smoking and staring at the car. 'Make sure you stay put,' she said.

Nightingale chuckled. 'You're such a snob.'

'It's nothing to do with snobbery, I just don't want to find my car on blocks when I get back.'

'They're just kids,' said Nightingale.

'Stay in the car,' said Jenny. Nightingale watched as she walked up to the front door. He took out his cigarettes and lighter but then remembered that she didn't like him smoking in the Audi. He put them away as the front door opened. A middle-aged woman in a flowered apron spoke to Jenny for several minutes and then closed the front door. Jenny came back to the car and bent down to talk to him through the open window. 'They're not there.'

'Who did you speak to?'

'Mrs Spradbery's sister. Tracey's aunt. She's in there to feed their dogs and give the place a clean.'

'Did she say where they've gone?'

Jenny shook her head. 'All she said was that the Spradberys have taken Tracey with them to keep her away from the press. They were ringing their doorbell every hour of the day and night.'

'Did she confirm the stigmata?'

'She said it's true. But she said the family don't want to talk to anybody.'

'Any idea when they'll be back?'

Jenny shook her head.

'Tracey has to go to school, right?'

'I asked her that. Apparently they pulled Tracey out of school when the bleeding started. They're home-schooling her. What do we do?'

'We talk to the neighbours.'

'That'll be the royal "we" I suppose.'

'Nah, I'll come with you this time,' he said. 'Ben Miller's family don't seem to mind talking about what's happened.'

Jenny looked around but the kids had gone from outside the off-licence.

'Your car'll be fine,' said Nightingale. He got out of the Audi and Jenny locked the doors.

'If my windows get smashed then you pay, right?'

'Cross my heart,' said Nightingale. 'But you worry too much.'

They walked by the Nissan and Nightingale rang the doorbell. There was no response and he tried again. 'Maybe they're not in,' said Jenny.

'The car suggests otherwise,' said Nightingale. He headed around the side of the house.

'Jack, where do you think you're going?' hissed Jenny.

'Let's check the back door.'

'I'm not up for breaking and entering,' she said. 'That's not in my employment contract.'

'No one said anything about breaking in,' he said. 'Let's just take a look.'

The rear garden wasn't much bigger than the one at the front, but was considerably more overgrown. There was a garden shed at the bottom of the garden and a washing line from which fluttered a sheet and a quilt cover.

'Jack, we shouldn't be doing this,' said Jenny behind him.

'It'll be fine,' said Nightingale. He reached for the handle of the kitchen door. He flinched as it moved just before his fingers touched it. The door opened and a woman holding a plastic basket of washing screamed. Nightingale jumped back and fell against Jenny as the woman dropped her basket of laundry. The woman staggered back into the kitchen and screamed again.

Nightingale recognised her from the newspaper article. It was Mrs Miller, Ben's mother. 'I'm sorry, I'm sorry,' said Nightingale. 'We're just here to talk to you.'

Mrs Miller stood staring at Nightingale, her chest rising and falling as she gasped for breath. 'You scared the life out of me,' she said. She was in her forties, a heavy-set woman with permed hair. She was wearing a shapeless dress with yachts and lighthouses on it.

'Mutual,' said Nightingale. 'Sorry. I did ring the bell.'

'I was in the laundry room,' she said, still panting. Sweat was beading above her upper lip, emphasising a slight moustache there. 'Who are you?'

'Jack Nightingale,' he said. 'This is my friend Jenny. Can we talk to you about Ben?'

'You're not journalists are you? We don't talk to journalists any more?'

Nightingale shook his head. 'I have a nephew who has Leukaemia,' he said.

'Oh, I'm sorry,' she said. 'What type?'

'Type?' repeated Nightingale.

'AML,' said Jenny, quickly. 'Acute myelogenous Leukaemia.'

'I'm so sorry,' said Mrs Miller. 'Let me hang these up and I'll make us some tea.'

She carried the laundry basket across the lawn to the washing line.

Nightingale opened his mouth to speak but Jenny silenced him with a wave of her hand. 'Don't,' she said. 'I'm not proud of myself for lying like that.'

'We don't have a choice,' said Nightingale. 'You heard her. Someone's told her not to talk to journalists.'

Mrs Miller came back and ushered them into her kitchen. The lino was threadbare and the gas cooker looked as if it was fifty years old. She told them to sit down at the kitchen table while she made tea. It was covered with a white plastic cloth and there were half empty bottles of Heinz ketchup and HP brown sauce standing in the centre.

'How is Ben?' asked Nightingale.

'As right as rain,' said Mrs Miller. 'Dr McKenzie says he's never seen anything like it.'

'Dr McKenzie?'

'Our GP. He's taken care of Ben since he was a baby. Lovely man. He's Tracey's GP too. He says it's a miracle, what happened to Ben.'

'It sounds like it,' said Nightingale. 'But he was treating Ben, right? Giving him medication and stuff?'

'He was, and he was helping us deal with the hospital,' she said. 'But Ben was getting worse. He'd lost all his hair, bless. Then...' She shrugged. 'It was a miracle. It really was. There's no other word for it.'

'Can you tell me what happened, Mrs Miller?' said Nightingale. 'I only know what I read in the newspaper.'

Mrs Miller turned away from the kettle and folded her arms. 'It sounds crazy when I tell the story,' she said, 'A lot of kids wouldn't play with Ben when he was sick. They thought they could catch it from him. Ignorant parents didn't help either. But Dave and Carla were different, they were more than happy to let Ben play at their house. He used to spend hours over there. Tracey would go through her schoolwork with him, helping him make up for the lessons he'd missed. She's an angel.'

The kettle switched off and she poured hot water into three mugs and popped in teabags. 'Then about two months ago, the thing happened.' She prodded the teabags with a teaspoon.

'The thing?' said Jenny.

'The stigmata. Ben came back and said that Tracey was bleeding. I thought maybe she'd hurt herself when they were playing so I went around. She had these wounds on her hands and her feet and another in her side.' She patted her own side. 'There was blood but not a lot. And Tracey said they didn't hurt.' She fished the teabags out of the mugs, dropped them into a bin and took a carton of milk out of the fridge. 'Dave and Carla were frantic, of course. They rushed Tracey to A&E and they bandaged the wounds and gave her antibiotics but other than that they didn't seem to know what to do. The doctor said she'd never seen anything like it. I think Carla was worried that they might call in social services.'

She put the mugs down on the kitchen table with the carton of milk and a bowl of sugar cubes. 'Help yourself,' she said, sitting down. She used her fingers to drop four sugar lumps into her tea and then slowly stirred it with a white plastic spoon. 'The next day, Ben went around to play. I said he should leave her be for a while but he didn't have anyone else to play with so he just kept on nagging. Well, that evening when Ben came back he was all excited and saying that Tracey had seen an angel.'

'An angel?' said Nightingale.

'I think she meant the Virgin Mary but the family isn't religious and I think Tracey was just confused. Ben said that the angel had cured him.'

'He said that?'

Mrs Miller nodded. 'He said that the angel had told Tracey that the cancer had gone. We thought it was ridiculous, of course. Maybe they'd been watching a DVD that had given them ideas or something. We told Ben not to be so stupid and to go to bed. But from that day on he started to get better. It was as if the Leukaemia had gone into remission, Dr McKenzie said. Then it was gone. Like he'd never been sick. Dr McKenzie said he'd never seen anything like it.'

'You said Dr McKenzie also treated Tracey?' said Nightingale.

'He went around to their house every day after the surgery closed to change her dressings,' said Mrs Miller. 'But the bleeding didn't stop. That's when a journalist found out about Ben and came around to write an article. The paper printed the story and then all sorts of journalists started coming around. TV, radio, the papers. They were knocking on our door at all hours. After a couple of days Dave came around and said they were moving. He wasn't sure how long they'd be away but he said they had to protect Tracey.'

'What did he mean by protect?'

'I don't know,' said Mrs Miller. 'He just said it was really important that they took her away. The next day they'd gone. Ben was distraught. But on the positive side, he's back in school now and doing really well.'

They heard the front door crash open and slam, and then rapid footsteps in the hallway. Mrs Miller looked up at a clock on the cooker. 'That'll be him now,' she said.

A schoolboy hurtled into the kitchen and tossed a backpack on the floor. 'What's for tea, mum?' he asked. Nightingale recognised the boy from the newspaper article. He was tall for his age and had a crop of freckles across his nose and cheeks.

'Fish fingers. But you need to get your homework done first.'

'Hi Ben, I'm Jack,' said Nightingale. 'This is Jenny.'

'Are you reporters? You look like reporters?' He looked at his mother. 'Tracey says we mustn't talk to the papers, you know that.'

'We're not reporters, Ben,' said Nightingale. 'I have a nephew who's sick like you.'

'I'm not sick any more,' said the boy. 'I'm cured. Tracey cured me.'

'I know, that's great news,' said Nightingale. 'Tracey helped you get well, right?'

The boy nodded. 'The lady made me better. She talks to Tracey.'

'Did you talk to the lady?'

The boy shook his head. 'Only Tracey can see her. Tracey's special, you see.'

'Upstairs with you now,' said Mrs Miller. 'I want all your homework done before you touch your PlayStation.

'Yes, mum,' said Ben. He headed for the door.

'Ben, before you go,' said Nightingale. 'Did Tracey touch you or do anything to make you better?'

Ben stopped and nodded. 'She put her hands on my head and said a prayer. The Lord's prayer. Our father who art in heaven. You know it?'

Nightingale nodded. 'Sure. And that was all? After that you were okay?'

'It was a miracle, Dr McKenzie said. He says he hopes that Tracey will be better soon, too.'

'Is Dr McKenzie still treating Tracey?'

The boy nodded enthusiastically. 'He takes letters to her from me and he brings letters from her.'

'Do you know where she is?' asked Nightingale.

'Ben, homework, now,' said Mrs Miller firmly. Ben ran out of the kitchen. 'Dave and Carla don't want anyone to know where Tracey is,' she said. 'I'm sorry, but I have to respect their wishes.'

'Do you have a phone number for them?' asked Jenny.

'I do, but they were quite clear that I shouldn't give it to anyone. Anyone at all.'

'We understand,' said Jenny. She took a pen and a notepad out of her handbag and scribbled a phone number on it. 'Could you mention it to Dave and Carla, tell them that we'd like their help, and get them to give us a call.'

Mrs Miller took the piece of paper. 'I will, but I'm pretty sure they won't contact you. I probably gave them two dozen numbers just like yours after they left and I know they didn't follow any of them up.'

'You'd think they'd want to help others the way that they helped Ben,' said Nightingale.'

'They were really worried about something,' said Mrs Miller.

'What exactly?' asked Nightingale.

'They didn't say. But I think they were worried about somebody wanting to hurt Tracey.'

'Who, do you know?'

Mrs Miller shook her head. 'It was just a feeling.' She looked at the clock again. 'I'm sorry but my husband's going to back soon so I need to get his dinner ready.

Nightingale finished his tea and stood up. 'Thanks for your time, anyway.'

'And we're really pleased for Ben,' said Jenny, standing up. 'It's great to see him looking so well.'

Mrs Miller nodded. 'I hope your nephew gets better,' she said. 'I really do.'

* * *

'I hate lying to people,' said Jenny as they walked back to the car. She was relieved to see that her wheels and windows were still intact. 'Now she's fretting over an imaginary nephew with Leukaemia.'

'She'll have forgotten it already,' said Nightingale. 'And let's be honest here. We told her that we have a nephew dying of Leukaemia and she just shrugged and said she couldn't help.'

Jenny pressed the fob to open the Audi's doors. 'That's not fair, Jack. She said she'd pass on the message but she didn't think the Spradberys would help. It's not her fault.'

'I'm just saying, there's nothing wrong with bending the truth a bit to get the information we need.'

'That was a barefaced lie, not bending the truth,' said Jenny. She climbed into the car and Nightingale got into the passenger seat. 'Now what?' she said.

'We need to find out where Dr McKenzie works,' he said. 'Can you do a bit of Googling on your iPhone?'

Jenny took out her phone. It took her less than two minutes to find the address of Dr McKenzie's surgery. It was a short drive away, and a few minutes later Jenny was parking across the road from the surgery, a detached bungalow that had once been a family home . The garden had been paved over to make a car park and there was a large sign saying 'DOCTORS ONLY, ALL OTHER CARS WILL BE CLAMPED.'

'I'll do this one,' said Nightingale.

'That's good because I think I've passed my quota of untruths today,' said Jenny.

Nightingale climbed out of the car and lit a cigarette. Jenny wound down the window and looked up at him. 'Seriously? You're going to go in there smoking?'

'No, I need a cigarette. I'll smoke it then go in.'

'You should try patches,' she said.

'I can't get them to light,' he said. He took a drag on the cigarette and walked across the road to the surgery. Through a window Nightingale could see half a dozen people, mainly pensioners, sitting on wooden chairs and beyond them a reception area. He took a final pull on his cigarette and then flicked it towards a drain before pushing open the door. He walked across a tiled floor to the reception. Two middle-aged women were sitting at desks staring at computer terminals while another woman was on the phone, explaining why it wasn't possible for the caller to have an appointment the following day, or the day after.

Nightingale stood and waited. The two women stared at the computer screens and he got the impression they were deliberately avoiding eye contact. To his right was a corridor that presumably led to the consulting rooms. There was a digital sign above the corridor that gave the name of the last patient and the number of the room they were to go to. Nightingale figured it saved the reception staff from having to talk to the patients.

'Because all our appointments are full,' explained the woman on the phone. 'The day after tomorrow is the best I can do.' There was a brief pause then the woman spoke again. 'Well I'm sorry you feel that way,' she said. 'You can always try A&E.'

To the left of the reception area there were framed photographs on the wall of the four doctors who worked for the practice. Dr Ron McKenzie was on the far right. He was in his fifties with grey hair, round spectacles and a kindly smile. According to the brief notes under the photograph he had been with the practice for ten years and specialised in young patients.

'By all means write to your MP,' said the woman on the phone. 'That's your right, of course it is.' She banged down phone. 'Just as it's my right to hang up on you. Silly woman.' She looked at Nightingale over the top of her spectacles. 'How can I help you?' she asked, in a tone that suggested she had zero interest in helping him in any way.

At the rear of the reception area a piece of chipboard had been nailed over a window. Nightingale flashed her his most boyish smile. 'What happened there?' he asked, pointing at the broken and patched window.

'We had a break in,' said the woman.

'Did they steal anything?'

'There's nothing to steal,' she said. 'Except the computers maybe. The police reckon it was drug addicts. Stupid because we don't keep any drugs on the premises. So how can I help you? There's no chance of a walk-in appointment today, I'm afraid.'

'I'm moving into the area and just want to check how easy it would be to have this as my local surgery.'

'Where are you living at the moment?'

'Near Kilburn, North London. I've got two children and I'm told that Dr McKenzie is good with kids.'

'He is, yes. He set up this surgery, actually.'

'So no plans for him to leave?'

'Dr McKenzie? Oh no, they'll have to carry him out of here.'

'Is he in today?'

'Yes, but he's far too busy to see anyone other than his appointments. Now, do you have your NHS number?'

'Not with me, no. I just wanted to know what I needed to move.'

'Your NHS number, some form of identification such as a driving licence or passport, and the name and address of your current doctor. Providing everything's in order it won't take long.'

'Brilliant, thanks,' said Nightingale. 'I'll bring my details in once I've relocated.' He took a last look at the photograph of Dr McKenzie and then headed outside.

Jenny had the engine running to keep the car interior warm and Nightingale rubbed his hands. 'He's in his fifties, grey haired, glasses.'

'Not my type then,' said Jenny.

'I was telling you so that you can keep an eye out for him. There's only four doctors there, two of them are women and the other guy's a Sikh with a full turban. Dr McKenzie is in there now.'

'So what's your plan?'

Nightingale looked at his watch. 'Ben said that Dr McKenzie is still in contact with Tracey. I'm assuming that means the good doctor is still treating her. Open wounds like you have with stigmata probably need cleaning every day so assuming she's not going to the surgery, he must go around to see her. Best time to do that would be after he's finished at the surgery.'

'Terrific. And what time does the surgery close?'

Nightingale sighed. 'Ah. Forgot to ask.'

Jenny shook her head sadly and took out her iPhone. She went to the surgery's website. The opening hours were on the main page. 'Eight o'clock tonight.'

'In two hours,' he said. 'Perfect. Fancy a curry? There was a curry house down the road. On me.'

* * *

Nightingale and Jenny were outside the surgery again at ten to eight, having polished off a lamb korma, a chicken vindaloo and a chicken biryani. Jenny was always loathe to let Nightingale behind the wheel of her beloved Audi so he had a couple of bottles of Kingfisher lager while she stuck to water.

'I'm going to tell you this just once, Jack,' she said. 'But if you break wind even once I'm kicking you out and you can get the bus home.'

'My bowels are sealed,' he said. 'But just to be on the safe side, how about I crack the window.' He opened the window a few inches and settled back in his seat. 'They had a break in, not long ago.'

'Who did?'

Nightingale nodded at the surgery. 'They did. There's a broken window at the back. And Connolly seemed to know an awful lot about Tracey's medical records.'

'You think he's behind the break-in?'

Nightingale shrugged. 'It could be a coincidence, I guess.'

'I can't see a priest breaking in anywhere, can you? Not in that cassock he was wearing.'

Nightingale laughed. 'Yeah, maybe you're right. But it's strange that he knew about her medical records but didn't seem to know that she'd moved.' He grimaced. 'Maybe I'm overthinking it.'

The last patient emerged from the surgery at eight and one of the receptionists turned the SURGERY OPEN sign around to read SURGERY CLOSED. The Sikh was first to leave, followed by one of the women doctors, then two of the receptionists, and finally Dr McKenzie appeared, wearing a beige raincoat and carrying a black medical bag. He walked around to the car park and got into a black BMW.

'Don't get too close,' said Nightingale, as the doctor drove out of the car park and down the road.

'Do you think?' said Jenny, putting the Audi into gear.

'I'm just trying to be helpful,' said Nightingale.

The doctor drove east along the A222 to Bromley, then turned off the main road into a side street of terraced houses. He slowed and was clearly looking for somewhere to park. 'Best I drop you near him so you can follow him on foot,' said Jenny.

'I'll find a place to park.' McKenzie had spotted a gap between two SUVs and switched on his turn indictor before slowly reversing.

Nightingale climbed out of the Audi and lit a cigarette as McKenzie parked the car. Jenny drove slowly down the road.

McKenzie got out of his BMW with his medical bag and headed down the street. Nightingale followed him on the other side of the road. The doctor walked quickly, his head down, deep in his own thoughts, until he reached a house with a blue door. He stopped, pressed the doorbell, and a couple of moments later slipped inside. Nightingale wasn't able to see who had let him in. He crossed over the road. The house was Number 26. He took out his phone and called Jenny.

'I'm parked up, not far away from where I dropped you,' she said.

'He's gone inside Number 26.'

'Can you see anything?'

'Nah. I'm going to try to get around the back.'

'Be careful, Jack.'

'Careful is my middle name,' he said, ending the call and walking quickly down the road. He counted the houses as he went. By the time he got to the corner, he had reached eight. There was a narrow alley running behind the houses. Nightingale flicked away what was left of his cigarette and headed down the alley. There were wooden gates set into the eight-feet high brick walls that ran either side of the alley. Few of the gates had numbers on them but Nightingale was able to count off the gates until he reached Number 26. He pushed the gate and it opened. He winced as the hinges squeaked. He opened it just enough to peer through. There was a small backyard with a rubbish bin and an oblong earthenware planter that seemed to be full of herbs. Or weeds. The backyard was illuminated by light from a frosted glass window upstairs, presumably a bathroom, and a softer light from a downstairs window. He pushed the gate again, wincing at the squeak from the hinges. He squeezed through the gap and gently closed the gate behind him.

He stood with his back to the wall, his heart pounding. The backyard was the width of the terraced house and about twelve feet long. There were two bikes leaning against one wall and a rotary clothes line from which were hanging half a dozen men's boxer shorts and several dresses that looked as if they would be worn by a twelve-year-old girl.

There were blinds over the window but they weren't fully closed, allowing light to spill out into the backyard. Nightingale moved forward on tiptoe.

Through the gaps in the blind he could see into the kitchen. A young girl was sitting at the kitchen table. She had rolled up the sleeves of her shirt and was holding her arms out. Dr McKenzie was sitting opposite her. His opened medical bag was on a chair next to him. A man in his fifties, bald and overweight, was standing by the cooker, his arms folded, a look of concern on his face.

The doctor was removing a dressing from the young girl's right hand. The dressing was bloody and when he pulled it away Nightingale could see a small wound in the girl's palm, not much bigger than a five-pence piece. The doctor put the dressing in a plastic bag and then removed a similar dressing from her left hand.

Nightingale realised that he'd been holding his breath. The girl was obviously Tracey Spradbery and the worried man by the cooker must have been her father.

A woman walked into the kitchen. It was obviously Tracey's mother. She was a few years younger than the man by the cooker, with dyed-blonde hair and a washed out face as if she hadn't been sleeping well. She sat down at the kitchen table and began talking to Tracey. Tracey nodded and said something to her mother and Mrs Spradbery laughed, showing a mouthful of crooked teeth.

Nightingale's phone buzzed in his raincoat pocket and he pulled it out. It was an SMS from Jenny. 'EVERYTHING OK?'

Nightingale sent her an SMS back. 'SHE'S HERE. STAY PUT.'

He put the phone back in his pocket. Dr McKenzie was dabbing a liquid on the girl's wounds. He said something to her and she laughed. She was a pretty girl, with shoulder-length chestnut hair and big green eyes.

Dr McKenzie reached into his bag and took out two fresh dressings. Nightingale jumped as the kitchen door burst open and a man appeared, holding a cricket bat. He was in his forties, tall with receding hair and a hooked nose and deep-set eyes that gave him the look of a hawk sizing up its prey. 'Who are you?' he said angrily.

'Nightingale. Jack Nightingale.'

'What are you doing here?' The man's eyes were blazing. He used both hands to hold the cricket bat.

'Who are you?' asked Nightingale.

'This is my house,' said the man. He held the cricket bat up in the air, ready to bring it crashing down on Nightingale's head.

'I want to write a story about Tracey and what happened to her.'

'You're a journalist?'

'That's right,' said Nightingale. He flashed the man a confident smile.

Mrs Spradbery appeared behind the man. 'Ricky, what's happening?' she asked. Nightingale couldn't make out her face as it was in shadow.

'Get back inside, Carla,' said the man. 'I'll handle this.' He kept his eyes on Nightingale and he took a step to the side, putting himself between Nightingale and the gate.

'Do you want me to call the police?' asked Mrs Spradbery.

'I can handle it,' said Ricky. 'Just close the door.'

The woman did as she was told. 'Who do you work for?' asked the man, still waving the cricket bat menacingly.

'Who do I work for?' repeated Nightingale.

'What paper?'

'I'm freelance,' said Nightingale.

'Yeah? Freelancing for who?'

Nightingale shrugged. 'One of the Sundays.'

'You've got a commission, have you?'

'Sure.'

'From who? Who commissioned it?'

Nightingale shrugged again. 'I'd rather not say.'

'Show me your NUJ card.'

'My NUJ card?'

The man smiled sarcastically. 'Have you got a hearing problem? If you're a journo you'd be in the NUJ, freelance or otherwise. It's the only card that the cops recognise.'

Nightingale took out his wallet, opened it, then made a show of looking through it. 'I must have left it at home.'

'Show me your notebook then.'

Nightingale grimaced and patted his coat pockets.

'You're as much a journalist as I'm Wayne Rooney,' said Ricky.

'That's not fair, I'm not calling your footballing ability into question.'

'I don't have any footballing ability,' said the man. 'Two left feet.'

'Then you really shouldn't be trying to pass yourself off as Wayne Rooney,' said Nightingale. He made a show of looking at his watch. 'Look, I've got work to do.' He moved to get by the man but he stepped in his way.

'What do you want with my niece?' he snarled.

'Your niece?'

'Yeah, my niece. I'm her mother's brother and this is my house. Now if you don't tell me why you're sniffing around my niece I'm going to detain you using a citizen's arrest and then I'm going to call the cops. And the cops don't pussyfoot around with paedophiles.'

'Alleged paedophiles,' said Nightingale. 'And you know that I'm as much a paedophile as you're a professional footballer.'

'So who are you?'

'I told you. Jack Nightingale.' He pulled out his wallet and gave the man a business card.

Ricky took it with his left hand and squinted at it. 'You're a private eye?'

'I can put two words together so it wouldn't be impossible for me to write an article for someone,' said Nightingale.

'That doesn't make you a journalist.'

'No. But last I heard saying you're a journo isn't a criminal offence.'

The man studied the card. 'And you're not local.'

'I'm from London.'

'Who's your client, Mr Nightingale?'

'I can't tell you that.'

Ricky lowered the cricket bat. 'Do you drink?'

'Do I drink?'

'Alcohol.'

Nightingale nodded. 'I've been known to.'

Ricky nodded and leaned the cricket bat against the back wall of the house. 'There's a pub down the road.'

'It'll take more than a drink to loosen my tongue,' said Nightingale. 'Two, possibly three.'

'You're a very funny man, Mr Nightingale.'

* * *

Ricky's full name was Ricky Hamilton. He was Carla Spradbery's elder brother and for the last five years he'd been working as a researcher for a TV documentary company. Prior to that he'd been a journalist for almost twenty years, with long spells as an investigative reporter on The Guardian and The Sunday Times. He'd written half a dozen books, mainly political biographies. As a joke Nightingale had asked to see Ricky's NUJ card and he'd happily produced it. The pub was a short walk from Ricky's house, a traditional boozer with oak beams and a real fireplace. Ricky turned out to be a fan of Corona and he paid for two bottles before they found a quiet corner of the pub and sat at a small circular table. Ricky pushed his slice of lime into the neck of the bottle, pressed his thumb over the top and then inverted it. The lime rose slowly to the top and Ricky waited for it to touch the bottom of the bottle before turning it the right way up.

'Why do you do that?' asked Nightingale.

Ricky shrugged. 'I saw someone else do it once. It runs the lime taste through the lager.'

'I was told that the reason they give you a slice of lime in Mexico is because it keeps the flies away.'

'Nah, that's an urban myth.'

'How do you know?'

'Because I've been to Mexico and they don't serve it with lime there. It was a marketing gimmick, that's all.'

'Well it worked,' said Nightingale. He clinked his bottle against Ricky's and drank.

'You followed the doctor to my house, didn't you?'

Nightingale nodded.

Ricky looked pained. 'I knew I should have got Tracey another doctor, but she loves Dr McKenzie.'

'He seems to know his stuff,' said Nightingale. 'And the stigmata is real?'

'Of course,' said Ricky.

'And she talks to the Virgin Mary?'

'That's what she says,' said Ricky. 'That's harder to prove. But the wounds, they're there, no question of that.'

'And she cured Ben of his cancer.'

'It was the Virgin Mary that told Tracey to get him over. She told Tracey to touch him, on the forehead, and to say a prayer. And that cured him.'

Nightingale nodded. 'I spoke to Ben's parents. They think it was a miracle.'

'It was a miracle, no doubt about it,' said Ricky.

'So why not tell the world?'

Ricky snorted. 'Do you have any idea what happens to people who perform miracles?'

'They become saints?'

Ricky nodded slowly. 'If they're Catholics, yes. If they're not Catholics...' He left the sentence hanging.

'What are you saying?' asked Nightingale.

'I'm saying that if you're Mother Teresa or Pope John Paul then the Vatican will be turning over every stone to prove it and get them a sainthood. But when you're not in the fold, when you're an outsider, well that's a game-changer.'

'In what way?'

'What do you know about the structure of the Catholic Church?' asked Ricky.

'Not much. I know the Pope's the big guy, obviously.'

Ricky flashed him a tight smile. 'You've got the laity at the bottom. The people. Then you've got the deacons who help out at mass. Then you've got the priests and above them the bishops and above them the archbishops and above them, the cardinals. And right at the top, the Pope. It's like an army. Hell, it is an army. And if any member of the army can perform miracles then they are fast-tracked to sainthood. But if anyone outside the army starts showing miracle tendencies – then it's treated differently. The church regards it as terrorism. And they stamp it out.'

'Stamp it out?'

'They kill them, Nightingale. Sometimes they make it look like an accident, sometimes they just disappear. But they die. They have to die otherwise their existence makes a complete mockery of the Catholic Church.'

'How do you know that?'

'Because I've done my research. I've spoken to people. I've looked into the last fifty cases of reported stigmata and I can tell you this much – the ones that aren't shown to be hoaxes either die or disappear. And that's a fact.'

Nightingale said nothing. His mouth had gone suddenly dry and he sipped his Corona, but that didn't seem to help.

'That's why I need to know who your client is,' said Ricky. 'If you're working for a newspaper or a magazine, or some reality TV show or other, then that's fine. If your client is sick and wants Tracey to lay her hands on him, okay, we can talk about that. But if you're acting for the Vatican, then we've got a big problem, Nightingale. One hell of a big problem.'

'What are you saying, Ricky? Are you saying they'll kill her?'

'I'm saying that when non-Catholics start to report miracles, it doesn't end well.'

'But if the miracle proves the existence of God, the Church would welcome that, surely.'

Ricky sipped his lager. 'Do you believe in God, Nightingale?'

'That's a tough question.'

'It's actually a very simple question.'

'Doesn't make it any less tough.' Nightingale picked at the label of his bottle with his thumb. 'I believe in devils,' he said. 'And angels. 'And I believe in The Devil. If I believe in The Devil then I have to believe in God. You can't have one without the other, can you?'

'You're asking the wrong person,' said Ricky. 'I'm an atheist. Have been for years.'

'Seriously? After what Tracey's been through?'

'Our mum was a Catholic and Carla and I were both baptised. When we were not much older than Tracey, she got cancer. We prayed, Carla and I, we prayed for hours on end, begging God to save our mum. He didn't of course. I became an atheist at her funeral. Carla did the same.'

'Understandable,' said Nightingale.

'There's no such thing as a God,' said Ricky. 'Not as an individual entity. It's impossible, how could one being control everything? The universe is huge and scientists can explain pretty much everything. God is a matter of faith, pure and simple.'

'But Tracey's stigmata?'

Ricky shrugged. 'Psychosomatic.'

'And the Virgin Mary?'

'Only Tracey sees her. No one else has.'

'You think she's making it up?'

'I don't know. And I don't know where she's getting it from. Her dad Dave's a confirmed atheist as well. There's no religion in the house. And none at the school, obviously.'

'I think that Tracey truly believes that she is talking to the mother of Christ,' said Ricky. 'I think somehow her belief is somehow manifesting itself in the stigmata. And while I can't even come close to understanding or explaining it, she can somehow cure people who are sick. But whatever she's doing, and however she's doing it, I don't think for one minute that God has anything to do with it.' He took another pull on his lager and wiped his mouth with the back of his hand. 'But that's not the point. The point is that she has the stigmata, she can work miracles, and she's not been baptised. That makes her a threat to the Catholic Church. So I'm going to ask you one last time, Nightingale. Is the Vatican your client?'

Nightingale said nothing.

'Because if the Vatican have hired you to find Tracey then you've put her life in danger.' He stared at Nightingale, his hand tightening around the bottle in front of him. 'You hear what I'm saying?'

Nightingale nodded slowly. 'I hear you.'

'Well?'

Nightingale took a deep breath and nodded slowly. 'I need a cigarette,' he said.

* * *

'He was definitely a priest?' asked Ricky. He and Nightingale were standing outside the pub, the collars of their coats turned up against the winter wind. There were two other smokers on the other side of the pub, young women with dyed blond hair and toddlers in matching McLaren pushchairs.

'He had the cassock and everything,' said Nightingale.

'That doesn't mean anything,' said Ricky. 'They do a lot of outsourcing.'

'You mean he might have been pretending to be a priest?'

'Don't look so outraged, Nightingale. It wasn't that long ago that you were claiming to be a journalist.' He blew smoke up at the darkening sky. 'Have you told this Connolly where Tracey is?'

Nightingale shook his head.

'That's something, at least. The problem is, if you found her, so could anyone else.'

'It wasn't difficult,' said Nightingale. 'You should have used a different doctor.'

'We didn't have much choice. We can't just pop into any A&E without questions being asked. And there's always some NHS employee wanting to make a few quid by tipping off a newspaper or Sky News.' He drew on his cigarette and blew smoke. 'The thing is, if you found her, others can, too.'

Nightingale flicked away what was left of his cigarette. 'I need a favour.'

'Yeah?'

'Can I talk to Tracey?'

* * *

Dr McKenzie had finished changing Tracey's dressing and had left the house by the time Ricky and Nightingale got back. They had picked up Jenny from the Audi. Ricky let himself into the house and asked Nightingale and Jenny to wait on the doorstep while he spoke to Tracey's parents.

'He seems nice,' said Jenny.

'He is. Just very protective of his niece.'

'What did he tell you?'

'He said the Vatican wants to hurt Tracey.'

Jenny's jaw dropped. 'What? Why?'

Before Nightingale could answer the door opened and Ricky ushered them in. 'Before you see Tracey, there's something I need to show you,' he said. He headed up the stairs and Nightingale and Jenny followed him. Ricky opened a door and showed them a small study. There was a desk and a computer and printer, and above it two bookshelves filled with reference books. There was a corkboard on the wall opposite the desk and there were several dozen newspaper cuttings pinned on it. Paragraphs and pictures had been circled in red ink and in the top right hand corner of the board was a map dotted with coloured pins. 'Once Carla told me what had happened to Tracey, I started doing some research on stigmata. And time and time again I discovered that within months of a stigmata case being reported one of three things happened. More often than not the person involved was shown to be a fake. That happens in more than ninety per cent of cases. Sometimes the Church sends an investigator and they prove fakery, sometimes the media exposes the fake. But it's the remaining ten per cent that concern me.

I looked at fifty cases in all. Of the five that weren't proven to be fake, two died and three have vanished.'

'Vanished?'

'They just disappeared. Along with their families. Now you might assume that they had just moved to avoid press attention, but trust me Nightingale, I'm good at tracing people. They vanished from the face of the earth.'

'And the two that died?'

'A teenage girl in France. She fell asleep in the bath and drowned. And a sixty-year-old man in Spain. Died in a car accident.'

'Accident's happen,' said Jenny.

Ricky smiled thinly. 'He had a spotless driving record and crashed into a tree on a perfectly clear day with zero alcohol in his blood. Like I said, one of three things happens: the case is shown to be a fake, the person with the stigmata vanishes, or they die. No one with stigmata lives happily ever after, and I think it's the Vatican that's behind it.'

'Ricky, are you absolutely one hundred per cent sure that Tracey isn't faking this, either deliberately or...' He left the sentence unfinished.

'You think Dave and Carla might be doing it?' Ricky shook his head. 'Definitely not. When a kid is shown to be faking stigmata it's usually because there's religion in the family. That's not the case here. There isn't a Bible in the house and Tracey has never set foot in a church.' He waved at the cuttings. 'Not a single one of the fake cases occurred in an aethiest household. Not one.' He took them downstairs to the kitchen. Tracey's mother was sitting at the kitchen table with the girl. They both looked worried as Ricky introduced them to Nightingale and Jenny.

'Would you like tea?' asked Mrs Spradbery.

'We're fine,' said Jenny.

Ricky pulled out chairs for Nightingale and Jenny and they sat down. Ricky stood by the door, his arms folded.

Nightingale smiled at Tracey. 'Your uncle says that you talk to the Virgin Mary. Is that right?'

The girl nodded solemnly.

'Who told you she was the Virgin Mary?'

'She did. At first I thought she was an angel but she isn't, she's the mother of Jesus.'

'But no one else can see her, is that right?'

'She doesn't let everyone see her. That's what she told me. Only special people.'

Nightingale nodded. 'Can I talk to her?'

'Only if you can see her. Can you see her?'

'Is she here now?'

'Of course,' said Tracey. 'She came in with you. She's over there, by the fridge.'

Nightingale and Jenny looked at the fridge, then at each other. Jenny shrugged.

'She's smiling,' said Tracey.

'I bet she is,' said Nightingale.

Tracey looked at the fridge and cocked her head on one side. She seemed to be listening intently, a worried frown on her face. Eventually she nodded. 'I'll tell him,' she said. She looked at Nightingale.

'She says you have to help.'

'She said that?'

Tracey nodded earnestly.

'Did she say why?'

'She said you know why. She says it's important.'

'Tracey, can she tell me herself?' asked Nightingale.

Tracey looked towards the fridge. 'Is that okay?' she asked, then stared into space for half a minute. She frowned. 'Can you say that again?' she said and stared at the fridge for several seconds before looking back at

Nightingale. 'She said you need to think about Astronomy Chapter Six Verse Sixteen.'

Nightingale frowned. 'Astronomy? You mean Deuteronomy?'

She nodded. 'That's right. That's what she said. Deuteronomy'

'What is it?' asked Jenny.

Nightingale smiled at her. 'You shall not put the Lord your God to the test, as you tested him at Massah.'

Jenny frowned. 'What?'

'It's a quote from the Bible. Deuteronomy Chapter Six Verse Sixteen. That priest said the same thing to me in my office. There's no way Tracey could have known that.'

Jenny leaned towards him. 'Are you saying she's really here? The Virgin Mary? She's in the room now?'

'She's there,' said Tracey. 'It's just that you can't see her.'

'Really Mr Nightingale, it's way past Tracey's bedtime,' said Mrs Spradbery.

'That's okay,' said Nightingale, standing up. 'I think we're done.'

'I'll show you out,' said Ricky. He took Nightingale and Jenny down the hall to the front door. 'You need to take her somewhere,' said Nightingale. 'You need to get her well away from here.'

Ricky nodded. 'I could do that,' he said. 'I've got a cottage on the edge of Dartmoor. It's a bit of a smallholding, I grow vegetables and stuff.'

'Bit of a farmer?'

'It's an eco-thing,' said Ricky. 'I use it as a bolt-hole when I'm working on a book. Tracey can stay with me. I'm pretty sure I can look after her wounds. It's mainly just a matter of keeping them clean.' He opened the front door.

'No one else knows about the cottage?' asked Nightingale.

'No one outside the family.'

'What about Tracey's parents? Can they go with you? I could do with the house to myself for a day or two. If that's okay with you?'

'What are you planning?'

'I'm going to try to get the Vatican off your back. So it would be best if you take Tracey and her parents and hole up in Devon for a few days until we see how it pans out. Okay?'

Ricky nodded. 'I guess so,' he said.

* * *

Jenny drove Nightingale to his flat in Bayswater. He went inside only to pick up his car keys and then he collected his MGB and drove to Clapham. He parked down a side street, turned up the collar of his raincoat and lit a cigarette as he walked to Perry Smith's house. He was halfway through the cigarette when he reached Smith's two-storey terraced house. Standing in front of the black railings around the steps that led down to the basement were two large black men and Nightingale grinned as he recognised the larger of the two. 'Bloody hell, T-Bone, doesn't Perry ever let you have a day off?'

The man grinned and opened his arms, inviting a hug. He was close to seven feet tall and despite the fact it was almost midnight he had on wraparound Oakley sunglasses. Like his companion he was wearing a black Puffa jacket over a dark tracksuit and had gleaming white Nikes on his feet. He hugged Nightingale hard and patted him on the back with shovel-sized gloved hands. 'The proverbial bad penny,' said T-Bone. 'Always turning up when you need something.' He released his grip on Nightingale and introduced him to his companion. 'Jack Nightingale, private dick,' he said. He waggled his little finger. 'He doesn't charge much because his dick isn't that big.'

'How are ya doing?' said the man, nodding at Nightingale, his blank eyes suggesting that he wasn't expecting an answer to his question.

'I need a favour from Perry,' said Nightingale, gesturing at the front door with his chin.

'Of course you do, that's the only time we ever see you. What do you need, Birdman?'

'Something from your lock-up in Streatham.'

T-Bone grinned and shook his head sadly. 'You treat us like a bloody hardware store, you know that?'

'I don't know many people who have what you have,' said Nightingale. He flicked his cigarette butt into the gutter and it sparked as it hit the tarmac. 'Is he in?'

'Yeah but he's busy. Busy in a way that we don't want to go interrupting him, if you get my drift.'

'I can wait,' said Nightingale.

'No need, Birdman,' said T-Bone. 'Perry says I can sort you out whenever you need sorting out.' He shrugged his massive shoulders. 'He's taken a shine to you. Dunno why, but he has.'

'That's good to hear,' said Nightingale. There was a black Porsche SUV parked across the road and he gestured at it. 'Can you fix me up now?'

'Where's that piece of shit Noddy car you drive?'

'My classic MGB? Parked up.'

'I'm not a taxi service, Birdman.' He grinned. 'But what the hell. You're practically family.' He clapped him on the shoulder. 'You've got money, right, because Perry's all out of freebies.'

Nightingale patted his pocket. 'I've got money.'

The two men walked over to the SUV and climbed in. 'Are you going to drive in them?' asked Nightingale, pointing at T-Bone's shades.

'You criticising my eye-wear, Birdman?'

'I'm just surprised that you can see anything at night.'

'I can see just fine. I wear them all the time.'

'Even during sex?'

T-Bone laughed. 'Especially during sex,' he said. It was short drive to the Streatham lock-up, in a row of six, tucked away in an alley between two rows of houses. It was brick-built with a metal door and a corrugated iron roof. T-Bone switched off the engine. 'What do you need?' he asked.

'You know what I need,' said Nightingale. 'A gun.'

'Calibre? Revolver or automatic? Silenced or not? Birdman, you're like a guy walking into Carphone Warehouse and saying he wants a phone.'

'Something threatening.'

T-Bone grinned. 'Threatening?'

'I want someone to know that I mean business.'

'Does it have to be concealed?'

'Not really,' said Nightingale. 'I plan to be indoors.'

'I think I've got just what you need,' he said. He took a Magnalite torch from the glove box, climbed out of the SUV and unlocked the door to the lock-up and pushed it up. He switched on the torch and motioned for Nightingale to follow him inside. There were a dozen or so wooden boxes on the concrete floor, and two rusting metal filing cabinets. 'Shut the door,' said T-Bone. 'We don't want anyone walking by and eyeballing us.'

Nightingale did as he was told. T-Bone tucked the torch under his arm then opened one of the wooden crates, pushed aside the Styrofoam packing and pulled out a bubble-wrapped package. He unwrapped it and handed it to Nightingale. 'That's as threatening as they come,' he said, shining the torch at the weapon.

It took Nightingale several seconds to realise what it was – a sawn-off shotgun. He grinned. 'Perfect,' he said, picking it up. 'Cartridges?'

'How many do you need? A box?'

'I won't be going duck-shooting, T-Bone. Just a half dozen.' He checked the action. It was a 12-bore with the twin barrels side by side. That meant it only held two cartridges but two would be more than enough. 'So how much?'

'Shall we say a monkey?'

'Five hundred quid for a sawn-off. How about we say a marmoset?'

T-Bone frowned. 'What's a marmoset?'

'It's a very small monkey. About a quarter the size of a regular monkey. So I'm thinking a hundred and twenty-five, a hundred and fifty at most.'

T-Bone laughed and held out his hand for the weapon. 'If you don't want it, Birdman, just say so.'

'I want it, T-Bone, but I want to pay a fair price. I'm not getting expenses on this job, it's pro-bono.'

'Pro-bone? What the hell's pro-bone.'

'Pro-bono. A freebie. For the public good.'

'Yeah, well I ain't in the mood for freebies. Let's call it two-fifty.'

'Including the cartridges?'

'Go on then,' said T-Bone. 'But next time you should go to Aldi or Lidl. I hear they're real cheap.'

'You're a star, T-Bone. A prince among men. Now have you got a holdall or something I can use to keep this away from prying eyes?'

* * *

Nightingale let himself into Ricky Hamilton's house. He locked the front door and slid a bolt across. The lights were all off and he left them that way, his eyes were already used to the darkness. He took out his mobile phone and called the number on Jonah Connolly's card. When the priest answered he sounded groggy. 'Did I wake you up?' asked Nightingale.

'What time is it?'

'About two. Sorry about the late hour but I've seen Tracey and yes, the stigmata's real. So's the whole cancer story. The neighbour, the boy, is fine and dandy. His cancer has completely gone.'

'That's good to hear, thanks. Where is she, the girl?'

'Staying with her uncle in Bromley. South London.'

'Can you email me a report?'

'Will do, as soon as I'm on the office. The reason I was calling so late is that they won't be in London after tonight.'

'What do you mean?' Nightingale could hear the tension in the man's voice.

'Tomorrow morning the whole family's leaving London. They wouldn't say where they're going. They say it's because she's still got the whole stigmata thing and they don't want it to become a media circus.'

'And you've no idea where there'll go?'

'Like I said, they won't say. I managed to get to see Tracey, but they weren't happy. Anyway, I just thought you should know.'

'I appreciate that, Mr Nightingale. Thanks. Do you happen to have the address to hand?'

Nightingale smiled to himself. 'I do, yes, Do you have a pen?'

* * *

It was just after three o'clock in the morning when Nightingale heard the sound of breaking glass from the kitchen, He was sitting in the hallway on a chair he'd taken from the kitchen, the loaded sawn-off shotgun in his lap. From where he was sitting he had a clear view of the front door and the open kitchen door, and he could see into the living room. He had been fairly sure that Connolly would come in the through the kitchen but he had wanted to keep his options open.

After a few minutes he heard the kitchen door open and a soft footfall across the tiled floor. He stood up and aimed the shotgun at the kitchen doorway. Connolly was dressed all in black and was holding a small torch in his left hand. He stiffened when he saw Nightingale. 'Surprise!' said Nightingale.

'What the hell are you doing here?' asked Connolly. He was wearing a black ski mask but Nightingale knew it was the priest.

'Take off the mask,' said Nightingale. 'And switch off the torch.'

Connolly did as he was told. He was wearing a black polo-neck sweater, black jeans and black trainers. On his back was a black backpack.

'Drop the torch on the floor. And the mask. Then put your hands behind you neck.'

'What the hell is going on?' asked Connolly.

Nightingale gestured with the gun and Connolly followed the instructions that Nightingale had given him.

'Back into the kitchen,' said Nightingale. 'If I end up shooting you it'll be easier to clean tiles than a carpet.'

'This is crazy,' said Connolly. 'I hired you, remember.'

'Walk backwards into the kitchen, slowly. Then kneel down.'

Connolly did as he was told. Nightingale kept the shotgun aimed at the priest's chest. A glass panel in the kitchen door had been shattered. 'I see you dumped the cassock but then I suppose it's not the best thing to wear when you're breaking and entering,' said Nightingale. 'I see you stuck with the black, though.'

'What's this about, Nightingale? What's going on?'

'Kneel down. Then put your hands behind your neck.'

Connolly obeyed. Nightingale switched on the lights.

'How many are with you?'

'Two men. They're in a van outside.'

'At the front or the back?'

'In the alley.'

'Are they priests?'

'Yes.'

'Are you?'

Connolly nodded. 'I'm a priest, yes.'

'And you work for the Vatican?'

'I told you all this when I hired you. You seem to have forgotten who's calling the shots. I'm the client and you're the hired help.'

Nightingale gestured with the shotgun. 'So far as calling the shots are concerned, I think the gun says it all. If you're a priest then what are you doing breaking into this house at this ungodly hour?'

Connolly took a deep breath and then sighed. He didn't answer.

'Cat got your tongue?'

'What do you want Nightingale? Are you going to call the cops? Are you going to shoot me? Or bore me to death?'

'I haven't decided yet,' said Nightingale. He gestured with his shotgun. 'Tell me something. If I pull the trigger, do you think God would save you?'

The priest shrugged. 'Probably not.'

'So God has saved the little girl but thrown you to the wolves. What does that tell you?'

The priest frowned. 'How has God saved her? You're the one with the shotgun.'

'That's right,' said Nightingale. 'But that depends on whether or not you believe in free will, doesn't it?'

Connolly raised his hands in surrender. 'To be honest, Nightingale I'm getting to the stage where I'd rather you pulled the trigger. I really can't be bothered listening to you any more.'

'Put your hands behind your neck.' Nightingale pointed the shotgun at Connolly's chest and the priest did as he was told. '. 'For God's sake be careful with that thing,' he said.

'For God's sake? You realise the irony in that statement.' Nightingale lowered the shotgun but kept it pointed at the priest's groin. 'You've done this before?'

'Is that a question or a statement?'

'Both, I guess. I think I know the answer already. It's what you do, isn't it?'

Connolly nodded. 'Someone has to.'

'To protect the Church?'

'The Church has been around a lot longer than you or me,' said Connolly. 'It's like a living organism, it fights to stay alive.'

'And it kills if necessary?'

'If it has to, yes. There's no arguing with that. The Catholic Church has killed hundreds of thousands of people over the years. Look at the Crusades.'

'And because Tracey Spradbery is a threat, you're here to kill her?'

'Is that what you think?' He laughed harshly. 'It's not about killing her. It was never about that.'

'What then?'

'We're going to take her to a safe place. Somewhere where she can be looked at by experts. People who understand stigmata.'

'Where exactly?'

'A convent in Spain,' said Connolly.

'A prison?'

'If she truly has been blessed by God, we need to know,' said Connolly. 'And we can't do that here.'

'So you're planning to kidnap her?'

'I am to take her to a safe place,' said Connolly.

'That's kidnapping. Pure and simple.'

'We need to know the truth, and we won't get the truth here.'

'I told you the truth. She has the stigmata, that's a fact. And she believes that she talks to the Virgin Mary. Take your bag off and slide it across to me.'

'What?'

'The bag,' said Nightingale, nodding at Connolly's backpack. 'I need to look inside it. Take it off very slowly.'

'You think I have a gun?'

'Or a knife. Either way, I'll know that you're lying and that you came here to do her harm.'

'And then what? You'll shoot me?'

'I'll call the cops.'

'You broke in here as well, remember?'

Nightingale shook his head. 'I was invited in by Tracey's uncle. It's his house. He gave me the key. Do you have a key? Oh no, of course not. You smashed a window to get in.''

Connolly nodded at the shotgun in Nightingale's hands. 'And you've got a licence for that sawn-off shotgun, of course.'

'Mate, I'll whack you over the head with it, hide it and then call the cops. Oh, and I used to be a cop so there's a good chance they'll listen to me.' He gestured at the backpack with his gun. 'Take it off.'

Connolly scowled, but did as he was told.

'Push it over here,' said Nightingale. 'Not to enthusiastically, I'd hate to pull the trigger accidentally.'

Connolly pushed the bag across the floor. Nightingale pointed the gun at his face. 'Now put your hands behind your neck again.'

Connolly obeyed the instructions.

'Now move your right foot over your left.'

Connolly did as he was told. Nightingale nodded his approval. In that position Connolly wouldn't be able to get the jump on him. He kept the shotgun aimed at Connolly's chest with his right hand while he used his left to root around the inside of the bag. He pulled out two rolls of duct tape and tossed them on to the kitchen table. Then he took out a small leather wallet with a zip running around the outer edge. Nightingale walked over to the table, put the shotgun down and quickly unzipped the wallet, never taking his eyes off Connolly. He opened it. Inside were two clear plastic boxes, each containing a syringe full of colourless liquid.

Nightingale picked up the shotgun again and levelled it at Connolly's chest.

'What are you going to do?' asked Connolly.

'I'm going to inject this into your arm. Or rather, I'm getting you to do it to yourself.' A look of fear flashed across Connolly's face. 'If you're right and it's a tranquiliser then you'll go to sleep,' Nightingale continued. 'If you're lying and there's poison in it, then you'll die. Either way, I'll go outside and tell your pals to come and collect you.'

'It's a tranquiliser,' said Connolly.

'Good to know,' said Nightingale. 'Good for you, anyway. Frankly I'm easy either way.' Nightingale placed one of the plastic boxes on the table.

And then what?'

'Assuming you're not dead? That depends on you.' Nightingale reached into his jacket pocket and took out a small digital recorder. A red light glowed on the side. 'If I ever see you again, this recording goes to the cops. Along with the CCTV footage from my office. And the DNA we took from the cigarette you smoked in my office.'

'You swabbed my DNA?'

'Your story sounded fishy even back then,' said Nightingale. 'We've already had the DNA profiled through a lab we use and we've got decent fingerprints off the business card you gave me. And on the cup you drank your coffee from. This tape is more than enough to have you sent to prison for a long, long time.'

Connolly nodded slowly. 'And I'm guessing there's a reason you haven't already called in the cops?'

'You read my mind,' said Nightingale. 'Can you figure it out for yourself?'

'You want to take the pressure off the girl.'

'She has a name.'

Connolly nodded. 'You want the dogs called off Tracey. And you need me to do that. Right?'

'Got it in one,' said Nightingale. 'You tell your bosses that she's faking it. She made up the whole thing to attract attention to herself. Most of the cases you look at are fakes, right?'

'That's true.'

'So that's what they'll be expecting to hear,' said Nightingale. 'You tell them that it's over. You do that and this recording stays in a safety deposit box along with the CCTV footage and the DNA profile, and a full statement from me just in case something happens to me. Can you do that for me, Jonah?'

Connolly said nothing for several seconds, then he forced a smile. 'It doesn't look like I have much choice, does it?'

'My Plan B is to call the cops now and have you and your pals charged with conspiracy to murder and to go public with as many TV and newspaper interviews as I can give over the next few days. There's a fair bit of hysteria out there about what's been happening to kids recently, and I think we can both agree that the Catholic Church has had more than its fair share of bad publicity.'

'I hear what you're saying, Nightingale.'

'And we have a deal?'

Connolly nodded slowly. 'We have a deal.'

'Get up slowly. And sit down at the table.'

Connolly did as he was told.

Nightingale grinned. 'Cool. Now inject that into your arm and we can all go our separate ways.'

'Are you serious?'

'Deadly serious,' said Nightingale. 'But if you don't want to do it, we've still got Plan B.'

Connolly stared at the plastic box and then slowly opened it. He took out the syringe, put the box down and carefully pulled off the small orange plastic cap off the needle. 'You don't have to do this. It's a sedative.'

'Then you've nothing to worry about.' He gestured with the shotgun. 'Don't spill any. And Jonah, maybe you should think about another line of work.'

'Offering career guidance now, are you?'

'You need to ask yourself why the Virgin Mary would appear to a little girl and not someone like you. And then you have to ask yourself what side of the fence your actions have put you on, and what the repercussions to that might be.' He wagged the shotgun at the priest. 'I have to say that the Virgin Mary is one lady I wouldn't want to get on the wrong side of.' He shrugged. 'I'm just saying, that's all.'

Connolly pulled up his left sleeve, then tapped on his arm to expose a vein. He opened his mouth to say something but Nightingale shook his head and pointed the shotgun at his face. Connolly sighed, inserted the needle into a vein and gently pushed the plunger and slowly injected the contents of the syringe into his arm. When he'd finished he removed the needle, replaced the orange cap, and put the syringe back into its box. Just as he closed the box his eyelids fluttered and he slumped forward. A few seconds later he was snoring softly.

Nightingale left the house through the front door, hiding the shotgun under his raincoat. He waited until he was back in his MGB before he phoned Ricky Hamilton. 'Where are you?'

'Almost at the cottage,' he said. 'It's been a long drive.'

'It's over,' said Nightingale.

'Are you sure?' asked Ricky.

'As sure as I can be,' said Nightingale. 'But you have to keep her away from South London. For a while, at least.'

'That's not a problem,' said Ricky. 'She can stay with me for as long as needs be.'

'No one can see her, you know that?' said Nightingale. 'The Vatican will be told that her stigmata was a fake. If she attracts attention again they might send someone else. So no healings, no Press, no nothing.'

'Will they send someone else?'

'I don't think so,' said Nightingale. 'I put the frighteners on the guy, and he knows that if anyone else threatens Tracey I have more than enough evidence to go to the police.'

'Evidence?'

'I have him on tape, but I also span him a line about CCTV, DNA and fingerprints. He'll run off with his tail between his legs and he won't be back. And the deal we've done is that he'll tell his bosses that the girl is a fake.'

'And they'll believe him?'

'Ninety-nine per cent of stigmata cases are fake, that's what they expect to hear,' said Nightingale. 'But you have to keep her under the radar from now on.'

'I hear you,' said Ricky. 'I'll take care of her.'

'I hope so,' said Nightingale. 'And Tracey? How is she?'

'Still bleeding,' said Ricky.

CURSED

Jack Nightingale figured that he had earned a day off. He'd worked pretty much non-stop over the weekend following a husband who'd told his wife he was attending a sales conference in Somerset when he was in fact giving his secretary a good seeing- to in a five-star spa just outside London. He had plenty of video of the pair together, and a copy of the bill, courtesy of a fifty-pound note he'd slipped to a Slovakian receptionist. It was the perfect surveillance job and since he didn't have much in the diary he decided to spend Monday getting his MGB serviced and collecting his dry-cleaning, with, hopefully, a few hours in the pub watching Sky Sports.

He phoned his assistant first thing and told her not to expect him in, then shaved and showered before pulling on a suit and tie out of habit. It was only when he was tying his tie that he realised he didn't need his office gear, but he couldn't be bothered changing so grabbed his raincoat and headed out in search of breakfast.

He was on his way to Costa Coffee for a cappuccino and an almond croissant when he heard the squeal of tyres behind him and he looked around to see two uniformed cops getting out of a patrol car. He carried on walking but then he heard rapid footsteps and felt a hand on his arm.

'Jack Nightingale?'

Nightingale stopped and turned to face them. They were both in their late thirties with tired eyes and bad skin, overweight and bored to death with the job. 'Maybe,' he said.

'Maybe?' said the taller of the two. He had a razor burn across his neck and a pimple on his nose that was about to burst. 'What sort of answer is that? Show me some ID.'

'What? You can't go around asking innocent passers-by for ID,' said Nightingale. 'Not unless we entered an alternative reality overnight and we're now part of Nazi Germany.'

'Under the Terrorism Act 2000 I have the right to detain you and ascertain your identity,' said the officer. He was a sergeant; Nightingale saw the stripes as he folded his arms and glared at him.

'So now I'm a terrorist?' said Nightingale. 'What, you think I'm a suicide bomber and under my raincoat I've got TNT ready to blow?'

'It's him, Sarge,' said the second policeman. No stripes. A constable. 'I was on a job with him about five years ago – a jumper on Battersea Bridge. He talked her down.'

'See, that wasn't so hard, was it?' said the sergeant. He jerked a thumb at the car. 'We need you to come with us.'

'Need? What's this about?'

'Don't shoot the messenger, Mr Nightingale,' said the sergeant. 'Superintendent Chalmers wants a word.'

'And what, he's forgotten how to use a phone? What does he want?'

'I'm having a bad day, Mr Nightingale,' said the sergeant. 'In fact this month has been bad and the year as a whole has been pretty shitty. The last thing I need right now is a former cop giving me a hard time just because I'm doing what my superintendent told me to do.'

'Understood, Sarge,' said Nightingale. 'Are you okay if I smoke in the car?'

'Providing you don't give me any grief you can burst into flames for all I care. Though strictly speaking, as the car is our place of work, you're prohibited from smoking under the 2006 Health Act.' He grinned. 'But if you don't tell anyone, we won't.'

They walked to the car and Nightingale climbed into the back and lit a Marlboro. He opened the window and blew smoke as the constable drove the car across the Thames and down through south London to Clapham. They pulled up on the west side of the common.

The sergeant pointed to a cluster of police vehicles parked on the grass. 'Chalmers is over there.'

'You're trusting me to walk over on my own, are you?' said Nightingale. 'What if I did a runner?'

'Then I'd Taser you,' said the sergeant.

'He would too,' said the constable. 'I've seen him do it.'

'I'll take your word on that,' said Nightingale. He got out of the car and walked over to the vehicles. There were two patrol cars, a grey saloon, a white van and an ambulance. Nightingale saw Chalmers standing with two uniforms as they watched a group of Scenes of Crime Officers working around what looked like two dead bodies lying face down.

Chalmers was wearing a black overcoat that glistened like it might be cashmere and there were flecks of mud over his gleaming black shoes. He looked disdainfully over at Nightingale. 'What took you so long?' he said, running a hand through his greying hair. Flecks of dandruff peppered his shoulders.

'I didn't know we had an appointment,' said Nightingale. He stood next to the superintendent and nodded over at the SOCO team as he took his cigarettes out of his pocket. 'What's the story?'

'Four black men shot two other black men and a dozen black men and women swore blind they didn't see a thing.' The superintendent shivered as a cold wind blew over the common. 'Welcome to multicultural Britain.'

'So why are you here and not Trident?'

'Trident have got their hands full with two shootings in Brixton and a knifing in Lambeth so I'm holding the fort until they can get someone out here.'

Nightingale lit a cigarette and blew smoke. 'I hope you're not planning to pin this one on me, because I was in Bayswater all morning.'

'You're here because you were a cop once and another cop is in trouble.'

'So you want me to lend you a few quid, is that it?'

Chalmers glared at Nightingale. 'Will you just shut up and listen for once in your life?' he said. 'And keep that bloody smoke away from me. I don't want to go home stinking of cigarettes.' He shoved his hands into the pockets of his overcoat. 'You ever come across a sergeant, name of Simon Roach? Based at Catford?'

Nightingale shook his head. 'Doesn't ring a bell.'

'He's with the TSG,' said Chalmers. 'At least he was. He's been off duty for months and there's no sign of him going back.'

'Stress-related?' said Nightingale. 'Holding out for a decent compo, is he?'

'This isn't about compensation, you insensitive bastard,' hissed Chalmers. 'Simon Roach is at death's door. Literally.'

'What's wrong with him?' asked Nightingale.

Chalmers took a deep breath and shrugged his shoulders. 'The doctors don't know,' he said. 'He's in the ICU at the Hospital for Tropical Diseases just off Tottenham Court Road. Before that he was on a ward in Lewisham. Before that he was in and out of A&E and before that he was seeing his GP pretty much every other day. And not one of all the doctors he's seen has any idea what's wrong with him.'

'Tropical diseases? They think he caught something?'

'They put him there because they don't know what else to do with him,' said Chalmers. 'They've tried every antibiotic, every treatment, but nothing works. The doctors in Lewisham just wanted to be rid of him, and most of the mystery cases end up in UCL.'

'UCL?' He blew smoke, turning his head so that it didn't go near the superintendent.

'University College London. They run the Hospital for Tropical Diseases The smartest doctors in the UK work there and they're stumped.'

'So why are you telling me this? Last time I checked my CV, doctor wasn't on it.'

'No, but arsehole was,' said Chalmers. 'You think I'm happy talking to you? You think I'd even piss on you if you were on fire?'

'I guess not.'

'And you'd guess right. But Roach is a good cop and his wife's an old school friend of the Deputy Commissioner's wife, so we've got to do something.'

'So again, I'm asking why me?'

Chalmers screwed up his face as if he had a bad taste in his mouth. 'Mrs Roach thinks that her husband was cursed.'

Nightingale's jaw dropped. 'What?'

'Cursed. By a gypsy.'

Nightingale laughed harshly. 'You're winding me up, right?'

'I don't have time for practical jokes, Nightingale. I've got about a dozen things on my plate at the moment and they're all urgent. It happened during the Dale Farm clearance. The Met supplied some of the teams for the operation. Roach was one of the first in and there was an incident with an old woman.'

'An incident?'

Chalmers grimaced. 'Look, I need you to talk to Roach's inspector. He was there at Dale Farm. He can talk you through it.'

'He was cursed by a gypsy, is that what you're saying? He was cursed and now he's in the ICU?'

'I'm just telling you what I've been told. You've got previous in the supernatural heebie-jeebie world so I need you to see what's going on.'

'And who'll be paying for this?'

'You'll be doing it out of the goodness of your heart,' said Chalmers.

'Yeah, well, I'd be happier with five hundred quid a day plus expenses,' said Nightingale.

'Like I said, you'll do it out of the goodness of your heart, and if you don't I'll make your life a misery. And that's in the short term. Long term, private investigators are going to be licensed, and getting the all-clear from the Met is going to be a necessity for any gumshoe planning to ply his trade in London.'

'Are you threatening me, Chalmers?'

Chalmers smiled cruelly. 'Damn right I'm threatening you. I'll do whatever I need to do to get Simon Roach out of that hospital bed. But I shouldn't have to threaten you, Nightingale. It wasn't so long ago that you were a cop. Simon Roach is a good cop who needs help and so far as I can see you're the only person who can save him. You can't walk away from that responsibility.' Two of the SOCOs walked towards Chalmers. The superintendent handed Nightingale a piece of paper. 'That's the number of Roach's inspector, Ian McAdam. He'll fill you in. Do what you can and keep me in the loop.'

Nightingale slipped the piece of paper into his pocket. 'How do I get home?'

'Tube? Bus? Taxi? How would I know?'

'You're a prince, Chalmers,' said Nightingale. He flicked the remains of his cigarette away and headed back to the road.

A West Indian nurse with a gleaming gold tooth in the front of her mouth and bright red lipstick showed Nightingale to the Intensive Care Unit.

Mrs Roach was already there, ashen-faced and watery-eyed. She was wearing a pale blue polo-neck sweater and a tartan skirt and while he figured she was probably in her forties she looked a good ten years older. She was sitting on an orange plastic chair, a newspaper unread on her lap, a paper cup of tea on the floor by her side. There was dark brown scum on the top of the tea, as if she hadn't touched it.

Nightingale introduced himself and she offered him her hand. There was no strength in it and he shook it carefully, almost afraid that it would break. He sat down beside her. 'Superintendent Chalmers said I should talk to you,' he said.

Mrs Roach sniffed and wiped her nose with the back of her hand. 'He said you might be able to help.' She looked at him, her eyes red and fearful. 'What can you do, Mr Nightingale? If the doctors can't do anything, how can you help Simon?'

'Where is he?' asked Nightingale, avoiding the question because he had absolutely no idea what he could do to help Roach.

Mrs Roach pointed at a glass window. Her fingernail was bitten to the quick. 'He's in there,' she said.

Nightingale stood up. There were white blinds on the other side of the window but they were angled so that he could see through into the next room. Two figures were moving around, wearing what at first glance looked like white spacesuits. Thick clear plastic tubes led from the back of the suits and up into the ceiling. One of the figures was stacking packs of ice around a patient while another was looking at a bank of instruments on a stainless-steel table.

'What's happening?' asked Nightingale.

Mrs Roach sniffed. 'He's hot, they said. They're cooling him down.'

Nightingale went back to sit next to Mrs Roach. 'How bad is he?'

She sniffed again. 'It's very bad, Mr Nightingale.'

'Jack,' said Nightingale. 'Call me Jack. What have the doctors told you?'

Before she could answer, a middle-aged Indian doctor came hurrying down the corridor, his white coat flapping behind him. 'That's one of the doctors,' said Mrs Roach. 'Dr Patel.'

Nightingale stood up and introduced himself. The doctor peered at Nightingale over the top of a pair of horn-rimmed spectacles. 'You are a family member?' he asked.

'Friend of the family,' said Nightingale. 'Can I ask you what's wrong with Mr Roach?'

The doctor toyed with a stethoscope that was hanging around his neck. 'He has some sort of infection but we're not sure of the nature of it,' he said.

'Like a blood thing? A virus?'

'No, not a blood thing. His blood seems perfectly normal. Whatever it is has targeted his skin. But his blood work is fine. He has the blood of a fit, healthy man.'

'So what's happening to him?'

The doctor sighed. 'Something is changing his skin cells. Hardening them, making them almost waxy. We've never seen anything like it before.'

'But what would cause that?'

'If we knew the answer to that question we'd be a step closer to knowing how to treat him,' said the doctor. 'We can't find a virus and there's no bacterial infection that we can see; he wasn't bitten by anything; there are no punctures in his skin that we can find.'

'Can I talk to him?' asked Nightingale.

'No one is going in there without a suit,' said the doctor. 'We don't know how he got it and we don't know how it's transmitted.'

'But I'm all right. I'm not infected,' said Mrs Roach. 'I was with him for four weeks until he was taken into hospital. And our kids are all right.'

'And we're grateful for that,' said the doctor. 'But the simple fact is that we don't know how your husband contracted this disease. It could be that most people have a natural immunity and that only certain people can be infected. It could be transmitted by contact, or through breathing. We just don't know.' The doctor turned to look at Nightingale. 'Frankly you'd be wasting your time anyway. He hasn't been able to speak for days, not since the infection reached his throat. Today he hasn't reacted to noise so we think it has also affected his hearing.'

'But what exactly is happening to him?'

The doctor wiped his hand down his face. 'As I said, I've never seen anything like it,' he said. 'The change in his skin cells is causing his body temperature to rise, but he's losing the ability to sweat and that means he's burning up inside. Literally cooking.'

Mrs Roach gasped and she sat down heavily.

'I'm sorry, Mrs Roach,' said the doctor, sitting down next to her. 'We're doing everything we can for him.'

'What have you tried so far?' asked Nightingale.

The doctor looked up at him. 'Pretty much everything,' he said. 'The previous hospital tried most antibiotics and they had just started him on steroids when he was moved here. We've used the most powerful antibiotic cocktails that we have and they had no effect. Now we're working our way through various combinations of steroids but nothing has worked so far.' He gestured at the window. 'The ice bath will lower his core temperature but we can't keep him cool that way for ever.'

'So what's next?'

The doctor took his glasses off and began polishing them with a handkerchief. 'We've contacted a skin specialist in Sweden and sent him the case file, and we're talking to skin hospitals around the world, but for the moment . . .' He shrugged. 'I wish I knew, really. In all my years as a doctor I've never seen anything like this.'

Nightingale caught a train from Charing Cross to Catford. It was the middle of the day and the carriage he was in had only four occupants, one of whom was an obese woman in a Day-Glo pink jumpsuit, with dyed blonde hair pulled back into a Croydon facelift. She was looking after three toddlers, though 'looking after' was stretching it as all she did was to scream at them in between talking at the top of her voice into her smartphone. Nightingale spent the journey wondering why the smartest phones seemed to be in the hands of the stupidest people. His own phone was a five-year-old Nokia and he only ever used it as a phone. He had no idea how to access the phone's GPS. He'd never even tried to connect to the internet, and if it had a camera he had never come across it.

He wanted a cigarette but, while he figured the pink harridan wouldn't notice if he lit up, he was mindful of the CCTV cameras watching his every move. He was going to Catford to meet the inspector who had led Roach's team at Dale Farm and figured that it wouldn't look good if he was arrested by British Transport Police officers as he got off the train.

The woman was explaining to a friend how she'd managed to get disability allowances for her children based on a series of afflictions that all seemed to consist of nothing but initials. She boasted that she was claiming close to two thousand pounds a month from the State, at which point Nightingale realised that perhaps she wasn't quite so stupid after all.

When he arrived at Catford he stood on the pavement outside the station and lit a Marlboro before phoning the inspector. McAdam told Nightingale to wait where he was.

Nightingale was finishing his second cigarette when he heard the dull juddering of a diesel engine seconds before a grey Sprinter van with police markings turned the corner and headed for the station approach. A group of black teenagers on BMX bikes scattered and a homeless man sitting by the side of a cash machine began gathering up his belongings. The van came to a halt and a side door rattled open. A uniformed inspector wearing a stab vest over his uniform stepped out and nodded at Nightingale.

'You Jack?'

Nightingale nodded, transferred his cigarette to his left hand and offered the right one. The inspector shook it then popped his head inside the van. 'Why don't you guys take ten?' he said. 'Grab a coffee and pick me up here.' The driver nodded and McAdam pulled the door shut. He rubbed his hands together as the van drove away. 'So you're going to help Scrambled, are you?'

'Scrambled?'

'Scrambled is Simon's nickname.' Nightingale frowned in confusion and the inspector smiled. 'Roach. Cock. Cockroach. Cock to chicken. Chicken to eggs. Eggs to scrambled.'

'You TSG guys do love your nicknames, don't you? What's yours?'

'They call me Sir,' said the inspector. He nodded at the cigarette in Nightingale's hand. 'Are you going to let me have one of those?'

Nightingale took out his pack of Marlboro and tapped one out. He offered the pack to the inspector and the officer took the cigarette. Nightingale lit it for him and the two men inhaled gratefully.

'Actually they call me Jack, too.'

'Because . . .?'

'Because my name's McAdam – so that's Tar McAdam and that's Jack Tar, so I'm Jack.' He took another pull on his cigarette. 'Have you seen him? Scrambled?'

'Yeah.' Nightingale shuddered. 'It's . . .' He shrugged. There were no words to describe how terrible it was.

'Yeah, me and the guys were in at the weekend but he was out of it. He didn't show any reaction at all.'

'They were using the ice, were they?'

'Loads of it. Said he was burning up.' He took a drag on his cigarette and then blew smoke up at the sky. 'You saw what was happening to his skin, did you?'

'They wouldn't let me into the room.'

'I went in. Had to show my warrant card and stretch the truth a bit, but they put me in one of those quarantine things and I had ten minutes with him.' He took another drag on his cigarette. 'His skin's turning into scales. Like a snake.'

'Yeah, the doctor said it was hardening.'

The inspector shook his head. 'They don't know what's happening. And we can hardly tell him the truth, can we?'

'The truth?'

'He was cursed. By one of the gypsies at the Dale Farm eviction. She grabbed him by his left arm and cursed him, and that's where he started having a problem. His left arm is where it started.'

'You're serious?'

The inspector's eyes hardened. 'What, you think this is some sort of practical joke, do you? You think we're making this up? Chalmers said you could be a bastard.' He jabbed what was left of his cigarette at Nightingale. 'You're Scrambled's last chance, mate, that's why I'm here talking to you. Chalmers said you knew stuff about curses and that.'

'Not exactly,' said Nightingale. 'But I know people who might know. So what happened?'

'You saw it on the news, right?'

'Who didn't?'

'Ninety families had to be evicted. It was a messy one, messy from day one. It was Green Belt and the travellers owned a piece of the land – they'd bought it legally – but they didn't have planning permission for Dale Farm so they had to be moved. They used every legal trick in the book, but once they knew we were serious about going in they started pulling in activists from all over Europe. Rentamobs. They got set for a battle, and that's what we ended up with.' He blew smoke as he cupped the cigarette in his hand.

'It took an hour or so to get through the barricades they'd set up, and they were pelting us with bricks and chunks of wood with nails in it. Not that you'd see that on the BBC – they were very selective about what they showed. They put poisoned meat down to try to get our dogs. And they used their kids as barriers. Hid behind the kids because they knew that would make us look bad.' He shook his head. 'The worst sort of scum. I mean, they call themselves travellers but they do bugger all in the way of travelling.

And they knew they had no legal right to be there. They'd used lawyers every step of the way. They could have just packed up and moved on but they wanted a confrontation.'

He took another pull on his cigarette. 'We went in at about seven in the morning and by midday we were ready to let the bailiffs in. But it was a bastard five hours, I can tell you.' He shuddered. 'I've been in some nasty situations over the years but Dale Farm was the worst. They hated us, make no mistake about that. For them it was personal. They swore at us, they spat at us, they said that they wished our families would die of cancer. I'll tell you something: if I ever got the chance to deal with one of those scumbags away from CCTV I'd beat them to a pulp for what they did to us. But of course that's never going to happen, is it? Human rights and all that. We're all geared up for protecting society's scum while they ride roughshod over decent people.'

He smiled ruefully. 'Sorry,' he said. 'Forget I said that. It's just that it was a shitty job, and a totally unnecessary one. The council should have nipped it in the bud when they first started moving in. Instead they let it get out of control and as always it's us cops that have to do their dirty work.'

'I was a cop, I know what it's like,' said Nightingale. 'So what happened to Scrambled?'

'We were among the hundred men first in,' said McAdam. 'That was to gain access to the site and secure the caravans. That was when we had most of the fighting. Then we had to gain access into each caravan to get the occupants out. It wasn't pleasant. And more often than not we'd have to go in with long shields. But Scrambled would always try to talk first. Scrambled always liked to lead from the front. His team respected him for that. He loved the TSG, too. Never wanted to work anywhere else.' He finished his cigarette and flicked it into the gutter. 'Chalmers said you used to be a negotiator,' he said.

'Yeah, I was in armed response. But I'd done all the negotiation courses.'

The inspector nodded. 'Scrambled would have made a good negotiator. He had the gift of the gab. He was good with people, too. You come in for a lot of shit in this job but for him it was water off a duck's back. He'd hold back the guys with shields and pop in himself, see if he could talk them out without having to get physical. That's what makes this so shitty. He was the last person anyone should have wanted to hurt.'

'I still don't understand what happened,' said Nightingale.

'It was the fifth caravan that we went into. This one actually was a caravan; it had wheels and could easily have been driven off the site. Scrambled was there with six officers from his bus.'

'Bus?'

'That's what we call the van. Now, standard procedure would be to announce ourselves then force the door before accessing the premises with two long shields, forcing any occupants back against the wall so that they can be restrained. But Scrambled wasn't having any of that. He knocked on the door, identified himself, and opened it. It wasn't locked so he went inside, on his Jack Jones. His team followed him but he was doing all the talking. There was an old woman lying in a bed, wrapped up in a blanket. Her grandson was there, a guy in his thirties. And his wife. Gypsies. The real McCoy.'

'I'm not sure I get the difference.'

'Travellers are mainly Irish. Tinkers. They're the ones that will sell you white heather or pretend to resurface your driveway or strip the lead off the local church roof. Gypsies, real gypsies, are the Roma. Now, I'm not an expert by any means, but I did some reading before we went into Dale Farm. There are four million or so of them around the world and there's a subgroup in the UK, the Romanichal, who've been around since the sixteenth century. They'd be the ones that used to travel around in the horse-drawn caravans, back in the day. These days they have transit vans and deal in scrap metal. Anyway, Scrambled tells them that they have to leave and the grandson says they're not going; he says they're Romanichal and that the legal action against the travellers has nothing to do with them.'

'And was that true?'

'The legal action specified which plots had to be cleared. It didn't matter who was on them. And, like I said, their caravan was mobile so they could have easily driven away. In fact they did later on, once the bailiffs were in and threatening to tow it.'

'So what happened?'

'Scrambled says the man pulled a knife. The problem is that he was between the guy and the team so no one else saw it. One of his team had a camera but again the view was blocked. But if Scrambled said the guy had a knife then he had a knife.'

'No argument here,' said Nightingale.

'So the guy lunges at Scrambled with a knife. They struggle. The guy falls back. The team crash the husband against the wall – don't ask me what happens to the knife. His wife takes a swing at Scrambled, damn near claws his eyes out. He falls against the old woman. And that's when it happened.'

'That's when what happened?' asked Nightingale.

'That's when she cursed him. She was grabbing his left arm, just above the wrist. And she said something to him, not in English. Then she spat in his face.'

'She was an old woman?'

'In her nineties. You're wondering how she was able to grab a cop a third of her age. Scrambled said she was strong, a grip like a vice. But you have to understand what Scrambled's like. He'd never get heavy with an old woman; it's just not in his nature. He managed to make her let go and the three of them were removed from the van. Social services were there and they looked after the old woman. The knife was nowhere to be seen so the guy wasn't charged, and once it was all over they drove off the site.'

'And Scrambled was okay then?'

'Right as rain. But the next day his arm was itching. Like he had a rash. He got some cream from Boots but that didn't help. It just kept spreading. After a week it was all over his arm. Then it went across his back. He was still working, mind. It was under his shirt so no one knew that he had a problem. He kept going to see his GP and they tried him on tablets and lotions and stuff, but nothing worked. And the more it spread the more his health deteriorated.' He shrugged. 'And now he's where he is. At death's door.'

'But I don't see why you're so convinced he was cursed. I'm guessing the camp was filthy; he could have picked up a bug. Got bitten by something. Or maybe it's just a coincidence. Maybe he'd have got sick anyway.'

The inspector shook his head. 'It started where she touched him. He showed it to me the next day. It was like you could see her fingerprints on his arm. And it spread from there.'

'So maybe she had some contagious skin disease.'

'I spoke to social services and they said she was okay. They had a paramedic check her out.' While the inspector was talking the van returned and parked a few feet away from them. 'What do you think, Jack? Can you do anything? He's dying. The doctors are no help.'

'I'll try,' said Nightingale. He realised he didn't sound confident, but then at that moment he didn't feel as if he had a snowball's chance in hell of helping Roach.

'The guy with the knife, the alleged knife, did you get his name?'

'Smith,' said McAdam. 'Sampson Smith. Not sure if that's his real name, though. Most gypsies are only in the system if they've committed a crime and even then we've no way of knowing if they're using their real name. Most of them don't even have birth certificates.' The inspector looked at his watch. 'Look, I've got to go. There are innocent members of the public out there waiting to be hassled solely on the basis of their colour.'

'I don't envy you your job,' said Nightingale.

'It has its moments,' said McAdam. 'Since the riots they've put us on a longer leash. The powers that be have realised what happens if we're too soft on the scumbags. It'll never be like the old days, and maybe that's no bad thing, but a lot of the street crime problems would be solved if we were allowed to smack a few heads and nip trouble in the bud.' He reached into his stab vest and pulled out a small grey thumb drive. 'You should look at this,' he said. 'We were videoed up when we went in. The picture's okay but the sound isn't great. I've put on the approach to the caravan and what went on inside. It's only about five minutes in all.'

Nightingale took it off him and slipped it into the pocket of his raincoat. The inspector threw Nightingale a mock salute and climbed into the van. Nightingale watched it drive away before heading back into the station.

Nightingale's office was in South Kensington, above a hairdresser's that offered him a fifty per cent discount if he allowed one of their trainees to cut his hair. Nightingale's assistant, Jenny McLean, was at her desk tapping away on her computer keyboard when he walked in.

She frowned and brushed a lock of blonde hair behind her ear. 'I thought you were taking the day off,' she said.

'Yeah, you and me both,' he said, hanging up his raincoat. He went over to her desk and gave her the thumb drive. 'There's a movie on that I need to see.'

'It's not porn, is it?'

'Of course not.'

'You're sure?'

'What sort of person do you think I am?'

'The sort who'd think it was funny to show his secretary porn in the afternoon.' She clicked the thumb drive into one of her computer's USB slots. 'So to what do I owe this unexpected pleasure?'

'Chalmers.'

'Your nemesis?'

'He's hardly that. But he needs a favour.'

'From you?' She tapped on her keyboard. 'Did hell freeze over and I missed it?'

'What do you know about gypsies?'

'Not much,' said Jenny. She clicked on an icon and the screen was filled with a grainy image of a group of caravans. 'Is this it?'

'I guess so,' said Nightingale, pulling up a chair and sitting next to her.

Jenny clicked her mouse and the picture began to shake. Two policemen in full riot gear – black fireproof overalls, blue helmets with Perspex visors and long Perspex shields – were moving towards a large white mobile home.

'It's not a home movie, then,' said Jenny.

'It's the Dale Farm clearance,' said Nightingale.

A uniformed sergeant moved into view. Unlike his colleagues he wasn't wearing riot gear, just a stab vest over a white shirt. 'All right, lads, stand back. Let the dog see the rabbit,' he said, walking towards the door of the mobile home.

Nightingale pointed at the sergeant. 'That's Simon Roach. He's in hospital now.'

'Who took the video? It's not TV footage, is it?'

'One of the cops had a camera. The Met uses them a lot these days in case they get accused of anything.'

Roach knocked on the door and identified himself, then pulled it open. He shouted something inside and then slowly went up a set of three metal stairs. The two officers with shields followed and the cop with the camera moved up behind them. The picture swung from side to side as the cop moved. First Roach, then the cops with shields, disappeared into the mobile home.

By the time the cop with the camera went through the door, Roach was already struggling with a large man in a stained T-shirt and baggy cargo pants. 'Can you see a knife?' asked Nightingale.

'I can't see anything,' said Jenny. 'I'm getting seasick just watching it. Why's it moving around so much?'

'The camera's clipped to his vest,' said Nightingale. 'He's not aiming it. It just shows what he sees, pretty much.'

The man in the cargo pants was shouting and swearing and then Roach staggered back. He moved to the side and the two officers with shields rushed forward and slammed the man against the wall.

'Police brutality?' asked Jenny.

'He had a knife,' said Nightingale.

The officers pulled back their shields and the man fell to the floor. A heavyset woman with bleached hair and wearing a blue Adidas tracksuit swung a punch at the sergeant and began screaming abuse at him.

'Nice to see a woman standing by her man,' said Jenny.

The sergeant put up his hands to defend himself but the woman began slapping him with both hands.

Another officer in riot gear appeared from behind the camera. He lunged at the woman and grabbed her arms, then wrestled her out of the picture.

The sergeant knelt down, took his handcuffs from a pouch on his belt and handcuffed the man's hands behind his back. The officers with the shields then grabbed the man's arms and dragged him away. He kicked out at the sergeant and spat at him.

'Why would you bother trying to fight trained cops in riot gear?' asked Jenny.

'Maybe they don't have TV,' said Nightingale. 'It probably passes for entertainment.'

The sergeant moved to the far end of the mobile home. Then he jumped as a figure sat up – an old woman who opened her mouth and screamed.

Jenny flinched and then laughed to cover her embarrassment. 'Where the hell did she come from?'

Nightingale didn't answer. He was staring at the monitor. The old woman was shouting at the sergeant. She had managed to grab his wrist and flecks of spit were peppering Roach's face as she screamed at him. She was ancient, at least ninety years old, with wispy white hair through which her skull was clearly visible in places. Her mouth was a pink toothless cave and her lips were thin and bloodless. But her eyes burned with a fierce fire and Nightingale could see that Roach was having problems pulling his arm away.

'What's she shouting?' asked Jenny. 'That's not English, is it?'

'She's a Romany gipsy. According to that guy's boss, she's cursing him.'

'And you believe that?'

'He's lying in the ICU as we speak,' said Nightingale. 'And the doctors have no idea what's wrong with him.'

The old woman was shrieking at the sergeant and he was trying to prise her fingers off his arm. The camera moved closer. Nightingale could make out one word being said over and over again. 'Sap.'

Eventually Roach managed to release her grip and he took a step back, talking to her in a calm voice. 'It's all right,' he said. 'We're not here to hurt you.'

'Sap!' screamed the woman, pointing at the sergeant. Her fingernail was several inches long, brown and gnarled.

'Please calm down. No one is going to hurt you,' said Roach.

Two women PCs in riot gear appeared either side of the camera and moved towards the old woman. One had taken off her helmet. She was in her early twenties, probably young enough to be the old woman's great-granddaughter.

Roach wiped his forehead and moved out of shot, then the camera moved slowly backwards and eventually left the mobile home.

The man in the T-shirt was being frisked next to a police van. Roach was standing some distance away, rubbing his arm where the old woman had grabbed him. The video came to an end.

'Is that it?' asked Nightingale.

'That's the lot,' said Jenny. She tapped on her keyboard then peered at her monitor. 'Snake,' she said.

'What?'

'The old woman was screaming "sap". That's Romani for snake. She was calling him a snake.'

'Or cursing him.'

'You think that's what happened? She put a gypsy curse on him?'

'I already told you that he's dying. And he was fit and well up until the moment she grabbed him.'

'And Chalmers expects you to what? Lift the curse?'

'Apparently.'

'So what's your plan?' asked Jenny.

'My plan? How can I have a plan? He gets cursed by an old gypsy and now he's at death's door. How could I possibly have a plan?'

'You could go to see Mrs Steadman.'

Nightingale grinned. 'Yeah, that was my plan.'

'Give her my best.'

'Do you want to come?'

'I've got work to do, Jack.'

'You think I'm crazy, don't you?'

She smiled sweetly. 'I know you're crazy,' she said. 'But I know that Chalmers is right. If he has been cursed then you're probably the one person that can help him.'

Nightingale caught a black cab to Camden and it dropped him outside the Wicca Woman shop, shoehorned between a shop that sold hand-knitted sweaters and a boutique that specialised in second-hand denim.

A bell chimed as he pushed open the door and Mrs Steadman looked up from the cash register. Her bird-like face broke into a smile. 'Mr Nightingale, I haven't seen you for ages,' she said. Mrs Steadman was in her sixties but she had the bright, inquisitive eyes of a young child. She was dressed from head to foot in black – a tight polo-neck sweater, leggings and elf-like ankle boots. She was barely five feet tall and Nightingale knew that she was standing on a wooden box to reach the cash register.

'I haven't needed much in the way of witchcraft supplies lately,' he said.

'Tea?' she asked.

'You read my mind, Mrs Steadman.'

'Do me a favour and turn the sign on the door around, will you?' she asked. 'I haven't had a break and neither of my assistants turned up today. Young people, they've no sense of responsibility, have they?'

'Definitely not,' said Nightingale, turning the sign around so that it was showing 'Closed'.

Mrs Steadman stepped down off her box and walked around the counter, her boots clicking on the wooden floor. She took him through a beaded curtain and waved him to a circular wooden table and chairs, illuminated by a brightly coloured Tiffany lampshade. A gas fire was burning and Nightingale took off his raincoat and sat down as Mrs Steadman busied herself making tea.

'I've got a bit of a problem, Mrs Steadman,' said Nightingale, and he told her what had happened to Simon Roach.

'That's awful,' she said as she carried over a tray on which there was a brown ceramic teapot, two blue and white striped mugs and a matching milk jug and sugar bowl. 'Simply awful.' She sat down and poured tea for them both. 'You have to be careful with the gypsies. They lack a certain . . . self-control.'

'Well, in this case I can tell you the policeman didn't deserve what happened. I saw a video of the whole thing and he wasn't being in any way aggressive towards her.'

Mrs Steadman nodded sympathetically as she stirred sugar into her tea.

'So can you help him?' asked Nightingale.

Mrs Steadman smiled. 'Perhaps,' she said.

'Perhaps? I was hoping for more than perhaps,' said Nightingale.

'Magic is not an exact science, Mr Nightingale. What works for some doesn't work for all. I can tell you what to do and how to do it, but the rest is up to you.'

'So what do I need to do?'

'First, I must sell you some Fiery Wall of Protection crystal salts, made to a recipe of my own.' She smiled. 'And I'm afraid they must be purchased because when the salts are given freely they lose their power.'

'And what's in them?'

Mrs Steadman laughed. 'I'm afraid we're a little like the Coca-Cola company in that respect,' she said. 'The ingredients remain a tightly controlled secret. I can tell you that I include sandalwood, black snakeroot and rue, but in all there are more than two dozen essences and herbs.'

Nightingale took out his wallet. 'Sold,' he said.

'That will be twenty pounds,' she said. She got up from the table and went through into the shop, returning a minute later with a purple paper sachet. She gave it to him, then took his twenty-pound note and tucked it under the teapot before sitting down again. 'It's a useful mix,' she said. 'You can use it for a ritual floor wash or sprinkle it on the path outside your house to attract good luck, and a small amount in your washing machine will keep your clothes smelling fresh all week.'

Nightingale thought she was joking and began to chuckle, but it was clear from the stern look she gave him that she was serious so he turned the chuckle into a throat-clearing cough. 'And how do I use it?' he asked.

'You need to run a full bath,' she said. 'When the bath is half full you add the salts and swirl them in a clockwise direction. That is important, Mr Nightingale. It must be clockwise. When the bath is full you place four small white candles at the corners of the tub and light them. You then put the person who has been cursed into the bath and you leave him in the water until the candles have burned down. When they have gone out you pull out the plug and he stays in the bath as the water drains away. The curse will flow away with the water.'

'That's it?' said Nightingale. 'He takes a Radox bath and the curse will go away?'

Mrs Steadman looked down her nose at Nightingale. 'It's hardly Radox,' she said. 'If you'd rather try that, of course, you're more than welcome to return my crystal salts.'

'I was joking,' said Nightingale.

'It's good that you have kept your sense of humour,' she said. 'But please don't think that a gypsy's curse is a laughing matter. A genuine gypsy curse leads to just one thing: death. Don't forget that.'

'I won't, Mrs Steadman.' He stood up. 'I don't know what I'd do without you.'

'Oh, I'm sure you'd muddle through,' she said. 'You usually do.'

The same West Indian nurse was at reception when Nightingale arrived at the ICU. When he asked her if she'd page Dr Patel she flashed him a smile that showed her gold tooth and said, 'Of course, honey, anything for you.'

Dr Patel arrived five minutes later and, unlike the West Indian nurse, had clearly forgotten who Nightingale was. 'I'm really busy, Mr Nightingale,' he said once Nightingale had re-introduced himself. 'I can't keep breaking off from work to speak to friends of patients. Mr Roach is getting worse but we're doing everything we can.'

'That's why I'm here, Doctor,' said Nightingale, taking the purple paper sachet from his pocket. 'This will help.'

The doctor frowned and took the sachet from Nightingale.

'You need to fill a bath with water and add the salts,' said Nightingale. 'Then you need to put him in the bath and light four white candles, and he has to stay in the bath until the candles burn down.'

'Are you insane?' said Dr Patel, looking at Nightingale over the top of his spectacles. 'What is this? You think because I'm Indian I'm some sort of witch doctor? You think I use mumbo-jumbo to cure my patients?'

'It'll cure him,' said Nightingale. 'He's been cursed and that will drive the curse away.'

'Cursed? What the hell are you talking about, man? He's got an infection, possibly an auto-immune disease.'

'Dr Patel, you have to listen to me. It's the only way of curing him.'

'Mr Nightingale, I was born in Southall. I studied medicine at Leeds University, where I came second in my year. I have worked in some of the best hospitals in the country. I am not some immigrant doctor who has only just got off the boat. How dare you attempt to tell me how to practise medicine!' He threw the sachet at Nightingale and it bounced off his shoulder and fell on the floor. 'Get out, now!' The doctor turned to the nurse, who had been watching the exchange. 'Call security and have this man escorted off the premises.'

'Yes, Dr Patel,' said the nurse.

The doctor walked off, his coat flapping behind him.

'Three bags full, Dr Patel,' she said.

Nightingale bent down, picked up the paper sachet and put it back in his pocket. 'You're not really going to call security, are you?' he asked the nurse.

'Do I need to?'

'Nah, I'm all done here.'

The nurse gestured with her chin at the departing doctor. 'Three years Dr Patel's been here and he still hasn't bothered to remember my name.'

'He's a very busy man.'

'It's not that. He thinks we nurses don't matter. Especially the ones like me who aren't graduates.' She leaned towards him and lowered her voice. 'You said that Mr Roach was cursed?'

'Why, are you going to tell me that I'm crazy, too?'

She shook her head solemnly. 'I believe in curses,' she said. 'I've seen what they can do.'

'What's your name?' asked Nightingale.

'Joyce,' she said.

He held out his hand. 'I'm Jack. And I'm very happy to meet you.'

They shook hands. 'The thing is, Dr Patel can't listen to you,' said Joyce. 'No medical man can. If they start to believe in curses then it takes away their power.'

'Power?'

'They get power from respect, and they get respect because they can heal people. But if someone can heal without medicine, then they will lose their respect.'

Two male nurses walked by and Joyce stopped speaking until they'd gone past.

'Doctors don't know everything, Jack. Not by a long way.'

'And if you don't mind me asking, Joyce, how do you know so much about curses?'

She looked left and right to make sure that no one was within earshot. 'Obeah,' she said. 'Jamaican folk magic.'

'Magic? You mean voodoo?'

Joyce laughed. 'It's called Obeah where I come from. Charms play a big part in it, and curses. Voodoo is something else. Now my grandmother, she knew all about voodoo. She was born in Ghana and she had the gift even when she was a child. She tried to teach my mother but my mother didn't have the gift.'

'And it works? Voodoo works?'

'Like a charm, Jack, like a charm.' She laughed but stopped when she noticed Dr Patel was standing at the end of the corridor, glaring at them. 'You should go,' she said. 'He'll want to know why I didn't call security.'

By the time Nightingale got back to the office, Jenny had already left. He sat down at her desk and called her mobile. 'Where are you?' he asked.

'First of all, I'm not twelve years old, and second of all, you're not my mother,' she said.

'Very droll,' he said. 'I just wanted to know if you can talk.'

'I've had that nailed since I was two,' she said.

'You're not driving?'

'No, I'm in a wine bar waiting for Barbara, with a very nice chilled Pinot Grigio on the table and a dark, good-looking waiter who keeps smiling at me.'

'Dark, good-looking waiters who smile a lot are usually gay,' said Nightingale. 'Or looking for a marriage visa. I need help.'

'Yes, you do,' said Jenny.

'I need to look at that video again. I'm sitting at your computer but the screen's blank.'

'It's asleep,' said Jenny. 'Wiggle the mouse. The mouse is that—'

'I know what a mouse is,' said Nightingale. He moved it and the screensaver appeared. A beach scene; palm trees leaning towards an azure sea.

'I'm pretty sure that the thumb drive is still in the USB slot,' said Jenny. 'Pop your head between your knees and take a look under the desk.'

Nightingale grunted as he did as he was told. 'Yeah, it's there.'

'Right, sit up straight and I'll talk you through it.'

Five minutes and three false starts later, Nightingale had the police video up on the screen. He thanked Jenny and ended the call. Despite the shakiness of the picture he was able to get the registration number of Sampson Smith's mobile home.

He called Superintendent Chalmers, who started speaking the moment he took the call. 'He's worse, Nightingale. When are you going to do something?'

'I'm on the case,' said Nightingale. 'But I need to track down the gypsy woman. I need to talk to her.'

'She's moved off the site, you know that. They were all cleared off.'

'I know, but I've got the registration number of the mobile home. They must have stopped somewhere, probably on another council site. Can you run a check for me?'

Chalmers didn't speak for several seconds and Nightingale began to think that he was going to refuse. 'It'll take some time,' Chalmers said eventually. 'A lot depends on whether they moved into another county.'

'That's what I figured,' said Nightingale. 'If I ring up then I'm just a nosy private eye and they won't tell me a thing, but if it comes through the Met they'll take it seriously.'

'Give me the number,' said Chalmers.

Nightingale's ringing mobile woke him from a dreamless sleep. He leaned over and groped for his phone. It was Chalmers. Nightingale squinted at the digital alarm clock on his bedside table. It was 8.10.

'We got lucky,' said Chalmers. 'They're still in Essex. They're on a small council site about twenty miles north of Dale Farm. I'll text you the address.'

'Thanks,' said Nightingale.

'Don't thank me,' said Chalmers. 'Just get it sorted.' The line went dead.

Nightingale rolled out of bed and phoned Jenny. 'At the risk of sounding like your mother again, where are you?' he asked.

'Just about to get into the car,' she said.

'Can you do me a favour and pick me up? We've got to go and see a gypsy about a curse.'

'You know my mileage rate? Plus lunch on you.'

'Agreed,' said Nightingale. 'And can you pick up a coffee and a Danish or something on your way?' He ended the call and padded to the bathroom.

Jenny rang to say she was outside just as he was pulling on the jacket of his suit. He grabbed his raincoat, hurried down the stairs and climbed into the passenger seat of her Audi A4. He grinned when he saw the Starbucks cup in the cup-holder. 'You really are a sweetie,' he said. There was bag containing a Danish pastry on the dashboard and he broke off a piece and ate it.

'So where are we going?'

'Oh, sorry,' said Nightingale. He fumbled in his pocket and gave his Nokia to her. 'The postcode's in this,' he said. 'Chalmers sent me a text.'

'Why don't you program the SatNav while I drive?'

Nightingale laughed. 'Yeah, that'll work. If you don't want to end up in the Thames you'd be better doing it yourself.'

Jenny fed the details into the SatNav. She sighed as she looked at the digital readout. 'Ninety minutes? You're sure you want to do this?'

'I don't have a choice,' said Nightingale. He settled back in his seat and reached for his coffee.

Jenny was a better driver than the SatNav realised and they reached the traveller site in just under an hour and twenty minutes. It was a small site on the outskirts of a shabby council estate, with room for a dozen caravans. The site was surrounded by a wire-mesh fence and in the centre was a toilet block with washing facilities. There were concrete foundations but only three were occupied. Two were prefab buildings without wheels but standing on the third was the mobile home that Nightingale recognised from the video.

'Home sweet home,' said Jenny. 'What do you want to do?'

'You stay here. I'll go and have a chat.'

'He had a knife, you said.'

'I'm just going to talk, Jenny.'

'It'll be safer if there are the two of us.'

'How does being two targets make us safer?' said Nightingale. 'Trust me. It'll be better if I'm on my own. It'll be less threatening and all I want to do is talk.'

She nodded slowly but he could see that she wasn't convinced. He climbed out of the car and walked towards the site entrance. There didn't seem to be anyone around but chained to the ground were two large black and white bull terriers that began barking furiously as soon as he entered the site.

To the left were half a dozen rusting cars, all on blocks with their wheels removed and their bonnets open like gaping mouths, the engine bays empty. T-shirts and underwear were hanging from a washing line and there was litter everywhere – crumpled-up newspapers, empty soft-drink cans, vegetable peelings and crushed cigarette packets. He saw a Marlboro pack and immediately the nicotine urge kicked in, but he ignored it.

He walked over to the mobile home and knocked on the door. There was no reply so he knocked again. He waited a full thirty seconds and tried the handle. It turned and the door swung open. 'Hello?' called Nightingale. There was no reply so he walked slowly up the metal steps. 'Hello?' he called again, then stepped across the threshold. If anything, the mobile home looked smaller than it had done on the police video. There was a folding table to the right, with a couple of chairs and a large LCD television that he didn't remember seeing in the video. There were built-in cupboards and at the far end was the bed where the old woman had been. There was a bump under a quilt but it wasn't moving. 'Mrs Smith? Are you there?' said Nightingale.

He moved carefully towards the bed. Dirty clothes were strewn across the floor. A threadbare pullover. A pair of boxer shorts. A football sock.

He reached the bed. 'Mrs Smith?'

The quilt was thrown back and the old woman sat up. Her eyes were milky and her face was so deeply wrinkled that it was sexless. Her hair was white and lifeless and so patchy that the thick blue veins threading her scalp were visible. She blinked and Nightingale saw that her eyelashes were virtually translucent and her eyebrows non-existent. She was wearing a faded pink nightgown that barely covered her pancake-flat breasts and as she raised her arms towards him folds of liver-spotted skin flapped back and forth. Her mouth worked soundlessly.

Nightingale took a step back. He heard a car engine outside and through a faded curtain he saw a battered blue Transit van pull up. Nightingale cursed as he saw Smith climb out and walk towards the mobile home.

He flinched as the old woman screamed and then something hit him in the middle of the back. She'd leaped at him, he realised, and he staggered forward, fighting to keep his balance. The woman began howling like a banshee and she clawed at his throat. Her legs wrapped around his waist and she gripped him so tightly that he could hardly walk.

The door to the mobile home was wrenched open and Smith stood in the doorway. 'Gran!' he shouted.

Nightingale tried to speak but she had a vice-like grip on his throat, her nails digging into his flesh like talons. He shook his shoulders from side to side and tried to force her hands away. She was screaming into his ear but Nightingale couldn't make out what she was saying.

Smith took a step towards Nightingale. He had a thick leather belt around his waist, with a buckle in the shape of an eagle with outspread wings. Smith grabbed at one of the wings and it came away in his hand, revealing a two-inch blade. Nightingale managed to prise the old woman's fingers from his throat but as she fell backwards Nightingale lost his balance and they both fell back on the bed. Smith roared and charged forward, holding the knife in front of him.

Nightingale lashed out with his foot and managed to knock the knife to the side but Smith's momentum carried him forward and he fell on top of Nightingale. The whole mobile home lurched under the weight of the three of them on the bed. Smith pushed himself up and brought the knife down hard, aiming for Nightingale's chest. Nightingale managed to get his left hand under Smith's wrist to block the blow and then he reached over with his right hand and grabbed the wrist and twisted. Smith roared in pain but he kept a grip on the knife. Nightingale brought his right leg up, put his foot against Smith's groin and pushed with all his might. Smith staggered backwards and his arm wrenched free from Nightingale's grasp.

Smith raised the knife again but Nightingale sprang off the bed and kicked Smith's left knee. As Smith's leg buckled Nightingale grabbed at Smith's right hand.

'Jack!'

Nightingale realised that Jenny was standing in the doorway.

'Jenny, get away!' he shouted. He twisted Smith around and pushed him towards the bed, then ran down the mobile home and out through the door.

He turned just as Smith burst out of the mobile home, swearing and waving the knife. The dogs went wild, barking and throwing themselves against their chains.

'I'm going to cut you!' Smith roared slashing the blade from side to side.

'Leave him alone, you bastard!' shouted Jenny. She was holding a small black cylinder in her right hand and as she pressed a trigger on the side a liquid sprayed out and splattered over Smith's face. Smith yelled in pain and staggered back.

Nightingale rushed forward, grabbed Smith's wrist and twisted it, then pulled the knife from his hand. Smith tried to grab the knife back but the blade ripped through the flesh of his palm and he screamed.

Jenny kept spraying the liquid onto Smith's face. He staggered against the mobile home, turned around and groped around for the door handle.

Jenny looked over to Nightingale. 'Are you okay?'

'I'm fine,' said Nightingale. He watched as Smith clawed the door open and stumbled up the steps into the mobile home. 'What is that? Mace?'

'Pepper spray,' said Jenny. 'My dad gave it to me years ago. First time I've had to use it.'

'And you always carry it with you?'

'My dad made me promise,' said Jenny, putting the spray back into her bag. She looked at the knife in his hand and grimaced at the blood on the blade. 'Did he cut you?'

Nightingale smiled thinly 'He cut himself. At least I found the knife. He must have shoved it back into his belt when the cops had him on the floor. Have you got a handkerchief or something?' Jenny pulled a handkerchief out of her bag and Nightingale used it to wrap the knife before slipping it into his raincoat pocket. 'Let's go,' he said.

They walked back to the Audi. 'Do you want to call the police?' asked Jenny as she climbed into the driving seat.

'There's no point,' said Nightingale. 'It'd be my word against his. And I was in his home. And he's the one who got cut. Better to let sleeping dogs lie.'

'And the curse? Did you get anywhere?'

Nightingale shook his head. 'Unfortunately, no.'

Jenny leaned over and stared at Nightingale's neck. 'What happened?'

'She grabbed me,' he said. 'The old woman.'

'Look at your neck, Jack.'

Nightingale pulled down the sun-visor and stared at his reflection in the mirror. He pulled his tie down and loosened his collar. There were four red patches on either side of his neck. Marks left by the old woman's fingers. 'They're just bruises,' he said. 'She was pretty rough.'

'They're not bruises,' said Jenny.

'By the time we get back to the office, they'll have gone,' said Nightingale. 'Trust me.'

The marks on Nightingale's neck hadn't gone by the time they got back to his office. If anything they were worse.

'Do you want to try some moisturiser on it?' asked Jenny.

'How bad does it look?'

Jenny fished a small mirror out of her handbag and gave it to him so that he could see for himself. The skin where the old woman had touched him had a waxy look to it. But the skin around the marks had reddened, and there was another patch of dry skin closer to his right shoulder.

'Do you want to see a doctor?'

'A doctor isn't going to help, not if it's what Roach has got.'

'Did she curse you?'

'She screamed at me, and she spat at me. How do I know if it was a curse or not? She wasn't a happy bunny, that's for sure.' He gave her back the mirror. 'It'll be fine.'

'How can you be so calm?'

Nightingale grinned. 'Because I've got one of Mrs Steadman's marvellous potions,' he said.

'And what if that doesn't work?'

'That's okay – there's a money-back guarantee.' He stood up and went over to the coffee-maker. 'Coffee?'

Nightingale got back to his flat just after half past six in the evening. He went straight to the bathroom and took off his tie and shirt. The marks had grown and were each the size of a fifty-pence piece. The skin marks were turning from red to a dark brown. There were other patches of hard skin on his shoulders and a mark the size of a fried egg in the middle of his chest. His heart pounded as he gingerly prodded and probed the blemishes. The skin felt waxy and it was definitely hardening.

He fetched white candles from the kitchen and ran a bath, poured in the powder and followed Mrs Steadman's instructions to the letter. He waited until the candles had burned down and the water drained away before examining himself in the mirror. The marks were still there. He checked again every ten minutes until midnight, but there was no change. At midnight he went to bed but he still got up every hour or so to examine the marks. If anything, they seemed to be growing larger.

Nightingale's whole body itched as if it was on fire and he tossed and turned on the bed. He rubbed his stomach and felt the hard rasp of scales, and when he touched his face there was no feeling – he could have been stroking metal. Every breath hurt because he could barely move his chest. It was as if he was slowly turning to stone, cell by cell.

He tried to roll onto his side but he couldn't move. He turned his head but it was an effort and each small movement was accompanied by an audible click, the sound of a snapping twig. There was a mirrored wardrobe to his left and he forced his eyes open. Slanted lizard eyes stared back at him, yellow with oval pupils. His face was covered in green scales and all he could see of his nose were two black holes which flared in and out in time with his tortured breathing.

As he gasped his thin black lips parted and a red forked tongue flicked out. He was about to scream but just as the sound began to build in his throat he woke up with a start. He lay staring up at the ceiling, his body bathed in sweat. He swallowed but his mouth was dry. It was still dark outside so he padded across to the bathroom and switched on the light. He blinked several times then took a step towards the sink. His eyes were still adjusting to the light so he could barely see his reflection. He ran a hand across his throat, expecting to feel hard scales there, but his skin felt smooth and soft. He leaned closer to the mirror and blinked again. The marks had gone. Gone completely, as if they had never been there. He sighed with relief and then took a deep breath before smiling at his reflection. 'Mrs Steadman, you're a marvel,' he said. He looked at his wristwatch. It was six o'clock. He'd fixed his own gypsy curse. Now it was time to do the same for Simon Roach.

Nightingale got to the hospital just after seven-thirty in the morning. He figured that Joyce was working the day shift all week and probably started sometime between eight and ten. He paced up and down for half an hour and then a coffee shop opposite the hospital opened up so he ordered a cappuccino, sat down at an outside table and took out his cigarettes. It was just before nine and he was on his fourth cigarette when Joyce appeared.

She was wearing a beige trench coat and carrying a large canvas shopping bag. He put out his cigarette and hurried across the road to her. She smiled when she saw him. 'You're not stalking me, are you, Jack?'

'Only in a good way, Joyce. How's Mr Roach?'

Joyce looked pained. 'He wasn't good when I left last night,' she said. 'I'm worried that when I get in . . .' She shuddered. 'The doctors are doing their best but every day he keeps getting worse.'

'That's why I'm here,' said Nightingale. 'I need to lift the curse from him. The gypsy curse.'

'Dr Patel won't let you near the ICU again, you know that.'

Nightingale nodded. 'I know. That's not what I had in mind. I need your help, Joyce.'

'Me? What can I do?'

'You can talk to me about voodoo. That's what you can do.'

Nightingale banged on the door of the mobile home.

'Who is it?' shouted a voice. A man's voice. Sampson Smith.

'The bogeyman,' said Nightingale. 'Now get your fat arse out here.'

The mobile home vibrated as Smith walked from the rear and Nightingale took a step back just as the door was flung open. 'What do you want?' snarled Smith. He winced and rubbed the side of his head.

'I want a word,' said Nightingale. 'Outside. I don't want Old Mother Riley making another grab for me.'

Smith chuckled. 'How's your neck?' he asked.

'Fine and dandy,' said Nightingale. He pulled down his shirt and tilted his head to give Smith a good view of his neck.

Smith frowned in confusion, then winced and rubbed his temple again.

Nightingale readjusted his tie. 'Tell her better luck next time,' he said. 'Except there won't be a next time.'

Smith looked over Nightingale's shoulder and squinted at the Audi parked near the entrance. Jenny was sitting behind the wheel. 'If that bitch comes near me I'm calling the cops,' he snarled.

'Of course you are,' said Nightingale. 'You always do when it suits you, don't you? But when the law's against you it's all about your human rights and persecution of gypsies, isn't it?'

'She squirted mace in my eyes.'

'It was pepper. And you were trying to stick a knife in me, remember?'

Smith grinned and then winced once again and rubbed his temples with the palms of his hands.

'I've still got your knife, don't forget that,' said Nightingale.

'How's that bad news for me?' asked Smith, folding his arms and leaning against the door frame. 'I'm not the one carrying it. That's the offence – carrying the blade. Owning it in the past isn't an offence.'

'There's blood on it.'

'Yeah, there's blood on it.' He held up his hand and waved the still-healing cut in front of Nightingale. 'And it's my blood. How does my blood on a knife you're carrying cause me any grief? You're full of shit.'

Nightingale grinned and reached into his raincoat pocket. Smith flinched and Nightingale chuckled. 'Don't worry, it's not a gun.' His hand reappeared holding a phone. 'It's one of those smartphone thingies. Borrowed it off my assistant. Mine doesn't do pictures.'

'What the fuck are you talking about?'

'No need for bad language,' said Nightingale. 'How're the headaches, by the way?'

'Headaches?'

'The migraines. You keep getting them, right? That's why you're rubbing your temples.'

'What the fuck are you playing at? What's this about?'

'I'm just asking after your health, that's all. They're bad, though, aren't they? The headaches. Like something stabbing right into your brain?'

A curtain twitched at the rear of the mobile home and Nightingale caught a glimpse of the toothless crone peering out at him. He pointed at her and the curtain fell back into place.

Nightingale tapped the screen of the smartphone. 'I can never get these bloody things to work,' he said. A picture filled the screen. 'There we go.' He held it out so that Smith could see it. It was a cloth doll with a crude face drawn on it and Smith's knife tied to its waist with white string. 'You know what that is, right?'

Smith said nothing but the colour drained from his face.

'That's right: a voodoo doll. And it's not one that I threw together myself. This is the real thing. Done by an old man who really knows his stuff. A Juju Man, who lives down in Brixton. He doesn't like gypsies much, I can tell you.' He pushed the screen closer to Smith's face. 'If you look really closely you can see the blood on the blade. Powerful stuff, blood. You can use hair or a bit of clothing but what we've used is as good as it gets. A personal possession and blood.'

'You piece of shit,' said Smith.

'Yeah, sticks and stones.' Nightingale looked at his watch. 'Right about now you're going to get a taste of just how bad it can get,' he said. 'Another thirty seconds or so.'

'You don't scare me,' said Smith.

'It's not about scaring you,' said Nightingale. 'The art of negotiation isn't about making threats or promises, it's about offering choices. That's what I'm doing now. I'm giving you a choice. You can get your grandmother to lift the curse on the cop, or . . .' He left the sentence unfinished.

'Or what?' growled Smith.

Nightingale held up a finger as he looked at his watch. 'I already told you I'm not one for making threats,' he said. 'Any moment now.' He put the phone away and looked at Smith expectantly.

Smith bunched his right hand into a fist and took a step towards Nightingale, but just as his foot touched the ground he screamed in pain and fell to his knees, his hands pressed against the sides of his head.

'There we go,' said Nightingale. 'Right on cue.'

Smith screamed again and this time he pitched forward into a foetal ball, his arms hugging his stomach. He lay there gasping for breath.

'It's not over yet,' said Nightingale.

'You bastard,' gasped Smith.

'Yeah, well, like I said, sticks and stones.'

Smith began to cough and choke and then blood oozed out from between his teeth and pooled onto the muddy ground. He spat and a stream of bloody phlegm slopped into the dirt.

Nightingale took a step back. 'Watch the shoes, mate,' he said. 'Suede is a bitch to clean.'

Smith rolled onto his back and lay there with his chest heaving as blood continued to trickle down his neck.

'That's it for a while,' said Nightingale. 'You can sit up now.'

Smith groaned and shook his head from side to side. Nightingale held out his right hand. Smith grabbed it with both of his and pulled himself up into a sitting position.

The door to the caravan opened and the old woman appeared, wearing a stained blue housecoat and holding a thick black walking stick. She came slowly down the metal steps, glaring at Nightingale and muttering darkly. She stopped a few feet from Nightingale and pointed a gnarled finger at him. She opened her mouth to speak but Nightingale held up his hand.

'Don't bother wasting your breath,' he said. 'There's nothing you can do to me. And if you even try cursing me I'll make your grandson wish he'd never been born.'

'Leave him, Gran, leave him be,' said Smith. He wiped his mouth with the back of his hand. The old woman hobbled over to him. She bent down and slowly rubbed the back of his neck, whispering into his ear. 'It's okay, Gran,' he said.

The woman glared up at Nightingale. If looks could kill he'd be dead there and then, but so far as Nightingale knew looks were just looks. If she touched him then that would be a different matter, but he was fairly confident that with Mrs Steadman in his corner there really wasn't much the old woman could do to him.

'So now we negotiate,' said Nightingale. 'And here's how it works. You tell your grandmother to take it back. I want the policeman back on his feet, fit and well, and that'll be an end to it.'

'The doll, you'll give me the doll?'

'The doll stays with me,' said Nightingale. 'And you can be sure I'll take good care of it.'

Smith nodded slowly.

'You and your grandmother stay away from me and you stay away from the policeman. And if I ever hear that she's cursed anyone else the way she cursed the cop, you know I won't have to come looking for you. I've got a direct line to your deepest, darkest pain.' He smiled amiably. 'And I know that sounds like a threat, but it's not. I'm just letting you know what your choices are.'

The old woman pressed her cheek against Smith's face and whispered to him.

'You've got what you want,' muttered Smith. 'Just go away and leave us alone.'

Nightingale stared down at Smith for several seconds, then turned and walked away. He could feel Smith and the old woman glaring after him, but as angry as they were he knew that there was nothing they could do. He'd won.

Nightingale watched as Simon Roach walked out of the ICU room and into the arms of his wife. They hugged and kissed. Dr Patel emerged from the ICU and began talking to Mrs Roach. Nightingale figured that he was probably taking credit for her husband's miraculous recovery.

Nightingale was standing at the reception desk and was just about to go when Joyce came out of a side room holding a clipboard. She chuckled when she saw him.

'So are you a believer now?' she asked, sitting down at a computer terminal.

'In the Juju Man? Oh yes.'

Joyce laughed. 'That's not what we call him,' she said. 'A voodoo priest is a Houngan.'

'Whatever you call him, he did the trick,' said Nightingale. 'I can't thank you enough.'

'No problem, Jack. I'm just glad that we were able to help Mr Roach.'

'I can't believe how quickly he recovered.'

Joyce laughed, giving Nightingale a glimpse of her gold tooth. 'Neither can Dr Patel. He's planning to write a paper on it.'

'That I'd like to read.' The lift door behind them opened and Superintendent Chalmers walked out, unfastening his overcoat. 'My boss,' whispered Nightingale.

'Best behaviour, then,' said Joyce, and she concentrated on her computer screen.

Chalmers walked over to Nightingale, his face hard. 'So are you going to tell me how you did it?'

Nightingale shrugged. 'I was always a good negotiator. Even you have to admit that.'

'That's what you did? You negotiated with the gypsies?'

'Pretty much.'

'Come on, tell me what you did.'

Nightingale grinned. 'That was never the deal. He's fine and he's going to stay fine. That's all that matters.'

Chalmers snorted softly, turned his back on Nightingale and headed down the corridor towards the ICU.

Nightingale flashed Joyce a smile. 'Honey, I'm going to have to love you and leave you. But I owe you one. If you ever need a private eye, I'm in the book.' He blew her a kiss and walked away.

BLOOD BATH

Jack Nightingale placed his camera on Jenny McLean's desk and grinned. 'Twenty-odd shots of Mr Clifford with his secretary, in her car, checking into the Holiday Inn Express and leaving ninety minutes later,' he said. 'Some nice video of them exchanging saliva.'

Jenny picked up the camera and began checking the shots as Nightingale took off his raincoat and hung it by the door. She was wearing a pale blue dress and had tied her hair back in a ponytail. 'How are you with haunted hotels?' she asked.

'I try to steer clear of them,' he said. 'Why?'

'There's a Mr and Mrs Stokes on their way in,' she said. 'They own a hotel in Brighton.'

'And it's haunted?'

'Apparently.' She connected the camera to her computer and began downloading the pictures and video that were about to make Mr Clifford's divorce much more expensive and have him out of the family home by the end of the week.

The door to the office opened and a middle-aged couple walked in. The man had a receding hairline that suggested baldness was only a year or two away and bifocal spectacles indicated that he had problems seeing things no matter how far away they were. He was wearing a Barbour jacket and had a red scarf wrapped around his neck. His wife was a small woman, barely over five feet tall, and was wearing a jacket and scarf that matched her husband's. She had a thin, drawn face and Nightingale noticed that her nails were bitten to the quick. 'Speak of the devil,' whispered Nightingale, but regretted it immediately when the woman flinched. She'd obviously heard him. He flashed them a beaming smile. 'Mr and Mrs Stokes?''

The couple nodded. Nightingale pointed over at a sofa by the window overlooking the street below. 'Why don't you make yourself comfortable?' he asked. Jenny stood up and took their coats and scarves and offered them coffee.

As Jenny made the coffees, Nightingale sat down behind her desk and asked them what their problem was. Mr Stokes did the talking. He sat with his legs and arms crossed and had a habit of grinding his teeth when he wasn't speaking. He explained that they had bought a hotel in Brighton six months earlier. 'We were getting by for a month or so,' said Mr Stokes. 'At least we were covering our costs, pretty much. But then a website called Haunted Brighton wrote about the hotel, saying that there had been a number of deaths there and that the hotel is haunted by a malevolent spirit.'

'A ghost?' said Jenny, her mug of coffee poised on its way to her lips.

'A ghost we could probably live with,' said Mr Stokes. 'The website said it was a vampire.'

Nightingale laughed out loud. 'A vampire?'

'It didn't actually say vampire,' said Mrs Stokes, flashing her husband a withering look. 'It described a demon that craves blood, that encourages suicides so that it can feed.'

'Complete bollocks, of course,' said her husband.

'But people believe what they read,' said Mrs Stokes. 'And the problem is that if you Google The Weeping Willow Hotel, Brighton, that bloody website comes up on the first page. So every potential booking is cancelled before it even gets started. I mean, who in their right mind would stay in a hotel that had had half a dozen suicides.' She glared at her husband. 'And who in their right mind would buy a hotel like that?'

'That's the name? The Weeping Willow?'

Mrs Stokes nodded.

'It's a nice name,' said Jenny.

'It's a lovely hotel,' said Mr Stokes. 'Everything about it is great. The rooms are lovely, we're close to the beach. It should be a goldmine.'

'Instead of which it's a money pit,' said Mrs Stokes. 'We have to pay the housekeeping staff and the night manager and the chef and the waitress.' She shrugged. 'It's a nightmare.'

'You said suicides,' said Nightingale. 'The website talks about suicides? I thought the website talked about a vampire?'

Mr and Mr Stokes looked at him in astonishment. 'There's no such thing as vampires,' said Mrs Stokes. 'You do know that, don't you?'

'Well...' said Nightingale hesitantly.

Mr Stokes shook his head in annoyance. 'The website said there was some sort of vampire killing guests. It was the first we'd heard about deaths in the hotel but once we looked into it we discovered that there had been several suicides. At least six over the past ten years. But there was nothing unusual or suspicious about them. Just suicides.' He shrugged. 'Sometimes people get to the end of their tether and they just want to end it all.' He looked over at his wife and she glared back at him.

'Theses suicides, were they all guests?' asked Nightingale.

'Five of them were guests but the wife of the last owner also killed herself in one of the bathrooms,' said Mrs Stokes. She began rubbing her hands together as if she was washing them.

Nightingale's jaw dropped. 'I'm sorry, the wife of the guy you bought the hotel from, killed herself there? And you still bought it?'

'We didn't know that at the time,' said Mrs Stokes. 'But yes, that's what happened.'

'The seller didn't mention it?' asked Jenny.

Mrs Stokes shook her head. 'Though to be honest, we never spoke to him, everything was done through the estate agent. Mr Dunbar had already gone back to Scotland.'

'Mr Dunbar was the pervious owner?'

'The estate agent said that he had health problems,' said Mr Stokes. 'Now of course we realise it was just a way of keeping him away from us.'

Nightingale nodded. 'I'm not a legal expert, but shouldn't your surveyor have picked up on something like this? Due diligence or whatever they call it. You made an investment on the back of a surveyor's report, presumably?'

'The building is fine,' said Mr Stokes. 'It's a hundred years old and will stand for at least another hundred. The roof is fine, there's no damp, the electrics and the plumbing were overhauled five years ago.'

'Don't sellers have to tell you about any negative aspects?' said Jenny. 'Things like noisy neighbours and dry rot.'

'Apparently suicides aren't covered,' said Mrs Stokes. 'That's what our solicitor tells us.'

'But you looked at the books, surely?' said Jenny, her pen poised over her notepad. 'Didn't they let you know that something was wrong?'

The couple exchanged a look and Mr Stokes flinched even before his wife spoke. 'I told you we should have done that, didn't I?' she said.

Mr Stokes threw up his hands. 'We were buying the building. The building is fine. I just assumed that the hotel would have guests. That's what hotels do, right?' He looked pleadingly at Nightingale as if he was begging him to agree with him.

'I guess so,' said Nightingale.

'Well guessing isn't good enough,' said Mrs Stokes. 'We haven't had a single booking since the website piece. And it turns out that the hotel had been doing badly long before we bought it.'

'So the seller knew there was a problem?' said Jenny. 'Doesn't that mean he conned you?'

Mrs Stokes shook her head. 'He never actually lied to us,' she said. 'And we didn't ask the right questions.' She flashed her husband a withering look leaving them in no doubt that by 'we' she meant him.

'When we looked around there were people in the restaurant so we assumed they were guests,' said Mr Stokes. 'And he said that we couldn't see several of the rooms because they were occupied.' He held up his hands again. 'With hindsight, I screwed up.'

'And the hotel has always been losing money?' asked Nightingale.

'I think things got worse about six months ago,' said Mr Stokes.

'About the time that Mr Dunbar put it up for sale,' said Mrs Stokes, glaring at her husband.

Before Mr Stokes could respond, Nightingale raised a hand, hoping to cut short any argument. 'So what exactly is it you want me to do?' he asked.

'First of all, get the website to take down its comments,' said Mr Stokes. 'We've tried emailing the website but no one will reply.'

'Have you tried setting a lawyer on them?' asked Jenny. 'If the website is libelling your hotel, you could sue them.'

'We spoke to our solicitor,' said Mrs Stokes. 'He says that we have to prove it's not true. But how do we prove there isn't a vampire in the hotel? It's ridiculous. But it's there on this bloody website for everyone to see.'

'Have you talked to the police?'

'About what?' asked Mr Stokes.

'To confirm that there have actually been deaths at the hotel. And that they were simple suicides.'

'They say that suicide isn't a crime so they are not bound to tell us if there have been suicides at the hotel,' said Mr Stokes. 'Here's what we need, Mr Nightingale. We need you to find out if it's true that there have been a spate of suicides at The Weeping Willow. If so, we need to know what we should do to put a stop to it. And we need you to get this website to take down the rubbish that's there. Can you do that?'

Nightingale smiled and nodded confidently. 'I don't see why not,' he said.

* * *

Detective Sergeant James Gracie was a dour Scotsman in his fifties with a greying beard and a bored expression that suggested there were a dozen things he'd rather be doing than standing in a bar with Nightingale. They were in a small pub a short walk from the John Street police station in Brighton. It was lunchtime, the only time that Gracie said that he had time to spare. The price of the meeting was fair enough – a double whisky and a ham sandwich, which Nightingale had ordered along with a bottle of Corona and a sausage roll for himself. 'I really appreciate this,' said Nightingale as they carried their food and drinks over to a corner table by a fruit machine.

Gracie shrugged. 'Colin Duggan vouched for you, grumpy old bastard that he is. Not sure how much I can tell you, though.' He sat down and looked at his watch. 'I've got to be back in the factory by one. Health and safety briefing followed by a diversity awareness survey. It's all go in the modern world of policing.'

'How long have you been in the job?' asked Nightingale.

'Coming up for thirty years,' said Gracie. 'Retirement beckons.'

'Got any plans?'

'I'm not going to be a private eye, that's for sure,' said the detective. He sipped his whisky. 'I'm planning to sail around the world.'

'Seriously?'

'Biggest regret of my life is that I didn't join the merchant navy. Always been a keen sailor and that's the plan, take my boat around the world.'

'Good luck with that,' said Nightingale. 'I get seasick walking over Tower Bridge.' He raised his bottle of Corona in salute and took a long drink before wiping his mouth with the back of his hand. 'There have been six deaths in The Weeping Willow Hotel, right?'

Gracie nodded as he picked up his sandwich.

'All suicides?'

'Yeah.' The detective took a big bite and chewed contentedly.

'That's a bit unusual, isn't it?'

Gracie swallowed and took another sip of whisky. 'Six in ten years? Not really. I mean, it's quite a few considering it's a small hotel, but I wouldn't say it's that unusual,' He sipped his beer. 'A lot of people choose to end it in hotels, you know that?'

Nightingale shook his head. 'I didn't.'

'Well it's true. Not the cries for help. They do it where there are people so that they can be talked out of it. But the ones who are really committed will often go to a hotel to do it. Smarter ones, anyway. The stupid ones will throw themselves under a train or step in front of a bus. But your average middle class suicide, he or she knows what's involved. You were in the job, you know what death smells like.' Nightingale nodded. Yeah, he knew. It wasn't a smell you ever forgot. The sphincters opened on death and bodily fluids and faeces made their own way out, then the insects would arrive and the body's own bacteria would start the decomposition process. Nightingale shuddered. 'There's a mess, with every suicide,' said Gracie. 'So if you know that and if you've got money, it makes sense to do the dirty deed in a hotel where someone else gets to clear up the mess. You book into a suite, have a bottle of champagne to wash the tablets down, maybe put on a porn movie.'

Nightingale grinned. 'Sounds like you've thought about it.'

Gracie pulled a face. 'Jack, if I had a terminal disease, I wouldn't let it eat me alive. My old man died of bowel cancer and it wasn't pleasant. If it happened to me, yeah, I'd choose the hotel route. There isn't a big hotel that doesn't get at least one suicide a year,' he said. 'The big posh London ones probably get one a month. No one talks about it, obviously. But it happens.'

'So you're saying The Weeping Willow isn't unusual?'

Gracie grimaced. 'I wouldn't say that. It's a smallish hotel and not that well known. But maybe word gets around.'

'What, that The Weeping Willow is a great place to end it all?'

'Hey, I'm just thinking out loud,' said the detective. 'It's less than one a year.' He took another bite of his sandwich.

'And what sort of suicides were they?'

The detective frowned. He swallowed. 'What do you mean?'

'Hanging, tablets, wrists?'

'Wrists. All wrists. In the bath.'

'Doesn't that seem a bit coincidental?'

'The fact they all cut their wrists?' He shrugged. 'Not really. A lot of people end it that way. Especially now it's harder to get the tablets.'

Nightingale took a long pull on his bottle of Corona. 'And what about the wife who killed herself? One of the owners?'

Gracie nodded. 'Yeah, I was actually on that night. Mrs Dunbar. Slit her wrists in a hot bath, bled out within minutes.'

'And nothing suspicious at all?'

'There were only five people in the hotel at the time. One guest, the night manager, the chef and a waitress. And her husband, of course. He was the one who found the body.'

'And nothing to suggest that there was anything untoward?'

'Untoward?'

'You know what I mean,' said Nightingale. 'Arguments with the husband, a guest on the sexual offenders register, a pissed-off member of staff?'

The detective shook his head. 'It was suicide, Jack. The razor was still in her hand.'

'What sort of razor?'

Gracie sighed. 'You're bloody persistent aren't you?' He finished his whisky and handed the empty glass to Nightingale. 'The least you can do is get me a refill.'

Nightingale went to the bar and returned with a fresh Corona and a double Scotch for the detective just as he was finishing his sandwich. 'I'm too long in the tooth to mistake a murder for a suicide, Jack,' said Gracie, brushing crumbs from his beard.

'I wasn't teaching you to suck eggs, James. Cross my heart. I was just asking. Razor blade? Straight razor? Kitchen knife?'

'Straight razor. Her husband liked a wet shave and wasn't a fan of disposable razors.'

'And there was no question of cause of death? The reason I ask is that he sold the place not long afterwards, right?'

'He'd spoken to the estate agent before she topped herself. They both did. We spoke to the estate agent, before you ask. He said there was no friction between them, other than the normal husband-wife stuff that we all go through. You married?'

Nightingale shook his head. 'And you don't think he decided to keep all the money for himself?'

'I saw Mr Dunbar within two hours of his wife dying and believe me, he was distraught. And he was having a drink with the chef when it happened. And the door was locked from the inside. They had to kick it in.'

'They being....?'

'The husband and the chef.'

'Locked or bolted?'

Gracie shook his head and took another sip of his whisky. 'You're bloody persistent, aren't you? Bolted.'

'Bolts can be slipped. Piece of dental floss and Robert's your mother's brother.'

Gracie frowned. 'Were you like this in the job?'

Nightingale laughed. 'No, not usually.'

'Mrs Dunbar killed herself.' He put up his hand. 'And before you ask, no, she didn't leave a note. But her doctor had prescribed anti-depressants.'

'Because?'

'Because she was depressed. Are you soft?'

Nightingale sighed. 'I meant what was she depressed about. Obviously.'

'The hotel was losing money. That's why they wanted to sell it.'

Nightingale sat back in his chair and pushed the slice of lemon down the neck of the Corona bottle. 'The other suicides. Were they cutters?'

The detective nodded.

'And you don't think that was a coincidence?'

'How could it be anything but? The alternative is what? A serial killer who makes it look as if his victims all killed themselves.'

'You've got to admit, it is possible.'

'In a Jeffrey Deaver novel maybe. But not in the real world.'

'And no connection between the victims?'

Gracie shook his head. 'Other than Mrs Dunbar they were all guests.'

'Sex?'

'No thanks, Jack. The ham sandwich and whisky is good enough for me.' He laughed at his own joke. 'All women,' he said. 'And before you ask, no that's not significant. Women tend to cut and take tablets, men tend to crash their cars or jump in front of trains.'

'Any of them leave a note?'

Gracie shook his head again. 'No, but you must know that most suicides don't leave notes.'

Nightingale wrinkled his nose and drank from his bottle. 'You don't happen to know which rooms they died in?'

'Mrs Dunbar was in Room 6, I know that. But I wasn't involved in the other cases. I can find out for you.'

'Nah, it's okay, I'm heading over there after this. I'll ask the new owner.'

Gracie raised his glass. 'Any problems, give me a call,' he said.

* * *

The Weeping Willow Hotel was about a hundred yards from Brighton Pier in a side road that ran at ninety degrees to the beach. It had been formed by knocking together two terraced houses and adding a main entrance. There was a sign in the window that said 'VACANCIES'. Nightingale pushed open the door and a bell tinkled. There was a small reception desk to the left and to the right a large staircase that ran around a chandelier with a couple of dozen electric candles in it.

Nightingale heard a door open and then Mr Stokes appeared behind the reception desk. 'Ah, Mr Nightingale,' he said.

'Are you okay to show me around?' asked Nightingale.

'It's not as if I have anything else to do,' said Mr Stokes. 'We don't have any guests.' He pointed at a rack of keys behind the desk. There were twelve room numbers and each had a brass key on an oblong key ring hanging underneath it.

'Mrs Dunbar killed herself in Room 6, right?'

'How do you know that?' asked Mr Stokes.

'I spoke to one of the cops who dealt with the case.'

'I didn't know it was Room 6.'

'How about we start with that room?' asked Nightingale.

Mr Stokes nodded and took the key. 'It's the Oriental Room,' he said. 'All the rooms have themes.'

'Was that your idea?'

Mr Stokes shook his head. 'I think it was done when the building was originally converted. Thirty years ago. It's been redecorated, obviously, but the themes haven't changed. There's a French room, a Spanish room, each has its own theme.'

Nightingale followed Mr Stokes up the stairs and down a landing. There was a small brass number 6 on the door. Mr Stokes unlocked it and ushered Nightingale inside. There was a double bed and above it a large picture of a dragon in a gilt frame. There was a Japanese-style cabinet housing a television and the carpet had a scattering of what looked like Chinese characters. There was a door to the left leading to a bathroom with a roll-top bath with feet made of dragon's heads and a large brass mixer tap where the water flowed out of a dragon's mouth.

'Unusual,' said Nightingale.

'The bath was imported,' said Mr Stokes. 'That's what Mr Dunbar told us.'

'He imported it?'

Mr Stokes shook his head. 'One of previous owners did that, I think. He did up all the rooms, spent a fortune on it, according to Mr Dunbar.'

Nightingale went over to the main window and looked out across the beach to the sea. Off to the right was the pier. Seagulls wheeled overhead, screaming at each other. 'And the previous owner was?'

'A chap called McDermid. Bit of a traveller. Used to work for an oil company all over the Far East. Came back here and converted the two buildings into a hotel.'

'How long ago?'

Mr Stokes frowned. 'Twenty years ago, I think. Maybe more.'

'And this Mr McDermid sold it to Mr Dunbar?'

'No, there were several owners in between.' He looked pained and shook his head. 'I know, the fact that it kept changing hands should have let me know that something was wrong, but I just fell in love with the place. '

The floor and walls were tiled with marble and there were several black candles with gold dragons on them.

'Do you know which rooms the other guests died in?' asked Nightingale.

'I never asked,' said Mr Stokes. 'I'd rather not know, to be honest. We only found out about the suicides when one of the neighbours dropped in for a drink. She asked us if we knew what had happened to Mrs Dunbar and when we said we didn't she gave us the whole story. My wife did ring up the police to confirm that there had been a number of suicides but they said they couldn't give us any information. But our neighbour's been here for years and she told us there had been six deaths in all.'

'Yeah, that's what I'm told. Six deaths, all women, and they all cut their wrists in the bath.'

'The cops will tell you but not me, even though I own the place? Why's that?'

'It's a data protection thing, I think.'

'It's bloody ridiculous,' said Mr Stokes.

Nightingale took out his mobile phone. 'No argument here.' He called Gracie. 'Hi, Jim, the owner isn't sure which rooms the suicides were in,' he said. 'Can you do me a favour and point us in the right direction.'

'Give me a minute,' said Gracie. 'I'll check the files and send you a text.'

Nightingale put the phone away. 'He'll get back to me,' he said. 'This is a nice room, isn't it?'

'They all are,' said Mr Stokes. 'Mr McDermid spent a lot of money on them.'

'Any idea where he is?'

Mr Stokes shook his head. 'There are some filing cabinets in the attic. Papers and stuff that he left. We haven't had time to go through them yet. Why are you asking about McDermid?'

'He spent a lot of money developing The Weeping Willow, I'd be interested to know why he sold it, that's all.'

'I'm happy enough to let you go through the files,' said Mr Stokes. 'Or I could do it. It's not as if I'm busy with anything else.'

'Still no guests?'

'And no bookings. And now we're getting shitty reviews on Tripadvisor website.' He shrugged. 'I'll be honest Mr Nightingale. If you don't sort this out the wife and I will lose everything.'

'Don't worry,' said Nightingale. 'My assistant is on the case as we speak. Once we've tracked down who's behind that website, I'll go and speak to him.'

Mr Stokes forced a smile. 'I hope so,' he said. 'Because believe me, I'm at my wit's end.'

* * *

Jenny looked up from her computer screen when Nightingale walked into his office with a bag containing two Starbucks muffins. 'Chocolate or banana?' he said.

'I'm easy.'

'So I heard, but what sort of muffin do you want?'

'Chocolate,' she said.

'Good choice.' He took out the banana muffin and handed her the bag before sitting on the edge of the desk. 'So what's the story?'

Jenny tapped on her keyboard and the Haunted Brighton website filled her screen. There was a scene of the famous pier with a spooky cartoon ghost over it.

'That's it?' said Nightingale. 'Looks like a spoof.'

'It's light-hearted, sure. Talks about all the haunted houses that have been reported, ghosts, ghoulies, things that go bump in the night.' She clicked her mouse and a photograph of The Weeping Willow Hotel appeared, taken at night with a full moon behind it. 'It says there's a Japanese demon haunting the hotel and that it has killed six people over the past few years.'

'A Japanese demon? How do you fight them? Wasabi and holy saki.' He popped a chunk of muffin into his mouth.

'The website doesn't go into details. It just says that there's a Japanese demon killing people.' She grinned. 'I know, it sounds stupid.'

'It doesn't mention suicides?'

She shook her head. 'There's very little detail about the deaths, but it definitely doesn't say suicide. Just that the hotel is haunted by a bloodthirsty Japanese demon.'

'Ridiculous, right?'

'Of course. But it's been picked up by several other websites and review sites. I can see why they're having trouble getting guests.'

'And who runs the site?'

'I've come up with a name and an address. Timothy Waites. He seems to have literally hundreds of websites. All generating advertising through Google and sponsored links. I've been running all the URLs through WHOIS. Most of the sites are done through proxies but I found an early one that gave me a name and address. Waites lives in Croydon. No phone number or email address.' Nightingale opened his mouth but she silenced him with a wave of her hand. 'Yes, I'll run you down, so long as you pay me the mileage and buy me lunch. When are you going to junk that MGB?'

'It's a classic,' said Nightingale, taking the last piece of banana muffin and popping it into his mouth.

'It's a rust bucket,' said Jenny. 'The soft top leaks when it rains and it's always breaking down.' She looked at her watch. 'We've got nothing in the diary, we could take a run down now and be back before the school runs clog up the roads.'

Nightingale pulled out his pack of Marlboro and got to his feet.

'And no smoking in the car,' she said.

'I'll leave the window open.'

Jenny pointed a warning finger at his face. 'If I'm driving you the Audi counts as my workplace which means it's against the law to smoke.'

Nightingale grinned and put the cigarettes away. 'Yes, miss.' His grin widened. 'I love it when you get all stern with me.'

'Yeah, well all joking apart, smoking kills. So does second-hand smoking.'

'Here's a statistic for you. About one third of people get cancer. One in three. And one in four people die from it. But seventy five per cent of smokers don't get cancer. So it looks to me as if cigarettes make little or no difference to whether you get cancer or not. In fact, the statistics tell me that smoking gives me a seventy-five per cent chance of not getting cancer, which I reckon are pretty good odds.'

Jenny sighed and picked up her bag. 'Maths was never your best subject, was it?'

'Too many numbers,' said Nightingale, following her out of the office. 'I was always happier with a good book.'

'Really? I always imagined you behind the bike sheds, smoking.'

* * *

Thomas Waites lived in a small terraced house on the outskirts of Croydon, not far from East Croydon railway station. As Jenny and Nightingale climbed out of the Audi they heard a train rattle by. There was a Crystal Palace football scarf draped across one of the upstairs windows. There was a small plastic doorbell to the right of the front door and Nightingale pressed it. An unrecognisable tune started playing somewhere at the back of the house. He was about to press it a second time when he heard the rattle of a lock and the door opened. A big, bearded man appeared, screwing up his eyes as he peered out. 'What do you want?' he growled. As soon as he opened his mouth, Nightingale was assailed by the smell of booze and curry.

'Mr Waites?'

The man screwed up his eyes even more as if he was having trouble focussing. 'Yes?' He was wearing a Chelsea football shirt and black Adidas tracksuit bottoms, but Nightingale was fairly sure it had been decades since Mr Waites had partaken of any sporting activity.

'I wanted a word about your websites,' said Nightingale.

The man rubbed the bridge of his nose, belched, and then looked down at Jenny. 'You Mormons?' he asked.

'No, we're not Mormons,' said Jenny.

'I hate Mormons,' said the man.

'I'm not exactly partial to them myself,' said Jenny.

'You're Tim Waites?' asked Nightingale. His phone beeped to tell him that he'd received a text message, but he ignored it.

'Always have been,' said the man. 'What do you want? I don't need double-glazing.'

'We looked you up on WHOIS,' explained Jenny.

'WHOIS?' repeated the man.

'It tells you who owns a particular domain. And you own a lot, don't you?'

The man wiped his nose with the back of his hand. 'I've no idea what you're talking about,' he said, and sniffed.

'Domains. You've got loads of them,' said Nightingale.

'Domains?' repeated the man. He rubbed the back of his neck as he frowned up at Nightingale. 'What the hell is a domain?'

'A website,' said Jenny. 'We want to talk to you about The Haunted Brighton website.'

Realisation dawned and the man nodded. 'Why didn't you say so? You want Timmy.'

'Timmy?'

'My son. He's upstairs. In his bedroom.' He narrowed his eyes as he looked at Jenny. 'It's not porn is it? This website? I keep telling him not to get involved with porn. Porn's trouble.'

'No, it's not porn,' said Jenny. 'Can we go up and speak to him?'

The man held the door open wide and gestured at the stairs. 'Suit yourself,' he said. 'I doubt you'll get much out of him. It's been years since I got more than a grunt from him.'

The smell of stale curry and beer was almost overpowering as Jenny and Nightingale walked past Mr Waites and into the hallway.

'Top of the stairs, turn left,' said Mr Waites as he closed the front door.

'Ladies first,' said Nightingale.

'Age before beauty,' said Jenny, motioning for him to go up first.

Nightingale headed up the stairs. Halfway up there was a framed picture of Jesus. The figure's coal-black eyes seemed to follow him as he went by.

The door to Timmy's bedroom was closed. Nightingale knocked and when there was no reply he knocked again. When there was still no answer, he reached for the door knob and gently eased the door open. Timmy was sitting in a high-backed chair facing three flat screens that were filled with websites, more than two dozen overlapping pages. 'Timmy?' said Nightingale. 'Can we have a word with you?'

There was no answer, just the click-click-click of Timmy's fingers playing over his keyboard. The walls of the room were plastered with posters, most of which showed pneumatic blondes in various states of undress. There were used fast food containers all around the room, and dozens of empty soft drink cans, most of them with high caffeine content.

'Timmy?' Nightingale walked around the chair and realised that the boy was wearing a pair of bright red over-the-ear headphones, bobbing his head in time to music that only he could hear. He jumped when Nightingale put a hand on his shoulder.

'Who are you?' he shouted. 'What are you doing in my room?'

Nightingale pointed at Timmy's headphones. Timmy took them off. 'Who are you and what are you doing in my room?' he repeated at normal volume.

'Jack Nightingale. I'm a private detective.'

'And I'm Jenny, his pretty young assistant.'

Timmy put his headphones on the desk and squinted at Jenny. 'You drive him around and do martial arts and stuff?' he asked.

'Pretty much,' said Jenny. She nodded at his computers. 'That's some amazing kit you've got there.'

Timmy shrugged but his cheeks reddened. 'It does the job,' he said.

Nightingale pushed a couple of sweat-stained t-shirts and an old pizza box off a chair and sat down. It was clear that Timmy was happier talking to Jenny so he figured he might as well take a back seat and just listen.

'You've got a nice little business here, haven't you,' said Jenny, nodding appreciatively. 'I bet the advertising money builds up nicely.'

'I got more than ten grand last month,' said Timmy, his eyes still on the middle screen. 'That's dollars, mind. Not pounds.'

'There's not many kids your age earning that sort of money,' said Jenny. 'What are you? Nineteen?'

'Sixteen,' said Timmy. 'Seventeen next month.'

'You're a regular entrepreneur,' said Jenny. 'It's a smart business. You set up loads of websites, force traffic to them and make money from click-throughs. But tell me, where do you get your content from?'

Timmy waved at the screens. 'It's all out there somewhere. I just cut and past most of the time. If it's something special I have freelance writers I can use to put stuff together.'

'What about copyright?' asked Jenny.

'There's no copyright on the internet,' said Timmy dismissively. 'Once it's out there, anyone can use it.'

'I'm not sure that's true,' said Jenny. 'Can you do me a favour and pull up the Haunted Brighton website?'

'Sure,' said Timmy, and his fingers played over the keyboard. A website flashed up on the right-hand screen. The main page was a picture of the pier with a cartoon ghost superimposed on it.

'And have a look at the article on The Weeping Willow Hotel.'

'Weeping Willow?' repeated Timmy as his fingers tapped on the keys. A picture of the hotel flashed up and Timmy read the accompanying article.

'You remember doing that page?' asked Jenny.

Timmy shook his head. 'I do hundreds of pages a day,' he said.

'Can you remember where you got that article from?' asked Jenny. 'The background, where you talk about the vampire.'

Timmy frowned. 'Vampire?' He scanned the text. 'It doesn't say vampire. It says demon.'

'Okay, demon then. Can you remember where the information came from?'

'Not off hand, but I can soon find out,' said Timmy. His hands played across the keyboard and various pages flashed across his left-hand screen, probably a dozen or so until he pointed at one and chuckled. 'Yeah, that was well-hidden, that was,' he said. 'Found it on a password-protected website. Some organisation called the Order Of Nine Angels.'

Nightingale's head jerked up. 'What did you say?'

'The Order Of Nine Angels,' said Timmy, still reading what was on the screen. 'Bunch of nutters but they have some good stuff tucked away.'

Nightingale went to stand behind the teenager. 'And you hacked their site and just what, downloaded the stuff on it?'

'Downloaded it and then gave it to a freelance to polish it, turn it more tabloid.'

'Timmy, you need to watch yourself,' said Nightingale. 'What you're doing, it's dangerous.'

'They won't know it's me, I do it all through overseas proxies.'

'Yes, but you're down as the owner of the Hauntings website. It won't take much to put two and two together.'

'What if they do? What are they going to do? I'm just a kid.'

'They won't sue you, Timmy,' said Nightingale. He took out his pack of cigarettes but put them away when Jenny flashed him a withering look. 'Look, it's not Nine Angels. It's Nine Angles. And they're not just a bunch of nutters. A bunch of very dangerous nutters. You need to watch yourself with them.'

Timmy sat back and ran his hands through his greasy hair. 'That doesn't make any sense,' he said. 'They're devil-worshippers, right? So Nine Angels. Fallen Angels, I guess.'

Nightingale shook his head. 'Nine Angles. They have a symbol that has nine points on it. Nine angles. It's a common mistake. But the name is neither here nor there. They're a dangerous group, Timmy. You need to be careful.'

'All I did was lift some stuff from their website. It's not as if I said where it came from.'

'Can you show me?'

'Sure. Last time I checked they hadn't even changed their password.' He tapped away on his keyboard, his face moving closer to the centre screen. It went black and then a small white nine-pointed star appeared, slowly rotating within a circle.

'That's the nine angle thing,' said Nightingale.

'Looks weird, like a pentagram but squished,' said Timmy. 'What's it mean?'

'I don't know,' said Nightingale. 'Most of what they do is a closely guarded secret. That's why I'm surprised that they have a website.'

'This isn't for public consumption,' said Timmy, his fingers moving again. 'This is just a portal. No one gets beyond this page without a password. And if you get the password wrong three times the portal moves to a different URL. But if you get the password right you have access to all sorts of information, most of it really spooky stuff.'

'How did you hack it?' asked Jenny.

Timmy grinned and tapped the side of his nose. 'That's top secret,' he said. 'I could tell you, but then I'd have to kill you.'

'You see, Timmy, that's not funny. Satanists generally are bad news but the Order Of Nine Angles are seriously dangerous. They do human sacrifice and all sorts of nasty stuff.'

'Take a chill pill,' said Timmy. 'They can't trace me. So far as they know I'm coming at them from an industrial estate in Kiev.' He sat back and tapped the 'ENTER' key. 'Here we go.'

The logo stopped rotating, then slowly grew in size until it filled the screen. Then it began to flash quickly. Timmy frowned. 'That's funny, it didn't do this last time.'

'What's happening?' asked Jenny, walking over to stand behind him.

As she put a hand on the back of his chair, all three of the screens went suddenly blank.

'Shit,' said Timmy.

Nightingale hurried over. 'What?' he said.

The screens all went white, and then they were filled with rows and rows of numbers that flashed across the screen so quickly that they became a blur.

Timmy's fingers began to pound on the keyboard as he muttered 'bastards, bastards, bastards,' under his breath.

''Timmy?' said Jenny, touching him on the shoulder.

Timmy ignored her and continued to bash at the keys. The left hand screen started flashing, white, black, white, black, as rows of numbers continued to scroll across the two other screens.

'Shit!' shouted Timmy. He leapt out of his chair, ran around behind the screens and began pulling plugs out a trailing socket. One by one the screens went blank. Timmy sat on the floor with his back against the wall, his head in his hands.

'What just happened?' asked Nightingale.

Timmy looked up at him. 'Some bastard just got to my server and I think they managed to get into my hard disc.'

'I thought you used proxies.'

'I did. Several. What they did shouldn't be possible but they did.' He banged his head against the wall. 'I'm going to have to delete all my drives, the works. Everything.'

'To be fair, I did warn you,' said Nightingale. 'Do you think they'll know where you are?'

Timmy shook his head. 'That's impossible,' he said. 'They might get my IP address but that won't do them any good. I change that every hour.'

'You be careful, Timmy,' said Nightingale.

'I'll be okay,' said the teenager.

'The last time you went to the Nine Angles site, did you make copies of what was there?'

'Some, sure.'

'Can you do me a favour and let me have a look at what you saw?'

Timmy shook his head fiercely. 'Didn't you hear what I just said? They got into my server.'

'Sure, but you can access your hard drive without going online,' said Jenny. 'Just dump what you have on a thumb drive and we'll get out of your hair.'

Timmy opened his mouth as if was about to refuse, but Jenny pre-empted him with a smile. 'Pretty please,' she said.

'Okay, okay,' said Timmy. He switched on one of his computers, inserted a grey thumb drive and tapped away on his keyboard. He rocked back and forth impatiently as the files downloaded, then switched off the computer, pulled out the thumb drive and handed it to Jenny.

'You're a star, Timmy,' she said. 'Now I hate to ask, but can you do me one other favour?'

'My equipment has just been totally screwed and you want a favour?'

'Yeah. Sorry about that,' said Jenny. 'But look, we'd be really grateful. And I could give you some interesting stories for your websites. I look after Jack's site and I'd be happy to send case details on to you.'

Timmy sighed. 'What do you want?'

'That information about the deaths at The Weeping Willow, can you take them off the site?' asked Jenny.

'Ah come on, it's good stuff,' said Timmy.

'Can you maybe just take the name of the hotel down? Leave the details there but just don't mention the name. It's really hurting our clients. They can't get anyone to stay there because as soon as they Google the hotel your site comes up.'

Timmy grinned. 'That's because of all the SEO work I put in.'

'And you do a great job,' said Jenny. 'But please, Timmy, can you just drop the name?'

'I tell you what,' said Timmy. 'I will, if you give me a kiss.'

'A what?'

'A kiss,' said Timmy. He tapped his cheek. 'Just here.'

Nightingale grinned but stopped when Jenny flashed him an angry look.

'Are you serious?' asked Jenny.

'It's up to you,' said Timmy, leaning back in his chair.

Jenny looked at Nightingale and Nightingale grinned again. 'It'd be for the greater good,' he said.

Jenny wagged a finger at Timmy. 'Only on the cheek, right?'

'Sure,' said Timmy. He turned his head and presented his left cheek to her. Jenny sighed and leaned forward to plant a kiss, but just as she got close Timmy turned and kissed her on the lips.

Jenny jumped back with a yelp as Timmy laughed. 'Got you!' he said.

Jenny looked over at Nightingale for support but he just grinned. 'I sort of saw that coming,' he said.

Jenny wiped her mouth with the back of her hand. 'You'd better keep your promise,' she said to Timmy.

'My word is my bond,' said Timmy, and his fingers tapped away at the keyboard.

Nightingale and Jenny let themselves out of the house. Nightingale checked his phone as they walked back to the Audi. The text message was from Gracie. 'That's interesting,' he said.

'What is?'

'All the suicides were in the same room,' he said. 'Room Six.'

'That's not good, is it?'

'No,' agreed Nightingale. 'It's not. How do you feel about a run down to Brighton?'

Jenny shrugged. 'If you pay my petrol and buy me dinner, I could be persuaded.'

'KFC?'

Jenny shook her head. 'I'll be insisting on a knife and fork, at the very least.'

* * *

Mrs Stokes was at the reception desk when Nightingale and Jenny walked into The Weeping Willow Hotel. 'Good news,' said Nightingale. 'The man behind the website has agreed to take down the story.'

Mrs Stokes beamed. 'Really?'

Nightingale nodded. 'We explained the situation to him and he said he would.'

'The pages might stay up on various caches for a while,' warned Jenny. 'But it'll all disappear eventually.'

'I can't thank you enough,' said Mrs Stokes. 'Seriously, that's the best news I've had all year. My husband will be delighted, and of course you must send us your bill. I have to say, it'll be one bill that'd I'll take pleasure in paying.'

'Is Mr Stokes around?'

Mrs Stokes shook her head. 'He's down at the cash and carry. He'll be an hour or so. Why, is there something wrong?'

'Nothing wrong,' said Nightingale. 'It's just that he mentioned there were some records in the attic.'

'From the previous owner,' she said. 'They're in filing cabinets. We're keeping them in case there's a problem with the taxman.'

'Could we go up and have a look?' asked Nightingale.

Mrs Stokes frowned. 'Is there a problem?'

Nightingale flashed her a reassuring smile. 'No, not at all. We're just interested in checking the receipts for the refurbishment.'

'Why?'

'There might be something significant in the bath that was installed in Room 6,' said Nightingale, but he could see from the look on the woman's face that his explanations were making her even more nervous. 'Really, it's nothing, I just want to find out where it came from.'

'To be honest, Mrs Stokes, I wouldn't mind ordering one myself,' said Jenny. 'It's lovely, and I've never seen one like it before.'

The lie seemed to make Mrs Stokes happier so Nightingale went along with it and nodded enthusiastically. 'It shouldn't take too long,' he said.

'It's a mess up there,' she warned.

'Not a problem,' Nightingale reassured her.

'Just go to the top floor and there's a pole against the wall you use to pull the ladder down,' said Mrs Stokes.

Nightingale and Jenny walked up to the top floor. The pole was where Mrs Stokes had said and Nightingale used it to grab a small ring in a wooden door set into the ceiling. He twisted and pulled and the trapdoor opened and a set of aluminium steps folded out. Nightingale went up first. There was a light switch in the wall to his left and he clicked it on before stepping off the ladder onto the bare wooden boards of the attic.

'What's it look like?' asked Jenny.

'A couple of vampires and a zombie or two,' said Nightingale. 'But I think I can take them.'

Jenny climbed the steps and joined him. The attic was filled with cardboard boxes, old mattresses and battered furniture. At the far end was a line of rusting green filing cabinets. The wooden boards squeaked and groaned as they walked around the stacks of boxes and unwanted furniture. 'At least they're dated,' said Jenny, pointing at small cardboard signs affixed to each drawer. 'We can assume the refurbishment was done in the first year, right?'

'Good call,' said Nightingale. The earliest year he could see was 1994 and he pulled it open. Inside were twelve pale blue files, each labelled with the month of the year. He took out January for himself and handed February to Jenny. 'Race you,' he said.

It was Jenny who found the receipts for the Japanese room, twenty minutes after they started their search. There were half a dozen receipts from companies in Japan including one, in Japanese, from an antiques shop in Tokyo. 'This is it,' she said, taking the receipt over to the single light bulb hanging from the roof.

Nightingale peered over her shoulder. 'You can read Japanese?' he asked.

'Some,' she said. 'This is for an antique roll-top bath. Believed to be from the eighteenth-century.' She frowned. 'That's strange.'

'What's strange?'

'The price. Two hundred thousand yen.'

'That's a lot?'

'No, that's not a lot. Just over a hundred pounds. That's cheap for an antique, don't you think?'

Nightingale took the receipt from her. 'Not if somebody was trying to get rid of it,' he said. 'And what better way of getting rid of it than selling it to someone on the other side of the world?'

* * *

Nightingale carried a cup of coffee over to Jenny's desk and put it down in front of her. She was frowning and squinting at her computer screen. 'What's wrong?' he asked.

She sat back and folded her arms. 'That thumb-drive that Timmy gave us. It's blank.'

'Do you think he's messing us around?'

She shook her head. 'I don't think so. He kept his word and took down any mention of the hotel. And we saw him put the files on the thumb-drive.' She frowned. 'It's as if something got onto the thumb-drive and deleted the files.'

'The Order of Nine Angles?'

'I can't think of anyone else, can you?' She picked up her mug of coffee and took a sip.

'So how are we going to get information on Japanese vampires?' Nightingale asked.

'Why do we need information? Just tell them to redecorate.'

'What, you think the vampire's connected to the bath?'

'Isn't it obvious? The bath's from Japan and so's the vampire.'

'But getting rid of the bath doesn't necessarily mean the haunting's going to end, does it?' said Nightingale. 'I'd just like a better understanding of what we're dealing with. I was hoping the thumb-drive would help, but clearly not.'

'There isn't much on the internet, either,' said Jenny. 'Why don't we go down to Aoki Sushi and talk to Mr Aoki?'

Aoki Sushi, close to Queensway Tube station, was one of Nightingale's favourite restaurants. The owner, Mr Aoki, was a small, bald man with a slight stoop from years leaning over his sushi counter. Mr Aoki took great pleasure in introducing Jenny and Nightingale to new tastes and sensations, from raw sea urchin to the infamous fugu puffer fish, which can be deadly if not prepared absolutely correctly. Jenny had introduced Nightingale to the restaurant and at first he'd been reluctant to eat raw fish, but Mr Aoki had won him over and now he visited at least once a month, usually with Jenny, 'Because he's Japanese?'

'Of course because he's Japanese. He knows a lot about Japanese folklore and history.'

'I didn't know that.'

'We were probably speaking in Japanese,' said Jenny.

'How many languages do you speak?'

'My Japanese is pretty basic,' said Jenny. She looked at her watch. 'Why don't we close up early and get there before his evening rush?'

When they arrived at the restaurant, there was a group of Japanese businessmen in a booth toasting each other loudly with beakers of saki. They were all in their thirties with their jackets off, shirt sleeves rolled up and ties askew and looked as if they were there for the night.

There was a line of eight empty stools in front of the sushi bar where Mr Aoki spent most of his time. Nightingale and Jenny sat down at one end. Mr Aoki was slicing tuna and he grinned when he looked up and spotted Jenny. He was in his fifties, squat and totally bald with a head that was pretty much spherical. They immediately began chatting away in Japanese, and it was clear that her proficiency in the language was way above basic. The restaurant stocked Corona and Nightingale ordered a bottle for himself and saki for Jenny. Jenny and Mr Aoki continued to chat in Japanese as he busied himself slicing raw salmon and tuna. He placed a dish of the succulent sashimi in front of them and waved for them to try. 'Flown in from Japan this morning,' he said proudly.

'Flying fish, how great is that?' said Nightingale, picking up a pair of chopsticks.

Mr Aoki frowned, not understanding the joke. 'It's not flying fish,' he said. 'Salmon and tuna. Top grade. Best in the world.'

Nightingale picked up a piece of tuna and popped it into his mouth. Mr Aoki was right, it was superb and virtually melted in his mouth. 'Delicious,' he said, and Mr Aoki beamed. He picked up a slab of grey fish and began expertly cutting it into oblongs as Jenny spoke to him in Japanese. The waitress returned with their drinks and they both toasted the sushi chef.

Mr Aiko put sushi hand rolls down in front of them. 'Jenny-chan tells me you are interested in the Gaki,' he said.

'I'm fine with any fish you put in front of me,' said Nightingale. 'I love your sashimi and sushi, you know that.'

Mr Aoki said something to Jenny in Japanese and they both laughed.

'The Gaki is the Japanese vampire,' explained Jenny.

'Not so much a vampire, more a corporeal ghost,' said Mr Aoki. 'A Gaki is a spirit that lived badly and failed to repent before death. It wanders around for eternity, cursed with a blood lust that is never satisfied.'

'And they attack people?' asked Nightingale.

Mr Aoki nodded. 'Some feed on blood, others on flesh. They are shape-shifters and can take many forms. Some eat samurai topknots, for instance. Other feed on sweat. Or incense. But blood is usually what they are after.'

A waitress came over with a written order and she handed it to Mr Aoki. He grunted and reached for a purple and white octopus tentacle.

'And if it is a Gaki, how do we go about killing it?' asked Nightingale.

'It's not easy,' said Mr Aoki, his knife poised in mid air.

'It never is,' said Nightingale.

Mr Aoki frowned. 'I don't understand.

'I was just...' Nightingale shrugged. 'In my experience, there's always a price to be paid when you take on the spirit world.'

Mr Aoki nodded. 'Let me do this and we'll go outside. I need a cigarette.' He made short work of the octopus, pushed two plates towards the waiting waitress and then nodded at a side door. 'We can smoke in the alley.'

He took Nightingale through the door, down a corridor and through a fire exit. Nightingale gave him a Marlboro and then lit a cigarette for himself. They blew smoke and the chef smiled over at Nightingale. 'You always smoke Marlboro?'

'Since I was a kid. It's a cowboy thing.'

'You wanted to be a cowboy?'

'I wanted to ride a horse. And fire a gun.' He chuckled. 'Actually, I got to do the latter.'

'The latter?'

'Fire a gun. I used to be an armed police officer. Fired all sorts of guns. Never rode a horse, though.' He took another long drag on his cigarette and blew smoke up into the night air. 'So, how do you kill a Gaki?'

Mr Aoki flicked ash away. 'It's best to simply keep it away,' he said. 'Shinto priests or Buddhist monks can perform the necessary prayers and rituals. You can leave scrolls with the image of Buddha on by all the doors and windows. And outside your home, you can leave offerings of food so that it feeds outside.' He shrugged. 'If you believe in that.'

'Do you?'

Mr Aoki shook his head. 'If I had stayed in Japan then maybe. But I have lived in London for more than twenty years. So no, I don't believe in ghosts.' He blew smoke up at the ceiling.

'What else can you tell me, though?'

'Okay, well they say that when a Gaki attacks it does it in a sort of mindless frenzy. Like a bloodlust. That makes it vulnerable.'

'To what?'

'To a sword or a knife, made of silver. But you have to strike when it's in physical form. It won't defend itself because it'll be in a mindless frenzy. But the fact that it's a frenzy makes it very dangerous indeed.'

'And when does it take on physical form?'

'When it is ready to feed.'

Nightingale nodded thoughtfully. 'Okay.'

'Then, when you have killed it, you have to burn it to ashes and scatter them to the four winds.'

'That's easy enough,' said Nightingale.

The chef flicked his cigarette away. 'I have to go back to work,' he said. 'Kouun wo inorimasu. Good luck.'

* * *

Jenny frowned at Nightingale. 'Tell me again why I'm the one who has to be in the bath?' she said. She was wearing a white hotel bathrobe and had clipped up her blonde hair.

'Because the Gaki only attacks women.'

'You could do it in drag.'

'Seriously?'

'Jack, this could be dangerous.'

'I'll be outside the door, listening. At the first sign of trouble, I'll be in.'

'And you're sure this isn't just a way of you seeing me with my kit off?'

Nightingale laughed. 'It'll be fine.'

'Six women have died in that bath, I don't want to be number seven.'

'The other six didn't know what was going on,' said Nightingale. 'Forewarned is forearmed.'

Jenny took a silver knife from her pocket. They'd bought it from a stall in Portobello market. The blade was about six inches long and the hand another four. According to the hallmark, it was more than forty years old. 'Forearmed with a fish knife?'

'The type of knife doesn't matter,' said Nightingale. 'What matters is that it's silver.' He picked up a silver carving knife off the sink cabinet. 'As soon as the Gaki appears you let me know and I'll take it from behind.'

'I'm not closing the door,' she said.

'You don't have to,' said Nightingale.

'Jack, are you sure there isn't another way of doing this?'

'This is the only permanent way of ending it,' said Nightingale. 'And the Gaki only attacks women.'

'You could dress up.'

Nightingale laughed. 'In the bath?' He took out his lighter and lit half a dozen small tealight candles in circular crystal holders, then turned on the taps. Water gushed into the large roll top bath. Steam billowed from the hot tap. 'Bath salts? Bubble bath.'

'I'll do it,' said Jenny. 'You wait outside. And at the first sign of anything, I want you in here. I don't want to face it on my own.'

'I'll be right outside, I promise.'

'I'm serious, Jack.'

'So am I. It'll be fine. I promise.' Nightingale took a final look around the bathroom. The mirror above the sink had already clouded over and he drew a smiley face with his finger. 'For luck,' he said.

'I don't want to rely on luck,' she said. She slipped the knife under the bath, then frowned. 'I'm not going to be able to reach it,' she said.

'Take it in the bath with you.'

'You'll be telling me to run with scissors next.'

Nightingale picked up a white flannel from the sink and gave it to her. 'Wrap it in this.' He headed out and pulled the door closed behind him before remembering what she'd said and opened it and left it ajar. He had placed a wooden chair in the hallway and he sat down. He could hear the bath still filling and then a soft splash as Jenny slipped into the water.

* * *

Jenny wiggled her toes and sighed. The bath was the perfect size for her, and the bath salts were doing their job, relaxing her muscles and filling the air with the scent of flowers. If it wasn't for the fact that she was being used as bait for a blood-sucking Japanese vampire creature she'd have been relishing the experience. She reached down into the water with her right hand to reassure herself that the knife was still there. She looked over at the smiley face that Nightingale had drawn on the mirror. It made her smile and she took a deep breath and sighed again. There were worse places to be than a lovely warm bath. She closed her eyes and luxuriated in the warm water. There was a quiet plop as water dripped from the hot top. She reached up with her right foot and ran her big toe around the top, but withdrew it when she realised it was hot to the touch. She shrugged her shoulders. There was another plop from the big tap. And another. The plopping sound was almost hypnotic. She sighed again, but realised she was close to sleeping and opened her eyes. The room was filled with steam now, and as she looked over at the mirror she realised that the smiley face had gone. She reached for the knife and her fingers tightened on the handle.

* * *

Nightingale looked at his watch. Jenny had been in the bath for more than half an hour and he hadn't heard anything for at least five minutes. He stood up and carefully put his ear against the door. He frowned as he realised the bathroom was in total silence. He pushed open the door a few inches and peered through the gap. He could see the shower and the medicine cabinet but that was all. He pushed the door a bit more, bracing himself for a torrent of abuse from Jenny if she thought he was spying on her. He took a step forward and moved his head to the side. He could just about see the mirror above the sink and as he moved his head a bit further he saw Jenny, lying in the bath with her eyes closed. He smiled as he realised that she had fallen asleep. But the smile froze when he saw the knife in her right hand. She was holding the blade against her left wrist and his eyes widened in horror as he saw her draw it across her skin. Blood flowed around the blade and Nightingale screamed. He threw open the door and stepped into the room and only then did he realise that Jenny wasn't alone. There was a figure crouched at the end of the bath, looming over her, part human, part, animal, part fog. Most of it was black but there were streaks of red and gold, there was what looked like a hand with talons and a bulge that might have been a folded wing.

Jenny's left arm flopped over the side of the bath and blood dripped down her palm and began to plop onto the floor. The creature had legs that were covered in glistening scales and feet with hooked claws that clicked against the tiles as it shuffled around the bath towards the pooling blood.

Nightingale groped in his pocket for the knife. The creature was so focussed on the dripping blood that it didn't appear to have noticed that Nightingale was in the room.

Nightingale gripped the knife tightly and thrust it into the closest thing the creature had to a neck. It was like stabbing rubber. The blade slid off the creature's skin. Nightingale cursed and lunged again, harder this time. The blade went in and yellow fluid gushed over his hand.

Something lashed out. A wing, or an arm. Whatever it was, it caught Nightingale under the chin and sent him spinning against the wall. The knife fell from his hand and clattered onto the floor. The creature moved towards him. A mouth opened and Nightingale's stomach heaved at the stench of sulphur. Something whirled towards Nightingale's head and he ducked. Tiles shattered behind him and fragments dropped down all around him. He fell to his knees and groped around for the knife but he couldn't find it.

Something smashed against the back of his neck, almost stunning him. He shook his head and then scrambled towards the bath. His eyes were watering from the stench emanating from the creature's mouth, making it difficult to see. The creature hit him again. A talon tore into his jacket, ripping the fabric apart. He felt a searing pain along his back and realised that the creature had drawn blood.

His head banged against the bath and he grunted in pain. He reached up and groped for Jenny's arm. His fingers touched her flesh and he ran them down to her hand and grabbed her knife. Talons raked his back again and he screamed. He fell to the floor, the knife in his right hand. He heard a hellish roar and as he rolled onto his back he saw the creature rearing up, more solid now. He saw a gaping maw and yellow cat-like eyes and then he was enveloped with a foul stench as it breathed over him. He could barely see through his tear-filled eyes but he saw movement as the creature lunged at him and he brought the knife up and plunged it into the left eye. The creature roared and the tiles vibrated beneath Nightingale. He gripped his right hand with his left and thrust the knife further into the eye socket.

Something wet and warm gushed over his hands as the creature began to shake and shudder. It reared up and Nightingale pushed up to keep the pressure on the knife and then the creature shuddered a final time and fell onto him like a dead weight. Nightingale let go of the knife and lay where he was, gasping for breath, his throat and nose burning from the noxious last breaths of the creature he'd killed. He tried to push the body off him but it was just too heavy. Something acrid dripped across Nightingale's face and his stomach heaved. He pushed up with all his strength and used his heels to push himself from under the dead weight. He managed to get his upper body out, then freed his left leg and used his foot to push the creature away.

He staggered to his feet and leaned over the bath. Jenny's eyes were closed and blood was trickling from her wrist and dripping onto the floor. He pulled out the plug so that the water would run away and then lifted her left hand and examined the cuts. There were two, about an inch apart, and they didn't appear to be too deep. He kept her hand above her head as he looked around for something to bind her wound. He could just about reach the medicine cabinet and he pulled it open. There was a pack of plaster and a crepe bandage on one of the shelves. He knew that the crepe bandage was better suited for sprains but figured it was better than nothing so he unwrapped it and wound it around the injured wrist before he lifted her out of the bath. 'Jenny, can you hear me?' he asked, but her eyes stayed closed.

He pulled the door open with his foot and carried Jenny down the stairs. Mr and Mrs Stokes were waiting in the hall.

'What happened?' asked Mrs Stokes.

'I need to get her to the hospital,' said Nightingale.

'I'll call an ambulance,' said Mr Stokes, pulling his mobile phone from his pocket.

'No, we'll drive her,' said Nightingale. 'Have you got a car?'

Mr Stokes grabbed for his coat. 'Outside,' he said. He picked up a set of car keys from a brass dish.

'Is she going to be okay?' asked Mrs Stokes.

Nightingale ignored the question. 'I need a robe or something she can wear.'

Mrs Stokes nodded. 'Of course. Yes.' She hurried upstairs. 'Whatever you do, don't go into the bathroom,' Nightingale called after her. 'I'll deal with it when I get back.'

'Deal with what?' asked Mr Stokes,

'Best you don't know,' said Nightingale.

Mrs Stokes came rushing back down the stairs holding a white towelling bathrobe. She and Nightingale helped ease Jenny into the robe. Mrs Stokes started when she saw the blood-stained bandage around her wrist. 'What happened?'

'I'll explain later,' he said. 'And remember what I said, stay out of the bathroom.' He nodded at Mr Stokes. 'We need to go.' Mr Stokes headed for the door and Nightingale followed him.

* * *

Jenny's eyes fluttered open and she frowned when she saw Nightingale standing by the side of the bed. 'Did I fall asleep?' she asked.

'Sort of,' said Nightingale.

Jenny looked around and her eyes widened. 'Where am I?'

'Brighton General Hospital,' said Nightingale.

'What happened?'

'What do you remember?' he asked.

She lifted up her hands and frowned when she saw the bandage around her left wrist. 'Jack?' she said, her voice trembling.

'It's okay, a couple of superficial cuts,' said Nightingale.

'So why am I in a hospital bed?' she asked, staring at the bandage.

'The thing put you under?'

Jenny stared at him in horror. 'What thing?'

'You don't remember anything that happened in the bathroom?'

'What bathroom? Jack, what's going on?'

'You were in the bathroom, waiting for the Gaki. I think it somehow drugged or hypnotised you. You remember the Gaki, right?'

'I remember talking about it, sure. So what happened?'

'It appeared. It made you cut yourself. I killed it. All's well that ends well. Or at least it will once I've burnt what's left of it and scattered it to the four winds.'

The door to the room opened and a doctor appeared, a dour woman in her fifties carrying a clipboard. She took a pen from the pocket of her white coat and looked at Jenny over the top of her bifocal spectacles. 'Well I'm glad to see that you've finally woken up, Miss McLean. You had us worried there for a while.' She frowned as she looked at the clipboard. 'We thought that you had swallowed something you shouldn't but your blood all seems good.'

'Swallowed something?' repeated Jenny as

'Sleeping tablets. Paracetamol. Weedkiller. There's no end to the things that people take when they want to hurt themselves.'

'I didn't try to hurt myself,' said Jenny.

The doctor walked over to the side of the bed and picked up Jenny's left arm. They both looked at her bandaged wrist. 'Of course you didn't,' said the doctor.

Jenny snatched her hand away. 'Anyway, I'm fine now,' she said. 'I'll be on my way home.'

'Before you go, I'd like you to talk to talk to one of our therapists,' said the doctor, scribbling a note on her clipboard.

'About what?'

The doctor looked over the top of her glasses again, like a teacher about to address a particularly stupid student. 'My dear, self-harming is nothing to be ashamed of. What matters is that we give you the tools to deal with it.'

'I haven't been self-harming,' protested Jenny. She looked over at Nightingale. 'Tell her, Jack.'

'Tell her what?' asked Nightingale.

Jenny opened her mouth to reply but then realised that even if she did tell the doctor the truth she'd more than likely think that she was crazy. She sighed and folded her arms. 'Fine,' she said. 'I'll talk to your therapist.'

'That's a good girl,' said the doctor, smiling encouragingly.

'She's had a difficult few months,' said Nightingale. 'We've all been very worried about her.' Jenny flashed him a withering look and he grinned as he headed out of the room. 'Give me a call when you're ready and I'll pick you up.'

'He seems like a very nice man,' said the doctor.

'Appearances can be deceptive,' said Jenny.

* * *

Nightingale sat at the bar and pushed the slice of lime down into the neck of his bottle of Corona. He sipped his lager and his eyes fell on the television set on the wall to his right. It was showing Sky News and an earnest red-headed reporter in a raincoat was talking into a hand-held microphone. Nightingale recognised the house behind her and he waved at the barman. 'Do me a favour, mate, can you put the sound up?'

The barman nodded, reached for the remote control, and turned up the volume.

'Police are treating the deaths as a murder-suicide,' said the woman. 'According to a source close to the investigation, Mr Waites stabbed his son to death in the bedroom and then went downstairs and slit his own throat. An inquest will be held but at the moment the police are not looking for anyone else in connection with the deaths.'

'Put the football on!' shouted a man at a table by the door.

The barman looked across at Nightingale and Nightingale shrugged. The barman pressed the remote again and changed the channel, then walked over to the sink and began polishing glasses. Nightingale smiled thinly and raised his bottle in salute at the television set. He was pretty sure that the death of the father and son had nothing to do with suicide and everything to with murder. The Order of Nine Angles was fanatical about keeping its secrets. He'd tried to warn Timmy Waites and his father but he'd known at the time that his warnings were falling on deaf ears. 'That's what you get when you mess around with things you don't understand,' he said. 'RIP guys.'

I KNOW WHO DID IT

The old man's eyes were closed and his chest wasn't moving. Mary Campbell wiped her eyes and looked over at the nurse. 'Has he gone yet?' she asked. She dabbed her eyes again.

'Not yet,' said the nurse. 'You'll know when it happens.'

'Is he in any pain?'

The nurse shook her head. 'None at all. The doctor has made sure of that.'

The man who was lying in the king-sized bed weighed barely more than thirty kilos, a quarter of what he'd weighed before the cancer had gripped him. It had moved quickly, as if making up for lost time, and in just three months it had reduced him to a shell. He had insisted on dying at home, and as J. Ramsay Campbell was a very wealthy man his wishes were respected. He had paid for round-the-clock nursing care and his doctor was always by his side within an hour of being called. But there had been no calls for the past few days because now it was just a matter of time. His morphine was supplied intravenously. For a while he had been able to adjust the amount of morphine himself but now the nurse did it for him. She had helped people die many times before and she knew exactly how much to increase the dosage by. She had learnt from experience that death was best not rushed.

Mary was J Ramsay Campbell's daughter. Her mother – J Ramsay Campbell's wife – spent most of the day sitting next to his bed but she was almost as old as he was and she needed her sleep. Mary caught what sleep she needed during the day and maintained her vigil throughout the night. Part of her knew that most people died at night and she wanted to be there when he passed away.

Mary barely thought of the dried husk as her father. The cancer had taken most of him away, all that was left was a shell. It was his face, just about, but his body had shrunk and she thought that she could, if she had to, scoop him up in her arms and carry him. His skin was almost translucent and she could see the veins and arteries that carried what little blood he had left in his system.

His chest moved, just a fraction, and there was a dry rattle from somewhere at the back of his throat.

'It won't be long now,' said the nurse. She was dark-skinned and barely more than five feet tall. Mary wasn't sure if she was from the Philippines or Thailand but she seemed to have a genuine affection for her patient. All his nurses did. There were five, working staggered shifts so that there was always one in the room and another close by.

'Do you think he knows I'm here?' asked Mary.

The nurse smiled. 'I'm sure he does,' she said. But Mary could see the lie in her eyes.

The nurse turned away and at that exact moment J Ramsay Campbell sat bolt upright. Mary shrieked and her hands flew up to her face. His eyes were wide and clear and his skin seemed healthy and liver spot-free.

'Dad?' said Mary, but her father didn't react.

He licked his lips as he continued to stare straight ahead

'I know who did it,' he said.

'What, dad? Who did what?'

The old man took a deep breath and then screamed at the top of his voice. 'I KNOW WHO DID IT!' He stiffened, his mouth fell open and then he collapsed back on the bed. The lines on the monitor went flat.

* * *

'And those were his last words? I know who did it?' Jack Nightingale was sitting at his desk, across from Mary Campbell. Jenny McNeal was sitting next to the client, taking notes. Jenny was wearing a dark blue dress that ended just above the knee and had her blonde hair tied back in a ponytail. Mary Campbell looked as if she was in her late thirties but was dressed as if she was in her sixties, in a tweed suit with sensible brown shoes. There was a large silver brooch close to her neck.

'He sat up, said it. Then shouted it. Then he passed away. It was the only thing he'd said over the past week.'

'People do get lucid towards the end,' said Nightingale. 'They often have a moment of clarity just before…' He shrugged, not wanting to finish the sentence.

'That's what the nurse said. And I understand that. But it was the way he said it, Mr Nightingale. It was as if he had solved a mystery.' She leaned forward, closer to him, and he could see that she was about to cry. 'The thing is, there is a mystery in our family. My sister, Emily. She died forty years ago. We never found out what had happened.'

Nightingale frowned, not understanding.

Jenny pushed a box of tissues towards Mary Campbell and she took one and dabbed her eyes. 'There was an inquest, surely, there's always an inquest when someone dies suddenly and unexpectedly,' said Jenny.

'They said Emily had killed herself, but my parents never believed that.' She dabbed her eyes again. 'Emily was their first child. I was born two years after she died.' She forced a smile. 'Mum was nearly forty then and they weren't expecting to have any more children.' She sighed, closed her eyes, and took a deep breath. She exhaled slowly before opening her eyes again. 'Emily was at boarding school, in Hampshire. She cut her wrists, they said. But my father never believed that. He always thought that someone had killed her. But the police insisted that she was found in a locked room, locked from the inside, and the coroner called it a suicide.' She took another deep breath to compose herself before continuing.

'My father hadn't mentioned it for years. And then three days ago, as he was dying, he sat up and said that he knew who'd done it. I can't think of anything else he could have been talking about.'

'But what is it you want me to do?' asked Nightingale.

'If my father knew who did it, if he'd remembered something, then I want to know too. I want to know who killed my sister.'

'But it was forty years ago.'

'My father was so sure. I could see it in his eyes. He knew, Mr Nightingale. Without a shadow of a doubt, he knew.' She fumbled in her bag and brought out a cheque book. 'I'll pay whatever you want, just find out what happened to Emily all those years ago.'

Nightingale looked over at Jenny. Business had been quiet for the last few weeks and it wasn't as if he had any pressing cases. Jenny nodded at him. 'I'll do what I can,' promised Nightingale.

* * *

Mary Campbell left the office after signing a cheque for a thousand pounds on account, and Nightingale phoned his friend Robbie Hoyle. He'd known Hoyle for more than a decade. He was a sergeant with the Territorial Support Group but was also a skilled negotiator. 'Jack, I'm a bit busy right now,' said Hoyle. 'I'm on my way to a jumper.'

'I need a quick favour when you've got the time,' said Nightingale.

'I assumed that's why you called,' said Hoyle. 'The only time I hear from you these days is when you want something.'

'That's harsh, Robbie.'

'Harsh but true. What do you need?'

'I need the name of an investigating officer in Hampshire. Forty-year-old case. A schoolgirl died at Rushworth School near Winchester. Her name was Emily Campbell.'

'A forty-year-old case, Jack? Seriously?'

'The client wants information, that's all. Can you get me a name?'

'I'll try. Call you later.' Nightingale put down the phone. Jenny was looking at him and shaking her head. 'What?' he said.

'You might have asked him about his wife. His kids. How he was getting on.'

'He was busy. He has a suicide to talk down. Anyway, Robbie and I go back a long way.'

'You use him, Jack. Like you use everybody.'

'I'll buy him a drink when I see him.' He held up his hands when he saw the look of contempt flash across her face. 'Fine, you're right, I'm sorry, I'll phone him back and ask him about his wife and kids.' He reached for the phone but she had already turned and walked out of his office. He sat back and lit a cigarette.

* * *

Hoyle didn't ring back that morning so Nightingale decided to drive down to the boarding school after lunch. He grabbed his raincoat and tossed it over his shoulder as he walked to Jenny's desk. 'If Robbie calls, tell him to try my mobile.'

'Have you got your hands-free fixed up?'

'Sort of.'

'What does that mean?'

'I tuck it between my neck and my shoulder. That counts as hands-free.'

'You'll lose your licence, Jack. The cops don't want you smoking and phoning while you drive.'

'To be fair, I don't do both at the same time. Why not come with me?'

She frowned up at him. 'Because?'

'Because I'll need a cover story. A guy on his own might look a bit out of place, but we could say we're parents looking for a school for our kid.'

Jenny's eyes narrowed. 'Parents?'

'It's just a cover story.'

Her eyes narrowed a bit more. 'How old is our child?'

Nightingale shrugged. 'I don't know. Eight? Nine?'

'You'd tell them that I'm the mother of an eight-year-old?'

'You married young.'

'You're an idiot sometimes. First, I doubt anyone would believe I was the mother of an eight-year-old. I bloody hope not, anyway. And second, I really hope that no one would believe for one minute that you and I were...' She shuddered.

'It was just an idea,' said Nightingale.

'A better idea would be for you to go on your own and say that your wife is overseas. You're looking at schools before she comes over with the kid.' She flashed him a tight smile. 'That sounds a lot more realistic.'

Nightingale raised his hands in surrender. 'Then that's what I'll do,' he said. 'Can you get me directions to Rushworth School?'

'Why don't you get yourself a GPS?' asked Jenny.

'I don't trust them,' he said.

'But you trust a computer printout?' She shook her head in amazement and turned to her computer. After a few minutes on the internet she printed out a map and gave it to him.

'What about running me out in the Audi?' asked Nightingale. 'I'll pay for the petrol.'

'As much as I'd love to, I've got to file our VAT returns today and I'm still working my way through the stack of receipts you gave me this morning.'

Nightingale took the map from her. The school was about sixty miles away. 'Suppose I'd better set off, then,' he said.

His MGB was in a multi-storey a short walk from his office and five minutes later he was heading west. Traffic was light and it took him just over ninety minutes to drive to the school. It was a large grey stone building, two wings either side of a columned entrance, with a grey-slated roof. Off to the left were tennis courts and a hockey pitch.

Nightingale parked in the staff car park and went to reception where he told a stern-faced woman the cover story that he'd been rehearsing on the drive down. He and his wife Jenny were moving back to the UK from Australia and bringing their nine-year-old daughter with them. Nightingale worked for a bank that meant he had to travel a lot, and Jenny was a high-powered lawyer so they had decided that Zoe would be best boarding. Nightingale actually felt quite sorry for the hypothetical young girl for being saddled with parents who clearly didn't give a toss about her. The stern-faced woman gave him a glossy brochure and a print out of the fees. He tried not to show surprise at the huge amounts being charged and asked if it would be possible to speak to the headmaster.

'Headmistress,' said the woman, archly. She waved him to a line of wooden seats. 'I'll see if Ms Cunningham is available.'

Nightingale was kept waiting for fifteen minutes but when Ms Cunningham did eventually arrive she was very apologetic. She was in her early thirties, with shoulder length blonde hair and bright red lipstick that matched her fingernails. She was wearing a dark green suit with a skirt that ended just above the knee, and matching green heels. She wasn't wearing a wedding ring or engagement ring but there was a framed photograph of her with a good-looking man holding a toddler on her desk. Nightingale gave her his cover story and she listened and nodded, then she gave him a five-minute sales pitch which she had obviously delivered a thousand times before. Then she asked him if he would like a tour.

'Perfect,' he said. As he stood up he saw a row of framed photographs on the wall by the door. Under each picture was a small brass plaque with a name and date. Ms Cunningham peered over his shoulder. 'Former heads,' she said. 'I'll be up there myself one day.'

'You'll certainly be the prettiest there, by a long way,' said Nightingale.

He felt Ms Cunningham stiffen and he held up a hand. 'I'm sorry, totally inappropriate,' he said.

She laughed. 'Actually, I'll take the compliment,' she said. 'I was brought in to liven things up. The school was getting a bit staid and I was very much the new broom.'

Nightingale looked at the last photograph in the line. It was Ms Cunningham's predecessor, a grey-haired man in his fifties with deep furrows in his brow and black-framed spectacles. He had the look of a teacher who still believed in corporal punishment, and probably relished it. According to the brass plate he had held the job for twelve years. He looked along the line of pictures. The head at the time of Emily Campbell's death was also a man. Charles Nelson was round-faced and balding with a small chip in one of his front teeth. He was smiling like a kindly uncle. The date on the brass plate suggested he had left the school the year after Emily had died.

Nightingale put his hand against the wall and shook his head from side to side.

'Are you all right?' asked Ms Cunningham.

'I feel a little dizzy, actually,' said Nightingale. 'I don't suppose I could have a drink of water, could I?'

'Of course,' said Ms Cunningham. She hurried out of the office. Nightingale took out his phone and snapped a quick photograph of Charles Nelson and was back in his chair when Ms Cunningham returned with a glass of water. She stood over him as he drank. 'Are you sure you're all right?'

'I'm been feeling a bit rough all day,' lied Nightingale. 'Maybe I'm coming down with a virus.' He handed her back the glass and smiled. 'But I think I'm well enough for the tour.'

Ms Cunningham looked at her wristwatch. 'I have a meeting coming up, but my secretary will show you around.' She took Nightingale through to the outer office and introduced him to the stern-faced lady who had given him the brochure. Her name was Sally and once she began taking Nightingale around her stern face vanished and she became quite chatty. She was very knowledgeable about the school and its history and Nightingale could barely get a word in as she talked away. She showed him around the classrooms and sporting facilities, and then upstairs to the bedrooms. The girls slept four to a room in bunk beds in bright, airy rooms. 'I'm sure your daughter will love it here,' said Sally. 'It's a magical place. And such a good mix of children. We have a lot from China and Russia, but they're all from good families.'

She took him out of the room and closed the door. 'That's pretty much the full tour,' she said, 'but is there anything else you'd like to see?'

'There is one thing,' he said. 'I know it sounds crazy but my wife has a thing about spirits.'

Sally frowned. 'Spirits?'

'Well, ghosts. She'd heard that a girl died on the premises.'

'Oh, that was years ago. It was in the seventies.'

'What happened? Do you know?'

'It was long before my time, obviously,' she said. She began walking down the corridor towards the stairs. 'All I know is what I was told by the caretaker when I first came to work here. Mr McGowan, he's long since retired. He said a young girl killed herself. Cut her wrists, I think.' She shuddered. 'Poor thing.'

'And where did it happen, exactly?'

She frowned again as she looked across at him. 'Why would you ask a question like that?' she said.

'I know it's crazy,' he said, and flashed her his most boyish smile. 'But as I said, my wife has a thing about spirits. She wouldn't want Zoe sleeping in a room where someone had died.'

'Oh, it wasn't a bedroom. I'm sure of that.'

'Where was it, exactly?'

'It was a store room.' She gestured down the corridor. 'It's used for storing spare mattresses and things these days. Back then I think it was empty.'

'Can I see it?'

'I suppose so,' she said. She walked down the corridor and opened a door on the left. Nightingale looked over her shoulder. It was a windowless room, about twelve feet by ten feet, and as Sally had said it was full of mattress and surplus furniture. The walls were painted white and the floor was bare boards. 'The children never come in here, your wife has absolutely nothing to worry about.'

'Did Mr McGowan ever tell you why the girl was in there when she died?'

'It really wasn't something we talked about,' she said. 'And as I said, it was a long, long time ago.' She closed the door and took Nightingale downstairs. She said goodbye to him at the main entrance and Nightingale thanked her and headed out. As he walked over to his MGB he saw Ms Cunningham looking at him through the window so he resisted the urge to light a cigarette. He climbed in and drove off.

* * *

Robbie Hoyle phoned just as Nightingale was driving away from the school. He pulled up at the side of the road and took the call. 'How was the jumper?' asked Nightingale.

'Cry for help,' said Hoyle. 'Husband had left her, one of her kids is on drugs, her benefits have been cut. She just wanted to talk to somebody. You know how it is.'

'Yeah,' said Nightingale. Sometimes people just wanted a shoulder to cry on, and if someone had no friends or family to, then a police negotiator would do. People who really wanted to kill themselves usually just went ahead and did it. Anyone who waited for a police negotiator to turn up more often than not wanted someone to talk to. 'Is she going to be okay?'

Hoyle sighed. 'She's back home but her husband is still off, her boy is still a junkie and I put a call in to the benefits office but you know what they're like. She's on anti-depressants so they might calm her down.' He sighed again. 'So, that case. You know it was a suicide, right?'

'That's what I was told.'

'So why the interest in a forty-year-old suicide?'

'I've a client who wants answers. I just need a chat with one of the investigating officers because it was all paper back then.'

'The guy you need is Inspector David Mercer. Retired fifteen years ago. I've got an address. He lives not far from Winchester.'

'You're a star, Robbie.'

* * *

David Mercer's house was a three-bedroom semi-detached on the outskirts of Winchester, with neatly-tended red roses growing around a small patch of grass, and a caravan parked in the driveway. Nightingale left his car in the road and walked past the caravan to ring the door bell. A grey-haired woman answered the door. She was a small woman, just over five feet tall. Her face was wrinkled but her eyes were a piercing blue and she stared up at him fearlessly. 'If you're trying to get me to change my electricity supplier, you're wasting your time,' she said.

'I'm not,' he said. 'Are you Mrs Mercer?'

'Yes?'

Nightingale flashed her his most reassuring smile. 'Is your husband in? David Mercer?'

'Why?'

'I'd like to talk to him about an old case.'

'Are you police?'

'I uscd to be.'

She wrinkled her nose. 'Private?'

Nightingale nodded. 'Is he home?'

'He's sitting with the fishes.'

'What? Is that like a Mafia thing?'

'I beg your pardon?'

'Sleeping with the fishes?'

She shook her head in confusion. 'Sleeping? Who said anything about sleeping? He's sitting with the koi in the garden. It's his hobby. He spends more time with the fish than he does with me.'

Now it was Nightingale's turn to be confused. 'Koi?'

'Koi. Carp. Big fish.' She sighed and pointed at the kitchen. 'Outside.'

Nightingale thanked her and let himself out through the kitchen door. Ron Mercer was sitting on a wooden bench by the side of a large pool surrounded by rocks and pebbles. He was a small man, bent over a Tupperware container full of brown pellets and he was tossing them a few at a time into the water. More than a dozen brightly coloured fish were snapping at the food.

'Inspector Mercer?' asked Nightingale.

Mercer peered up at him with watery eyes. His skin was as wrinkled as old leather and he had a large mole on his nose that looked pre-cancerous. There was a flesh-coloured hearing aid tucked behind his right ear. 'No one's called me that in years,' he said. His voice was surprisingly powerful, deep and authoritative. 'You in the job?'

'Used to be,' said Nightingale. He nodded at the bench. 'Mind if I join you?'

'Go ahead,' said Mercer. Nightingale sat down and Mercer held out the Tupperware container.

Nightingale took out a handful of pellets and began throwing them one by one into the water.

'I was a firearms officer in the Met,' said Nightingale, 'And a negotiator. Jack Nightingale. He offered his hand and Mercer shook. He had a firm grip. Mercer let go of Nightingale's hand and joined him in throwing food to the fish. 'They're expensive, right?' said Nightingale. 'Most expensive fish in the world, I heard.'

'Can be,' said Mercer. 'They can go for thousands. Some of these are worth a couple of hundred.'

What makes them valuable? I'm guessing it's not the taste.'

'You don't eat these lovelies,' said Mercer. 'Most of the value is in the colour and the pattern. The most valuable is the fish that most resembles the Japanese flag – a red spot on a white background. The closer the red spot is to the head, the more valuable.'

'You like feeding them, huh?'

'I'm checking them,' said Mercer. 'I check them all every day, This food is designed to float so they have to come to the surface to feed. That way I can see if they've got ulcers or parasites. They recognise me, you know. When I walk up to the pond, they come to the edge to be fed. But the wife, they ignore her.' He chuckled. 'That drives her crazy, it does.'

Nightingale threw a couple of pellets and a large orange fish snapped up both of them.

'They eat according to the temperature,' said Mercer. 'The warmer it is, the more they eat. And in the middle of winter they don't feed, other than to nibble a bit of algae from the bottom.' He threw in some more food. 'They can live for more than a hundred years, if you look after them.' He chuckled. 'They'll outlive me for sure.' He began to cough and dabbed at his lips with a handkerchief. 'So what do you want, Jack? I'm assuming you want something?'

'An old case of yours,' said Nightingale. 'Forty years ago. Emily Campbell. She died at the Rushmore Boarding School.'

Mercer frowned, his liver-spotted hand lying on top of the fish pellets. 'Emily Campbell,' he repeated.

'She was sixteen. One of the pupils.'

Mercer shook his head. 'I remember the name, but the case was closed. She killed herself, right. It was a suicide.' He shuddered. 'Are you a smoker?'

Nightingale grinned. 'Sure am. You?'

'Used to be. The wife made me stop ten years ago.'

Nightingale took out his cigarettes and offered the pack to Mercer. 'I won't tell her if you don't,' he said. He lit the cigarette and one for himself. Both men blew smoke contentedly up at the sky. Mercer looked nervously over at the house.

'It was definitely suicide?' asked Nightingale.

Mercer looked back to him, eyes narrowed. 'You think I'm senile?'

'No, but it was a long time ago. What can you tell me about the case?'

Mercer frowned. 'Young girl, she cut herself. Bled to death. There was a black magic thing going around at the time and she was a vulnerable kid.'

'Black magic?'

'You know how kids like to mess with that sort of thing. There was some magic circle drawing on the floor.'

'And no one else was involved?'

'The door was locked from the inside. The staff had to break in to get to her.'

'Were photographs taken at the time?'

'Of course.'

'Where would they be now?'

'Long gone,' said Mercer.

'The files weren't kept?'

'No computers back then, everything was paper,' said Mercer. 'It wasn't a case so it would have been thrown away. No point in keeping it.'

'What about your notebooks?'

'My notebooks.'

'Every cop I know keeps his notebooks,' said Nightingale. 'I did for sure. You never know when an old case might come back to bite you in the arse.'

Mercer laughed. 'That's the truth,' he said. He gestured at the house. 'In the attic. But I've not looked at them for years.'

Nightingale grinned. 'Would you mind?'

'Are you serious? For a forty-year-old suicide?'

'It'd be a big help.'

Mercer bent down, stubbed out his cigarette on the soil and buried it. He nodded at Nightingale. 'You'd better do the same. My wife would have made a great murder squad detective.'

Nightingale followed his example while Mercer put the top back on his Tupperware container and stood up. He placed the container on the bench, then led Nightingale down the path to the kitchen door. Mrs Mercer was watching a quiz show on television and she looked up as her husband walked by with Nightingale. 'I'm just taking Mr Nightingale up into the attic,' he said.

'For heaven's sake, why?'

'An old case,' he said.

'Well don't bring any dust and dirt down with you,' she said, and looked back at the TV.

The attic was reached through a small trapdoor above the landing. Mercer used a pole with a hook on the end to open the trapdoor and pull out an extendable ladder. It rattled down and Mercer leaned the pole against the wall before slowly climbing up. Nightingale waited until Mercer had disappeared through the trapdoor before following him up.

Mercer flicked a switch and a fluorescent light flickered on. The attic was windowless and lined with plasterboard. There were cobwebs around the ceiling and dust everywhere. There were several metal chests to the left of the trapdoor and against the wall that marked the boundary with next door there were a dozen cardboard boxes. 'My police stuff is in there,' said Mercer, nodding at the boxes. They went over to them. They were all labelled with dates written in felt-tipped pen. Mercer took a pair of spectacles from his shirt pocket and he put them on and peered at the boxes.

'There we are,' he said, pointing at a box on the floor. Nightingale moved the two boxes on top of it and Mercer opened it. It was full of manila files and black notebooks. There was a sticker on each of the notebooks, also with felt-tip writing, and Mercer went through them until he found the one he was looking for. 'Got it,' he said, waving it in triumph. He went over to stand underneath the fluorescent light and slowly flicked through the pages. 'The father kept calling me. Every week, regular as clockwork. J Ramsay Campbell, his name was but he never told me what the J stood for. Kept asking how the investigation was going. I suppose he's been dead for years.'

Nightingale shook his head. 'He died last week. Eighty-five.'

Mercer looked up and grimaced. 'I felt for him. My youngest had just been born. No parent wants to bury his child. What about you? Kids?'

Nightingale shook his head again. 'No wife.'

'Playing the field?'

Nightingale grinned. 'I guess so.'

Mercer continued to flick through the pages of his notebook. Then he stopped and frowned. 'I'd forgotten I did that.'

'Did what?'

'I made a drawing of the thing on the floor. The magic circle thing.' He held out the notepad. The diagram filled one page. It was a circle with a five-pointed star inside, similar to a regular pentagram. But in the spaces between the points of the star were filled with strange symbols, the like of which Nightingale had never seen.

'Did you ever work out what it is?' asked Nightingale.

'Some black magic thing, obviously. We figured she'd made it up. Just squiggles.' He frowned. 'You think it's significant?'

Nightingale shrugged. 'I've seen similar circles. But not as complex as this one.'

'Well we got nowhere. I did speak to someone at the British Museum but they weren't much help.'

Nightingale held up the notebook. 'Can I borrow this?'

Mercer looked pained. 'I'd rather not. I feel happier knowing that I have them, you know.'

'Can I copy it, then?'

'I don't see why not but let's do it outside, the dust isn't good for my lungs.'

Nightingale went down the ladder first. Mercer switched off the light and followed him down before closing the trapdoor. This time Mrs Mercer didn't look up as they walked down the hallway to the kitchen but she shouted 'I hope you didn't bring down any mess'.

'We didn't,' said Mercer as he led Nightingale through the kitchen. He grabbed a sheet of paper and a pen from a drawer and took Nightingale into the garden. They sat on the bench while Nightingale copied the drawing from Mercer's notebook.

When he'd finished he handed the notebook back to Mercer. 'So who discovered the body?'

'A member of the cleaning staff found the door was locked from the inside and she called the headmaster. Now what was his name?' He flicked through the notepad. 'Charles Nelson. He was called and he broke down the door.'

'So it was locked?'

Mercer nodded. 'From the inside. The key was in the lock.'

'And the girl?'

Mercer grimaced. 'She was lying on the floor. There was a cut in her left wrist. Deep. And a knife on the floor.' He shuddered. 'Don't suppose you've got another cigarette, have you? I smoked like a chimney back then and all this talking about it is bringing back the craving.'

Nightingale took out his cigarettes and lit two. 'There must have been a lot of blood.'

'Now that's a cop question.'

'I was just wondering if she died in the room or if the body was moved.'

'The door was locked from the inside. I told you that. But there wasn't as much blood as you'd have expected.'

'Did you think it was significant?'

'I thought it was but my boss didn't. It was an old building and the floors were bare wood. He said the blood had probably just drained through the floorboards. Possible, I suppose.'

'Was there a note?'

Mercer shook his head. 'And no social media back then. We spoke to her friends and they said she was worried about her exams.'

'Do you think she killed herself?'

'You're asking me that after forty years?' He sighed. 'She didn't seem the type to kill herself.' And the blood thing worried me. But the headmaster was a Mason and so was my Chief Superintendent so I think a secret handshake was done and I was told to put it down as suicide and move on.'

'What made you think it might not be suicide?'

'The whole magic circle thing seemed out of character. She hadn't expressed any interest in the occult, the girls weren't using Ouija boards or any nonsense like that. And who goes to all that trouble, drawing something like that, before killing themselves?'

'But the locked door?'

Mercer smiled. 'Yeah, the locked door. The key was on the inside, but that doesn't mean that the door was locked from the inside.'

'I don't follow.'

Mercer took a long drag on his cigarette. The kitchen door opened and he put the cigarette down guiltily. His wife appeared in the doorway. 'Do you want tea?' she called over.

'That would be great, love, thanks!' shouted Mercer. He looked at Nightingale. 'How do you take your tea?'

'White, one sugar.'

'White with one sugar for Jack!' shouted Mercer. The kitchen door closed and Mercer resumed smoking.

'What did you mean, the door didn't have to be locked from the inside?' asked Nightingale.

Mercer screwed up his face. 'I always thought Nelson was off.'

Nightingale took out his phone and showed Mercer the photograph he'd taken at the school. Mercer nodded. 'That's him. He just wasn't right, you know. They call it a copper's sixth sense, but it's more than that. I'd been a copper for ten years, three as a DC, and I could tell when someone wasn't right. He was upset, but it was like he was pretending to be upset. It didn't feel right. I knew at the time he was off but I was just a DC and my DS was ten years older than me and our Chief Super wore a funny apron and rolled up his trouser leg, so I just did as I was told.' He took a long drag on his cigarette and blew smoke before continuing. 'We signed it off as a suicide and I didn't give it much thought until a few years later. I was watching some TV show, one of those detective things, can't remember which one. It was a locked room thing. Guy dead in a study, locked from the inside. He'd stabbed himself is what it looked like. Turned out it was the guy's brother who'd done it. Stabbed him, put the knife in his hand and then left, locking the door as he went.'

'From the outside?'

'Sure. From the outside. But he comes back later with the guy's wife and knocks on the door. The door's locked, right? So he kicks down the door and they go into the room. As the wife rushes over to the body, the brother slips the key into the lock. So when the cops come, it looks as if the door had been locked from the inside. That's when I remembered the Emily Campbell case. Nelson was first through the door, he could have put the key in the lock after he'd broken it down. But as I said, that was years later. The horse had bolted, right?' He took a long drag on his cigarette, then leaned over, stubbed it out and buried it in the soil.

'Any idea what happened to Nelson?'

Mercer shook his head. 'It wasn't a case to be followed up. What about you? Why are you so interested?'

'I've a client who wants to know what happened.'

'Family member?'

Nightingale nodded. 'The dead girl's sister. She just wants answers. Closure.'

'Forty years is a long time.'

'You're telling me.'

The kitchen door opened. Nightingale followed Mercer's example and buried what was left of his cigarette in the soil before Mrs Mercer came over with their tea.

* * *

Nightingale got back to the office with a couple of Starbuck coffees and two chocolate muffins. 'Any joy?' asked Jenny as he put a coffee and muffin down in front of her.

'Thirty grand a year for a boarding school, does that sound right?'

'Education isn't cheap,' said Jenny.

'But thirty grand,' said Nightingale. 'That's serious money.' He went through to his office and dropped down on his chair. Jenny got up and followed him through.

'The cop thinks that she was killed,' said Nightingale. 'I'm going to ask Robbie to check out the headmaster. He might have been involved.' He sipped his coffee and then called Hoyle. Hoyle answered on the third ring. 'Robbie, it's Jack.'

'Ask him about Anna,' mouthed Jenny.

'How are Anna and the girls, by the way?' asked Nightingale.

'What?'

'Anna. And the girls. Are they good?'

'They're great,' said Hoyle. 'Anna keeps asking when you're coming around for dinner.'

'This weekend works,' said Nightingale.

'Why don't you bring Jenny?'

'I'll ask.' He put his hand over the receiver. 'Robbie and Anna want you to come to dinner at the weekend.'

Jenny grimaced. 'I can't, my parents have a shoot. Tell them I'd love to but sorry.'

Nightingale nodded and put the phone back to his ear. 'She's shooting peasants this weekend.'

'I think you mean pheasants,' said Robbie.

'Peasants, pheasants. I think they're pretty much interchangeable among the upper classes.'

Jenny shook her head contemptuously and walked out of his office.

'So what do you want, Jack?'

'Another favour.'

Hoyle laughed. 'I took that for granted,' he said. 'What in particular do you need?'

'I'm trying to trace the headmaster of a boarding school from forty years ago. If I give you a name and a photograph, do you think you could find him?'

'Bloody hell, Jack, you don't ask much do you. Is it an unusual name?'

'Not really. Charles Nelson.'

'There'll be hundreds with that name,' said Hoyle. 'Have you got a date of birth?'

'Just the name and a photograph. Can't you run it through DVLC or the Passport office.'

'Why the interest?'

'There was a case forty years ago that was put down as suicide. I went to see that cop you told me about – Mercer – and he said he thought this guy Nelson might have killed her.'

'Forty years ago? That's one hell of a cold case, Jack.'

'I know, but can you do it for me? I'd really like to talk to this Nelson if he's still alive.'

'Even if you find him, what are you going to do? He must be seventy or eighty now, unless he right out confesses I don't see the CPS being interested.'

'The client is more interested in finding out what happened,' said Nightingale. 'Closure.'

Hoyle sighed. 'I'll see what I can do. But don't expect miracles.'

* * *

Nightingale drove to Camden in his MGB. It was a sunny day so he took the top down and let the wind blow through his hair. He parked in a multi-storey close to Camden Lock market and smoked a Marlboro as he walked to the Wicca Woman shop. Mrs Steadman's shop wasn't easy to find unless you knew what you were looking for, it was in a narrow side street wedged between a shop selling exotic bongs and t-shirts promoting cannabis, and another that offered hand-knitted sweaters.

The Wicca Woman window was filled with crystals, candles and pendants, plus crystal balls of differing sizes. There was also a display of books with titles such as 'Love Spells to Catch Your Man' and 'How Wicca Can Fulfill Your Dreams.'

Nightingale flicked away what was left of his cigarette and pushed open the door. The tinkling of a tiny silver bell announced his arrival and he smelled lavender and lemon grass and jasmine.

Alice Steadman was arranging a display of incense sticks next to an old-fashioned cash register and she beamed when she saw him. 'Mr Nightingale, this is a lovely surprise.' She was in her late sixties, with pointy features that always reminded Nightingale of a bird. Her grey hair was loose around her shoulders. It was the first time he'd seen her hair like that, usually it was tied back in a ponytail. Her skin was wrinkled and almost translucent but her emerald green eyes burned like coals. She was dressed all in black, a long tunic over a floor-length skirt and a thick leather belt with a silver buckle in the shape of a quarter moon.

'Would you like tea?' she asked.

'I would love some,' he said.

Mrs Steadman pulled back a beaded curtain behind the counter and shouted up a flight of stairs. 'Shona, you can leave that for the time being, can you mind the shop for me?'

Nightingale heard the soft pad of bare feet on the stairs and a pretty blonde girl with full tattooed sleeves and several stainless steel face piercings appeared. She avoided looking at Nightingale as she took her place at the cash register while Mrs Steadman ushered him through the curtain into a small room where a gas fire was burning, casting flickering shadows across the walls.

As Nightingale sat at a circular wooden table under a brightly-coloured Tiffany lampshade, she went over to a kettle on top of a pale green refrigerator and switched it on. She looked at him over her shoulder. 'Milk and no sugar,' she said.

'Perfect.'

'So how can I help you, Mr Nightingale,' she said as she spooned PG Tips into a brown ceramic teapot. 'I'm assuming this isn't just a social visit.'

'I do love your tea,' he said. 'But yes, I could do with some advice.' Nightingale took the drawing of the magic circle from his pocket and spread it out on the table. 'Have you seen something like this before?'

Mrs Steadman walked over and frowned down at the drawing. 'Now where did you get that from?' she asked.

'It was done in a school,' said Nightingale. 'A boarding school.'

'Oh dear,' sighed Mrs Steadman. 'Dear, dear, dear.'

'What does it mean?'

'Nothing good, Mr Nightingale,' she said. 'Nothing good.'

She went back to the kettle and stood with her back to him, her shoulders hunched. When the kettle had boiled she poured water into the teapot and carried it over to the table on a tray with two blue and white striped mugs and a matching milk jug and sugar bowl. She sat down and poured tea for him, then added milk. Only when she had handed him his tea did she speak. 'Mr Nightingale, you really shouldn't be messing with things like this.' She nodded at the paper. 'And please, put that away.'

Nightingale picked up the paper, folded it, and put it back in his pocket.

'What does it mean, Mrs Steadman?'

'Just walk away from this, please.'

'You know what it is, don't you?'

'So do you. It's a pentagram.'

'But it's special, isn't it. I've never seen those markings before.'

'They're…special.' She shuddered.

'Special in what way?'

'Why do you want to know, Mr Nightingale.'

'A young girl was found dead by one of these circles.'

'Inside or outside?' asked Mrs Steadman quickly.

'Outside.'

Mrs Steadman winced as if she had been struck.

'Please, I need to know what the significance is.'

'Of the girl? Or the circle.'

Nightingale frowned. 'Both, I guess.'

Mrs Steadman took a deep breath, then poured herself more tea. 'The circle is used to summon Paimonia, one of the kings of Hell.' She pointed at one of the symbols. 'This is his sigil. His symbol. He is a demon of the first rank with two hundred legions of followers and really, you don't want to have anything to do with him. He is powerful, Mr Nightingale. Really powerful.'

'I just need information, Mrs Steadman. I'm not planning on summoning him.'

She stared at him with her bird-like eyes. 'I do hope that's the truth,' she said eventually. 'Paimonia is different to most of the demons in that doing a deal with him requires a sacrifice.'

'A human sacrifice?'

Mrs Steadman nodded. 'Generally a deal can be struck with a demon once summoned. A quid pro quo. But Paimonia requires more. And because of what he offers, many are prepared to make the sacrifices that are required.'

'What does he offer?'

'Eternal life, Mr Nightingale. 'Or as close to eternal as is possible.'

'You can live for ever?'

'At a price, Mr Nightingale. At a terrible price.'

Nightingale sipped his tea and waited for her to continue.

'Demons are devious, as you know. Paimonia is more devious than most. He offers you immortality, but demands a sacrifice. That sacrifice means that only the most committed move forward. Which is when the rest of the deal is made clear. The sacrifice is not a one-off. It has to be repeated. If it isn't repeated, the immortality is lost.'

'So the person has to keep on killing?'

'Not necessarily doing the actual killing, but they have to supply the sacrifice. The only negotiation is how often the sacrifices have to occur.'

'I don't understand, I'm sorry.'

Mrs Steadman sipped her tea. 'The person who summons Paimonia often doesn't know about the sacrifice. Those who do a deal with him are sworn to secrecy. When they do realise that a girl has to be killed, they often back out. Those that decide to continue then negotiate how often the sacrifices have to occur. Paimonia has some flexibility. If it's a soul that he really wants, perhaps the sacrifices take place every fifty years. Or a hundred. If a soul is less valuable, then perhaps Paimonia would insist on a sacrifice every year.'

'But if the deal is for immortality, Paimonia would never collect. That doesn't make sense.'

'Devils have patience, Mr Nightingale. They view time differently.'

'But if the person never dies, Paimonia won't get the soul.'

Mrs Steadman smiled sadly. 'No one wants to live forever, Mr Nightingale. Not really. They think they do, but birth, life and death form a cycle. You can't fight the cycle for ever. Sooner or later everyone decides it's time to go.'

Nightingale felt a sudden craving for a cigarette but he knew that Mrs Steadman didn't approve so he picked up a biscuit and nibbled it.

'Time means nothing to the likes of Paimonia. He just waits for as long as it takes. And he's happy to wait because he takes pleasure from the sacrifices.'

'Always a girl?'

Mrs Steadman nodded. 'A girl, the younger the better. Sometimes that will be spelled out during the negotiation. Paimonia might insist on a virgin, for example.' She leaned towards him and stared into his eyes. 'Mr Nightingale, please don't even think about getting involved with Paimonia.'

'I'm sort of involved already,' he said. 'It's a case. I have a client who wants answers.'

'You won't get answers from Paimonia. Only grief.'

Nightingale forced a smile. 'I understand.'

She leaned even closer. 'I hope you do,' she said.

Nightingale realised for the first time how dark her eyes were. The irises were almost as black as the pupils. As he stared into her eyes he saw his own reflection, then suddenly his reflection was gone and he was looking at something else, something with a gaping mouth and pointed teeth and slanted red eyes. He flinched and jerked backwards, tea slopping over his hand. He apologised and Mrs Steadman scurried away to fetch a towel. She used it to mop up the spilled tea.

'I'm so sorry,' he said.

'Don't be silly. There's no point in crying over spilled tea.' She sat down opposite him and refilled his mug.

Nightingale smiled. Her eyes were brown now, her pupils clearly defined. 'This Paimonia, he's all-powerful, is he?'

'Most devils are,' said Mrs Steadman. 'But Paimonia is especially strong. He's cunning and careful. The only time he takes physical form is at the moment of sacrifice.'

'Could he be killed then?'

Mrs Steadman's eyes narrowed. 'Mr Nightingale…' she sighed.

He held up his hands. 'I'm just curious,' he said.

'I'm serious about this, Mr Nightingale. You really don't want to go anywhere near Paimonia.'

'I'm not planning to. I'd just like to know.'

She sighed and sipped her tea. 'Then the answer to your question is yes. In theory, Paimonia could be killed at the moment of sacrifice. But you know about the magic circle. You have to stay within it while the devil is present. Or your own life is at risk.' She waved her hand in front of her face. 'I really don't like talking about this, Mr Nightingale. It makes me very uncomfortable.'

'I'm sorry, Mrs Steadman. Let's drop the subject.' He sipped his tea and smiled brightly. 'So, what's new in the world of Wicca?'

* * *

Nightingale was eating duck noodles in Mrs Chan's Chinese restaurant on the ground floor of the building where he lived when Robbie Hoyle called him. 'You screwed up with that photograph, it's not from forty years ago.'

Mrs Chan put a bottle of beer down in front of him and smiled.

Nightingale waved his thanks. 'Why do you say that?' he asked Hoyle.

'Because his name isn't Charles Nelson and he's thirty-nine years old.'

'You must have the wrong guy.'

'One hundred per cent match on facial recognition,' said Hoyle. 'I'm looking at both pictures now, Jack. It's the same guy, same chip in the front tooth. Where did you get your photograph from?'

'It was on the wall of the school. He was the headmaster there, forty years ago.'

'Somebody is messing with you. His name is Richard Hall and like I said, he's thirty nine.'

'Have you got an address?'

'Sure. He's in north London. But if your guy was a headmaster forty years ago, it's definitely not him.'

'You're a star, mate, thanks.'

Nightingale ended the call and a few minutes later, just as he was finishing his noodles, his phone beeped to let him know he had received a message. Attached to the message was a picture of a driving licence belonging to Richard Hall. The address on the licence was in Highgate, not far from the cemetery where Karl Marx was buried.

* * *

'Exactly what are you going to say to him?' asked Jenny. She was behind the wheel of her Audi sports car, parked a short distance from the house in Highgate where Richard Hall was supposed to live.

'I'll ask him if he's Charles Nelson,' said Nightingale. He was in the passenger seat. She had picked him up in Bayswater at just after seven o'clock in the morning, the idea being that the early bird would catch the worm.

'And if he denies it, what then?'

'The picture evidence is pretty convincing,' said Nightingale.

'You'd need DNA or fingerprints to be sure,' said Jenny. 'Face recognition isn't an exact science, not yet anyway. And if you're right – what then?'

'What do you mean, what then?'

'Suppose he admits to being Charles Nelson? And that he changed his name to Richard Hall? And that he hasn't aged a day over the last forty years? You think he'll just put his hands up to murdering Emily Campbell.'

'You'd be surprised how many people do confess when confronted with the evidence.'

'Jack, all you have is a photo on your phone. And the change of name means he wants to cover his tracks.'

Nightingale sighed. 'I could do with less negativity, frankly.'

'Yeah? And I could do with a boss who doesn't use me as a chauffeur before the sun comes up.'

'You get what this guy has done, right? He's done a deal with a devil to live forever and in return he has to offer up regular human sacrifices.'

'You really believe that?'

'If I didn't, I wouldn't be up at sparrow's fart, would I?'

The front door opened and a man in a suit stepped out. He was carrying a briefcase. 'Is that him?' asked Nightingale, peering at the picture of the Richard hall driving licence on his phone.

'Hard to tell,' said Jenny.

The man pulled the door shut and walked down the path towards the pavement.

'It's him, no doubt,' said Nightingale. He climbed out of the car. 'You stay where you are.'

'That's exactly what I was planning to do,' she said.

Nightingale walked towards the man. He kept his head down and tried to get by but Nightingale held out his arms to block his way. The man stopped, confused. Only then did he look at Nightingale. 'Mr Nelson? Charles Nelson?'

Nightingale had been a cop long enough to recognise guilt when he saw it, even though it flashed across the man's face in less than a second. 'I'm sorry, no, you have the wrong person.'

He tried to get by but Nightingale moved to block his way again. 'You were headmaster at Rushworth School forty years ago.'

The man froze and his eyes burned into Nightingale's. 'Are you stupid? How old do you think I am?'

'We both know how old you are, Mr Nelson.'

'Are you mad?' sneered the man.

'I'm not mad enough to do a deal with Paimonia,' said Nightingale. 'Not now I know what that entails.'

The man's eyes narrowed. 'Who are you?' he asked.

'The name's Nightingale.'

'Have you got a card, Mr Nightingale?'

'Why do you want my card?'

'I'm in a bit of a rush right now, I'll call you later.' He looked over Nightingale's shoulder at the Audi. 'The blonde, she's with you?'

'All I want is for you to confirm that you used to run Rushworth School. And that you left after Emily Campbell died.'

The man thrust his face close to Nightingale's. 'Who the fuck are you?'

'I told you. Nightingale.'

'What the fuck do you want?'

'I wanted you to confirm that you're Charles Nelson. And you've pretty much confirmed that.'

The man moved even closer to Nightingale so that their noses were just inches apart. Nightingale could smell the man's breath. It was sour, like milk that had gone off. 'I've confirmed fuck all, now you need to get the hell out of my way or I'll rip your fucking arm off.' His eyes went completely black and Nightingale flinched as he saw his own face reflected in them. He took a step back and the man pushed past. Nightingale watched him go, then walked over to the Audi. Jenny looked over at him as he climbed in. 'How did it go?' she asked.

'Not great.'

'He was looking at the car, wasn't he?'

'Yeah. Sorry.'

'If he knows my registration number he can track me down.'

'He'd have to know the right people, Jenny.'

'If he's who you think he is, he probably does.' She sighed. 'Jack, what the hell have you done?'

* * *

Jenny stopped the Audi in front of the gates to Gosling Manor and Nightingale climbed out to open them. She drove through and waited while he closed the gates and got back into the car. She put the car in gear and drove along a narrow paved road that curved to the right through thick woodland and parked next to a huge stone fountain, the centrepiece of which was a weathered stone mermaid surrounded by dolphins and fish. They climbed out and looked up at the two-storey mansion, the lower floor built of stone, the upper floor made of weathered bricks, topped by a tiled roof with four massive chimney stacks.

'You should sell it,' she said. 'It's not as if you're living here.'

'I will,' said Nightingale. 'Once I've worked out what to do with all the stuff in the basement.'

Nightingale fished the key from his raincoat pocket and unlocked the massive oak door. The hallway was huge, with wood-panelled walls, a glistening marble floor and a large multi-tiered chandelier that looked like an upside down crystal wedding cake. There were three oak doors leading off the hallway, but the entrance to the basement library was hidden within the wooden paneling. He clicked it open and reached through to flick the light switch. Jenny followed him down the wooden stairs.

The basement ran the full length of the house and was lined with shelves laden with books. Running down the centre of the basement were two lines of display cases filled with all sorts of occult paraphernalia, from skulls to crystal balls. At the bottom of the stairs was a sitting area with two overstuffed red leather Chesterfield sofas and a claw-footed teak coffee table that was piled high with books.

Nightingale waved at the bookshelves. 'We need something about summoning demons,' he said. 'Specifically a demon called Paimonia.'

'Is there an index or something that lists the books?'

'Not that I know of,' said Nightingale.

'So we browse through, what, two thousand volumes?'

'Do you have a better plan?'

She sighed. 'Unfortunately not.' She took off her coat and draped it over the back of one of the sofas, then walked over to the bookcases closest to the stairs. Nightingale started on the bookcase next to hers. As always he was amazed by the variety of titles in the library, all devoted to witchcraft and the occult. The books had been collected over more than fifty years by Nightingale's genetic father, Ainsley Gosling, a Satanist who had put Nightingale up for adoption at birth.

It took them the best part of two hours before they found what Nightingale was looking for. Like most of the books on the shelves, there was no title on the spine. It was bound in the skin of some long-dead animal, a reptile maybe. It was a small book, six inches by four inches just about, with fewer than a hundred pages, most of which were blank. The pages weren't paper, they were more like yellowed cloth, and the words had been handwritten in capital letters. The only title was on the first page – THE SUMMONING OF DEVILS and underneath was a list of twelve names. Paimonia was the last name.

Nightingale took the book over to one of the sofas and sat down. Luckily the book was in English – the volumes on the shelves came from all over the world, and a lot of them were written in Latin.

'Does it tell you what you need?' asked Jenny.

Nightingale nodded. 'The whole thing. Though it skates over the details over what the deal involves.'

'The deal?'

Nightingale was about to explain when he realised that Jenny was better off not knowing the finer points of negotiating with demons. 'It's complicated,' he said. 'But I'm guessing that Nelson found a book like this.'

'What are you planning, Jack?'

'What do you mean?'

'You've got that look in your eye that says you're up to something.'

Nightingale grinned. 'I'm just doing my research, that's all.'

Jenny looked around the basement and shivered. 'Can you do it somewhere else, this place gives me the heebie jeebies.'

'The heebie jeebies?'

'You know what I mean. The sooner you sell this place, the better.'

* * *

Nightingale was about to clean his teeth when his phone rang. It was Jenny. 'He's here, outside my house,' she said, her voice trembling.

'Who is?'

'Nelson. Or Hall. Or whatever his name is. He's parked in a grey Toyota.'

'Has he said anything?'

'He's just sitting there.'

Stay inside, keep the door locked, I'll be right around.'

Nightingale hurried downstairs to the street and flagged down a black cab. Jenny's three-bedroom mews house was just off the King's Road in Chelsea. Nightingale had the cab drop him at the entrance to the mews. Jenny's Audi was parked outside her house. The grey Toyota was four houses along. There was someone sitting in the driver's seat, hands on the wheel. Nightingale walked towards the car, trying to stay in its blind spot. He grabbed at the passenger door handle and pulled the door open. Hall looked over at, mouth open in surprise. Nightingale climbed in and slammed the door shut. 'What the hell are you doing?' he said between gritted teeth.

Hall sneered at him. 'It's a free country. You came around to my home, I thought the least I could do was return the favour.'

'I don't live here.'

'I know that. The lovely Ms McLean does.'

'You go near here and I'll…'

'You'll what, Nightingale? And I'm already here so do what you think you have to do?'

'I just want you to leave her alone. She's nothing to do with this. If you've got a problem with me then face me, man to man.'

Hall chuckled. 'First things first.'

'What do you mean?'

'You haven't worked it out yet? I'm due a sacrifice, and Ms McLean fits the bill. It's a pity she's not a virgin, but…'

Nightingale grabbed Hall by the throat but the man continued to smile at him. 'What do you think you can do to me, Nightingale?' he said, his voice strangled but firm.

'I can stop you. That's what I can do.'

Hall reached inside his jacket and pulled out a knife. It had a blade almost six inches long, pointed and with a jagged edge along one side. Nightingale stiffened and released his grip on Hall's throat. Hall handed the knife handle first to Nightingale. 'Take it. Kill me. Go on.'

Nightingale shook his head. 'That's not what I meant.'

'So what are you going to do? Tell the cops?' He laughed. 'I'm sitting in a car in a public street.'

'With a knife,' said Nightingale.

Hall tapped him on the chest with the handle. 'Take it. You know you want to. Take it and kill me. Go on.' Nightingale shook his head and Hall laughed. He turned the blade around and quickly plunged the knife into his own chest, grunting through gritted teeth.

Nightingale jerked back and Hall continued to smile. 'What do you think you can possibly do to me if I can do this to myself,' said Hall. He slowly pulled the knife out. There was no blood, not on his chest or on the blade. Hall took a deep breath then put the knife back inside his jacket. 'You can't kill me, Nightingale. That's the deal I have. I'm immortal.'

'In exchange for your soul? And regular sacrifices?'

Hall shrugged. 'It's a small price to pay, in the grand scheme of things.'

'And Emily Campbell was the first?'

'Why do you care?'

'Her sister wants to know what happened. They said it was suicide. But she didn't believe it.'

'If it makes her feel better, it was Emily's fault. She shouldn't have been there. It was midnight, I'd done the ritual. Paimonia was explaining the small print. I didn't know about the sacrifice, or that the sacrifice had to be repeated. All I knew was what I'd read in this old book I found among my grandmother's things after she died. She was a bit of a witch, though I never realised that. Anyway, the book explained the ceremony and what I could get, but there was stuff missing.' He shrugged. 'Emily came into the room. I think she was sleepwalking, maybe. Or maybe Paimonia had done something to her. Anyway, she walked into the room, the door slammed behind her and that was that. She was the first.' He grinned. 'Does that help you, Nightingale? Does knowing what happened help you in any way? Because it isn't going to change anything. I'm going to arrange for your friend Jenny McLean to be the next sacrifice and there's nothing you can do about it. Now go.'

'You can't do this.'

Hall reached for the knife inside his jacket. 'Get the fuck out of my car or I swear I'll kill you now and fuck the consequences.'

Nightingale glared at the man but knew there was nothing he could do. He cursed and got out of the car. Hall grinned and drove away.

* * *

Mrs Steadman could see from the look on Nightingale's face that he was worried so she didn't make any small talk or offer him tea. 'What on earth has happened?' she asked.

'I've made a huge mistake,' he said. 'I confronted a guy who'd done a deal with Paimonia and I told him that I know what he did.'

Mrs Steadman frowned. 'Why would you do that?'

'I guess I wanted to know for sure, so that I could tell my client what she wants to know.'

'Client?'

'It's a lady whose sister died forty years ago. She was told it was suicide but she never believed it.'

Mrs Steadman's hand flew up to cover her mouth. 'The sister was a sacrifice?'

'I think so, yes.'

'Oh Mr Nightingale, what have you done?'

'It gets worse, Mrs Steadman. This man is now threatening me, and my friend Jenny. And there's nothing I can do to stop him.'

Mrs Steadman sighed. 'I warned you, didn't I? I told you not to mess with Paimonia.'

'This man can't be killed, can he? That's part of the deal.'

'I thought I explained that to you.'

'I knew the deal was that you could live for ever. I didn't appreciate that meant you couldn't be killed. What can I do, Mrs Steadman? How can I put a stop to this?'

Mrs Steadman looked at him fearfully. 'You can't, Mr Nightingale. If this man has the protection of one of the strongest demons in Hell, there's nothing you can do.'

Nightingale sighed. He wanted a cigarette, badly.

'You need to run, Mr Nightingale. You and your friend need to get as far away from this man as you can. That's your only hope, to be somewhere where he can't find you.'

'I can't do that, Mrs Steadman.'

'You have to.'

Nightingale rubbed the back of his neck. 'There's no way of stopping this man? No way at all.'

Mrs Steadman swallowed nervously. 'I'm afraid not. So long as he has the protection of Paimonia, there is nothing you can do.'

'What if this Paimonia were to die. What then?'

Mrs Steadman's eyes narrowed. 'What do you mean?'

'If Paimonia were to die, what about the people who had done deals with him?'

'Those deals would no longer be valid, obviously. But Paimonia is all-powerful, only Satan himself is stronger.'

'I have to go,' said Nightingale, heading for the door. 'Thanks for your help.'

He hurried out, leaving Mrs Steadman staring forlornly at the door. 'Mr Nightingale, I didn't help you at all,' she whispered.

* * *

Nightingale drove south to Streatham, through the town centre and made a right turn and then a left and then drove down an alley between two rows of houses. There was a row of six brick-built lock-up garages with metal doors and corrugated iron roofs. A large black man was waiting for him, next to a black Porsche SUV. He was wearing a black overcoat and impenetrable wraparound sunglasses. T-Bone worked for a South London gangster but had a sideline in supplying illicit weapons to the criminal community. T-Bone grinned as Nightingale climbed out of his MGB. 'You still driving that rust bucket, Birdman?'

'It's a classic,' said Nightingale.

'It's a piece of shit,' said T-Bone. 'If I sold guns as shit as your motor, I'd be out of business.' T-Bone pulled out a set of keys from his coat pocket, unlocked the door of one of the lock-ups and pushed it up. There was an old Jaguar there, its boot facing outwards. T-Bone pulled the door halfway down behind them. 'Don't want anybody looking in,' he explained. He used another key to open the boot of the car. Inside were a dozen or so packages, covered in bubble-wrap. T-Bone picked up one of the packages and unwrapped it. It was a Glock, similar to the one Nightingale had used when he was with the Met's firearms unit. T-Bone held it out to Nightingale but

Nightingale shook his head. 'Have you got anything smaller? More concealable?'

'A lady gun, you mean?'

'I was thinking of something I could hide.'

T-Bone nodded and rooted through the packages before selecting one and unwrapping it. 'Smith and Wesson 638 Airweight?' he said. 'Aluminium so it's light, small frame so it's, well....the clue's in the name, innit?'

Nightingale nodded and took the revolver. He held it in the palm of his hand. T-Bone was right, the 638 Airweight was a near-perfect lightweight revolver. It weighed less than a pound and the barrel was just two inches long. That meant it wasn't especially accurate beyond a few yards but it could easily be carried in a jacket pocket. It only held five rounds but there were thirty eights so would do a lot of damage.

'Five rounds be enough for you?' asked T-Bone as if reading his mind.

'Five should be overkill,' said Nightingale. 'I was never one for spray and pray. How much?'

'I was thinking six hundred.'

'Four?'

'Five-fifty. And if you don't fire it, I'll buy it back for three.'

'I'll be firing it,' said Nightingale. 'Five, and I only need five rounds.'

T-bone pulled out a plastic bag of bullets and counted out five. He slammed the boot shut and gave the rounds to Nightingale. 'Deal,' he said.

Nightingale took out his wallet and handed over ten fifty-pound notes. Always a pleasure doing business with you, T-bone,' he said. He shoved the gun into his pocket then tried to raise the garage door. It seemed to be stuck and he couldn't get it to budge.

T-Bone chuckled and forced it up with one hand. 'You take care, Birdman,' said T-Bone, as Nightingale walked back to his MGB.

* * *

According to the book, Paimonia was best summoned during the day. There were other peculiarities of the ceremony. The candles had to be a mixture of black and blue, and among the herbs and compounds that had to be burned were mercury and bindweed, both of which he managed to find in storage jars in a display case in the basement. The book also emphasised that the summoner had to look to the northwest during the ceremony and he had used a small brass compass to check which way that was. He put everything he needed into a cardboard box and carried it upstairs. He chose a large bedroom that had been stripped of all its furniture and furnishings. He closed the door behind him, placed the box on the bare floorboards, then used consecrated chalk to draw a circle in the middle of the room, about twelve feet in diameter. Then he used a birch branch taken from the garden to slowly outline the circle. Then he used the chalk to draw a five pointed star on top of the circle, with two of the five points facing northwest. So far it was a standard pentagram. Nightingale sprinkled consecrated salt water around the perimeter of the circle before studying the diagrams in the book. They were a pretty close match to the page he'd copied from Mercer's notebook. In a standard pentagram the letters MI and then CH and then AEL were written around the circle, spelling out the name of Michael, the archangel, but for Paimonia the letters were replaced by complex symbols. Nightingale spent more than an hour making sure he drew them perfectly, then he went through to the bathroom and stripped off his clothes.

He had already filled the claw-footed cast iron bathtub with water and he slid into it. He held his breath and slid down under the water, holding his breath until he felt his lungs start to burn, and then he pushed himself up and scrubbed himself clean with a small plastic brush and a bar of soap. He washed and rinsed his hair twice, then climbed out of the bath and towelled himself dry. He put on clean clothes and a pair of new trainers. Finally he combed his hair, checked himself in the mirror over the sink, and went back into the bedroom.

He picked up five candles, three black and two dark blue, and placed them at the five points of the pentagram. He lit them with his lighter, picked up the cardboard box, then stepped inside the circle.

He took a couple of deep breaths then used the birch branch to go over the chalk outline again. He sprinkled consecrated salt water around the perimeter of the circle, then set fire to the contents of a lead crucible. The herbs and spices and bits of wood hissed and spluttered. He added bindweed and mercury salt and the room filled with cloying smoke.

He took the book out of the box and opened it at the chapter on Paimonia. He began to carefully recite the words that would summon the demon. They were written phonetically, they weren't English or Latin, they were something in between. The candle flames flickered as warm wind started to blow through the room, even though the windows and door were shut. The air was getting thicker as the fumes billowed up from the lead crucible. He tried not to think about the damage the mercury might do to his lungs and he concentrated on the words he was saying. His eyes began to water and he blinked away the tears.

There were flashes of light above his head, like lightning strikes. He ignored them and kept his eyes on the book. It was getting harder to see, his eyes were tearing and the smoke was getting thicker by the minute.

He reached the end of the incantation and closed the book. He peered through the smoke. There was no sign of any demon. He frowned, wondering if he had missed something out. Then there was a loud boom that hit him in the chest like a punch and he staggered back. There was a second boom, even louder than the first and then something appeared in front of him. It had no real form, it was greyish-green and constantly shifting. Nightingale saw a glimpse of what might have been a claw and then a wing but they were there only for a few seconds.

'Who are you?' asked a surprisingly soft, almost feminine, voice.

'My name is Jack Nightingale and I have summoned you to offer my respects and to respectfully request you bestow on me the gift of everlasting life. Are you Paimonia?'

'You summoned me, so you should know.'

'Then can you grant me my wish?'

'That can be done,' said Paimonia. 'But there is a price that has to be paid.'

'My soul?'

'Yes, of course. But the gift of immortality does not come so cheaply. You were baptised?'

'Why do you need to know that?'

'Because a baptised soul has more value.'

Nightingale shook his head. 'No. Not baptised.'

'Are you Jewish? Or a Muslim?'

Nightingale shook his head. 'I'm a Christian.'

'I shall require a sacrifice.'

'I will do whatever you ask,' said Nightingale.

'A girl.'

'You want me to kill a girl?'

'No, merely to provide the sacrifice. I will do the rest. All you need to do is to bring her to me.'

Nightingale nodded. 'And then I get to live for ever?'

'For ever and ever. For as long as you want, anyway.'

'And you take my soul?'

'Only if you die.'

'Let's do it, then,' said Nightingale.

'It's not as straightforward as that,' said Paimonia. 'I will require more sacrifices, in the future.'

Nightingale frowned. 'What? So we don't have a deal?'

'We have a deal, my friend, you give me your soul and I grant you eternal life. But I require a sacrifice first and then sacrifices at regular intervals. Every five years.'

'So I have to provide you with a sacrifice every five years? And if I do, I live forever?'

'Yes.'

'And I don't get any older?'

'Not a day.'

Nightingale nodded thoughtfully. 'What about every ten years?'

'Ten years?'

'How about I get a sacrifice for you every ten years?'

'You want to negotiate with me?'

'It's a deal, right? So let's deal. I'll get you a sacrifice every ten years.'

'Ten is not acceptable.'

'What is acceptable?'

'I told you. Every five years.'

'Nine.'

Paimonia sighed. 'Seven. And that is my final offer.'

'When? When do you want the sacrifice?'

The door opened and Jenny McNeil stood there, a look of surprise on her face. She was wearing a leather flight jacket with a sheepskin collar and blue jeans. Her hair was tied back in a ponytail. 'What the hell are you doing, Jack?' she said.

'Jenny, what are you doing here?'

'You've summoned Paimonia? You did it?'

Paimonia roared and the floorboards shuddered. 'She is perfect,' he said. The grey-green shape began to harden. It became darker, and smaller.

'No!' shouted Nightingale. 'Not her.'

Paimonia laughed again. There were wings now, grey and leathery, and a reptilian jaw, lined with teeth. Eyes opened, a fiery red, that glared at Jenny. 'She is the price,' said Paimonia. 'She is the sacrifice.' There were legs now, covered in scales with large hooked talons. And a tail, with a vicious barb at the end.

Jenny turned to run from the room but the door slammed shut. She whirled around, her eyes wide in terror. 'Jack, what's going on?'

'What are you doing here?'

'Your phone's not working. I thought you might be in trouble.'

Paimonia laughed and the walls and floor vibrated. 'You're the one in trouble, my dear,' he said. 'But if it's any consolation, you'll be helping Mr Nightingale to get his heart's desire. Eternal life.'

'Jack, what's happening? Tell me?' She was stood with her back against the door, her arms outstretched.

The creature was fully formed now and it moved towards Jenny, its claws reaching for her.

'Jack!' she screamed.

'He can't help you,' said Paimonia. 'He can't and he won't.'

'I wouldn't bank on that,' she said. She reached inside her jacket and took out a small canister of mace. She pointed it at the demon's head and pressed the trigger. A tight stream of mace sprayed over its eyes and mouth and it roared in anger. Jenny took a step forward, continuing to spray the burning liquid at the eyes.

Nightingale bent down and pulled the Smith and Wesson revolver from the box. He brought the gun up, supporting his right hand with his left and fired twice at the back of Paimonia's head. Both bullets hit their target, the first shot blowing off a chink of green skin and bone, the second burying itself in the skull. The creature roared in defiance and turned. Nightingale waited until it was facing him before firing again. Two quick shots to the throat then as the creature staggered to the side he fired into its eye at point-blank range. Green blood spurted from the wound and it began to stagger. Then there was a loud bang and space seemed to fold in on itself and the creature disappeared.

Nightingale stood with the gun in both hands, breathing heavily. Jenny was leaning against the door, still holding the can of mace.

'That worked out well,' said Nightingale.

'Do you think?' asked Jenny, her voice loaded with sarcasm

'It could have gone worse. I wasn't a hundred per cent sure that bullets would kill it.' He put the gun back in the cardboard box.

Jenny's jaw dropped. 'Please tell me you're joking.'

Nightingale grinned. 'I was joking.'

She tilted her head on one side. 'Really?'

'Mrs Steadman said he took on physical form at the moment of sacrifice, so assuming that was the case, bullets should have worked.'

'And if they hadn't?'

Nightingale looked uncomfortable. 'I'm afraid I didn't have a fallback position.'

'Good to know, Jack. Good to know.' She glared at him, put the can of mace in her pocket and then turned on her heel and walked away.

'You're going to run me back to London, aren't you?' he shouted after her.

He heard the click of her heels as she headed downstairs, the front door open and slam shut, followed a few seconds later by her Audi starting up. 'I guess not,' said Nightingale. He took out his cigarettes and lit one as he walked over to the window, just in time to see Jenny drive off in her Audi.

* * *

Nightingale was walking back to his flat when his phone rang. It was Robbie Hoyle. 'What have you been up to?' asked the detective.

'This and that,' said Nightingale. 'Why do you ask?'

'Seen anything of that guy you wanted information on? Charles Nelson? Or that guy who looks like him? Richard Hall?'

'Nah, I let it drop,' said Nightingale. 'It couldn't have been him, obviously. No one stays the same for forty years, right?' Nightingale didn't like lying to his friend, but on this occasion he didn't have a choice. There was no way he could explain that Charles Nelson had sold his soul to a demon from Hell in exchange for immortality, and no way that Hoyle would ever believe him.

'So you just let it drop?'

'It was a dead end.'

'Because Richard Hall is dead.'

'Dead?'

'You know what dead means, Jack. Deceased. No longer with us. You sure you didn't go to see him?'

'What's happened, Robbie? Why not just cut to the chase?'

'Okay. Richard Hall was found dead in his house today. His cleaner turned up and found him in his bed.'

'People die in their beds all the time.'

'Not like this, Jack. The doctor who came in to examine the body says Mr Hall shows all the signs of having been dead for forty years.'

'What?'

'How is that not clear, Jack? The body was mummified, pretty much. Dental records proved who it was but even so... forty years. How does that happen, Jack? His driving licence was issued four years ago. And his cleaner said he was alive and well two days ago when she was last in the house.'

'It's a mystery, no question.'

'So why do I get the feeling that you're not telling me everything?'

'I'm off the case,' said Nightingale. 'I couldn't find Charles Nelson so I just assumed he'd died or left the country. I'm trying to find other people who worked at the school but I'm not having any joy. Forty years is a long time, like you said. So is it a murder enquiry?'

'According to the doctor, Hall died of natural causes. Forty years ago. I can't see my bosses being happy if I start a murder investigation on the basis of that. So no, it goes down as death by natural causes. There don't seem to be any relatives to cause a fuss so I guess Mr Hall's secret will be buried with him.'

Hoyle ended the call, clearly less than satisfied with the answers that Nightingale had given him. Nightingale waited until he'd got back home and drunk two bottles of Corona and smoked three cigarettes before phoning Mary Campbell. He took a deep breath and began talking. 'I know who did it,' he said. 'And I'm happy enough to tell you who did it. But I warn you now, you're not going to believe it.'

'I just want to know what happened, Mr Nightingale.'

'Then I think you'd better sit down,' he said, reaching for his cigarettes.

MY NAME IS LYDIA

She woke up exactly at two a.m. It was always easy to take control while the bitch slept, though in time she would be able to overcome all resistance no matter what the time. Enough moonlight filtered through the thin curtains to allow her to inspect the naked body. The budding breasts were developing nicely, and she cupped each one in turn, feeling the nipples harden. She ran her fingers between the legs, lingering long enough to feel the moisture start to flow. This body would be so much more fun, now that the transition to womanhood had begun. Still, time enough for that later, once she'd started on the process of subjugation. And spread a little more unhappiness. She took a slow, deep breath, enjoying the feel of the warm night air entering and leaving her lungs. It was good to be alive.

She sat up and stretched. She found the packet of cigarettes in the top drawer of the bedside table, placed one between her lips and lit it with a plastic lighter. It had been easy enough to persuade one of the Year Ten boys at school to buy them for her, especially with the suggestion of a little reward to come. She inhaled deeply and blew a smoke ring up towards the ceiling. The parents might smell the smoke, but that would be the least of their worries. She smiled at the thought of what was to come. She was going to have such fun.

She crushed the last of the cigarette out on the top of the clock-radio, which read 2.08. She swung her feet onto the floor and stood up, a little unsteadily at first because being in control still took some getting used to. She took a long look at the body in the mirrored door of the wardrobe. Yes, it would do. It would certainly do, and it held the promise of much more to come.

The room was warm, the window open to the August night air, and she ignored the dressing gown hanging behind the door. She turned the knob and walked out onto the landing, past the door of the parents' bedroom and on into the bathroom. She closed the door behind her before turning on the light, then opened the medicine cabinet over the basin. What she needed was on the top shelf, and the eleven-year-old body wouldn't stretch that far, so she pulled over the wicker towel box and stood on it. She pushed aside the mother's sleeping pills and Prozac to ensure they wouldn't fall as she reached for the father's Gillette Fusion razor and the box of spare blade cartridges. She stepped down from the box and pushed it back to its usual place by the wall.

She slipped off her nightdress and sat on the edge of the bath as she loaded one of the cartridges into the razor, just as she'd seen the father do many times before, as she'd watched through the bitch's eyes. She carefully ran the blade across the left wrist, pressing just hard enough to open three shallow cuts that ran the whole width of the arm. There was hardly any pain at all. Blood started to seep out, and she transferred the razor to the left hand and repeated the procedure on the right wrist. As the blood started to cover the wrists, she wiped them across the breasts and stomach, leaving ragged red trails.

She climbed into the bath, leaned forward to put the plug into its hole, placed the lever of the mixer tap into the middle position, then lifted it to start the flow of water into the bath. She lay down in the deepening water and watched as it slowly turned red and waited. She didn't think it would take long before they heard and the fun would begin.

She was right. Inside two minutes, she heard the sound of the parents' door opening and the pad of slippers along the landing. The door knob rattled as the father spoke. 'Christine? Are you all right in there, sweetheart?'

She said nothing, just continued to watch as the reddening water crept slowly around the body.

'Christine? What are you doing in there? What's the matter?'

She heard another set of feet as the mother joined him, and her voice rang out. 'Christine? Open the door, darling. Please.'

The water was covering the stomach now. The head rested against the back of the bath, still well clear of danger. She heard the whispered conversation outside the door, though she couldn't make out the words. Finally the father spoke again. 'Christine, you need to come out now, or we'll have to come in. Please, darling. You're worrying us. Please open the door.'

Still she waited, and then she smiled as the doorknob turned. She heard the impact of a shoulder against the door. The door itself was strong, but the tiny bolt was held in by shallow screws and burst away from the frame as fifteen stone of the father's full weight smashed against it. The parents tumbled into the room, stopping in horror when they saw the small figure in the bath.

'Christine,' screamed the mother. 'Oh my God, Christine.'

She raised the head a little further out of the water and stared malevolently at the two adults, her eyes flashing contempt. The voice was harsh, deep and angry 'Don't you fucking dare to call me that. My name is Lydia.'

* * *

Jack Nightingale knew that it was illegal to smoke in a place of business. On the other hand, with a complete absence of cases for the last two weeks, he was beginning to doubt whether his office fitted that description any longer. He decided to open the window before lighting up a Marlboro, which he figured probably let in fumes far more harmful than his cigarette produced. He sat down at his computer and continued checking his emails, most of which seemed to be offering him dates with Russian women and Chinese Viagra pills to make his relations with them last longer. No sign of anything that would top up his bank account. In fact he was starting to wonder why he'd bothered to show up at the office at all today, when the door swung open and Jenny McLean walked in.

Nightingale just had time to notice her dark blue blazer and light blue jeans before she pointed an accusing finger at him. 'Seriously? You promised not to smoke in the office anymore.'

'Well, to be fair, I think what I actually said was that I wouldn't let you see me smoke here anymore.'

'That wasn't what you said. You promised.'

'I had my fingers crossed. This is the last one for the day. In here anyway. Now sit down and I'll make you a coffee.'

'Coffee isn't actually an infallible way to get round me, you know.'

Nightingale raised an eyebrow. 'So, you don't want one?'

'Well…yes.'

Nightingale crushed out his cigarette and did the necessary with the coffee maker. By the time he handed Jenny her cup she was sitting at her desk with her computer fired up, checking invoices and payments. Not many of either recently. She sipped her coffee and looked up at him.

'Jack, I need a favour.'

'Ask and ye shall receive,' he said. 'Unless you need a loan in which case you're out of luck. My bank balance is under some strain at the moment.'

'No, it's not money. I just want you to see a friend of mine, well, more a friend of my mother's really. He's in a bit of a quandary apparently, and he says it sounds like your sort of thing. I sort of gathered it's to do with another friend of mother's but…'

'Hold on a minute,' said Nightingale. 'You're losing me already. Why don't you start from the beginning and take it slowly.'

She sipped her coffee. 'Well, I'm not sure I can really, he didn't tell me all that much about it. It would be easier if you talked to Maurice yourself. That's his name, Maurice Mahoney.'

'So it's a case?'

'Not really, he just needs some advice. Pro bono.'

'You know I hate that band, Jenny.'

'You make the same U2 joke every time I mention Pro Bono.'

'I have a limited repertoire,' he admitted. 'Bit like U2. Sure, bring him in. It's not as if I'm worked off my feet at the moment.'

Jenny smiled. 'He'll be here in twenty minutes. I knew you wouldn't mind.'

'You sneaky madam. Gives you just enough time to nip over to Starbucks and get the muffins in. One for your mate too if he's the muffin type.'

* * *

Nightingale's detective skills hadn't been given much exercise in recent weeks, but they were still up to the task of deducing that Maurice Mahoney was a Catholic priest. The long black cassock and dog collar were a dead giveaway. Mahoney looked to be in his mid-fifties, the brown in his hair losing the war to the grey. He was quite a big man still in pretty good shape. Nightingale waved him to a chair. 'Sit down, please, Father.'

Nightingale didn't miss the quick glance the priest gave to the packet of Marlboro and the ashtray on the desk as he sat down. A lot of Catholic priests seemed to smoke and drink. Nightingale wondered if that was because it helped make up for the vow of chastity thing. 'You a smoker, Father Mahoney?' he asked, though the nicotine stains on the fingers of his right hand were a dead giveaway.

'When I can find a place where it's still legal. We even have to put up "No Smoking" notices in the church now.'

'Well, I've got one of those notices too, but I'm the boss so I think I have some leeway.' He pushed the packet and lighter across the desk despite the angry look from Jenny.

'I won't say no,' said Mahoney. 'My nerves need a little soothing at the moment.' The priest lit a Marlboro, blew smoke at the ceiling, and sighed. 'Jenny's talked about you a little, so I know I can rely on your discretion. This has to stay between us, Jack. This concerns a friend of hers, or at least her parents, and it couldn't be more personal. My friend's name is Susan Warren.'

Nightingale nodded, though the name meant nothing to him. He had met Jenny's parents but only knew a few of their friends.

The priest continued. 'She's quite a prominent solicitor, works for a firm in London, though she lives in Twickenham. I met her at one of Jenny's parents' dinner parties.'

'Married?' asked Nightingale.

'Oh, yes. Matthew's a doctor. Very nice chap. Devoted to each other. And to their daughter, Christine. She's eleven now. And that seems to be where the problem lies.'

He flicked ash into the one ashtray on Nightingale's desk. 'It seems that Christine has been displaying some …rather…unfortunate behaviour lately.'

'Teenagers can be difficult, I'm told.'

'Yes, I've been told that too. But this seems to go a little further than sullenness and defiance. If the Warrens are to be believed, it seems that Christine has developed a complete alternate personality, and an extremely dangerous and unpleasant one at that.'

'For example?'

'For example, she's started to associate with much older boys, to smoke, swear and abuse her parents, she damaged her father's car and the most recent incident involved her cutting her own wrists.'

'A suicide attempt?'

'Not a serious one, apparently. More a gesture. As her mother puts it, her new personality seems determined to make their lives a misery.'

'So she's changed completely?'

'No, that's the strange thing. Most of the time she's her normal self, a lovely girl. The new and nasty persona only takes over occasionally. When it does, she even refuses to answer to her own name. Insists on being called Lydia.'

'So what has all this got to do with me?' asked Nightingale. 'Or, come to that, with you? Sounds like a job for a child psychologist, rather than a priest and a private detective.'

Father Mahoney closed his eyes and shook his head. He opened his eyes after a few seconds and took a long pull on his cigarette. 'The parents sent her to a psychiatrist but he said there was nothing wrong. Absolutely nothing. He gave her a completely clean bill of health. That was the day before she cut her wrists.'

'She fooled the psychiatrist? Is that what you're suggesting?'

'Or maybe when she went to see the psychiatrist there wasn't a problem. The girl the psychiatrist saw was perfectly well-adjusted. But maybe the psychiatrist didn't get to see Lydia.'

'I'm not sure I follow you,' said Nightingale.

'Susan wants me to perform an exorcism.'

'A what?' said Nightingale incredulously. 'You can't be serious. A few behavioural problems and the mother thinks she's possessed by the Devil? What century is she living in?'

The priest gave a wry smile.

'It's not quite as medieval as you might think, Mr Nightingale. You might be surprised to learn that the Roman Catholic Church introduced a modernised Rite of Exorcism in 1999. There is even an International Association of Exorcists within the Church which has over two hundred members.'

'Fair enough, but it still seems pretty drastic for an eleven year old girl's behaviour problems.'

'I entirely agree,' said Mahoney. 'Which is where you come in. Jenny says you're something of an expert in supernatural matters.'

'I've seen more than my share of odd stuff,' said Nightingale. 'Though I wouldn't claim expert status.'

'I'd like you to come with me to see the girl.'

Nightingale shook his head. 'I'm not interested in watching an exorcism. I don't believe in them.'

'No, no. And I certainly can't contemplate carrying out an exorcism without the express authority of the Bishop. I'd be hoping that together we could persuade the parents to abandon the idea, and perhaps seek more conventional help.'

'Well, as it happens, I do have a few holes in my current schedule,' said Nightingale. 'When were you thinking?'

'No time like the present,' said Mahoney with a smile. 'Shall we take my car?'

* * *

It took just over an hour for Father Mahone's grey Kia to get to the Warrens' house in Strawberry Hill. Nightingale took in the double frontage, the large garage, the immaculately tended front lawn and flower beds, and decided that the family definitely weren't short of money. Father Mahoney parked on the drive, the two men got out and headed for the front door, where the priest rang the bell.

The woman who answered the door was tall and slim, wearing a neat pink suit that looked as if was probably Chanel. Her hair was an immaculate golden-blond, but it didn't disguise the fact that she was in her mid-fifties.

Christine must have been a very late arrival in her life. She smiled at Mahoney, and offered her hand. They shook, formally, as if she was thanking him for a stirring sermon. 'This is Mr Nightingale,' said the priest by way of introduction. 'I mentioned him. He's very experienced in matters like this.'

She nodded and flashed Nightingale a worried smile. 'Susan Warren, Mr Nightingale.'

'Call me Jack, please.'

Another nod, but she made no attempt to use his first name, just showed them into the hall. Nightingale took a look around. The hall seemed bigger than his whole flat in Bayswater. The Warrens definitely had money. A lot of it.

'Father Mahoney said you have had some experience in possession,' said the woman.

'Susan, we're not sure that Christine is possessed,' said the priest.

'How else can you explain what's happening to her,' said Mrs Warren.

'That's why Jack is here,' said Mahoney. 'Let's let him talk to her and we can see what he thinks.'

'She's in her bedroom.'

'She didn't go to school?'

'We're keeping her at home until this is resolved,' said Mrs Warren. 'Last night she...' She shuddered and didn't finish the sentence. She led the way upstairs, past three closed doors, then opened the fourth with a key which she took from her jacket pocket.

'You keep her locked in her room?' said Nightingale.

Mrs Warren flinched as if he'd struck her. 'Christine is my daughter and I love her with all my heart, but you don't understand what she's like.'

'What happened last night?' asked Nightingale.

Mrs Warren continued to stare at the door, the key in her hand. 'We have a dog. A small dog. A Jack Russell. Lovely little thing. So loyal. Loved Christine to bits.' She shuddered. 'She killed it last night. We're not sure how. But at some point she used a kitchen knife. She cut Poppy up and spread her insides around the kitchen.' She shuddered again, then took a deep breath and composed herself before opening the door. 'Christine, some people to see you,' she said. 'You remember Father Mahoney, and this is Mr Nightingale.'

The girl lay on the bed, watching 'Frozen' on a wide-screen TV on the opposite wall. She clicked the mute button as they entered, then stood up to meet them, shaking her long, blond hair over her shoulders and straightening her skirt. 'Hello, Father Mahoney,' she said. 'Hello Mr Nightingale.'

Nightingale's eyes were drawn to the bandages wrapped round both of her wrists, but, apart from them, she looked a normal, cheerful eleven year-old, her smile showing perfect teeth and her blue eyes lively and intelligent.

'Why have they come to see me?' Christine asked her mother.

'They'll explain,' said Susan Warren. 'I'll leave you with her, gentlemen.'

'Mummy, I want to go outside and play.'

'Maybe later,' said Mrs Warren.

'And where's Poppy. I keep calling her but she won't come.'

She opened the door to leave but Father Mahoney held up his hand. 'No, no, Susan, we shouldn't be alone with Christine without a parent present, please stay.'

'Well, it'll be rather crowded,' she said. 'Perhaps we should go downstairs?'

'Fine,' said Mahoney, and Mrs Warren led them all down to a large drawing room which looked out onto the rear garden. Christine and the priest sat on the long dark-green leather Chesterfield sofa, with Nightingale and the girl's mother in the matching armchairs facing them. Mrs Warren looked at Father Mahoney and nodded.

'So, Christine,' he began. 'How have you been?'

'Fine thank you, Father.'

She held up her bandaged wrists.

'Except this. I was sleepwalking, and mummy says I fell and cut myself. It hurt a bit at first, but it's healing up now.'

'Do you often sleepwalk?' asked Nightingale.

'I don't think so, do I mummy? But I don't know really, I'd be asleep when it happens. I don't remember.'

'Sometimes she does,' said her mother. 'But she's never hurt herself before.'

'Do you know anyone called Lydia?' asked Mahoney.

'Lydia?' repeated Christine, wrinkling her face into a puzzled look. 'I don't think so. She's not in my class.'

The priest opened his briefcase and took out a well-thumbed copy of The Bible, opened it and handed it to the girl. 'I wonder if you could read that for me Christine, where it says Twenty Three.'

She smiled.

'Oh yes, I know that one. Mrs Hemmings reads it in assembly quite often. The Lord is my shepherd. I shall not want...'

She read confidently and fluently, and Mahoney let her carry on to the end of the psalm before resuming his questions. 'Do you believe in Jesus, Christine?'

'Oh yes,' she said. 'I really like Bible stories.'

Father Mahoney nodded and took a small vial out of his pocket, took off the top, sprinkled a few drops of liquid on his hands, then drew the sign of the cross on the girl's forehead. 'May God bless you and keep you safe, my child,' he said.

Christine smiled again. 'Thank you, Father,' she said. 'Do you think if I pray enough, He might stop me sleepwalking?'

'Maybe He will, my dear.'

Father Mahoney looked at her mother and nodded.

'That's fine, Christine,' said Mrs Warren. 'You can run along upstairs and finish your film now.'

'Thanks, Mum,' said the girl. 'Nice to see you, Father. And you, Mr Nightingale. Are you a priest too? You don't dress like one.'

'Not quite,' said Nightingale. 'Though today I'm a priest's assistant, I suppose. Nice to meet you, Christine.'

The girl left the room, and her mother turned her attention to Father Mahoney.

'Was that it?' she asked. 'That was the exorcism? Surely there's more to it than that?'

'That wasn't an exorcism, Mrs Warren,' said the priest. 'And I won't be performing one. Whatever's wrong with Christine is nothing to do with demonic possession.'

'But how can you tell?'

'She took the Bible and read it aloud, I crossed her with Holy Water and she accepted Jesus. No demon would ever do any of those things, much less all three. There's no grounds at all for recommending an exorcism. It's not a priest you need, but a doctor.'

The woman slumped forward and buried her face in her hands. 'But what am I going to do? I'm at my wits' end. She killed our dog. Killed her and mutilated her. What 11-year-old behaves like that?'

This time it was Nightingale who spoke.

'Why don't you tell me a little more about what has happened, Mrs Warren. Perhaps I could offer some suggestions. When did these episodes start?'

The woman raised her head and looked over at him as if she'd almost forgotten his presence. She took a deep breath before answering him.

'She's always been prone to nightmares, ever since she was a toddler. Maybe once a month or so, she'd wake up screaming in the small hours, never anything coherent, just babbling nonsense. Once she woke up properly, she never remembered anything about it. In fact the nightmares got less frequent after about the age of eight. But all of this new stuff started about four months ago.'

'Did anything seem to cause it?' asked Nightingale.

'Not directly. Though, it was around the time of her first... well, when she reached puberty.'

'So what exactly has been happening?' he asked. I've heard about the self-harming. And the dog. But what else has happened?'

'Well, about three months ago, she started having nightmares again and would wake up screaming, but this time there was a pattern to it. One of us, Matthew my husband or I, would go into her, and she'd sit bolt upright in the bed and start cursing us. Really foul language, stuff we had no idea she knew. And wishing such awful things on us. That was bad enough, but what really drove her to hysterics was when we used her name. She'd scream torrents of bile at us, and insist we called her 'Lydia'. Then after half an hour or so, she'd slump back exhausted and sleep through till morning. In the morning she'd have no recollection of anything, and just be her normal self again. As sweet and caring as ever.'

'Have you seen a doctor?'

'My husband is a doctor...but neither of us want...want to have her labelled. As you can probably tell, she came to us late in life, and she means the world to both of us. We don't want to involve psychiatrists.'

Nightingale found that a little hard to believe. If a much-loved child was showing evidence of a psychological disorder, then surely the parents would seek professional help?

'But your husband would know specialists, surely? Him being a doctor.'

'Matthew says it wouldn't be a good idea.'

'But it hasn't just been nightmares and hysteria, has it?' he asked.

The woman nodded. 'That's right. We were told by a family friend that they'd seen Christine hanging around with a group of older boys on her way back from school. They even thought she was smoking.'

'What did she say to that?'

'Denied it absolutely. Said she didn't have any friends at school except the ones in her class, and she hated smoking. That part's true, she nagged Matthew for months until he gave up. But after...after the time she cut herself, we found a packet of cigarettes in her room...and her breath smelled of smoke. It's just not like her. It makes no sense.'

'And the car? Father Mahoney said she'd damaged a car?'

'Yes. Matthew's Jaguar. One night we heard the garage door open, and we found her in there with a front door-key, scratching every panel of it. She just hurled abuse at us when we tried to stop her, she scratched Matthew with her nails when he pulled her away. Again she said she couldn't remember anything about it in the morning. And then this last thing. Cutting herself.'

'Tell me.'

'We found her in the bath. It looked worse than it was because it doesn't take much blood to discolour the water. Matthew said the cuts were superficial, across the wrist rather than up. As if she wanted to make us worry. And then she started screaming and swearing at us again while we were bandaging her. In the morning she was crying and wanted to know what happened. We just made up the sleepwalking story to calm her down.'

Nightingale nodded, looked across at Father Mahoney, shrugged his shoulders and shook his head. He had no idea what was going on.

'Susan,' said the priest. 'There really is nothing either of us can do here, it's out of our area. Honestly, I can only suggest again you seek medical advice for her.'

The woman nodded. Her lower lip quivered and she was clearly close to tears. 'I'll talk to Matthew,' she said. 'Thank you both for at least trying.'

'I'll just pop up and say goodbye to Christine,' said Nightingale. He headed up the stairs. Christine's door was open. She was sitting on her bed, her hands in her lap. 'We're off now,' he said. 'Nice to have met you.'

'Bye,' she said, then looked up at him and frowned. 'Do you think there's something wrong with me, Mr Nightingale?'

'Not really,' he said. 'Perhaps you just need some help to sleep better. Anyway, you have a good day, Christine.'

She growled and bared her teeth at him like a feral dog. Her voice dropped an octave and her eyes flashed hatred. 'My name is Lydia. And if you or that fucking old fool of a priest come near me again, I'll rip your fucking throats out. Now fuck off and leave me alone.'

* * *

As Father Mahoney drove back towards Central London, Nightingale told him what had happened in the bedroom. The priest frowned. 'And she wasn't playing? Pulling your leg?'

'She sounded as if she meant it,' said Nightingale. 'It wasn't the girl we spoke to. Her voice was completely different.'

'It sounds as if she is possessed,' said the priest. 'But that isn't possible.'

'You're sure about that?'

'No demon could hold a copy of the Bible or not react to holy water,' said Mahoney. 'And the way she spoke about Jesus.' He shook his head. 'No, possession is out of the question.'

'I have to say that whoever was threatening to kill us seemed a completely different person to the one we spoke to downstairs. But you know way more about possession than I do.'

The priest lit a cigarette and handed his pack to Nightingale who helped himself.

'She can't be faking it, though. She's only eleven, for pity's sake.'

Nightingale lit his cigarette. 'The person who spoke to me in her room seemed a lot older than that. And a hell of a lot more dangerous.'

'This is definitely out of my field, Jack. I'm not even sure I believe in demonic possession, but even so this girl shows none of the classic signs.'

'It's not my field either,' said Nightingale, without committing himself to an opinion on demonic possession. 'I really feel they need a psychiatrist or psychologist rather than a priest and a detective. But we told them that. So did you.'

'I suppose so. And you're right. It's up to the parents to get the right help. I have to say I'm rather glad I won't be needing to ask the Bishop to let me do the bell, book and candle casting-out stuff.'

'No problem. Look, Father, no point you driving me all the way, drop me up here at Putney station and I'll get the train home.' The Kia pulled up outside the station. Nightingale climbed out and gave Father Mahoney a final wave before heading inside.

* * *

Nightingale was sipping coffee and frowning at the Daily Mail's Sudoku puzzle when the office doorbell rang. Jenny had popped out to get toner for the printer so Nightingale crushed out his cigarette and headed for the door. His visitor was a tallish grey-haired man of around sixty, wearing a dark suit and a rather garish red spotted bow-tie. He studied Nightingale through a pair of gold-rimmed bifocals, before clearing his throat and speaking. 'Mr Jack Nightingale?'

'Just like it says on the door. Can I help you?'

'My name is Matthew Warren. I'm Christine's father. You were at my house yesterday with Father Mahoney.'

Nightingale showed him into his office and sat down. He reached for his pack of cigarettes but dropped them when he saw the look of disapproval that flashed across the doctor's face.

'My wife told me about your visit yesterday,' said Dr Warren. 'I wasn't aware she'd asked him to see Christine...much less that he was planning anything as ridiculous as an exorcism.'

'He isn't planning on it. He doesn't really believe in demonic possession, and Christine has none of the recognised symptoms.'

'So my wife says. She says you recommended psychiatric help.'

'It's not really my place to recommend anything. I'm a private detective, I'm no doctor. I have to say I'm a little surprised that you didn't go the psychiatrist route. Presumably you know people, professionals. From the little I've seen, it's as if there are two personalities inside her. I wondered if you'd considered schizophrenia?'

'Christine is not schizophrenic, I'm sure of that. It's as if she has multiple personality disorder, but outside of cheap novels that's incredibly rare. Almost non-existent as far as proven cases go.'

'Could Christine be inventing all this?'

'No, I really can't see that. She's a normal eleven year old, the 'other' personality seems far older, more sophisticated as well as more cunning and malevolent. Did my wife tell you what she did to our dog?'

Nightingale nodded. 'She did.'

'Christine loved that dog. I mean really, really loved it.'

'So you are sure there is a different personality at work?'

Doctor Warren's eyes seemed not to want to meet Nightingale's, focusing on different parts of the scantily furnished office as he spoke. Nightingale recognised the signs. The man was hiding something.

'I think you have a theory, Doctor,' said Nightingale. 'Why not tell me? I'm a good listener.'

Doctor Warren clenched his fists, took a deep breath before speaking. 'Christine was...is a very special child. My wife and I had tried to conceive for over twenty years without success. Finally we tried IVF. Three courses on the NHS and then three more that we paid for ourselves. We decided to give up after the last one seemed not to work. Then, suddenly, almost later than seemed possible, the final try worked, and Christine was the result. I couldn't begin to describe how thrilled we were, especially since she seemed so happy and healthy. Never any of the childhood illnesses, I can't remember her ever even having a cold. And now this. It's devastating.'

Nightingale nodded, but didn't interrupt.

'What I am going to tell you is in strict confidence, Mr Nightingale.'

'Of course,' said Nightingale.

Dr Warren took another deep breath before continuing. 'Last week I wanted to rule out anything physical, so I took a blood sample from Christine and had it analysed. I did it without telling my wife.'

'And was there anything wrong?'

'No sign of any physical problem. She's perfectly healthy. Except that her blood contains two different groups, and she has two separate sets of DNA.'

Nightingale gaped at him. 'But that's not possible. Everyone has unique DNA...don't they?'

'Apparently it isn't impossible, but almost unheard of. Do you know what a Chimera is, Mr Nightingale?'

Nightingale frowned.

'Rings a bell. Wasn't it some monster in Greek myths?'

'Originally. Made out of parts of different beasts, a lion, dragon, snake and a goat. Well a human Chimera is much the same. One person made up of parts of two different people.'

'That's surely not possible, it sounds like something out of Frankenstein.'

Warren grimaced. 'It's actually not as dramatic as it sounds. Apparently it's more common in IVF pregnancies than any other. What happens is that the pregnancy starts off as twins, but one zygote fails to develop properly and is absorbed into the other.'

'Zygote?' repeated Nightingale. 'You'll have to explain that, I'm afraid.'

'A zygote is the first stage between fertilisation and a foetus. When the weaker zygote is absorbed into the stronger, often some evidence of its cells remains. Hence the twin blood groups and DNA. It is rare, but it's a recognised medical phenomenon.'

Nightingale was struggling to get his head around the idea. It still sounded like some mad scientist's experiment gone wrong. 'You can't mean that two separate people have been developing inside Christine? Like Dr Jekyll and Mr Hyde?'

The Doctor sighed. 'No, that's not what I mean,' he replied. 'I just wonder whether there may be some sort of conflict within Christine, but I can't see how that could happen. I'm clutching at straws.'

'But, if she is a Chimera, could the other cells be removed?'

'Quite impossible. They'll be spread throughout her body, and impossible to localise. Besides, they can't possibly be causing these episodes.'

'So what's your plan, Dr Warren? What are you going to do?'

Dr Warren stared out the window and blinked. Nightingale thought the man was on the verge of tears. 'I don't think there's anything anyone can do,' he said eventually.

'So what do you plan to do?' asked Nightingale.

Warren sighed. 'What we should have done when it started, I suppose. Seek professional help. The medical profession I mean.' He looked at his watch. 'I'm sorry, I have a surgery at the hospital. I'm late already.' He stood up and forced a smile. 'Thank you for listening, Mr Nightingale. I'd like to pay you for your time. Yesterday and today.'

Nightingale shook his head. 'Pro Bono,' he said. 'I was doing a favour for Father Mahoney. And, truth be told, it's not as if I did anything.'

He showed Dr Warren out and lit a Marlboro, only to stub it out when Jenny arrived back less than a minute later.

'Jack, what was Matthew Warren doing here?'

'A chat about Christine. He's at his wit's end. Did you know they used IVF to conceive?'

Jenny nodded her head. She went over to the printer and installed the new cartridge. 'They tried so hard to get pregnant. That's what makes this all so horrible.'

'IVF does cause problems sometimes.'

'You're an expert on children now?'

'I had a case a year or so back. An unfaithful husband who was threatening to throw his wife and kid on the streets. The kid had autism and I spent a lot of time with the wife. They'd used IVF to conceive and she always blamed the autism on the IVF.'

'What does Matthew think?'

Nightingale shrugged. 'He doesn't know what to think.'

'It's so unfair,' said Jenny. 'I remember talking to her ages ago, when I was at university, I think. I'd come back for Christmas. She and Matthew were at my parents house, one of their shooting weekends. I remember her hugging me so tightly and saying that she'd sell her soul to have a child like me. I thought it was a bit scary, actually.' She finished installing the printer cartridge and turned around to face Nightingale. She saw the look on his face and her eyes widened. 'Please don't tell me you're thinking what I think you're thinking.'

'Those were her exact words?'

'It's an expression.'

'Sometimes it's more than that, Jenny. Sometimes people follow through.'

She shook her head. 'She wouldn't be that stupid.'

'Sometimes people get desperate. They tried to have a kid naturally, and that didn't work. Then they tried IVF and that wasn't working either. Finally, just as her biological clock is about to stop ticking, she gets pregnant. Not long after she said she'd sell her soul for a baby.'

Jenny's hand went up to her mouth. 'What are you going to do, Jack?'

'I'll have to talk to her,' said Nightingale. 'And hope that she tells me the truth.'

* * *

Nightingale's MGB had recently had an expensive service and a new set of tyres, so there was no drama as he drove out to Strawberry Hill and parked in the road outside the home of Dr and Mrs Warren. He knew that Dr

Warren was at his hospital and he assumed that his wife was at home taking care of Christine. He parked his car and walked up to the front door. He rang the doorbell and less than a minute later she opened the door. She was wearing a dark skirt and a grey blouse and didn't look as if she'd slept well. The make-up was a little more thickly applied than the last time he'd seen her and it was caking in the wrinkles around her eyes and mouth.

'Mr Nightingale? Was I expecting you?' Her voice trembled a little as she spoke.

'No, but I have a couple of questions for you, if you don't mind. Could I come in?'

For a brief moment she looked as if she was about to refuse, but then her shoulders sagged and she opened the door. She led him through the hall and into the sitting room, waved him to the same chair as the previous day and sat on the sofa. She didn't offer him anything to drink which Nightingale took as a sign that she wanted him gone as quickly as possible.

'So,' she said, flashing him a tight smile. 'Ask away.'

Nightingale stared at her for several seconds, wondering what the best approach would be. From the look of her, she wasn't going to put up with a lengthy interview so he decided just to go straight in for the kill. Her reaction alone would tell him all he needed to know. 'I need to know which demon you made your pact with, and what they promised you.'

Her jaw dropped and she flinched as if she had been stung. She shook her head and tried to speak but all she could do was repeat one word. 'How... how ... how?' Her right hand moved up as if it had a life of its own and began to massage her scalp just behind her ear.

'How I know isn't the issue,' said Nightingale. 'But if you did a deal to have a baby, you need to tell me.'

'I can't tell anyone,' she said. 'Not even Matthew. No one must ever know.'

'That ship has sailed,' said Nightingale. 'I'm guessing that you have a pentagram behind your ear, just under your hair.'

The look of astonishment on her face and the way her hand fell back into her lap let Nightingale know that he was right. 'You need to tell me everything,' he said.

Tears began to run down her face and she leaned forward and pulled a handful of tissues from a box on the coffee table in front of her.

'Yes,' she whispered. 'Yes. I would have done anything for children. Given anything.'

'Did you meet Marcus Fairchild at the McLean house? During one of their weekend parties.'

Her eyes narrowed. 'You know Marcus?'

Nightingale nodded. 'I know he's a dangerous man. A high-ranking Satanist. Did he tell you that?'

'He didn't say Satanist. He said he practised Wicca. A sort of witchcraft.'

'He lied,' said Nightingale.

'He said he could help. Or rather, he said he could show me how to ask for help.'

'Black magic?'

She shook head and wiped her eyes. 'He didn't say black magic. He said Wicca. Of course I didn't believe he could help at first. Matthew and I had tried everything. We'd spent thousands of pounds and got nowhere. Marcus was so convincing, so persuasive. Finally I decided to try.'

Nightingale was pretty sure he knew how it had gone, but he asked anyway.

'You summoned a demon, and sold your soul. Want to tell me about it?'

Her eyes widened. 'What? No! Of course not. Sell my soul, that's ridiculous.'

'But you did a deal, right?'

She dabbed at her eyes. 'I went to a meeting with Marcus. A ceremony. It was all... very strange. We all drank from this metal goblet and...' She shuddered. 'I think I was drugged.'

'I'm not sure you were,' said Nightingale. 'Deals have to be done when you are sober and your mind is clear. It has to be that way. Tell me what happened next.'

'I can barely remember,' she said.

'Try.'

She shuddered again and stared at the carpet. 'We were in a circle. There were braziers burning. I could hardly breathe. They were banging drums and blowing trumpets, it was so noisy. And then Marcus began shouting stuff, Latin I think it was. I wanted to leave, I wanted to get away, but I couldn't. I couldn't move.' She blew her nose. 'Then she appeared.'

'She?'

'The angel, Marcus said. The angel who can grant wishes. The angel who gave me my babies.'

'Babies? Plural?'

'I was promised twins. That was the deal. I swore eternal allegiance to Proserpine and I would get twins. But she lied.'

Nightingale stared at her. 'Proserpine?'

She nodded. 'A young girl, black hair, black eyes, dressed as a goth.'

'With a dog? A black and white dog?'

Her eyes narrowed. 'How do you know that?'

'I've come across her. She's not an angel.'

'Marcus said she was. He said she was a force for good.'

'Yeah, well Marcus was lying. So Proserpine promised you two babies?'

'I didn't think I'd be able to do it twice. I was running out of time.'

'And tell me again what the deal was?'

Her hand went up to her ear. 'I had to swear on a black book that I would do Proserpine's bidding, and that I would agree to carry her mark.'

'And you didn't think that maybe it was a bad idea?'

'I wanted babies. And when it was all happening, it was like a dream. Even now, looking back, I'm not sure that it was real. Except that two months later I found out I was pregnant and seven months after that Christine was born.' She forced a smile. 'I've never told anyone this. Not even Matthew.'

'And you mustn't,' said Nightingale.

'I've made a terrible mistake, haven't I?'

Nightingale looked pained. There was nothing he could say that was going to make her feel better.

'Why did Marcus lie to me?' she asked.

'He wanted you in Proserpine's power.'

'How do I get out of that?'

'By talking to Father Mahoney. You were lucky – she could have had your soul, then there'd be no hope for you.'

She began crying again and dabbed at her eyes with a new tissue. 'And what about Christine?' she said between sobs. 'What can I do?'

'Proserpine tricked you. She promised you twins and she gave you twins. It's just that they're in the same body.'

'Can't we get Father Mahoney to do an exorcism? Cast the evil presence out of her body?'

Nightingale shook his head. 'This isn't a possession. Lydia isn't a demon who has invaded your daughter. Lydia IS your daughter. The evil twin, if you like. And it looks as if she's going take control. Which is probably what Proserpine wanted from the start. That's why the deal was so easy, why she didn't press for your soul. She wanted you to give birth. It feels as if you were set up from the start.'

'This is a nightmare,' sobbed Mrs Warren.

'That's why you went to Father Mahoney for help in the first place, isn't it?' asked Nightingale.

Mrs Warren nodded. 'I couldn't tell him why, though.'

Nightingale took out a cigarette and lit it. He studied her as he inhaled and held the smoke deep in his lungs. He blew smoke and then nodded slowly. 'I don't think we can cast Lydia out. But maybe there is something we can do.' He took out his phone. 'I'm going to call my assistant. When do you expect your husband back?'

'Not until late,' she said. 'He has his surgery and then he's got a business dinner. He'll be out until nine at least.'

Nightingale nodded. 'Hopefully that'll give us enough time.'

* * *

Mrs Warren went upstairs to see her daughter while Nightingale phoned Jenny. 'Is everything okay?' she asked.

'Not really,' said Nightingale. 'But I have a plan. Can you get over here with Barbara?'

'I'll call her. Why?'

Barbara McEvoy was an old friend from Jenny's student days, now a trained psychiatrist and hypnotherapist. 'I'm pretty sure that there are two personalities sharing Christine's body. It's not possession, they both belong. But one is good and one is evil. I'm hoping that Barbara might be able to use hypnotic suggestion to keep the evil personality supressed.'

'How did that happen?' asked Jenny.

'It's a long story. I'll explain everything but at the moment I need you to get Barbara here as soon as possible.'

'I'll call her and pick her up,' said Jenny. 'If there's a problem I'll let you know.'

Half an hour later, Jenny's Audi sports car pulled up in front of the Warren house. He had the front door open for them as they walked up to the path. Barbara was wearing a sheepskin flying jacket and tight blue jeans. Nightingale grinned. 'You look like you've been flying a Sopwith Camel,' he said.

'Nice to see you, too, Jack,' she said, air kissing him on both cheeks. She brushed a lock of dark brown hair over her ear. 'What's going on? Jenny said you wanted help.'

As Nightingale ushered them into the hall, Mrs Warren came down the stairs. 'Jenny!' she said. 'What on earth are you doing here?'

Jenny kissed Mrs Warren and introduced her to Barbara.

'I think Barbara might be able to help,' explained Nightingale. 'Let me take her into the garden while I have a cigarette. Perhaps you could take Jenny up to see Christine?'

As Mrs Warren and Jenny went upstairs, Nightingale took Barbara down the hall, through the kitchen and into the back garden. There was a white-painted gazebo next to a small pond and Nightingale walked over to it as he lit a cigarette. He quickly explained the problem, but didn't mention the Satanic pact, Marcus Fairchild or Proserpine, the demon from hell. He stuck to the basics – that Christine Warren was struggling to cope with a second personality that was threatening to overwhelm her.

When he'd finished, Barbara shook her head. 'Jack, Christine isn't a patient. I can't go treating people willy-nilly.'

'It's hypnotherapy, not brain surgery,' said Nightingale.

'Thank you very much.'

'I didn't mean it like that. Look, Christine needs help. There's a second personality that's trying to take over and I think you can stop it.'

'That doesn't happen, Jack. Really. There's no real evidence of multiple personality disorder. We only have the one brain, the one consciousness. Okay, your subconscious might try to fool your conscious, but the idea of two personalities inhabiting one brain has been pretty much discredited.'

'Then humour me, please. Just put Christine under and have a root around.'

Barbara smiled. 'A root around?'

'Just see what you can find.' He flicked his cigarette away. 'These people need help, Barbara. They're at their wits end.'

* * *

Barbara decided to do the session in Christine's bedroom, figuring it was where the girl would be most at ease. Mrs Warren stood by the window, watching nervously as Barbara helped Christine make herself comfortable.

'Draw the curtains, please, Mrs Warren,' said Barbara. 'And Jenny, light those candles.'

Jenny borrowed Nightingale's lighter and lit three vanilla-scented white candles on Christine's dressing table.

Barbara sat on the edge of Christine's bed and talked to her softly, explaining what was going to happen. Nightingale was sitting on an armchair on the other side of the bed. Jenny finished lighting the candles, gave the lighter back to Nightingale and sat on a wooden chair by the dressing table.

Barbara lowered her head so that she was whispering into Christine's ear. The girl seemed totally relaxed, her eyes were closed and her golden hair had spread like a halo across the pillow. Nightingale couldn't make out Barbara's words, but the tone was soothing and he had to keep shaking his head to stop himself falling asleep.

Eventually Barbara looked across at him and nodded. 'She's under.'

Nightingale stood up and walked over to the bed. 'Can you ask her to talk to me, and to do what I tell her?' he whispered.

'Yes, so long as it's not something that sets up a resistance in her.' She turned back to Christine and whispered in her ear. 'Christine, Jack's going to talk to you now, and I want you to do what he asks. Is that alright?'

The girl said nothing, but gave an angelic smile and nodded. Barbara got up and went to stand next to Mrs Warren.

'Christine,' said Jack, sitting down on the bed. 'Can you hear me?'

'Of course,' she said quietly.

'I want you to move aside, Christine, I want to talk to Lydia. Can you do that?'

'I don't know anyone called Lydia.'

'Okay, just relax. Let Lydia talk to me.'

'Who is Lydia?'

Nightingale said nothing for several seconds. 'Lydia?' he said.

There was no reply.

'Come on Lydia, talk to me. There's no need to hide. I know you're there.' He put his mouth close to her ear. 'I'm a friend of Proserpine's.'

Christine opened her eyes. 'What the fuck do you want, fool?'

'I just want to talk to you.'

'About what?' Her voice was a harsh rasp, almost metallic.

'About what you're doing. The way you're hurting Christine.'

'Don't worry, the bitch will be gone soon,' said Lydia.

Mrs Warren gasped but Nightingale flashed her a warning look and pressed his finger to his lips.

The girl tried to sit up but Nightingale pushed her back. 'Stay lying down, Lydia. And listen to Barbara. She has something to tell you.'

He waved Barbara over. 'You need to put her under,' he whispered.

'I already did.'

'No, you put Christine under. This is Lydia. Now you need to hypnotise Lydia.'

He moved out of the way and Barbara sat down on the bed again. She began to talk to the girl in a soft, low voice. At first the girl seemed to fight it, moving her head from side to side and gritting her teeth, but gradually she relaxed. It took much longer to hypnotise her this time, and it was half an hour before Barbara looked over at Nightingale. 'She's under,' she whispered.

'Tell her to talk to me,' said Nightingale.

Barbara nodded, and put her face next to the girl's ear. 'Lydia, Jack's going to talk to you now, and I want you to do what he asks. Is that alright?'

'Yes.' The voice was still lower, but had lost its aggression.

Nightingale and Barbra switched places. 'Lydia, listen to me. You're going to go to sleep, and you won't wake until I tell you to. Do you understand?'

'I understand.'

'You're to go to sleep and stay asleep. You're not to bother Christine again ever. You just sleep until I tell you to wake up.'

And that's never going to happen, he thought.

'Do you understand?'

'Yes.'

'Then sleep now. And stay asleep.'

A shudder ran through the girl's body. Nightingale spoke again. 'Christine?'

'Yes?'

'Are you okay?'

'Yes.'

'Is Lydia there?'

'Who?'

'Let me talk to Lydia.'

'Lydia isn't here.'

Nightingale stood up. He smiled at Barbara. 'Can you bring her out of it now?'

'It that it?' asked Mrs Warren. 'Is it over?'

'I'm pretty sure it's worked,' said Nightingale. 'Though I guess time will tell. To be honest, all we can do now is to hope for the best.'

* * *

It was two weeks later that the envelope arrived. Nightingale and Jenny were in the office trying to decide whose turn it was to make coffee when the post arrived. Jenny sorted through it, filing the bills, binning the junk and opening anything which looked interesting. She passed the long white envelope across.

'Says "Personal" and you know I'm not one to pry,' she said.

'We both know you'd have opened it if I'd been out.' Nightingale ripped open the envelope and pulled out a letter and a cheque. He looked at the cheque first and whistled.

'Who's it from?'

'Susan Warren. Listen to this. 'Please accept this with our heartfelt thanks. Christine's entirely back to her old self and we really can't thank you enough. It seems our nightmare is over, and it's all due to you. Once again, thank you so much.' Looks like it worked.' He grinned at Jenny and passed her the cheque. 'Better get that in the bank as soon as possible.'

As Jenny headed out, Nightingale lit a cigarette and blew smoke up at the ceiling. It was good to hear that Christine was okay, but it was Mrs Warren he was worried about. He hoped that she had gone to Father Mahoney for help. Her soul had been tainted, but at least it was still hers. And the pentagram was still behind her ear, the mark that showed she had sworn allegiance to Proserpine. He tried to blow a smoke ring but failed miserably. He still had a bad feeling about the Warren family, but he'd done all he could.

* * *

Christine was walking home from school with two of her friends, Emma and Olivia. She tried never to walk home alone, since a couple of older boys from year ten seemed to think she might want to talk to them. She didn't, of course, didn't even know their names. The three girls were chatting about how awful the school lunches had become when Christine heard someone call out her name.

'Hey, Christine. Over here.'

Christine looked around and saw a young woman dressed in a long black leather coat over leather motorcycle boots. An upside-down silver cross hung round her neck, and her earrings were five pointed stars. She had long straight black hair and the blackest eyes imaginable. Sitting by her side was a cute collie dog, its tongue lolling out of the side of its mouth.

'Christine, I need to talk to you.'

Christine frowned. 'I don't know you,' she said. 'You're a stranger.'

'My name's Proserpine. Lydia knows me. Let me talk to Lydia.'

Christine turned to look at her friends. They were standing motionless, staring blankly ahead, almost as if time had stopped for them.

Then she shuddered, closed her eyes and opened them again. She smiled at Proserpine. 'Mistress Proserpine. How may I serve you?' Her voice had dropped an octave.

Proserpine walked over and patted the girl on the head. 'It seems I took my eyes off you for a while, and you made your presence felt rather too early. What did Nightingale tell you?'

'He said I should sleep till he woke me.'

Proserpine laughed. 'He really is an idiot, he has no idea what he's doing most of the time. Still perhaps a period of silence might be no bad thing. Bide your time Lydia, let's have no more manifestations, just watch and wait. I'll have work for you to do soon enough.'

'How soon, mistress?'

'Be patient, girl, your time will come. And don't call me Mistress. You're my daughter. My one and only.'

'Can I kill Nightingale for you, mother? Please let me.'

'Nightingale, no. But that interfering priest, yes, I think so. But not just yet. I'll be in touch when I need you.'

Lydia gave a blissful smile and a shudder of pleasure. 'I'll be waiting to serve you.'

Proserpine stroked the girl's blonde hair, then gently pinched her cheek. 'Be seeing you, darling.'

She blew a kiss at the girl, and Christine shook her head, smiled at her friends and then walked off down the street with them flanking her. Just a normal, happy eleven-year-old, heading off home to her loving family.

THE CREEPER

The sun set over the Gulf of Mexico with rays of pink light. Along the coastline palm trees shuddered in the breeze, their fronds whispering. Sand was kicked up in the wind and blown over the dunes. The air was thick, the sky swollen black with the threat of rain. In Everglades Campground – more of an R.V park than a place to pitch tents – Mitchell was strolling back from the corner store carrying a shopping bag full of beer, smoking a cigarette and murmuring to himself as he went. Lizzie was back at the campsite, getting drunk. All it would take were a few more beers until she reached the point of oblivion. Then, as Mitchell well knew, he would make his move. He'd have to get her away from her brother Charlie to get the deed done properly, but that could be arranged. He could offer to take her on a romantic walk around the campground. Yeah, that's what he'd do. Take her for a walk. Maybe offer her some weed. She liked the weed, did Lizzie. Weed and booze were two of her favourite things.

On his way back to the campsite Mitchell followed the swamp, a wasteland stretching on for miles, home to all the creepy things that haunted his imagination. Snakes. Alligators. Spiders. He shuddered and tried not to think about the creatures that called the swamp their home. He hadn't always been so squeamish. When he was a kid he'd liked snakes and pestered his parents to buy him one. Eventually they'd agreed and given him a pet boa constrictor for Christmas. He'd named it Sally He also had a couple of hamsters that he liked to play with. One morning, after handling the hamsters for an hour or two, he decided to take Sally out of her cage to let her slither around his arms, as he usually did to give her exercise. Only this time he smelled like the hamsters, so when he reached down to pick her up, Sally distended her jaws and latched onto his hand with her teeth, causing him to cry out with pain. It was only when his big brother came along and pried Sally off him that he finally stopped screaming. He'd never gone near the snake again and begged his parents to take it away. It ended up back in the shop they'd brought it from, though the shopkeeper refused them a refund.

Mitchell walked along the riverbank. The wind was doing a number on the palm trees, making them bow to and fro. A storm's coming, he thought. I'd better hurry this up. Lizzie was laughing when he reached the fire, a group of college seniors on spring break gathered around it, drinking. She was laughing so hard she almost fell into the fire pit. Mitchell laughed. Too easy, he thought. Mitchell tossed a few beers to Charlie and Luke, sat on the ground beside Lizzie and draped his arm around her; she eyed him with mock suspicion.

'You, mister,' said Lizzie, poking a finger into his chest. 'Are trying to get me drunk?'

'Me?' asked Mitchell. 'Not at all.' He held up one of the cans and winked. 'Hey, want a beer?' Lizzie feigned surprise as he opened the can and passed it to her. He leaned towards her as she took a sip. 'I've got some weed if you want it,' he said.

'Hell yeah,' she said.

He put his finger on his lips. 'But keep it a secret,'

She shrugged, glanced quickly at Charlie and back at Mitchell. 'Okay,' she said. She put her finger against her lips. 'Shhhh!' she said, and burst out laughing.

It was getting dark now. Beyond the campground the swamp was filling up with the songs of peepers and the silence of hunters. The cypresses and mangroves that grew in the swamp were a breeding ground for predators, providing a million different places to get lost and trapped and eaten. Alligators prowled the waters of the swamp, scanning with yellowed eyes for easy prey, submerging themselves for a time and reappearing farther down the river.

In Everglades National Park giant pythons swallowed deer whole. The smaller of them split open when it was too much to handle. People saw it all the time – pythons sprawled in the grass with perfectly-preserved deer spilling out of their bellies. Some of the deer were still alive, their eyes sealed with pink mucus from the snake's belly. After an hour they'd be galloping around again. But that kind of luck didn't happen often.

Charlie was talking about the recent headlines: an alligator horde found in the Everglades City sewage system. Apparently the alligators had been living down there for years, eating all manner of things from flushed-down kittens to human waste. Some were over twelve feet long. They were blind; their eyes the color of milk. The alligators had been discovered after a sewage worker went missing; he still hadn't been found.

'Crazy shit, huh?' asked Charlie, but Mitchell wasn't listening, he was whispering something into Lizzie's ear. She giggled. He tightened his hold around her waist, slipping a hand under her jeans and grasping her butt.

'Mitchell!' shouted Charlie.

Mitchell wheeled around. 'What?'

Charlie was glaring at him. 'I said that's some crazy shit.'

'Ok...' said Mitchell, looking around. 'Who cares?'

'I care, asshole, hence the comment coming from my mouth.' Charlie stood up, swayed a little, but kept his footing. 'Know what else I care about? My sister. So get your fucking hands off her before I break them.'

'Fuck you man,' whined Mitchell.

'All right you two,' said Luke. 'Take it easy. Just relax.'

Lizzie spoke up. 'Charlie, I'm a big girl,' she said. 'I think I can handle it,'

Charlie didn't pay her any attention. He pointed a beer at Mitchell. 'You,' he said. 'Get up.' He slugged the beer and let it fall to the ground. 'I'm gonna kick your ass.'

Mitchell shook his head nervously. 'No,' he said.

'I said get the fuck up!'

Charlie tottered towards him. Luke stood up and prepared to break up the fight. Mitchell tried to break free as Charlie grabbed the collar of his polo and prepared to sock him in the face. Lizzie screamed.

And then they heard it.

Charlie let go of Mitchell's collar and looked at the swamp. They all looked at the swamp. 'What the hell is that?' he said.

The sound came again. Gurgling, like something was taking in a mouthful of water and drowning.

'What the fuck?' said Charlie. He'd backed away from Mitchell and forgotten their argument. Something was thrashing in the water. Something big.

An old wooden dock jutted out into the swamp. Some of the boards were missing, and the rest were water-logged and damp; the source of the commotion seemed to be coming from under it.

'Luke,' said Charlie, distracted. 'Come on, let's go check it out.'

'Fuck that,' said Luke. 'Are you crazy? I'm not going anywhere near it. It's probably a crocodile or something.'

'Alligator,' corrected Lizzie. Everybody was watching the darkness where the sound was coming from.

'What do you mean? It could be a crocodile, couldn't it?'

'They're alligators in Florida,' said Lizzie.

Luke shook his head. 'They've got both. Alligators and crocodiles.'

'Come on, Mitchell,' said Charlie with a wave of his hand.

'Nah, man, I don't think it's a good idea.'

Charlie pointed at him. 'Either you be a man and come with me or I remember our little argument and kick your ass. Your choice.'

Mitchell stood up warily and started to go with him.

'Guys, don't!' cried Lizzie, but they didn't stop. Mitchell turned and gave her a scared look, and then they passed beyond the light of the fire. A crash of thunder hit nearby. As if by magic, rain began to fall.

Drawing close, the thrashing intensified. Whatever was doing it was strong, that much was obvious. The dock was elevated ten feet above the swamp; the sound was coming from the end, where the water was deepest.

'This isn't safe,' said Mitchell. 'I think we should turn back.'

'Don't puss out on me now,' said Charlie.

Just as they were about to reach the source of the noise, it stopped. The sudden quiet made them uneasy, the woods had gone completely still. Not even the crickets were singing.

'I think we should go back now, man,' said Mitchell, trembling. 'For sure. Come on. Let's go.'

Charlie motioned for him to be quiet. He bent down, clutched the sides of the dock, and peered over the edge to look at the water. 'Shit!'

Mitchell jumped. 'What?' he said. 'What is it?'

'That's so weird...' said Charlie, shaking his head.

'What's weird?'

Charlie looked up, frowning. 'It's an alligator,' he said. 'But it's been ripped apart.'

A powerful crash erupted against the wood pilings holding the dock. One of them dislodged, causing it to lean. Mitchell fell into the water with a splash. Charlie watched as a round fleshy head rose from the water a few feet from him, then dove under and began swimming towards Mitchell.

'Mitchell! Get out of the fucking water!'

Luke was hollering, demanding to know what was happening. Mitchell had never been a good swimmer but he swam as hard as he could now, harder than he'd ever swam before in his life. He was taking mouthfuls of water and whimpering, paddling towards the riverbank as fast as his limbs would carry him.

But something grabbed his leg.

Sharp nails tore into Mitchell's flesh and he let out a piercing scream before he was dragged underwater. Bubbles floated to the surface; the swamp became silent and calm, and a red cloud formed where Mitchell had been.

Charlie froze. He kept blinking as though his eyes had fooled him, as though Mitchell would reappear any moment. But he didn't.

'Charlie!' cried Luke from the shore. 'Where's Mitchell? What the hell is going on, man?'

As Charlie turned to face him the mangled body of Mitchell shot up through the water like a rocket. Beside it emerged a disfigured creature with lolling eyes, a gory mouth full of teeth, two tiny holes for a nose. Its eyes darted around, taking in everyone at once as if deciding who to attack next. It decided on Charlie.

'Run!' cried Luke.

The creature climbed out of the water onto the dock, its pale body crisscrossed with purple scars – misshapen limbs and fleshy lumps. Charlie ran down the dock and the rest of the campers took off screaming for the woods. The creature loped sideways after them like a human crab, making a strange sound as it went.

Charlie reached the woods but it was too late: the thing was upon him. As it tore into him with its teeth he understood what the strange sound was.

The creature was cackling.

* * *

Jack Nightingale lit a cigarette and reclined against the soft leather of Joshua Wainwright's Humvee. Wainwright was smoking an expensive cigar and twirling a crystal tumbler of whiskey; every now and then he poked at the ice cubes with his finger to give it a stir. They were leaving Naples, Florida. When Wainwright called, Nightingale had been on vacation in the Florida Keys, enjoying a couple of hard-earned weeks under the hot sun.

'We've got a situation,' Wainwright had said over the phone.

Nightingale had sighed; there on Key Largo with the cool ocean breeze and the tropical drinks, he never wanted to work another day in his life. 'What kind of situation?'

'The murder kind,' said Wainwright. 'Six campers in the Everglades. Five dead. Eaten, I should say. The survivor says they were attacked by a demonic creature. Lizzie Harris. She's missing most of her face. The feds called me, they think it's an alligator, but someone in the department, Taylor, who took the girl's deposition, thinks it's supernatural.'

That's all Nightingale needed to hear.

Less than ten hours later they were driving at breakneck speed down the highway surrounded by tropical vegetation, headed to the Everglades.

The Humvee changed lanes, sped up. Wainwright took a drink of whiskey and passed Nightingale a fat wad of cash. Nightingale didn't bother to look through it before stuffing it into his jacket.

'Supernatural?' asked Nightingale, exhaling a puff of smoke. 'What reason does Taylor have to think that?'

'Everglades City is a spooky town, my friend. Lots of strange goings-on. A few years ago a Satanic cult was caught trying to kidnap illegal immigrants who came in over the Gulf. Apparently they'd been abducting these people, since there was no record of them in America, and making offerings of them to the Prince of Darkness Himself.'

'Were they friends of yours?' said Nightingale, but Wainwright ignored his attempt at humour.

'I'm just saying, this town isn't all sunshine and rainbows. And whatever did this…' he held up a picture and Nightingale winced, 'has got a lot more in store for the people of this town, I'm afraid.'

Nightingale looked at the picture. It was the girl, Lizzie Harris, in her hospital bed, though her sex could no longer be determined. She was missing her ears, her nose, her lips, her breasts. Her entire body was patched with gauze. Nightingale shook his head. 'Bloody hell.'

'I know. She probably won't be around for much longer.'

Nightingale took a few last drags of the cigarette and put it out in the ashtray. 'Got any leads?' he asked.

'A couple,' said Wainwright. 'The coven I mentioned? Not all of them were taken into custody. There's still a guy who's been practicing the craft, let's just say. He's outside Everglades City by the swamp. Lives in an old colonial mansion. This one,' Wainwright opened a large file and handed it to Nightingale – a picture of a two-story white colonial with columns and a shaded veranda. 'Winston Tollhouse, 83, still up to no good. The authorities took pity on the old man and instead of jailing him they put him under house arrest. He haunts the mansion wearing a bracelet around his ankle, unable to walk past the porch.'

Wainwright filled his empty glass, took a drink. 'My suspicion,' he continued, 'is that old Mr Tollhouse has been cooking up some black magic, refining his summoning skills, if you will. I think whatever's out there, whatever it is that killed all those kids, is nothing less than the results of the demonic. After all, some of the kidnapped illegals have never been found.'

'Never been found?'

Wainwright shook his head, his eyes studying Nightingale as if waiting for him to piece it together.

'So,' said Nightingale, 'you think this monster is the result of possession?'

Wainwright shrugged. 'It's certainly not beyond the realm of possibility.'

'Maybe,' said Nightingale, leafing absently through the file, through missing persons reports. Young, white males. He looked at one – John Seward. Wife. Kids. – 'Hang on a second.' Nightingale held up the photo. 'What about these guys?'

'Six men, all white males, have gone missing in the last two months,' said Wainwright. 'I don't know whether these incidents are related but one can't be too careful.' He stubbed out the cigar. 'Talk to Taylor and the girl before heading out to see the old man. Get some info. I don't need any more college kids dying on account of some demon. It's bad for business.'

Nightingale looked at him. 'So the practice of Satanism is now a business, is it?'

Wainwright cracked a smile. 'How else do you think I got to be so rich and powerful?'

'I thought it was because you were pals with your new President. That's something I was meaning to ask you, is the Donald...'

Wainwright silenced him with a warning finger. 'Don't go there,' he said. 'Really, just don't go there.'

* * *

From the outside, Nightingale's rented bungalow looked like a dump – a clapboard thing standing on stilts above the reeking swamp, leaning to the left like some abandoned house in the wilds of Detroit. Inside was no better. The room was spartan – a dusty spring bed, a corner table, and a lamp made up its furnishings. Aside from this the place stank like mold and Nightingale's hand fit between the slats in the walls. 'Joshua,' he muttered, shaking his head. 'You're too good to me.'

It was just past noon. Nightingale drove a rented car to town, bought a cappuccino and an almond croissant at the Island Café, then drove to Everglades City Police Department. He finished his cigarette and flicked it to the ground before heading inside.

At the front desk the receptionist told him he could find officer Taylor in the mess hall where all the officers were eating lunch. Nightingale checked his watch; he might have enough time to see both the officer and the girl before nightfall. He didn't want to visit Tollhouse after dark, not where Satanism was concerned.

'Thanks,' he said, and began to head for the cafeteria, but he was stopped by a woman's voice.

'You sound like a Brit.'

Nightingale turned around. A female officer stood in front of him, arms crossed. She was wearing a beige uniform and had a gun on her hip.

'Oh, here she is,' said the receptionist. 'Officer Taylor, this man's been looking for you.'

'She?' thought Nightingale, but he didn't say it out loud. He hadn't been expecting a woman.

Officer Taylor was striking in her slim blue police uniform, blonde hair held back in a ponytail, her eyes blue and sparkling like sapphires. She looked more like one of those beach girls on the cover of Sports Illustrated than a police officer.

'What's the matter?' asked Taylor. 'Never seen a female police officer before?'

Nightingale stammered. 'Oh, uh, sure I have. You just surprised me is all.'

'You are British.'

'I am. And thanks,' he said. 'Most Americans tend to think I'm Australian.'

Taylor frowned as if taking offense. 'What's wrong with being Australian?'

'Nothing! Nothing at all, what I meant was…'

Taylor's frown turned into a wide grin. 'Relax. I'm just goading you.'

Nightingale took a deep breath. 'Right,' he said. This was not going to be easy. Why hadn't Joshua told him she was a woman?

'So… you wanted to see me about something?'

'Yeah. I've got a few questions about the girl that was attacked. You thought it was supernatural the way—'

Taylor's hand shot up, silencing him. The receptionist was watching intently.

'Let's go to my office where you'll be a little more comfortable.'

Without another word Taylor turned on her heels and strode down the hallway. Nightingale followed her to a cramped office at the end of the hall. She held the door open for him, closed and shuttered it when he'd entered.

'I wish you wouldn't have said that,' said Taylor in a low voice. She sat behind her desk and put her feet up.

'Said what?'

'That word – supernatural. I'm already a laughingstock around here for being the only female officer, I don't need my colleagues thinking I'm some witch-hunter on top of it all.'

'Sorry. I wasn't thinking. I should have been more discreet.'

'It's all right, you couldn't have known. Let's just keep this between us from now on, deal?'

'Of course.'

Taylor stood up and went to the coffeemaker. 'Coffee?'

'Please.'

She poured two cups, black, and handed one to Nightingale.

'You don't have milk, do you?'

'Milk?'

'Milk. For my coffee.'

She grimaced. 'We drink our coffee black here.'

'Ah, Right. Sorry.'

'No need to apologise,' she said, settling down and propping her feet back on the desk. 'That's a British thing, isn't it? Always saying sorry. Like that Hugh Grant. Always apologising. She grinned. 'Anyway, the Harris case. That's what you wanted to ask me about?'

'That's right.'

'And who are you again, exactly?' She sipped her coffee, studying him. 'Mr Wainwright wasn't specific.'

'Nightingale, Jack Nightingale. I'm a PI.'

'And you work for Mr Wainwright?'

'Sometimes. It's an ad hoc arrangement. How do you know him, by the way?'

'I was in something of a supernatural bind myself a couple years ago and Mr Wainwright stepped in and helped me through it.'

'I see.' Nightingale sipped his coffee, winced, and set it on the desk. 'Was it the Satanic cult?'

Taylor furrowed her eyebrows. 'He told you about that?'

'Just about the case, briefly. He didn't mention your name.'

Her body relaxed. 'Good. If you don't mind, I'd like to keep it that way.'

The harshness in her voice and the way her face darkened told Nightingale this mystery was best left alone. 'Of course,' he said. 'Anyway, I just want to know about the Harris case. When was the girl found and what were the circumstances?'

We found her and the others a good quarter-mile outside the campground in the woods. She looked as if she'd fallen into a meat grinder. Every part of her body had been mauled. She was unconscious and had lost a lot of blood; she was barely alive, holding on by a thread.'

'And the others?'

'Dead on arrival. It took us two days just to find all the body parts scattered around the woods. It was a massacre.'

'And the state of the injuries?'

Taylor paused, her face a tight scowl, as though she was smelling something awful. 'Animal,' she said.

'Animal?'

'Whatever attacked those kids wasn't human, not by any stretch of the imagination. It ate them, ripped them apart with its teeth like a goddamned lion. We found one, by the way. A tooth.'

'You found a tooth?' Nightingale straightened in his chair. 'Why isn't it in the report?'

Taylor looked up defensively. 'What report is that?'

Nightingale flushed. 'I have access to certain information,' he said. 'It's part of my job.'

'Well you best keep that information to yourself. You go spouting that around here and you'll be driven out of town ahead of a squad of police cruisers. ECPD has jurisdiction here, and aside from myself they aim to keep it that way.'

'I'll be more discreet. Joshua says you think it's supernatural. Why is that?'

'First you asked about the tooth. Right now it's being analyzed over at Dr Jacobsen's office on Key Lime Drive.'

'And this doctor, who is he?'

'A veterinarian.'

'A veterinarian? Why would you send the tooth to a veterinarian?'

'We're a small operation here, detective. We don't have a forensics lab, the nearest one is up in Naples and to pass the tooth along to them would be to compromise the jurisdiction of this case. Dr Jacobsen will do just fine.'

'Ok, well... by what you've told me so far, officer Taylor, all this seems to be the work of an animal, not a demon. So why is it that you think it's supernatural?'

Taylor's face dropped, as if a dark cloud had passed over it. She opened a drawer and set something on the desk between them: a wooden doll made from moss and sticks and held together by sinew. It looked grotesque, like some crude folk art a child might put together, and for some reason just the sight of it filled Nightingale with dread.

'Witchcraft,' said Nightingale.

'There were six of them. Five on the ground next to the bodies and one hanging by the Harris girl, as though they, or it, knew we'd find her alive. I believe the murder of these kids was premeditated. And I believe someone or something demonic is controlling it even now, luring us into the case, but I'm not sure why.'

As Nightingale held the strange wood configuration in his hands, horrible pictures flooded through him. Rotting corpses in mass graves. Fire sweeping across the countryside. Grotesque creatures dancing nude under the full moon, stuffing their mouths with human flesh. Nightingale gasped and dropped the stick figure to the floor.

Taylor leaned forward. 'It speaks to you, doesn't it?' she asked. 'The same thing happens to me when I touch it.'

Nightingale sighed deeply and nodded. He massaged his temples. 'I need a cigarette,' he said.

Officer Taylor stood up. 'I've got to go check on the Harris girl to see if she's ready to give a full statement. Then I'm headed to the vet to get the lowdown on that tooth. Wanna join me?'

Nightingale nodded. 'Sure. But can I smoke a fag first?'

'You know that's illegal in this State? In all States, actually.'

Nightingale frowned. 'I can't smoke?'

She laughed. 'I'm messing with you again,' she said. 'Having a cigarette is fine, it's killing homosexuals that we don't allow.'

Nightingale got the joke and smiled. 'Ah, two countries separated by a common language.'

'Who said that?'

'I did. Just then.'

She grinned. 'I can see we have the same sense of humour,' she said. 'I must watch too much British TV. But seriously. Who said that about us speaking the same language but differently?'

'Depends who you ask,' said Nightingale. 'It's been attributed to Oscar Wilde, George Bernard Shaw and Winston Churchill.' He took out his pack of Marlboro. 'Can I smoke in the car?'

'Only if you open the window.'

* * *

Lizzie Harris sat upright in the hospital bed, her body a mess of bloody bandages. A nurse bent over to change her dressings while Nightingale and officer Taylor sat at her bedside with open notebooks in hand. Lizzie had trouble speaking – her lips were gone, as well as part of her tongue, and whenever she spoke she seemed to have that horrifying skeletal smile shown in the worst kind of horror films, like a death's head.

Nightingale had trouble looking her in the eye – the one that remained. But it didn't matter; Lizzie avoided eye contact with everyone in the room.

'I told you,' she said. 'It was a monster. A thing. I don't know how else to explain it.'

'Yes,' said Taylor gently, 'you've told us that, honey. But can you remember anything specific? Height, eye color, hair color?'

'It was taller than him,' she gestured towards Nightingale. 'Way taller, like, seven or eight feet probably. Its eyes were bloodshot and scary-looking, like it had lost its mind. It almost looked human but everything was deformed. It had gills or something, on its neck. No hair.'

'And fast,' said Taylor. 'You said it was really fast.'

The nurse rolled gauze over Lizzie's arm and she winced. 'Yeah,' she said. 'Insanely fast. And the way it moved was…' she paused, shook her head.

'Go on, honey,' said Taylor. 'You're doing great.'

Lizzie struggled with the words. 'It was strange… 'cause it didn't move like anything I've ever seen. It moved sideways. Its legs were bent but in the wrong direction, like its joints were all messed up. It ran sideways like a crab.'

Nightingale raised his eyebrows. Sideways? How is that possible?

'What else, honey? Can you remember anything else?'

Lizzie was silent a moment. 'Yeah,' she said. 'The thing was...' she broke off and shook her head stiffly. 'It was horrible,' she said, sobbing.

'What was it doing, honey? It's ok. You're safe now. You can tell us.'

Lizzie took a few deep breaths, composed herself, then turned to face them.

'It was laughing,' she said. 'Laughing while it ate us.'

The room fell silent. The nurse finished changing the dressings and closed the door softly behind her as she left. Nightingale gazed out the hospital window at the endless swamplands.

Taylor closed her notebook. 'I think that's everything, Lizzie. You're so brave, honey. Thank you.'

Lizzie said nothing. Officer Taylor and Nightingale stood up and headed for the door.

'Lizzie,' said Nightingale from the door, and for the first time the girl turned and met his eyes. 'We're going to catch whatever did this to you, no matter what it takes. I promise you that.'

Lizzie's expression hardened. 'If you wanna make promises then promise me this: Promise me that when you catch it, you'll kill it.'

Nightingale didn't speak, but he nodded.

Lizzie turned away.

* * *

Back in the police car, Taylor buckled her seatbelt and turned to face Nightingale. 'You're going to kill it, that's what you promised her?'

'Sure.'

'And how are you going to do that? With your bare hands?'

Nightingale shrugged.

'Are you carrying, Nightingale? Do I have to frisk you?'

He grinned. 'I'd love you to frisk me, Officer Taylor.'

She didn't smile. 'This isn't funny, Nightingale. You can ride along, that's fine, you can help with the investigation, that's also fine. But what isn't fine is a civilian pulling out a gun and blasting away when I'm not expecting it.'

'I hear you,' said Nightingale. 'And no, I don't have a gun.'

'Good to know.'

She started the engine.

'But can I borrow yours, if necessary?'

'Wipe that smirk off your face. This ain't no joke.' But even as she said this Nightingale noticed a faint smile on her lips as she faced the road.

They pulled out of the hospital parking lot and swung onto Route 1. Nightingale held up a pack of Marlboro. 'Mind if a smoke?'

'Go ahead.'

He rolled down the window and lit a cigarette, watching the jungle landscape drift by. 'It sure is pretty out here,' he said, taking it in. 'You like it?'

'Florida?'

'The Everglades.'

Taylor shrugged. 'Sure. It's all right, but it wouldn't be my first choice or anything.'

'What's your first choice then?'

'Where I was stationed before. Tennessee. That's where I'm from.'

'I didn't hear an accent.'

'You mean I don't talk like a hillbilly?' She shrugged. 'I lost the accent after moving here. People calling me 'cornpone' and things like that. It wasn't fun, let me tell you.'

'I have no idea what that is.'

'Cornpone? She chuckled. It's a type of bread. But when you use it about a person, you're saying they're a hick.'

Nightingale studied Taylor, her blonde hair, her blue eyes. Everything about her was stunning. The way she wriggled her nose every now and then when focusing on something. The bright smile. She was gorgeous, and as far from being a hick as he could imagine.

'It's probably their way of flirting with you,' he said.

'What?'

'I'm just saying, calling you a cornpone is probably what passes for flirting down here.'

'What about you, Nightingale? Do you have a significant other?'

He shrugged. 'Not really.'

'A rolling stone gathers no moss, is that it?'

He laughed. 'More that it's harder to hit a moving target,' he said. 'But yeah, I move around a lot.'

'Working for Mr Wainwright?'

'Yeah, more often than not.'

* * *

The veterinary clinic was a small building with a stuccoed roof in the center of town. Stout palm trees grew from the corners of the yellow lawn. Stray sand covered the walkway. They went inside and met with Dr Jacobsen outside his office, a small old man in blue scrubs with the friendly smile of a pediatrician. 'Shall we?' asked Jacobsen, motioning down the hall.

In a spotless operating room full of stainless steel tables and trays of crude surgical instruments, Jacobsen picked up a manila folder and under the bright glare of the overheads showed them photographs of the recovered tooth, both X-ray photos and close-ups. 'I should preface this conversation by saying that this tooth does not belong to any known creature in the animal kingdom. That being said, I did find some identifying characteristics which could aid in your investigation.'

'Oh?' said Nightingale, exchanging glances with Taylor.

Jacobsen slid a picture of the tooth across the table. It was long and pointed like a shark's tooth, but also thin and brittle-looking. The clear porcelain color reminded Nightingale of a fish bone he'd once had to pick out of his gums in a seafood restaurant in London. 'It seems quite obvious why this tooth was left behind in one of the victims, don't you think?'

'It's fragile,' offered Taylor. 'It broke off during the attack.'

'Precisely my first thought,' said Jacobsen. 'In fact, at first I was surprised you found only one.'

'At first?' asked Nightingale.

'Yes. A creature with teeth as seemingly fragile as this ought to leave behind far more than one when engaged in such vicious activity. Some sharks lose over 30,000 teeth in their lifetimes, after all – each time they feed, they lose dozens.'

'But...?' said Nightingale.

'But this tooth is anything but fragile, quite the opposite, in fact. Here, take a look at this—' he took out another photo, a close-up of the bottom of the tooth, where a tiny hole was. '—See the perfect hole? It came from a small diamond core drill bit. I know this because on the side I'm an amateur jewelry craftsman. I collect seashells on the beach and turn them into necklaces and earrings, sell them at fairs, that kind of thing.' His face flushed and he shrugged. 'My wife likes them.'

Taylor shook her head. 'A drill hole...?'

'Hang on,' said Jacobsen, taking another photo from the folder, the tooth inverted to show a silver center. 'I took a scraping from the tooth's interior—it's titanium.'

'Titanium?' said Nightingale, aghast. 'Why the hell would it be titanium?'

'There's only one reason,' said Taylor. 'It's man-made.'

'That's not possible,' said Nightingale.

'I'm afraid it is possible, detective,' said Jacobsen. 'Furthermore, the drill-hole, upon closer inspection, seems to have housed a small screw. I believe this indestructible tooth was in fact screwed to a metal jaw of some kind, something man-made. That it came loose at all was purely accidental.

The maker of this artificial tooth did not screw it in properly and consequently it was dislodged during the creature's mad feeding frenzy.

'But that's not all I discovered. Most perplexing and disturbing of all is the fact that whatever murdered those kids is human. A man, in fact.'

'What?' said Nightingale and Taylor. They stared blankly at him.

Dr Jacobsen nodded slowly. 'I'm afraid so. You don't see it here because it's been removed, but there was a piece of pink gum tissue stuck to the titanium center. I had it analyzed; it's human. In fact, mitochondrial DNA testing revealed it to be none other than John Seward, the man who went missing a few months ago.'

* * *

Taylor drove to the precinct, her foot heavy on the gas pedal. She was staring ahead, her knuckles blanched white as her hands gripped the steering wheel. 'I don't understand,' she said. 'It just doesn't make any sense. How could the thing be human? Seven or eight feet tall? Looks like a monster with gills?' She was driving over eighty miles an hour, flying past cars on the inside and hurling the cruiser back in the lane in a wave of dry white dust.

'You really don't need to drive so fast,' Nightingale said nervously. 'We'll get there.'

'You heard Dr Jacobsen,' said Taylor. 'whatever it is, it's unlike anything he's ever seen before. But the tissue is evidence enough. It's John Seward. I was wrong to think it was anything supernatural.'

'How could it be human? By all accounts the thing is a monster!'

She looked across at him. 'Even after all this you still think it's supernatural?'

Nightingale threw up his hands. 'Look, I don't know what to think. Honestly I have no idea. I'm just not sure how it could possibly be John Seward. I mean, maybe it is, maybe he's been possessed, dramatic transformations are known attributes of the possessed. But sprouting eight feet tall? Titanium teeth? I have never seen a case like this before, and trust me, I've seen a lot of cases.'

'What about vampires and werewolves ... you know, what do they call it, shape-shifting?'

'You believe in vampires?' said Nightingale. 'Seriously?'

'I'm starting to question what I do believe,' she said. 'But I meant could it be similar to a vampire. Or a werewolf. I didn't say it was a vampire.' She shook her head as she realised how ridiculous she sounded but she finished the chain of thought anyway. 'Or a werewolf.'

'Some sort of shape-shifting monster, maybe. I suppose. But how did John Seward become a monster? And why? Something like that doesn't just happen. Something must have caused it.' Nightingale was silent for a while. He rolled down the window, took out his pack of cigarettes and lit one. 'So it's a man, but not a man. It's a tooth but not a tooth.'

Officer Taylor breathed a deep sigh. She flicked on the blinker and turned right onto the Everglades City exit. They navigated the streets and parked at the town bar. 'Well,' said Taylor. 'I don't know about you, but I need a drink.'

* * *

The bar was called the Thirsty Gator; its sign had a picture of an alligator guzzling a pint of beer. The interior was small and cramped, each dusty corner dominated by a real-life stuffed alligator standing on its own two feet and smiling with powerful jaws, a sign in its clawed hands: HI, I'M THIRSTY!

Nightingale and Taylor sat at the deserted counter; it was not yet five o'clock, people were still at work. Nightingale was pleasantly surprised to find that the bar sold Corona lager; he'd already had one and was nursing his second. The two of them stared off into the oblivion of the paneled wall behind the counter, sipping their beers and picking at the bowl of nuts.

'It's a cannibal,' said Nightingale finally. 'If you and the doctor are right about it being human, and it's eating people, then that makes it a cannibal. At least we know that much.'

Taylor winced. 'Gross.'

Nightingale thought for a moment. 'Hey, weren't there a few cannibalism cases in Florida recently?'

Taylor set down her beer. 'Yeah, a guy recently killed someone and ate his face off, then there was the Miami Cannibal Attack, which is pretty famous. And another one over the summer, actually…'

'Cannibalism sure is featuring in the news pretty often around here.'

'Yeah,' said Taylor. 'I guess so.'

'And what were the motives for these crimes?'

'I don't remember.'

'Have you got one of those smartphones?'

Taylor chuckled. 'Yes, Nightingale, I've got one of those smartphones.' Nightingale was persistent. 'Do me a favor and look up what the motives were for those crimes, please. Just a hunch.'

'Okay,' she said, taking out her phone and tapping the screen. After a minute she looked at him. 'All three investigations were inconclusive. No motives could be established. No one was ever caught.'

'Interesting,' said Nightingale.

'You think they're connected?'

'Maybe,' said Nightingale. He looked outside. 'What time does it get dark around here?'

'Seven-thirty or so. Maybe eight o'clock, tops.'

Nightingale nodded. 'We've got time, then.'

'Time for what?'

'You've heard of Winston Tollhouse?'

'The Warlock?'

'You have heard of him, then.'

'He's just a crazy old man,' said Taylor. 'He's under house arrest. He was involved with a coven of witches a while back. They were accused of human sacrifices, but nothing was ever proved.'

'Illegal immigrants, I heard.'

Taylor nodded. 'A few bodies were found and the media got all excited because of what they said were Satanic markings burnt into the flesh. A reporter went undercover and wrote about witnessing a sacrifice but that body was never found and a few weeks later the reporter vanished. Most of the people in the newspaper story left the county soon after it was published, Tollhouse stayed behind. The newspapers call him The Warlock. But it's more of a joke than anything. He's not considered a serious threat to anyone, he's just a sad, deluded old man.'

Nightingale stood up and grabbed his jacket. 'Time we had a chat with Mr Tollhouse.'

* * *

They parked on slushy grass outside the huge white colonial that was home – and prison – for Winston Tollhouse. Large mangrove trees grew on all sides, casting an abundance of shade. Fitting home for a Satanist, thought Nightingale. A tad luxurious for a prison.

He and Taylor left the car and approached the house, knocked on the front door. The white lead paint was peeling off the siding; it had fallen in chips onto the porch. The door opened and a tall wiry man stood scowling at them, the lid of his left eye drooping. 'The hell you want?' he asked in a thick southern drawl. He was glaring at officer Taylor. 'I ain't broke no curfew. I been in my house.'

'We'd just like to ask you a few questions, Mr Tollhouse,' said Taylor. 'About the recent killings.'

Tollhouse's face knotted, and for a moment Nightingale thought he seemed nervous, even suspicious, but then Tollhouse spit out a brown glob of tobacco which sailed past Taylor's head and fell onto the porch with a thud. 'I heard tell of them,' he said, running his tongue over stained teeth. 'Real mess, that was.'

Nightingale didn't know what to say, but Taylor didn't miss a beat. 'Why don't we step inside a minute, ask you a few questions about it. My colleague here might have a lead, but we need your help. You're not under any suspicion whatsoever.'

'Well that's a relief,' said Tollhouse, stepping aside and letting them in. 'You folks might not like my beliefs too awful much but I ain't no murderer, sincerely. I can hardly cook my own breakfast in the morning, how could I kill a fella?'

Tollhouse led them through the house to a dark sitting room – the whole house was dark, for that matter, all of its windows shuttered. Tollhouse was a hoarder. In every room there lay huge piles of old mildewed books and stacks of magazines dating as far back as the 1960s. Mouse droppings littered the floor. Layers of dust coated everything like fungus – when they sat on the couch, a thick cloud of dust shot up and perfumed the air with age. Nightingale sneezed.

'So,' Taylor began, looking at Nightingale. 'You wanted to ask Mr Tollhouse some questions.'

'Right,' said Nightingale, sniffling. 'You were part of the Satanic cult arrested for kidnapping a few years ago?'

The old man raised a bushy eyebrow. 'Maybe,' he said. 'But I told the police all about that.'

'Forget the police for a moment, you're not in trouble of any kind. We're just talking.' The old man nodded, working the tobacco around his mouth. Nightingale went on. 'They were performing rituals, practicing the dark arts, bequeathing gifts of sacrifice to Satan.' The old man said nothing. 'My question is… did you ever have to turn anyone away? I mean, people who wanted to be a part of what you were doing, but didn't fit the mold?'

'Well sure! We turned folks away. Not a whole lot, mind you. People wasn't knocking at our doors and asking to become part of the clan every fine Sunday afternoon.'

'And were any of these people practitioners of Santeria? Of voodoo, or hoodoo?'

Tollhouse squinted with one eye. 'I ain't heard tell of none of that, you seem to be speaking in tongues, mister.'

Nightingale tried a different approach. 'Why'd the clan turn away those people? What was it about them specifically that didn't align with your beliefs?'

Tollhouse paused. 'Well, most times it was just a matter of we didn't see no reason to trust 'em. Once or twice, though, we came across a couple of real crazies, real weirdos.'

Nightingale leaned forward. 'Like who?'

'Black fella named Parker, he wanted to join us one time or another, I seem to remember. But there was somethin about the man that just wasn't right. I think he was schizophrenic or some such. Sincerely though, I hear he's good and locked up in the loony bin by now.'

Nightingale gritted his teeth in frustration but forced himself to smile.

'Then there was this other one, guy named Cole. White fella, older, maybe a few years younger'n me but then maybe time's just been good to him. He was asking about joining us once. We heard tell of him, though, he was a doctor, some kinda big shot surgeon from New York fired on account of some weird experiments he was doing with the hospital facilities. The public was none too pleased about that, let me tell you. Look it up if you don't believe me. Sincerely!'

'Was Cole his first name?'

Tollhouse shook his head so vigorously that Nightingale feared it might come off. 'No, that was his family name. Bob or Bobby, I think. Bobby Cole.'

Nightingale looked over at Taylor but she was already scribbling in her notepad.

* * *

Taylor's police car peeled out of Tollhouse's driveway, leaving behind a trail of rubber on the asphalt. Taylor's police computer screen showed a mugshot of a white man named Robert Simpson Cole, M.D, arrested in New York for stealing a cadaver from his hospital and trying to reanimate the corpse.

The sun was setting, casting a sheen of fire over the blue sky to the west. Taylor was speeding again, and Nightingale's stomach lurched. 'You know,' he said, 'for a cop you drive pretty bloody fast.'

'So Cole's been trying to bring back the dead,' said Taylor, ignoring him. 'He kidnapped Seward, killed him, and brought him back. Is that what you're telling me?'

'Maybe,' said Nightingale. 'We have a motive. Cole got sacked from his job and is trying to finish what he started. Sounds like he already has.'

'But the creature is eight feet tall. Read the report, John Seward was six feet.'

'I don't think he used one cadaver, I think he used a couple of them.'

'A couple of them? Forgive me Nightingale, but what the hell are you talking about?'

'You ever read Frankenstein?'

Officer Taylor groaned and shook her head. 'This is just too much.'

'How many men have gone missing in the past several months around here? Think about it. Cole's a surgeon. He obviously knows how to piece together body parts. He probably learned how to reanimate when he traveled abroad, maybe to Cuba, West Africa, the Far East, I'm not sure. But he learned it from somewhere and took the knowledge back home with him to add to his own private practice. I think he's created some kind of super-creature.'

'Why?' asked Taylor. 'I still don't get it. Reanimating corpses, sure, but releasing the damn thing to prey on townsfolk?'

'I don't know why,' said Nightingale. 'But we're going to find out.'

* * *

They pulled into a long driveway that carved a strip of island into the swamp. Taylor had gotten on the radio dispatch to call for backup and the squad car was on the way. Bordering the road were cypresses and cedars growing straight up from the swamp. They towered over the car, green bushy leaves blotting out the setting sun. The road to Cole's house was the only stretch of dry land. The rest was mushy swampland.

Only one way in, thought Nightingale, and only one way out.

At the end of the driveway was a modern mansion; it sat on the edge of a peninsula surrounded by swamplands. No sunlight shone on it. If not for the brand new SUV parked in the lot, it would look completely deserted.

The sun had fallen below the trees and it was starting to get dark, but no lights came on inside the house. They climbed out of the cruiser and walked towards the house. By the time they reached the front door, Nightingale's Hush Puppies were spotted with mud. Taylor unholstered her Glock and knocked on the door. No answer.

Taylor knocked again.

'Mr Cole, it's the police, open up. We'd like to ask you a few questions.'

'No one's home,' said Nightingale.

'I don't buy that for a second. There's a car.'

'He probably has more than one. Look at the house.'

Taylor pounded on the door several more times. Crickets were singing in the swamp. Nightingale felt a queer chill come up his spine – he hadn't wanted to be caught out here after dark. He stepped away and paced the side of the house, peering through windows at the deserted rooms. In a window he caught the reflection of something swinging and he turned around.

Hanging from a mangled tree in the swamp was a stick figure, like the one Taylor had shown him earlier, rotating slowly on a clear string. Nightingale scanned the swamp and saw several more stick figures hanging from the trees.

'Bloody hell,' he said.

Taylor looked at him. 'What?'

Nightingale pointed to the stick figures, dozens of them. 'It's all very Blair Witch, isn't it?'

Taylor's eyes grew wide. 'We've got him.'

'Not yet we haven't.'

Taylor's cellphone rang, causing them both to jump. She breathed a sigh of relief and answered the phone.

'Taylor,' she said.

'Damn it, Taylor, where have you been!' It was Chief Jackson from the precinct. Before she could answer, he said, 'Lizzie Harris is gone. The thing came back and took her!'

The blood drained from Taylor's face. 'What?'

Nightingale joined her and bent his head to the phone, trying to listen.

'The fucker climbed up to the third floor and bashed her window in. There's blood everywhere, it looks like a fucking slaughterhouse in here.'

'You're at the hospital?'

'Yeah. Officer Dennings is leading a search and rescue team out on the swamp. I don't think they're going to find her. You need to get over here right now.'

'I'm on my way.'

Taylor hung up the phone and punched the door. 'Fuck!'

Nightingale hovered beside her. 'The Harris girl... she's gone?'

Taylor nodded gravely. 'It got her. Seward, or whatever it is, came back, climbed the building and got her. What kind of monster is this?' Nightingale didn't answer. 'Listen, we gotta go. We'll come back for this asshole after we find that creature and shoot him. Come on.' She jogged towards the car.

'Hold up a second,' said Nightingale. 'What if you don't find him? What if he comes back here?'

Taylor turned around. 'What do you mean?'

'Someone should be here just in case. I'll stay. Besides, I can take a look around, see if there's any evidence I can find.'

'And if whatever it is does come back. It's a monster, Nightingale. It eats people.'

'It's the only plan we've got. What if the creature brings Lizzie back here?'

Taylor took in a deep breath, let it out. 'All right, Nightingale, but come here.'

They went to the squad car and Taylor took a shotgun that was mounted on the ceiling, a semi-automatic Benelli M-1.'

'You know what this is?' she asked.

'Duh. Is it a gun?'

'Don't screw around,' she said. 'Do you know how to fire a gun?'

'I was an armed cop in a former life, so yes,' he said, suddenly serious. He nodded at the weapon. 'It's a Benelli, Italian-made, semi-automatic shotgun with an aluminium alloy receiver and tubular magazine.'

Taylor grinned and handed it to him. 'Keep this with you, just in case,' she said. 'It fires buckshot, but it's devastating in close quarters. There are only nine rounds, so use it wisely.'

'Thanks.'

Taylor got into the front seat and started the engine. 'You sure you want to stay out here?' she asked through the window. 'Alone?'

'I'll be fine,' said Nightingale confidently, but he felt a lot less confident as he watched the police cruiser drive away.

* * *

Jack Nightingale stood outside Cole's empty house in the dark, holding the shotgun and listening to the night sounds coming from the swamp. His eyes were playing tricks on him. He thought he saw something moving to his right, then to his left an alligator vaulted off the peninsula and sank into the water. Predators were all around him, and he knew it. What's more, they knew it.

Starting from the front door, he walked around the house, flicking off the shotgun's safety switch. Behind the house was nothing but an endless expanse of swamp. Water slopped against the trees – the wake of some large animal. The crickets chirped, and an owl crooned in the darkness.

Still no lights came on in the house. No movement from inside.

Nightingale wasn't happy about breaking into the house, but decided he didn't have much choice. He needed to know what was going on and he wasn't learning anything standing outside. He went to where he'd seen a laundry room, held up the butt of the shotgun and rammed it into the window. Shattered glass fell to the floor. Again he flicked the shotgun's safety switch and tossed it inside the room, crawling in after it, careful not to cut himself on the jagged edges sticking up from the windowsill.

Once inside he retrieved the gun and took out his Zippo cigarette lighter, flicked it on inspecting the rooms a few feet at a time. They were largely empty, or looked like storage rooms full of boxes. Nightingale opened one and flicked through medical records and printouts of drugs reports he'd never heard of, paperwork on various clinical trials. He closed the box and proceeded into a cramped hallway. No pictures lined the walls.

He came upon a kitchen reeking of chemicals. Dark brown bottles lined the sink, unlabeled. No dishes or cups, no remnants of meals, nothing to suggest human habitation. He opened the refrigerator and what he saw caused vomit to rise in his throat.

Standing upright on a large dinner plate was a human head – it had been perfectly severed just above the collar with surgical precision. Its dead eyes gazed out at Nightingale longingly, as if pleading with him to reverse the unthinkable. He stumbled backwards, almost tripping and dropped his lighter. It went out immediately, plunging the room into darkness.

He got down on his hands and knees and scrabbled around for the lighter. He found it and flicked the flint wheel. The flame spluttered and as he stood up his breath caught in his throat as he realised someone was standing in front of him.

'I don't recall inviting you into my home.'

Before Nightingale could lift the shotgun, something solid smashed into the side of his head and he fell to the floor.

* * *

Officer Taylor was briefed outside the hospital room. Chief Jackson said there was no reason to hold out hope that Lizzie Harris was still alive and when Taylor saw Harris's hospital bed, she understood why. Blood and gore covered the bed and walls, messy puddles all over the linoleum. It looked like a pack of starving wolves had been turned loose in the room. In all her years on the force, Taylor hadn't seen anything like it.

'This is search and destroy,' said Jackson. 'You find that thing, you kill it no questions asked. Do you understand me, Taylor?'

Taylor nodded. For the first time since she'd met him, the Chief, standing six-foot-four with tree trunks for arms, seemed genuinely afraid, and the fact that even this beast of a man was not immune to the evil in evidence here made Taylor's own fear skyrocket. 'I'll do my best, sir,' she managed.

'Got a pair of boots?'

Taylor frowned. 'Sir?'

'We've got a team out there in those swamps. We're going after them.'

A few minutes later they were both trudging through the swamp holding flashlights, their Glocks at the ready, trying to ignore the sounds of slithering snakes and splashing water as the gators slipped in after them.

Taylor felt goosebumps crawling on the back of her neck; she hurried out of the water just in time to see a pair of golden eyes and a long snout on the surface behind her.

'Shit, Chief, I think we're being followed here.'

Jackson aimed his gun at the alligator and fired. The gator snapped its jaws, beat at the water with its tail and swam swiftly away. 'Not anymore,' he said.

After thirty minutes they were far beyond the glow of the hospital and their flashlights were the only source of light. The stars and the moon were half-hidden by the treetops. The radio on Jackson's shoulder crackled. A static voice came through.

'Hey Chief, you out there? Over.'

Jackson took the receiver, spoke into it. 'Dennings, what's your position? Over.'

'Roughly two miles south of the hospital in a big clearing. And Chief? We found her. She ain't pretty. Over.'

Jackson swore under his breath. 'Dennings, any sign of the perp? Over.'

'No sir. No sign of the perp. But there sure is a lot of water out here where he could've disappeared into. Over.'

'Listen to me,' said Jackson. 'Hang tight and wait for Taylor and me. Call the medical examiner and wake his ass up. You said there's water near you? Over.'

'Yes sir, plenty of water, over.'

'Good. I'll get a boat out there to get the girl. Just hang tight. As of this minute the search is over. Over and out.'

Dennings crackled back, 'Over and out.'

Taylor stepped forward. 'What do you mean the search is over? We've got to find that thing, Chief. It's not going to stop.'

'I know that, Taylor, but without mobility out here we're sitting ducks. This is too big for any of us. We did the best we could, now we've got to bring that girl, or what's left of her, back to the hospital. I've got to make a call to the FBI. This is just too big.'

Taylor spoke slowly and carefully. 'Chief, what I'm about to tell you is going to sound crazy, but I need you to listen to me.'

They stopped walking and Jackson listened to her story of the afternoon with Nightingale. When she had finished, his face flushed red and he began swearing at the top of his lungs. 'Are you fucking nuts? On what authority did you go to that house? And you brought a fucking civilian along with you? What were you thinking!'

'I'm sorry, Chief, I just didn't think the precinct would buy it. I'm not even sure I buy it. A zombie? A monster? It sounds crazy.''

'That was not your call to make, goddammit!' Jackson kicked at a fallen branch, sending it into the air. He was fuming, his chest pumping. He put his hands on his hips and shook his head, eyes closed.

'I'm sorry, Chief,' said Taylor. 'I should've told you sooner.'

'Those wooden things. The stick figures? You swear you saw them?'

Taylor nodded. 'I swear,' she said. 'Dozens of them, all over the swamp around Cole's house. I don't know what his level of involvement is, not for sure, but I know he has something to do with the murders. Nightingale's still out there.'

Jackson thought it over for a few seconds, deep furrows in his brow. 'All right,' he said. 'Let's call back the team and head to that house. But when this is all over, Taylor, you and I are going to sit down and have a long chat about honesty and respecting one's superiors. Is that clear? Good. Now let me get ahold of Dennings before he gets his ass bit off by a gator.' He paused, and cursed under his breath.

'What is it, Chief?' asked Taylor.

'I should've brought the thrower.'

'The thrower?'

'Flamethrower. I keep one in my trunk.' He shrugged. 'You never know.' Jackson took the receiver from his shoulder, clicked the button. 'Hey

Dennings, Chief. Listen, we've got a new lead. It's an odd lead... but it's a lead. I need you guys back here ASAP. We'll get the girl later. Over.'

Jackson held the receiver in his hand, his ear bent toward it. Coming through the radio was nothing but static. The Chief tried again.

'Dennings. I need you back here now. Please report. Over.'

Again, steady static.

Jackson glanced worriedly at Taylor. For a moment static was the only sound in the swamp – not even the crickets were singing. Then, a few meters to the left, something began thrashing in the water.

Something big.

* * *

Jack Nightingale was floating in ether, suspended in darkness. His body felt weightless, like a balloon. His thoughts were vague and distant; he wondered how much time he'd spent there, how long he'd remain. He wondered if this was any place at all.

Something tore into the ether's dark awning. A blade of some sort. Cutting diagonal across the ceiling – or was it the floor? – and spilling white light into Nightingale's eyes, blinding him. He screamed but no sound came.

He screamed again and woke up.

* * *

Officer Taylor and Chief Jackson leveled their pistols at the thrashing form in the water, ready to fire. Coming into the flashlight beams was a haggard creature – bloodied, bruised, clothes torn to pieces.

'Oh shit,' said Taylor. 'Dennings!'

Officer Dennings stumbled through the water and fell to his knees, his eyes blinking against the glare of the flashlights. He seemed confused.

Jackson reached down, clutched Dennings by the shoulders and lifted him out of the water. 'Dennings,' he demanded. 'Where are the others?'

Dennings stared blankly at him – through him – and suddenly his face became an awful grimace. He whimpered, cried out.

Jackson shook him by the shoulders. 'Answer me goddammit! Where are they?'

At last Dennings seemed to register their presence. He looked at each of them in turn like a frightened child, afraid of being reprimanded. 'Dead,' he whimpered, and then his mouth opened, closed, opened again as though he were chewing some phantom food. 'Eaten,' he said.

Jackson let go of him and Dennings fell sobbing to the wet grass. He faced Taylor. 'You need to take him back.'

'And you?'

Jackson popped the magazine from his pistol, inspected the rounds and clicked it back. 'I'm going to find the team.'

'Are you insane?' said Taylor. 'Chief, they're gone! You heard Dennings. If you go out there, you're dead, simple as that. You said so yourself, this thing is bigger than us. We can't do it anymore. We need to go back, all of us, and drive to Cole's house with a shitload of firepower. That's where the creature is headed. That's where it lives.'

Jackson shook his head. 'I'm giving you a direct order, Taylor. Take Dennings and get out of here. Call the Collier County Sheriff's department and get all the firepower you need. I'll touch base when I find the team.'

With that he left, his flashlight bobbing in the darkness. For a moment Taylor watched, then she took Dennings from under the armpits and helped him to his feet. 'Come on,' she said. 'Let's go.'

The going was painfully slow. Dennings fell into crying fits and had to be coaxed like a child. Finally he sank to his knees in the mud and refused to go any farther. Taylor slapped him hard across the face, sobering him. 'Ok,' he said, rising to his feet. 'Ok.'

They reached the clearing and the hospital lights. Gunshots exploded behind them: six shots in rapid fire, followed by silence.

Taylor swore. Chief Jackson was dead, she was certain of it. Dead and probably being eaten at that very moment.

'Come on Dennings,' she said, holding him up. 'Faster.'

They limped along at a slow pace. Taylor was thinking of Nightingale and hoping he was ok when something splashed in the water behind them.

Dennings cried out and fell. Taylor groaned, tried to help him up; he squirmed out of her grip and crawled through the tall grass, crying, 'No, no, no.'

Taylor looked around; nothing was there. She was not impressed. 'Dennings,' she groaned. 'Get up.'

Behind Taylor came a low, gurgling growl. She wheeled around. The thing stood in front of her on slanted knees, eight feet tall or more, the most wretched of God's creatures. It looked like a giant disfigured infant crisscrossed with purple scars, its body pulpy in some places and flat in others. But it wasn't the creature's body that paralyzed her, it was the face: the lopsided bloodshot eyes, the missing nose, the mouth full of long, sharp teeth glistening with blood.

Before she even had time to scream, the creature was on her.

* * *

When Jack Nightingale woke up the side of his head felt like it was on fire. He squinted in the harsh light. A man's fuzzy head bobbed in the afterglow, revealing a worn face with glasses and tired mud-colored eyes. Robert Cole, Nightingale realised. He'd been in the house all the time. 'I thought I'd lost you,' said Cole.

Nightingale looked around, blinking as he tried to clear his vision. He was in a windowless basement, a bizarre science lab and an operating room all rolled into one. On the many shelves were Mason jars with small deformed figures curled into themselves, pale naked bodies with enlarged craniums, clawed hands, bulbous yellow eyes, all of them floating in a murky green liquid – formaldehyde. Beyond the shelves were stainless steel tables and surgical instruments. Bone saws. Scalpels. Knives.

Nightingale was standing spread-eagle, nude except for his underwear. His ankles were shackled to the cement floor, his arms spread wide, wrists held tight by leather straps from the ceiling beams. Cole aimed a small flashlight into his eyes.

'No, I did not strike you deaf and dumb – your pupils tell me that. There's nothing you can hide from me, Mr Nightingale.'

Nightingale frowned at the mention of his name. He wanted to speak but the side of his skull ached, he felt nauseous and faint.

'Yes, that's right,' Cole said. 'I know who you are. I know everything about you, everything worth knowing, that is. Isn't that right, Winston, my old friend?'

Winston Tollhouse came into view. 'Howdy d'tective.' Then the old man dropped his accent: 'Or shall I say, hello again, Mr Nightingale.'

Nightingale cursed under his breath, annoyed at himself for having been taken in by the old man.

'You underestimated me,' said Tollhouse. 'You took me for a dumb, powerless country hick. A mistake, I'm afraid, which will prove fatal.'

Finally Nightingale spoke. 'You can't be here! Your ankle bracelet… they're going to find you. They're going to find all of this!'

Tollhouse propped a leg against a stainless steel table and lifted his pants to show the bracelet. 'You mean this?' He chuckled. 'I'm afraid not. The police department is gone; Kalmyra saw to that.'

Kalmyra? What the hell was Kalmyra?

'And by the time the authorities get to this house,' said Cole, 'there'll be nothing left. We'll be long gone. You as well. Well, not you, per se, but what's left of you.'

Cole brought over a stool and sat on it.

'What the hell is going on?' asked Nightingale.

'I'm going to kill you, that's what's going on' said Cole. 'Then bring you back. With alterations, of course. You saw the head upstairs in the kitchen? That will be your new head. We only need your body. Or parts of it.'

Nightingale's mind was racing. 'The missing persons...'

'We kidnapped them. Well, Winston didn't, of course, but I did. You have not yet seen the creature, but when you do you'll see certain resemblances.' Cole nodded to Winston. 'Turn that on, will you?'

There was a large monitor against the wall; Tollhouse took a remote control and pressed a button. Nothing happened. 'Winston, the red button,' Cole said irritably. Tollhouse hit the red button and the screen came on, showing a picture of a tall robust man, mid-thirties, good looking.

'My first subject. The foundation on which I built the creature. Now the right arrow, Winston.' Tollhouse pressed a button and the picture was replaced by one of a stout, muscular man. 'Subject two... Again.' Now came a picture of John Seward – Nightingale didn't need Cole to tell him that; he remembered the face from the missing persons report.

'Subject three. Notice the eyes, Nightingale. Notice the face. You will be seeing it soon enough. Go ahead and set the remote down, Winston.'

'Where did you learn to raise the dead?' asked Nightingale.

'I lived among a Hoodoo tribe in Ghana for many months, healing the sick and the lame. I learned from them. But I was never able to actually do it – after the unfortunate incident with the hospital I was forced to go into exile. I came here, not because of its tropical beauty, but because of this fellow you see before you now, good old Winston, who is adept at bringing back the dead.'

'You practice hoodoo and he practices Satanism,' said Nightingale. 'You put them together, and...'

Cole nodded. 'In a nutshell. Though I wasn't able to successfully raise the dead until I met Winston. As it turns out, hoodoo has its flaws, at least for a white practitioner. Satanism is much easier. After all, there are a great many demons and devils that wish to come into this world to have a bit of fun. All one must do is provide a viable means of access: a body.'

'That thing out there is a demon?' Nightingale gasped. Joshua was right all along.

Tollhouse nodded. 'Kalmyra is its name, from the seventh circle of Hell, guardian of the outer ring of murderers and those who've inflicted severe violence. It is said that the denizens of that ring are submerged in a river of boiling blood and fire for all eternity. Kalmyra ensures they stay there. At least, he did, until we summoned him through the creature.

'I fear Hell will miss him,' said Cole, almost sadly. 'He is a worthy torturer and executioner, but he has far more potential on this plane of existence, I can assure you.'

'What do you get out of it?' said Nightingale. 'Aside from sick pleasure.'

Cole smiled sardonically. 'I get a blank canvas on which to paint my masterpiece—the culmination of science and the occult. But mostly, I get power, courtesy of Lucifer Himself – I get immortality.'

Nightingale laughed. Tollhouse and Cole exchanged a confused glance. 'Devils are the biggest liars in existence,' said Nightingale. 'They're using you as they use everyone else. You idiot. You've opened a portal for them and the moment they're done with you, they'll kill you. If that thing's a demon as you say, he doesn't need you anymore, he can raise the dead all by himself without kidnapping anyone. Don't you see what you've done?'

Cole shook his head. 'Don't be ridiculous. When you make a deal with a devil, any devil, that deal is inviolate.'

'That's what you think, is it?' said Nightingale. 'Well good luck with that.'

Cole seemed momentarily troubled by what Nightingale had said. 'You are mistaken,' he said coldly. 'I have spoken to the Dark Lord Himself, and we have drawn a pact.'

Tollhouse looked over at him. 'A pact? What are you talking about?'

Cole blinked as if waking from a trance. He turned to regard Tollhouse. 'Oh, right,' he said. He took a revolver from his belt and aimed it at him. 'Sorry, Winston. The Master says there's only room for one.' He shot Tollhouse in the head. Tollhouse's head exploded in a shower of blood and brains and he fell to the floor with a dull thud.

Nightingale fell back in his restraints. 'What the fuck!' he said. 'Are you mad?'

Cole shrugged. 'No,' he said. 'I'm practical.'

There was a hatch in the floor on the far side of the basement, full of water. Something was crawling out of it, splashing, making a mess. The creature walked towards them, carrying Taylor in its arms.

'Ah,' said Cole, turning. 'Kalmyra, my son, you've arrived. And you've brought another worthy subject for the cause. A woman, no less. The Master will be pleased!'

The creature set Taylor on the ground. Her head rolled to one side; she was unconscious.

'Taylor, wake up!' cried Nightingale. 'Wake up!'

Taylor stirred, moaning, but didn't wake. There was a deep gash across her left eyebrow.

Nightingale hurled against his restraints, trying to break free.

'Ah, ah, ah,' said Cole, turning a scalpel in front of Nightingale's eye. 'I'd remain calm if I were you. I have yet to apply the anesthesia and I would hate to see you in pain. Though of course you will be watching the entire thing – you've earned that, at any rate.'

'You sick bastard,' whispered Nightingale.

'Enough talking,' said Cole. 'Let's get started.' Cole went for the electric saw and turned it on. The creature stood off to the side and watched Nightingale hungrily. Cole seemed to notice this, because he said, 'Kalmyra. Once the procedure is over you may have the leftovers, as it were.'

The creature's eyes lit up and it began cackling madly, wheezing and snorting. It crawled on all fours to Tollhouse's corpse, dipped its ugly head and began to feed on his stomach. A wet slopping sound filled the room. Then the electric saw came to life, raw and piercing. Nightingale was frantically working his right hand in the restraint. He felt it loosen a little around his wrist but he knew there wasn't enough time.

'Forget the anesthesia,' said Cole. 'This is going to be so much fun!'

Cole was wearing goggles now. He came forward and held the saw just below Nightingale's left kneecap. Nightingale felt cool air on his skin, the hairs on his leg standing straight up. He felt the pain as the saw found his flesh. Tearing the skin like fire. Another moment and it would start digging into the bone.

Nightingale closed his eyes and prayed.

A wave of hot air blew against his body.

That's it. Pain and shock. He was going to lose consciousness. And then he was going to die.

The wave came again, this time followed by a gut-wrenching scream. Nightingale opened his eyes.

Chief Jackson, bloodied and haggard, was wielding a flamethrower at the base of the stairs. A huge gust of liquid fire poured out of it and coated the creature, which flailed and screamed as its entire body went up in flames.

Cole stared, dumbfounded. The saw clattered to the floor and sent up sparks. Nightingale kicked his left foot away just in time. He worked his hand through the leather strap and punched Cole in the face, sending him sprawling to the floor.

The creature was smoldering, whipping its body in circles and screeching.

Nightingale loosened the other straps while Cole groaned on the ground by his feet.

'Nightingale!' screamed Jackson. 'Move!'

A splash of fire surged onto Cole just as Nightingale flung himself away. Instinctively he rushed to Taylor's side, picked her up. Several containers of Formaldehyde had smashed open and fire was rapidly spreading throughout the basement. The stairs were blocked off by a wall of flame reaching up to the ceiling. The stairs were on fire.

'We gotta go through it!' screamed Jackson, but Nightingale shook his head and went for the floor hatch. Jackson followed. Without thinking, Nightingale pressed his mouth to Taylor's and dropped into the water. Blackness filled his vision. He allowed gravity to guide him, floating, rising, breaking the surface just beyond the house. Jackson soon followed.

'Swim away from it!' screamed Jackson. 'Swim away from the house!'

Just then the house exploded, the many jars of formaldehyde igniting like a miniature atomic bomb. Glass, wood, and blocks of concrete rained down on them. Nightingale gave Taylor his air and dropped below the surface for what felt like an eternity.

When they emerged, the house was gone.

* * *

It was late morning. Sunlight streamed through the curtains and fell on the linoleum. The light splashed officer Taylor's face, hitting her eyes. She squinted and turned away from it.

'Here, I'll draw the curtains,' offered Nightingale, but Taylor stopped him with her hand.

'No,' she said. 'It's nice to see the sun. Didn't think I'd ever get another chance when that creature came down on me.'

'I didn't think I would either,' said Nightingale, gesturing towards his bandaged head, still throbbing from where Cole had hit him. 'What a night.'

Taylor chuckled. 'Yeah. What a night.'

'Hey,' said Nightingale, holding up a pack of cigarettes. 'You mind?'

'No, just crack a window.'

Nightingale lit a cigarette. 'So what now?' he asked. 'Are you going back to the precinct?'

'I have to, I'm sergeant now. Not that it means anything with half the precinct gone…'

Nightingale nodded. 'I'm sorry,' he said.

'That's law enforcement for you.'

'Sure,' said Nightingale. 'Law enforcement is all about fighting flesh-eating zombie-demons and killing mad scientists with flamethrowers, no doubt. What's that expression Americans use? All in a day's work.'

Nightingale smiled, and Taylor did, too.

'Hey,' said Taylor, sitting up. 'You wanna go get dinner later? I mean, once they let me walk out of here?'

Nightingale tilted his head as if weighing his options. 'Will there be beer involved?'

Taylor laughed, and for the first time in twenty-four hours, Nightingale felt good.

'Yeah,' she said.

'Dinner it is, then,' said Nightingale.

CHILDREN OF THE DARK

The small New England farmhouse was cast in a shroud of falling snow. Surrounding it on all sides was a dense forest of spruce, hemlock and pine, their heavy boughs weighted down by piles of snow, soft and glistening like vanilla ice cream. The dirt road leading to the house was barren and unplowed. Outside nothing was visible beyond the dull amber porch light, which extended a glow several feet beyond the door before being cut off by the darkness of the starless winter night.

Inside, nestled in comfortable chairs by the fireplace, an elderly couple were drinking cups of coffee. It was early; they'd just awoken. The woman was knitting a quilt for her new grandbaby and the man was staring impassively into the flames, watching them lick at the blackened hearth stones, his eyelids drooping, his breathing slow and deep. The only sounds were the clicking knitting needles and the howling of the wind.

'Wonder how long this'll keep up,' said the woman. 'Lord knows we don't need any more snow. My goodness, just think, when we went to sleep last night there were clear skies. And now this.' The man grunted in answer, keeping his eyes on the fire, which he'd just stoked. His wife looked at him for a moment and went back to her knitting. 'The least you could do is talk to me, Lester,' she said reproachfully, shifting in her seat.

Lester pried his eyes away from the flames and turned to her. 'And the least you could've done was ask me before you went and sold my damn truck, Loretta.'

Loretta rolled her eyes and set down her knitting. 'So that's what this is about? You're still sore about the truck?'

Lester looked back at the fire, saying nothing.

Well come on now,' said Loretta. 'Let's have it out. I won't be walking on eggshells in my own house. I'll have none of that.'

Lester mumbled something under his breath.

Loretta continued. 'You know well enough May couldn't pay the tuition this year and you yourself came up with the idea about the truck, so don't go blaming me on account of your own self. You did a good thing, Lester, but if you want to go on grumbling about it then you best leave me out of it.'

'Fine,' said Lester.

'Humph,' said Loretta with a roll of her shoulders. She went back to her knitting.

Lester got up to retrieve more wood for the fire. He walked across the open living room to the front door, noticing for the first time that all six candles had been blown out.

'Weird,' he muttered to himself.

Beside the door a pile of year-old cedar was stacked in a neat pile as high as his shoulders, but a few pieces had fallen to the floor. With a deep sigh, he bent over to pick one up. He froze mid-reach.

Outside, the wind was howling and pummeling the house, but beyond the wind there was another sound. Something strange. Lester held his breath and listened. Against the door was a faint scratching noise, as if a couple of sharp claws were raking across the wood in a frenzy.

'What the hell...?' He leaned closer. A chill crept up his spine and he was suddenly struck by a heavy sense of foreboding. He'd felt something like this before, back when his brother George was killed. They'd been burning blueberry fields on his father's property when the wind changed and George got caught in a circle of fire. His father was off burning a different part of the fields with a team of men and couldn't hear Lester's hollering. Lester tried to get to George but the flames were too high and too thick. Everything was alight. He caught a glimpse of his brother's eyes just before he lost consciousness from the smoke; they were full of fear and urgency, and they filled Lester's heart with dread because he knew there was nothing he could do. He had the same feeling now and he shuddered.

The scratching grew more fervent. Lester thought two sets of claws were now ravaging the door. He shuddered again. But he couldn't fight the urge to bring his ear closer.

Moving slowly, carefully, he rested his ear against the part of the door where the scratching was loudest. He listened as the fingernail seemingly attacked the wood, as if it were trying to claw its way in. Something about the sound, aside from the sheer strangeness of it, struck Lester as unholy and terrifying.

The scratching grew more frenzied. Lester was sweating and his heart was beating in his chest, fit to burst. Without thinking, he reached up and pulled the latch across the door, locking it.

The scratching stopped.

Lester jumped back from the door, staring at it.

The wind howled and the windows rattled, but the scratching was gone. Without knowing why, and in spite of being an atheist, Lester made the sign of the cross over his heart. He then walked quickly to the rear of the house and latched the back door.

Loretta heard the sound of the latch and looked up. 'What in the Lord are you doing now, Lester?' she asked.

'There's somebody outside.'

Loretta laughed. It was a bright, cheerful laugh.

'Oh, quit foolin around and come sit down,' she said, chuckling. 'Your coffee's getting cold.'

'I ain't foolin,' said Lester, quickly switching on the light to the back porch and gazing out the window at the whitewashed haze. Far off, he could see the dark outline of the trees. The snow on the ground was white and featureless. No people. No animals. 'Somethin's out there,' he said. 'I just know it.'

Loretta watched her husband peering out the window, his eyes unusually alert, his back straight as he scanned the backyard. A loose clapboard banged against the house and made Lester jump. 'Christ!' he said. 'Loretta where's my gun?'

She thought of telling a joke but decided against it. She wanted to impart some sense of calm to the situation, but she, too, was feeling something cold and dark welling up inside her. 'Lester,' she said. 'You're scaring me now.'

'I said where's my gun!'

That was when there was a knock on the door.

Three knocks. They were soft, almost imperceptible. Both Loretta and Lester faced the front door, wide-eyed. They exchanged glances.

The knock came again, more adamantly this time, more forceful. Loretta stood.

Lester looked at his wife, his face clouded with fear. 'Don't,' he said.

'Lester,' she said. 'Someone's outside in the cold and they need our help.'

'Loretta, don't you open that door. Y'hear me?'

But she had already crossed the living room. Lester, for all his age and creaky bones, dashed across the room until he was right behind her. He clutched her arm and said desperately, 'Whatever's out there needs to stay out there.'

The knock came again. Loudly.

Loretta brushed off his hand. 'Nonsense,' she said. 'Someone's out there. What if they're hurt?'

'Loretta, I didn't tell you this before because I didn't wanna scare you, but just a couple minutes ago I heard this ungodly scratchin at the door as though somethin was trying to claw its way in here by force. That's why I went and locked the back door.'

'There's a storm coming,' Loretta said. 'What you heard was just the wind.'

She unlatched the door and reached for the handle.

'Loretta!'

But it was too late. By the time Lester had grabbed hold of her arm she'd already turned the handle and opened the door. The wind grew louder. A rush of cold air swarmed into the house.

Standing on the porch were a boy and a girl, both no older than eight. They were dressed in strange clothes that looked as if they belonged to the eighteenth century. The boy had on a black conductor's cap and the girl was wearing a bonnet caked with snow. Their hair was black – black as the night. And, noted Lester and Loretta with a cold sense of dread – so were their eyes. Behind the children there were no footprints in the snow.

The children did not speak. They merely looked up at Lester and Loretta with those shiny black eyes, unsmiling, their skin so pale as to be translucent.

'Shut the door,' whispered Lester. 'Quick!'

The snow had piled atop their shoulders but the children didn't seem to notice.

'Who are you?' asked Loretta, overcoming her shock, but not her fright. 'Where are your parents?'

The boy spoke. 'Don't worry,' he said. 'They will be here soon.'

His voice was dull, lifeless.

'Please,' said Lester. 'Close it.'

'Hush, Lester! These children are alone and cold and they're in need of our help. Come on in, children. Go warm yourselves by the fire. I'll fetch a pot of water for some tea. Are you hungry?'

The children didn't answer; they brushed past Lester, walking toward the fire stiffly as if their legs were made of wood. Lester and Loretta saw this, but still Loretta closed the door and latched it. She went to the kitchen and began filling a pot of water from a plastic jug with a spigot, and while her back was turned she quickly made the sign of the cross.

With great difficulty Lester pried himself away from the door and joined the children in the living room. They were sitting straight-backed on the rug in front of the fireplace. It was strange, noted Lester. They looked more like stone carvings than living, breathing people.

Since they'd entered the house, the feeling of foreboding had amplified. Lester and Loretta felt an unnamable dread clawing inside them, as if something terrible was happening but they were powerless to stop it.

He watched the children. They didn't move. Not a muscle.

'What happened to you two?' he asked, taking not his usual seat but the one far away from the children.

The children didn't answer. Lester flashed Loretta a worried glance but her back was turned to him. He couldn't see, but her hands were shaking so badly she was having trouble setting the tea packets into the cups.

'Was there some kind of accident?' prodded Lester.

'Yes,' said the boy.

Lester nodded. 'Was anyone hurt?'

Nothing.

They were staring into the fire, taking no apparent notice of the two adults in the room. It now felt as if it was their house and Lester and Loretta were the imposters.

Loretta came over and set two mugs of tea on the floor beside them. 'Here, drink this. You must be frozen to the bone.'

The children said nothing. They did not reach for their tea but continued to stare into the fire.

Loretta took her seat. She moved her knitting onto the table. Lester was looking at her. He pointed to his eyes, mouthing the words, 'Did you see their eyes?'

Loretta nodded. Lester turned back to the children.

'Were you in a car accident?' he asked.

'No,' said the boy.

'What kind of accident was it then?'

No answer. Lester and Loretta shifted uncomfortably, waiting.

'Your clothing,' said Loretta, her voice trembling, 'is so... different. Are you kids from around here?'

The boy shook his head.

'There's an Amish community up north a ways,' offered Lester. 'Is that where you're from?'

'Our parents will be here soon.' This time it was the girl who spoke.

'Ok, that's good. Are you hungry?' asked Loretta.

'Our parents will be here soon,' said the boy.

His voice was toneless, dispassionate, as though he were reading lines from a script that bored him intolerably. Or worse – it was as though he were a corpse possessed with speech. Lester shuddered as he realised that the children's chests didn't rise and fall; it was as if they simply weren't breathing.

Outside the wind screeched and howled. The fire crackled in its hearth, shooting glowing sparks out onto the floor. One of the sparks landed on the girl's lap and started to burn its way through her dress, but she took no notice.

Instinctively, Lester hopped off his seat to help. 'Careful!' he said, and went to brush the ember away, but the girl looked slowly up at him with those dead black eyes, and suddenly Lester felt a sharp pain in his chest. It was as though some invisible hand were clutching his heart and squeezing. He gasped and fell over.

'Lester!' cried Loretta, rushing to his side. She helped him back to his seat where he slouched heavily, moaning and rubbing his chest. 'What's the matter? Where does it hurt?'

'My chest…' he moaned. 'I think… I think I'm having a heart attack.'

Oh, Lord!' cried Loretta, getting up and rushing to the kitchen. Cabinet doors swung open and slammed shut. Drawers flew open and Loretta plunged her hands in, searching frantically in the dark. 'Hold on, Lester!'

While she looked for his heart medication the boy and girl stood up slowly and soundlessly. It was unnatural, the way they moved. They floated toward Lester, hunched in his chair and panting heavily. The fire was dying quickly the farther they advanced, the embers turning from orange to black, the flames shrinking down to nothing.

The children's eyes were like tiny black pools reflecting Lester's anguished face. He couldn't move, couldn't speak. He was frozen with fright.

Loretta was fumbling through another drawer. 'Found them!' she cried as she grabbed for the bottle of white tablets.

The front door slammed open and snow began to pour into the house. The wind screeched like a maddened beast. A mighty draught of cold air extinguished the fire and the light until everything was in total darkness.

Lester couldn't see the children in front of him but he could feel their presence like the closeness of death. The boy lay his hand on Lester's trembling cheek. It was icy cold.

'Look,' said the boy. 'Our parents are here.'

And then Loretta screamed.

* * *

Jack Nightingale stood in the cathedral's stone archway and cupped his hand around his cigarette to light it, puffing twice before blowing out the smoke and letting it merge with the snow and the wind. The city of Boston was a wonderland of snowy tundra. The blizzard had started early the night before and had not abated. It was almost noon. People had been warned by FOX News to stay in their homes and wait out the storm, but there was no end in sight. Half the city's power was out and the other half, North Boston, was so caked with ice people couldn't nudge open their front doors. The official death toll was over two dozen already, and probably much higher, considering how many people were trapped in their homes without heat. It was mayhem.

Nightingale had just arrived on a plane from San Francisco. He'd flown on many planes, but none had been so cursed with turbulence, swooping right through the eye of the storm. He was pretty sure they'd been the only plane left in the sky, and he was right – all the others had made emergency landings in Philly and New Jersey. But not his. Throughout the final two hours of the flight everyone had been utterly convinced they were going to die. The plane had lurched horribly and went into free falls like a roller coaster ride. Several people threw up their breakfasts into the aisles. A lot of people called out for God to save them. Or Jesus. Nightingale had just closed his eyes, clutched his armrests and hoped for the best.

He lit a cigarette and shivered helplessly in the cold. The cathedral door opened and a pair of black-robed priests shuffled out. They saw Nightingale smoking and shook their heads silently before bowing and trudging through the snow in the direction of the rectory. Nightingale tossed his cigarette into the snow, where it fizzled out and was quickly buried, and then he went inside.

The cathedral was almost deserted. Three worshipers sat in the pews, all women; colored light filtered through the stained glass windows and fell softly on their grey heads. Another figure was present. Sitting in the rear of the church in the shadows, he had open a newspaper and kept checking his wristwatch. He was dressed all in black. Nightingale sat behind him and the man passed him the newspaper with one hand tucked under it, the other on top.

'Paper?' asked the man.

'Thank you,' said Nightingale, opening the paper and carefully inspecting the file within, then flicking through the wad of cash stuffed in an envelope. 'I'll see what the Red Sox are up to.'

'The postseason was in October,' the man said without looking at him.

'Right.' Nightingale new little about American sports. He was more a fan of soccer, though he preferred to call it football. The whole point of football was that it was played with the feet. The American version made no sense to him.

'Mr Wainwright thought the cash might be useful,' said the man. 'Not everywhere takes credit cards where you are going.'

'Where is he?' asked Nightingale.

'Mr. Wainwright is otherwise engaged. But he wants this dealt with as a matter of urgency.'

'Happy to help,' said Nightingale.

Joshua Wainwright was Nightingale's employer, and protector, a billionaire and Satanist who went to a great deal of trouble to make sure that Satanic events stayed out of the mainstream press.

'His secretary briefed you on the case?' asked the man.

'Brief is an apt word. I barely know anything. All I know is there's been a murder in the Berkshires. I wasn't given any details.'

The man lowered his voice. 'Then allow me. In the early morning of December 11th, an elderly couple, Mr. and Mrs. Woodruff of Pine Ridge, were allegedly paid a visit by a couple of kids with jet black eyes. Mr. Woodruff was found lying in a pentagram made with his own blood. Someone had robbed him of his eyeballs and certain other organs which have yet to be accounted for. He'd been carved up like a Thanksgiving turkey. Mrs. Woodruff was found later that morning by a plowman who saw her front door wide open and streaks of blood in the snow. She was cowering in a corner and clawing at the wall with what remained of her fingernails, muttering unintelligible nonsense. She's now in an asylum awaiting trial for the murder of her husband, but just two nights ago she regained enough composure to tell a nurse about the children.'

'She says that children did it?'

The man nodded. 'Black-eyed children, she called them.'

'Children killed and mutilated her husband?'

'That's what she claims, yes. Anyway, Mr. Wainwright wanted you to look into the case so here you are. But personally, I think it's just a load of crap.'

'What do the police think?'

'They think the crazy old bat did it, and I can't say I blame them with her ravings. It doesn't look good. I think she did it and made up the whole black-eyed kids story.'

Jack pursed his lips and was silent a moment. One of the worshipers, a small stout lady with a scarf wrapped around her throat, stood up, crossed herself before the statue of Jesus and wearily began her exit down the aisle, shuffling slowly. They waited for her to pass and for the door to close before they resumed their conversation.

'So,' the man said. 'You ready to head up there?'

Nightingale's eyes widened. 'Now? There's three feet of snow out there. The whole city's been shut down. I don't think anyone will be on the roads for a couple of days.'

The man grinned. 'We got it covered.'

* * *

Nightingale was shivering as they made their way through the blizzard, his eyes clamped shut against the whipping wind and snow. There was no way they were leaving the city. It was impossible. No one was going anywhere. The man took him to a side street completely cleared of snow, and Nightingale looked in awe at the shiny black Humvee with huge studded snow tires and at the massive plow truck parked in front of it. It was the biggest plow truck he had ever seen.

'Mr. Wainwright owns a plowing business,' said the man.

'Of course he does,' muttered Nightingale, who had been hoping to get a night of rest before starting on the case.

'Come on. Daylight's burning.' He got into the rear of the Humvee and Nightingale sat next to him. The driver switched on the engine and flashed his headlights. The plow truck flashed back and started to move. The Humvee followed.

The plow truck did its job; it smashed through the deserted streets, huge white waves splashing away on either side. The Humvee sauntered along easily on the icy roads until they were out of the city and on a road surrounded by snow-covered trees.

The sun set. Floodlights beamed from both vehicles. The man, who still hadn't given his name, was sitting in the passenger seat while a stocky man in black fatigues drove the Humvee. The man passed Nightingale a folder with pictures of Mr. Woodruff's mutilated corpse. They were not pretty. Nightingale read the coroner's report. Missing from the body were both eyes, the liver and the heart. He knew from past experience just how often these organs featured in occult rituals, but he couldn't figure out what business black-eyed children would have with them. But it made even less sense that the man's wife would have carried out the mutilations. Something else must be going on – but what?

Ritual killings had been a common practice in Cameroon – a small country in Africa - up until the 1970's. Some voodoo cultures believed human organs, when eaten, imparted mystical powers. Some believed the taking of organs could bestow great riches and luck. It was a bloody practice that had been used around the world for thousands of years, but in a secluded farm house out in the middle of nowhere in 21st century America? It just didn't make sense. Nightingale supposed there could be other options - such as an illegal organ trade. But who would want the organs of a seventy-five-year-old man? And again, why go through all the trouble of traveling to rural Pine Ridge Massachusetts to get them? There was something evil at play here, something primordial, but Nightingale couldn't figure out what it was. Not without first talking with Mrs. Woodruff and visiting the site of the murder.

'We're making good time,' said the man.

Nightingale took off his coat, bunched it into a ball, and set it against the window to rest his head. His eyes closed and he fell into a dreamless sleep.

* * *

The motel parking lot was empty. Dim light was shining from only one room throughout the entire building: the office. The snow was still falling heavily but at least the roads had been plowed and sanded. A couple of slow moving cars passed as Nightingale grinned at the man in the back of the Humvee. 'You sure you don't want to stick around?' asked Nightingale.

The man shook his head. 'Black-eyed kids, mutilated corpses and a town full of hicks – I think I'll pass.'

Nightingale laughed. 'You take care now,' he said. The man pulled the door shut and the driver gunned the engine. They merged onto the road and went back the way they'd come, soon disappearing around the bend. The plow truck had already left, heading back to Boston.

Nightingale went to the front desk and rang the bell several times before the sleepy proprietor showed his face. Nightingale used one of Wainwright's credit cards to pay in advance and the man gave him the key. His room was dark and cold, with a single bed, an old dresser, and a small round table covered in black cigarette burns and coffee stains. The sheets smelled strongly of bleach. 'Lovely,' muttered Nightingale, but truth be told he'd stayed in worse places. There was a well-thumbed Gideon bible on the bedside table and a small wooden crucifix on the wall by the bathroom door. He was in God-fearing country.

He turned the heat as high as it would go. The radiator made a strange metallic coughing noise before kicking on. He took a hot shower and came out in a towel, checked the fridge, and, seeing it empty, called up the front desk. It rang several times before the proprietor answered in a cranky voice.

'What?'

'Hi,' said Nightingale. 'I was wondering if there's a place nearby where I could get dinner.'

'If you don't mind the chance of getting splattered by a semi, sure.'

'Semi?'

'You Australians don't have semis?'

'I'm British. A semi is a small house to me.'

The man chuckled. 'To us it's a big truck. Whatever. Listen, there's a bar down the road a piece. Hang left and you should be able to walk there in about five minutes.'

Before Nightingale could thank him the line went dead.

The walk was indeed fraught with danger. Each time a car or truck passed he had to hop into a snow bank to avoid being struck. His shoes sloshed with water as he made his way into the dimly-lit tavern on the side of the road, where four old trucks sat parked in the driveway.

'Do you have a Corona?' Nightingale asked an elderly bartender.

'Don't sell that Mexican shit,' said the bartender gruffly.

'A Budweiser will be fine,' said Nightingale as he took off his raincoat and sat at the bar. 'And the menu. Please.'

The bartender pointed at a single sheet of paper on the bar and went to get his Budweiser. There were two things on the menu – steak and fries or a burger and fries – he chose the steak. While he ate he studied the file that he'd brought with him tucked inside his coat. A couple of rough-looking fellows were laughing and drinking at the far end of the bar, watching him. Nightingale kept looking at the file and shaking his head; he couldn't figure out who the black-eyed children were or why they had done what they'd done. There was no logic to it. And yes the violence clearly wasn't random.

He finished his meal, ordered another Budweiser and asked whether he could smoke. The bartender said no.

'Hey whatcha got there?' said one of the men, who'd come up to order another round of drinks. He peered at the photos in the file and grimaced; Nightingale quickly covered them up.

'Oh, sweet Jesus,' said the man. 'Was that ole Woodruff lying there in all that blood?'

'I shouldn't be talking about this,' said Nightingale, tucking the file back into his coat.

The man got his drinks but didn't move. 'Well jeeze, mister, if you're looking at them in a public place I think that makes them public property in a way.'

'Sorry,' said Nightingale. 'My bad.'

The man shrugged. 'Suit yourself. I was just gonna say maybe I know something you don't. But you have yourself a good night now.' He winked sarcastically and turned back to his friends but Nightingale stopped him.

'Hold on. What is it you know that I don't?'

'Any number of things, really.'

Nightingale rolled his eyes. 'I meant about the case.'

The man smiled, and, taking this as an invitation, set the tray of beer down and sat on the stool beside him. 'Well, the fact that ole Woodruff was a die-hard atheist, for one.'

'He was?'

'Yes indeed. That man never went to Church a day in his life. The missus did, of course, went every Sunday, never missed a service. But ole Woodruff didn't believe in God.'

'That's interesting,' said Nightingale, watching the stranger closely to check if he was lying. His years as a police negotiator taught him how to look for tics, but this man wasn't showing any. 'What else?'

The man averted his eyes and shrugged. 'Oh, well… I don't know. I'm forgetful, see.'

Nightingale reached into his pocket with a sigh and took out a couple of bills, laid one on the counter. The man quickly pocketed it and started talking. 'But now I'm really thinking about it, I do remember something. Not about ole Woodruff, because apart from the heathenism he's – was _– as straight as they come. It's about the property they live on. An urban legend old folks used to tell us when we was kids, keep us from going out in the woods at night and that sorta thing.'

Nightingale leaned in, watching him. 'Go on,' he said.

'They said folks used to practice witchcraft in those woods. Long time ago. They used to take the bad children, them ones who misbehaved and wouldn't be missed too awful much, and then they'd, you know… sacrifice them.'

The bartender had been listening in while carelessly polishing a glass. 'Oh yeah,' he said. 'That old wives' tale. Man, those were some creepy stories, I'll tell you that much.' He slapped the cloth on his shoulder and leaned towards them, lowering his voice. 'When I was a teenager and used to go smoke pot up in those woods with my friends, we found all these old kids' shoes. They were tiny, leather, with buckles, you know, like in the olden days.' The bartender shuddered. 'It was just plain creepy, man.'

The guy with the beer smiled mischievously. 'And I might know one more thing,' he said. 'I just might.'

Nightingale set another bill on the counter and again the man snatched it.

'There's this woman in town, old crazy hoot name of Lyda, lives in some dump on the edge of town. She's always making these tinctures and things, keeps to herself though, mainly. No friends, no family. Anyway, there's always been rumors she's a witch. Last fall when all those cats and dogs disappeared and then wound up dead, entrails taken out and all that, a lot of the townsfolk blamed Lyda. I know it was her, personally.'

'How?' asked Nightingale, unable to conceal his interest.

The man shrugged. 'Dunno. Just do,' he said. 'Anyway, food for thought.'

'Lyda, you said?'

'Lyda. Lyda Cornthwaite. You planning to talk to her?'

'I might.'

The man's eyes hardened. 'Well if you do, Mister, you keep my name out of it.'

'I don't know your name,' said Nightingale.

'Let's keep it that way, then,' said the man. He took the beers and sat back down with his friends.

Nightingale finished his Budweiser, paid the tab, and walked back into the snow.

* * *

The next morning Nightingale rose early, rented a car and drove to the local library. The locals hadn't been lying – tales of disappearing children, human sacrifice, and mutilated animals went as far back as the Salem Witch Trials of the late 17th century. One recent case, the subject of a popular film called 'The Blair Witch Project,' told of a man named Rustin Parr, an old hermit who, in 1940s Maryland, lured seven children to his remote cabin with promises of candy and then brutally murdered them. Parr claimed that prior to the murders he'd been visited in the woods by a figure in a black-hooded cloak called the Blair Witch. He said the witch had instructed him to commit the murders. But there was no mention of black-eyed children that he could find.

The snow finally stopped falling as Nightingale made his way down the forest road leading to the Woodruff house. His was the only car on the road. When he arrived he found yellow tape cordoning off the area. He was the only person on the scene. The forensics team had probably already wrapped things up, finding no traces but for those belonging to Mr. and Mrs.

Woodruff. In the eyes of the local police, it was an open and shut case. Mrs. Woodruff was the murderer.

Nightingale ducked under the crime scene tape and opened the door. At his feet was a large red stain. He was in the living room. A portion of the rug had been removed and a bloody pentagram spread across the floor as large as a human body.

He knelt beside the pentagram and inspected the floor carefully. No black candlewax. No visible signs of a satanic ritual.

And then he saw it.

He knew immediately this wasn't the result of an old woman who'd suddenly lost her mind. It wasn't the result of a madman who'd entered the house, either, or of an organ thief looking to make some money. No. This, Nightingale thought, as he looked down at the three deep gouges in the floor which the report had written off as inconsequential, was the work of demons. There was only one problem.

Who let them out of Hell?

* * *

Jack Nightingale knew demonic activity when he saw it. Scratching in the walls, loud knocks, poltergeist activity, sudden cold draughts and smells of sulfur, excrement, or rotten flesh – these were the demons' calling cards. Things always happened in threes. This was to mock the Holy Trinity: the Father, the Son, and the Holy Spirit. Oftentimes demonic activity didn't begin until three o'clock in the morning, not only to mock God, but also because it was the witching hour. Nightingale checked the coroner's report – Mr. Woodruff had died just after 3 a.m. The report mentioned the marks on the floor but didn't say how many there were. The time and the marks told Nightingale that demons were involved – but were the black-eyed children demons? Or children of demons?

He tried to visit Mrs. Woodruff at the Pine Ridge Health Center but was ushered away; they said she'd been trying to take chunks out of the orderlies with her teeth. Nightingale wondered just how devastating it must be to have lost a man she'd been married to for over sixty years.

He decided to investigate the forest surrounding the town. At an old hardware store he asked the man at the cash register if he could point him in the direction of where the children's shoes had been found. He laughed at Nightingale and said he was off his rocker. But an old woman stepped forward and took his arm. 'Those woods are haunted, son,' she said. 'There're ghosts.'

'That's just what I'm hoping to find,' said Nightingale, and the man at the register snickered; the woman ignored him.

'On the road to Chase's Mill,' she said, 'there's an old carriage path in the woods. You'll see it about a quarter mile after the mill. You wanna park there at the edge of the forest and hike your way in. Two, three miles. You'll come to a clearing. That's where you'll find it.'

'Find what?' asked Nightingale.

'What you're looking for.'

An hour later Nightingale had parked his rental car and was walking up a snowy path in a dark wood. Huge pines and spruces swayed over the path, looming like giants and blocking out the sunlight. He could smell pine sap, crisp air and sodden leaves. The first half of the walk was actually quite pleasant, and he had to keep reminding himself that he wasn't on vacation; this was a case he had to solve. But it didn't last long. Soon the air seemed to change; it got colder, and the woods were darker and the trees grew more thickly together so he couldn't see into the woods. He felt a strange tingling sensation creeping up his spine, and gooseflesh stood out on his arms and rubbed against his coat – something was following him. Watching him.

He looked around but saw nothing.

The farther he went, the more he had an urge to go back, but he fought against it. He'd come too far to turn around.

His sense of unease amplified as he stepped out into a clearing and the sun started to set below the trees. There were standing stones arranged in circles throughout the clearing, small ones, large ones; he suspected the entire clearing was just one big circle.

But that wasn't what disturbed him: in every circle lay a rotting animal corpse.

There were foxes, cats, dogs, squirrels, birds. All of them flayed, their jaws open in skeletal grins and screams. It was a killing grounds.

A pack of coyotes began to howl as the sun's light faded through the trees. Nightingale felt a sudden chill course through him. They'd been tracking him all along, he realized. And he had to leave. Now.

He looked around but didn't see anything, so he started walking briskly to the path; when he reached it he took off in a full sprint. All around him the woods were darkening quickly. He thought he heard the sound of paws trampling through snow. He caught quick glimpses of the coyotes through the trees: six of them, their eyes glowing yellow in the dark.

He ran, his Hush Puppies slapping on the wet ground. There was a different feeling in the forest now, as though other eyes were upon him. He felt an ancient evil pursuing him, not the coyotes but something stronger, something overflowing with hatred, something hungry for blood. Every now and then as he looked into the trees, he thought he saw snatches of children in old period clothing, standing perfectly still and watching him with black eyes. But before he could know for sure, they vanished.

He slipped and fell, scraping his hands and knees on the ground. He pushed himself up and ran on. It was dark and ahead the path was fading. He kept tripping into the snow banks on the side of the path. There were no stars or moon above him. The coyotes were close. Just yards away from him. He screamed at them in anger and frustration. The coyotes split up. Two on the left, two on the right, one pursuing him from the back – the alpha in front.

Nightingale stopped in his tracks, gasping for breath. The alpha was massive, its hair greasy and grey. It snarled at him and walked closer, growling. They were circling him now, and the black-eyed children were watching from the forest. They were smiling.

The alpha broke into a run and leapt straight at him. Nightingale reacted instinctively stepping to the side and punching the animal on the nose. It was a good punch, more by luck than judgement, and it had his full weight behind it. Blood spurted from the animal's nose, the coyote yelped and ran off. The others followed.

Nightingale stood and watched them go, his fists still clenched. 'That's it?' he shouted. 'One punch and that's it?' He shook his head. 'Pussies!' He looked around. The coyotes had gone and so had the black-eyed children. He turned and took off down the path.

The rental car had been vandalized. The windows were smashed in, the leather seats were torn, and wires were sticking out from under the steering wheel. It looked as if they'd been chewed. But no animal had done the damage. There were scratches that could only have come from a child's fingernails, though Nightingale had no idea what sort of child had the strength to gouge paintwork. Nightingale swore out loud. It was a ten-mile walk to town, and it was freezing cold. Night had fallen.

* * *

Ten miles away, on the outskirts of Pine Ridge, Clint Broadbent, a middle-aged lumber yard worker, was nursing a glass of whiskey in front of the wood stove and falling into a stupor. Clint's wife had left him several months ago for another man, so, having never learned how to cook, he decided he'd start eating liquid dinners instead. He had almost fallen asleep when he heard a faint scratching in the walls. His eyes opened, and suddenly he felt very threatened. The scratching grew louder. He stumbled to the gun cabinet and withdrew a .22 long rifle he used for hunting deer. He released the safety and aimed at the ceiling where the scratching was coming from, and fired.

The scratching stopped.

Sheetrock dust fell through the hole.

Silence.

Clint smiled in triumph. He set the gun on the kitchen counter and went back to his La-Z-Boy, but then there came a knock at the door. Then another knock. And another. Three loud knocks.

'Jesus Christ, who is it!' bellowed Clint, opening the door.

Standing in front of him were the most disturbing children he'd ever seen in his life – their eyes were pitch black and their faces blank. When the little boy asked him in a toneless voice, 'Can we come in?' he shook his head and tried to close the door. But the boy had nudged his shoe in the doorjamb.

'Please,' said the boy. 'We're hungry. We need your help.'

Clint's voice was shaking: 'Who… are you?'

'Our parents are coming.'

'Good. You can wait for them outside.'

The boy pushed and despite using all his strength, Cliff could not close the door. He turned and hurried to the rifle on the counter. But before he got there he heard a loud roar and felt his body being torn to pieces.

* * *

Nightingale didn't have to walk the full ten miles. Police cruisers were speeding down the main road. One of the cruisers stopped and a policeman got out and leveled a gun at him. Nightingale had blood on his hands from where he'd hit the coyote.

'Freeze!'

Nightingale froze.

'Put your hands on your head!'

Nightingale did as he was asked. 'I'm a detective,' he said weakly, shivering from the cold. The cop was clamping cuffs around his wrists.

'We'll see about that.'

An hour later after the cops had tested the blood and realised it wasn't human, he was released from the police station and offered a lift to his motel. Apparently there'd been another murder in town. A man was found with his arms, legs and head torn off and placed in another bloody pentagram. The town was mortified. The police were on edge.

'Sorry about that,' said the officer as they drove back to the motel. 'I just saw the blood and didn't know what to do. I thought you were the killer. Man, a coyote pack?' he said in disbelief. Nightingale nodded. 'I ain't never heard tell of that before. These are strange times, when a man can't even go on a stroll through the woods without being attacked by animals.' He looked at Nightingale suspiciously. 'Is there something going on here? I mean, really going on?'

'How do you mean?' asked Nightingale.

The policeman shrugged, tapping the wheel. 'I just feel it, you know? Like this whole damn place is about to go up in flames. You ever felt that way before? In your heart? Hell, scratch that, in your soul?'

'Yes,' said Nightingale. 'I've felt it.'

'Well whatever it is, I just hope it's over soon.'

The cop dropped Nightingale at his motel and drove off. Nightingale's jaw dropped when he opened the door. The room had been ransacked. The furniture was torn, broken, flipped over. Large concussions had been made in the walls and ceiling and the stained carpeting had been ripped up. Broken glass was everywhere. And there scratches on the walls that could only have been done by a child's hand. The crucifix was untouched, though, as was the Gideon bible. Nightingale took the small crucifix off the wall and slipped it into his raincoat pocket. He had a feeling the way things were going it might come in useful.

Nightingale rubbed his fingers against his temples and closed his eyes, sitting on what remained of the mattress. There was one thing for sure, he thought. This was no ordinary case.

* * *

The motel proprietor was furious the next morning. At first he blamed Nightingale, but then he checked the CCTV footage and eventually found two children, a boy and a girl, letting themselves into Nightingale's room the previous evening. The picture was blurry so their faces couldn't be seen, nor could they see how they had gained access to the room.

'Did you give them the key?' asked the proprietor.

'Of course not,' said Nightingale. He took his key from the pocket of his raincoat and showed it to him.

'So how did they open the door?'

'That's a good question. Are you going to call the cops?'

The proprietor shrugged. 'They won't do nothing. Just kids. And the damage is superficial. The maid will sort it out.'

Joshua Wainwright paid for the totaled rental car – in full – and they supplied Nightingale with another. Nightingale hadn't eaten since yesterday morning, having decided to fast. He also drove to the local church to attend confession in the hopes that his soul might be purged when the time came to battle the demons or devils plaguing this town. There was no question it would be soon.

That afternoon Nightingale pulled into Pine Ridge Health Center, a large brick building with an American flag flapping in the wind. He lit a cigarette outside and smoked, watching the locals go about their daily routines, picking up the mail, redeeming bottles, buying groceries, delivering loads of firewood. Nightingale couldn't help noticing the expressions of fear plastered on their faces.

When he'd finished his cigarette he went in and asked an orderly about seeing Mrs. Woodruff. The young nurse said they weren't taking any more police visitors; the poor woman had gone through enough already, contrary to popular opinion. Nightingale said he wasn't police but family and that he hadn't been allowed in to see her yesterday either. The nurse eyed him up and down, as if trying to find a fatal flaw in his story to turn him away.

'You're Australian?' said the nurse.

'British. Well, English.'

The nurse frowned. 'What's the difference?'

'English is, well, English, But British can be English or Scottish or Welsh. And Northern Irish.'

'The Irish are British?'

'The Irish in the north are, yes. It's complicated.'

'But Mrs Woodruff isn't English or British or Irish.'

'She's British on her father's side,' lied Nightingale. 'We're distant relatives, but relatives nonetheless. I was in Boston when I heard what happened; I'm just appalled.'

The nurse's face was grave. 'Well, Lord knows she needs family in a time like this,' she said. 'Her granddaughter came in to see her few days ago and left in a hurry. When I asked what was the matter, she just kept saying, 'That ain't Granma! That ain't Grandma!' Now what do you make of that Mr...'

'Nightingale.'

'What do you make of that Mr. Nightingale?'

Nightingale shrugged. 'Grief,' he lied. He certainly knew what to make of that... and if his suspicions were correct, it was not good.

The nurse led him through a series of corridors with drugs posters lining the walls, their shoes sticking to the linoleum as they walked. They stopped at a door and the nurse looked at him sorrowfully. 'We've had to sedate her,' she said. 'She was just too darn violent. She tried jumping out the window yesterday afternoon. She's very disturbed, I'm afraid.'

Nightingale said nothing. He simply nodded as if distracted.

'Well,' said the nurse, biting her bottom lip as if to indicate this was a lost cause, but she was glad he was trying. 'Good luck.'

She turned on her heels and walked back down the hallway. Nightingale took a deep breath and opened the door.

Mrs. Woodruff was lying in bed, her eyes closed, a thin line of drool glistening on her chin. Nightingale sat in a chair beside her. She appeared to be sleeping. He took a napkin and gently wiped the drool away. She stirred, opened her eyes.

'Sorry to disturb you,' said Nightingale.

'Who're you?'

Nightingale was surprised by the direct question. Relieved, even.

'My name's Jack Nightingale,' he said. 'I'm a private investigator. I want to find out what really happened to your husband.'

The woman sighed and turned around, facing the window. 'So you're not one of them,' she said.

'Who?'

Nightingale knew she was old, but he couldn't help noticing how much older she looked than in the photographs he'd seen of her. Her face was ashen, her brown eyes hovering in pools of shadow, everything about her sunken and wrinkled. It was as if she was... dead.

Mrs. Woodruff turned and looked him in the eyes, smiling. Her eyes were wide and childlike, and set in that ancient face with the wide grin, it gave Nightingale the creeps. She suddenly looked insane.

'The cats,' said the woman pleasantly. 'The cats, the cats, the cats,' she moved her head from side to side as she said this. 'You know, little felines, little furry things, with flesh and blood and gore!' She had raised her voice so that she was almost shouting.

Nightingale jumped back abruptly at this outburst, but Mrs. Woodruff didn't seem to notice; she was flicking her fingers madly and moving her head as if she was singing a tune, and for the first time Nightingale got a glimpse of the bloodied stubs where the fingernails had broken off. She smiled like an excited little girl, now singing a nursery rhyme in a broken, gravelly voice that turned Nightingale's blood cold: 'There was an old lady who swallowed a fly. I don't know why she swallowed a fly. I guess she'll die.

'There was an old lady who swallowed a spider that wiggled and jiggled and tickled insider her. She swallowed the spider to catch the fly. I don't know why she swallowed a fly. I guess she'll die.

'There was an old lady who swallowed a bird. How absurd! To swallow a bird! She swallowed the bird to catch the spider that wiggled and jiggled and tickled inside her. She swallowed the spider to catch the fly. I don't know why she swallowed a fly. I guess she'll die.

'Cat . . . Imagine that! She swallowed a cat. Dog . . . What a hog! She swallowed a dog. Goat . . . She opened her throat and in walked a goat. Cow . . . I don't know how she swallowed that cow.

'There was an old lady, she swallowed a horse. She died of course!'

Mrs. Woodruff sat up straight and glared at him. Her eyes were black. She laughed maniacally in a deep baritone voice. For the first time Nightingale noticed she wasn't wearing restraints, and he was afraid.

'You can't have her!' the voice bellowed. 'She's mine!'

In a fraction of a second, Mrs. Woodruff was out of her bed and grasping Nightingale by the throat, choking him. An IV stand fell to the floor with a loud clatter. Two nurses rushed into the room and tried to subdue her, but with superhuman strength she flung them across the room and they smashed into the walls. She peered into Nightingale's face. Her mouth was full of froth. Her features had transformed into those of an animal, she wasn't human any more

'I killed him, Nightingale,' the thing said. 'And I'll kill others too.'

She jumped up and burst through the door, knocking over another nurse, and took off down the hallway faster than any eighty-year-old woman ever ran.

* * *

Night had fallen. The woods were silent, and a gentle snowfall descended from the sky. In the old shack at the edge of town, Lyda Cornthwaite was chanting an incantation, hunched over a human heart boiling in a pot. The language she spoke was ancient and dead, but the black-eyed children understood it; it was their language, after all.

They stood in a dark corner of the shack while Lyda spoke the words that would summon their parents from Hell.

* * *

Nightingale was shaken. He didn't know what to believe anymore. Mrs. Woodruff was clearly possessed by an extremely powerful entity – probably a devil. Was it the same devil that had killed her husband? Did it possess her and then kill her husband? Were there more of them? And what part did the black-eyed children play in all this? These were the questions he asked himself as he drove to Lyda Cornthwaite's house. The one piece of good news was that it was a possession that he was dealing with, and almost certainly an involuntary one. He doubted that Mrs Woodruff had wanted her husband dead, so whatever it was that had possessed her had been acting on its own. A forced possession was always easier to deal with than an entity that had been invited in. The town had gone completely mad. Everybody had heard that a murderous psychopath was on the loose. Police cars with sirens and flashing lights sped by on the roads as they were called in to investigate potential disturbances – whether they were real or imagined, Nightingale didn't know, but he prayed for the second one. Something horrible was happening to this town. And according to the man he'd met in the bar, Lyda Cornthwaite was a witch who might know what was going on.

Pulling into Lyda's house, he saw a light on. He parked the car and walked towards the house he noticed he didn't hear any sound. No animals. No cars. No townsfolk. Nothing. It might have been peaceful under normal circumstances, but it felt creepy now, as though the whole forest had eyes that were watching his every movement, taking stock of him, summing him up as if preparing to devour him.

He went up to the door and knocked. There was no answer. Nightingale knocked again, louder. He thought he could hear something from inside, some vague mutterings. He leaned his head closer and listened: a strange guttural voice was reading off an incantation. He recognized it immediately – it was a summons.

He kicked the door open to see an old haggard woman covered in blood. She was bent over a pot that was spewing a disgusting scent throughout the cabin, waving her clawed fingers in the air and chanting the summons. Seeing Nightingale, she bared her rotten teeth and growled. Two children in the corner were gazing at him with pitch black eyes. They moved towards him.

'Stop!' shouted Nightingale. 'You don't know what you're doing!'

'She knows,' said the boy.

'Yes, she knows,' echoed the girl.

They were coming around the table from different directions. The witch kept chanting, louder, faster.

'It's too late,' said the boy, his voice dream-like and far away. 'It's finished.'

'I said stop!'

'Our parents are on their way to the house now. They'll kill everyone. The mother. The father. The two children asleep in their beds. They'll butcher them while they're still alive.'

'Where?' asked Nightingale. There was a kitchen knife on the table and he grabbed it. The children were two yards away now, drawing closer.

'Cedar Street,' said the boy. 'But it doesn't matter. You're coming with us.'

Nightingale ran towards the woman. The children clawed at him. He felt icy cold pain seizing his entire body. The woman raised a long bloody knife, shrieked, and went after him. The children's cold hands were on him, trying to pull him down to Hell.

The woman lashed out with her knife but Nightingale was quicker. He shoved his knife into her throat and she fell back, blood spurting from an ugly wound. She span around, blood spraying over the wall, and then slumped to the ground, a nasty gurgling sound coming from her throat, which gradually subsided as she went still.

The hands still grabbed at him but he pulled the crucifix from his pocket and they vanished immediately. He stood where he was gasping for breath, the crucifix in one hand, the bloody knife in the other.

* * *

The devil that possessed Mrs. Woodruff was positively ravenous for blood. It wanted to taste it, the warmth, the sweet candy, gushing from the flesh of an innocent. It didn't have much time; it knew that. The witch-lady was dead. The incantation had fallen through, preventing its masters from rising. But it would summon them. Yes, it would.

The devil ran with lightning speed across the deserted yards. It crouched on all fours like an animal, its mouth slobbering a mixture of mucus and blood. It wailed from time to time, moaned with excitement, squealed like a pig. Its movements were erratic and unpredictable.

All the lights were on in the homes on this street. No one was outside. They were too afraid.

Too afraid of me, the devil thought.

Finding the house, the devil smashed through a back window and crawled inside, its flesh getting lacerated by the broken glass, but it didn't mind; it didn't feel pain like humans did.

It heard a commotion as someone came down the stairs. It was the husband, wielding a baseball bat. He saw the devil and started shaking. 'Oh my God,' he said, gripping the bat uncertainly. 'Honey call the police! Now!'

The devil began its strange clucking noise, which came from so deep in its throat it seemed disembodied, not belonging to the creature.

It used to be a woman, an old woman, but now it was something else entirely. It's face was a grotesque scowl. Its teeth were long and sharp and slick with blood. Its eyes were black like oil and evil; staring into them made the man wail in despair.

Still crouched on all fours, it started galloping towards the man, galloping like a horse, its body soaring high in the air. It reached the stairs with a cunning grin and opened its mouth wide. The man shouted, dropped the bat and fumbled up the stairs, but the thing was on him, teeth and claws tearing into his flesh. His screams filled the house.

It bit into his throat.

At the top of the stairs a woman was holding a phone to her ear. Now she screamed, too.

The thing looked up, craned its head. 'I've come for the children,' it growled, and began chasing the woman screaming down the hallway. The children appeared from the doors in time to see the devil pounce on their mother and raise its slobbering jaws.

'Stop!'

A man's powerful voice echoed through the corridor. The devil's head shot up and it began to sniff the air.

'In the name of the Lord Jesus Christ I command you to stop!'

The devil dropped the woman. It turned around.

Jack Nightingale was standing at the top of the stairs. He was holding a crucifix in one hand a Gideon Bible in the other. He began to recite the Lord's prayer. The devil charged at him. It hooked its fingers into claws and leapt in the air, its jaw distended to reveal a row of razor sharp teeth. In that moment Nightingale raised the crucifix and the devil came crashing into it, then sprawled backwards in a flash of white light. Nightingale advanced.

'I cast you out, unclean spirit, along with every Satanic power of the enemy, every specter from hell, and all your fellow companions; in the name of our Lord Jesus Christ. Begone and stay far from this creature of God. For it is He who commands you, He who flung you headlong from the heights of Heaven into the depths of hell. It is He who commands you, He who once stilled the sea and the wind and the storm. Hearken, therefore, and tremble in fear, Satan, you enemy of the faith, you foe of the human race, you begetter of death, you robber of life, you corrupter of justice, you root of all evil and vice; seducer of men, betrayer of nations, instigator of envy, font of avarice, fomenter of discord, author of pain and sorrow. I cast you out!'

The devil was writhing and squealing on the ground. The mother and children watched in terror as Nightingale pressed the crucifix to the creature's forehead and its flesh smoldered.

'Depart, then, impious one, depart, accursed one, depart with all your deceits, for God has willed that man should be His temple...'

The devil stopped squirming and went limp. Nightingale's voice softened.

'Tell me your name, devil,' he said.

'Boliath,' whispered the creature. 'Leave me! Leave me!'

'Boliath, creature of Satan, I command you in the name of the Lord Jesus Christ, depart from this child of God and never return! I cast you out!'

The horror in the woman dissolved. The claws were reduced. The black hollows around the eyes went grey. The fangs sank down. Mrs. Woodruff looked up at Nightingale with glossy eyes. She moved her hand up to his face and touched his cheek softly.

'It's gone,' she said.

'I know.'

'Lester... I see Lester. Oh, my! He's so handsome, and young again!'

'Go to him,' Nightingale said gently. 'Go be with him now.'

Mrs. Woodruff smiled and closed her eyes. A moment later her hand fell from his cheek and she was at rest.

Nightingale stood up. The mother and children were staring at him.

'You're going to be ok,' he said. 'It's over.'

The mother gathered her children in her arms and they began to cry together. Nightingale went to check on the husband and was amazed to see he was still breathing. His throat was bleeding badly, so Nightingale took off his coat, ripped a piece of his shirt and bound it tightly over the wound. He held it with both hands until the police and the paramedics arrived.

* * *

Back at his motel, Jack Nightingale fell onto his bed with a groan. Less than a minute later, his mobile rang. 'Hello?' he answered.

'Jack?'

Nightingale sat up. He recognized the Texan drawl. 'Hi, Joshua,' he said.

'I hear you had one hell of a time,' said Wainwright. 'No pun intended.'

'How'd you hear about that so fast? I just got back to my motel room.'

'I've got my ways, Jack, don't worry about it. So... is everything settled then? The children are back in the nursery, so to speak?'

'Yes,' said Nightingale. 'They're gone. It's over. And I'm in need of a vacation. A long vacation.'

'You're one tough sonofabitch, you know that?'

Nightingale didn't answer; he heard something in the bathroom.

Something like scratching.

'Sorry, Joshua. I'm going to have to let you go.'

'But Jack I—'

Nightingale picked up the crucifix. He heard it again. Scratching. Like fingernails raking across the bathroom wall.

Cautiously he moved to the door and nudged it open.

The black-eyed children were standing in the tub, fully-clothed, scratching away at the wall with elongated fingernails. They turned to Nightingale and growled. He held the crucifix up in front of him. The children raced towards him, but they disappeared just at the moment they were to collide with his body.

They were gone.

On the wall behind the bathtub they had scrawled one word: Soon.

Nightingale took a deep breath and slowly let it out.

'Well,' he said. 'You know where to find me.'

He put on his coat and went out the door in the direction of the nearest bar. He needed a drink.

TRACKS

The two people in the rear of the black SUV had been married a total of four times in between them, but never to each other, which was why they'd driven out to The Tracks in separate vehicles. Chris had parked the Crown Victoria sedan a hundred yards back down the track and walked to the SUV where Ronnie sat waiting in the driver's seat. Ronnie had turned off the headlights, got out, opened the rear door and they'd both climbed in. They shared twenty urgent minutes behind the heavily tinted privacy glass, no sound leaking from the vehicle into the moonless night.

When they were done, they returned to the front of the SUV, lit cigarettes and smoked in silence for a while, from time to time turning to look at each other by the dull red glow of the dashboard lights. It was Chris who spoke first.

'Where's this gonna take us? Two years now, and we're still sneaking round like a couple of thieves.'

Ronnie shrugged. 'We've both got kids. Do you want to destroy two families?'

'I hate living a lie.'

'That lie keeps you in your job. Do you think they'd let you stay on if this got out?'

Chris grimaced. 'Of course not.'

'And I doubt I'd be allowed to keep my job either. This is a small town. It's not like I could move across a city and find another job.'

'So what do we do?'

Ronnie sighed. 'I don't know. Seems we can't go forward and we can't leave it alone.'

'You'd think... Holy shit, what the Hell is that?'

The two of them gaped through the windscreen in the direction of The Tracks as a thunderous roar overwhelmed their ears and a blinding light approached at frightening speed. No, not a light, a collection of lights, red, blue and green, flickering through the trees racing towards them as the noise grew to a deafening pitch and volume. And then it was gone.

The night was plunged into blackness once again, and simultaneously a heart-rending scream of agonized terror cut through the sudden silence.

'What the hell...' said Ronnie, grasping Chris's arm. 'What was that?'

'It looked like a train, but that's impossible. I'll go take a look.'

'Don't be crazy. Let's just get the hell out of here.'

'I'm the Chief of Police, babe. I have to see what's going on. That scream could have been human.'

'It was a coyote.'

'You don't know that.'

'Please, let's just go. You can call it in later anonymously if you want?'

'And say what? We saw a train down at The Tracks? Come on Ronnie, there's nothing out there to hurt us, there can't be. I'll get the flashlight out of the back.'

'You're not leaving me here alone?'

'Then come with me. I've got my gun, don't worry.' Chris fetched the flashlight and they walked in the direction the scream had come from. The powerful flashlight showed the trees ahead of them and the glint of the tracks beyond. It took them nearly ten minutes to pick their way across the rough ground to the tracks, and then to walk east along them. Two hundred yards further down, they found what they were looking for. Chris bent over it and cursed. 'What the hell happened?'

There was a body lying on the tracks, a body that had probably once been a man but which was now a mass of mangled meat and clothing.

Ronnie stared at the remains in horror. 'Looks like he hasn't got an unbroken bone left in his body.'

'What could do that to him?' asked Chris.

'You ask me, it looks like he was hit by a train.'

'How could that be?' Chris stood up and shone the beam of the flashlight along the tracks, to where the rusty rails came to a sudden stop fifty yards away, to be replaced by grass, weeds and bushes. 'There hasn't been a train along here in fifty years.'

* * *

Nightingale was asleep, but he wasn't asleep. In fact, he wasn't sure where he was. Everything was misty, or cloudy, or somewhere between. He had been asleep, he was fairly sure of that, then he thought he had woken up but then it became clear that he was still dreaming. The mist was heavier, closer to the ground so he couldn't feel his feet. Then he realised he actually couldn't feel anything, it was as if he was wrapped in cotton wool. He couldn't hear anything either. He sniffed and wasn't in the least surprised to discover that he had no sense of smell.

'It takes some getting used to, the astral plane,' said a voice. He turned and saw the tiny bird-like figure of Alice Steadman behind him. She was smiling up at him, dressed in a long black shirt and black leggings with a thick leather belt with a silver buckle in the shape of a quarter moon. Her grey hair was tied back in a ponytail and her skin was wrinkled and almost translucent but her emerald green eyes had the burning intensity of a teenager.

'You could have phoned, Mrs Steadman.' He wasn't sure how to greet her so he just gave her a small wave.

She smiled showing tiny white perfect teeth. 'You are forever changing your number,' she said. 'And this is so much more personal. So where are you?'

'Just outside of Denver, Colorado.'

'Working for Mr Wainwright?'

Nightingale smiled. He knew that Mrs Steadman didn't have an especially high opinion of his employer. 'I'm afraid so.'

'I wonder if I might ask a favour of you,' she said, and waved at a white wrought iron bench that seemed to have appeared from nowhere.

'Of course,' said Nightingale. They sat down on the bench.

Mrs Steadman put her tiny hands in her lap. 'A friend of mine has a problem. More than a problem. Her father has died in circumstances that are somewhat strange. The local police don't seem to know what happened and my friend feels they are being less than helpful.'

'I'd be happy to help.'

'Excellent. She is in a place called Scarsdale, in Utah. I believe it's not too far from Denver.'

'I'll go tomorrow,' said Nightingale. 'So tell me what happened?'

'I'd rather you heard it from Annette.' She reached over and gently touched the back of his hand. Instantly Nightingale realised that he knew Annette Carson's name, address and telephone number.

'That's a great trick, Mrs Steadman.'

She giggled girlishly. 'Why Mr Nightingale, that's not a trick. It's magic.'

'Is this Annette a Wicca person, like yourself?'

'Just a friend,' she said. 'I sold her a candle once and she became a regular visitor to my shop. She knew of my interest in the Wicca world, of course, and she called me today for some advice. The best advice I could come up with was for her to talk with you.'

With that, Nightingale awoke. He glanced at the clock radio on the table next to his bed. It was just after six o'clock in the morning. He groped for his iPhone and Googled Annette Carson's address. It was about six hundred miles from his motel on the outskirts of Denver, so he figured it would be at least a ten-hour drive. He sighed, rolled off the bed and headed for the bathroom.

* * *

Nightingale had picked up an Avis rental when he'd arrived at Denver airport. It was a large white SUV and more than up to the eleven hour drive to Scarsdale, a small town just outside the northern border of the Navajo Nation reservation. Nightingale relied on the SatNav to guide him and it did a fine job of getting him there, ordering him around in a voice that reminded him of one of his primary school teachers, Mrs Ellis, who thought that one way of making him more attentive during lessons was to force him to stand in the corridor in his duffel coat whenever he spoke out of turn.

Nightingale had never been to Utah before, nor really ever heard of it all that much. It seemed to sit in the middle of The USA without doing too much, except, as he'd discovered from Google, being the only state in America which had a majority religion - The Church Of Jesus Christ Of Later Days Saints. The Mormons.

He drove into Scarsdale from the north, past a tower and machinery which was fenced off and bore the legend 'G&L Hydraulic Fracturing Company'. It was a little after five o'clock in the evening when he arrived in front of Annette Carson's trim wooden house set back a little from the road. He parked and walked up to the front door. It opened just before he reached it. 'Are you Jack?' asked a woman who looked to be in her late forties now, elegant and attractive in a maroon skirt and jacket over a white blouse. Her chestnut hair hung loose over her shoulders.

'Jack Nightingale, yes. Mrs Steadman told you I was coming?'

'I was starting to get worried,' she said, holding the door open for him.

'I had to drive from Denver,' he said.

'You could have flown.'

'I'm not a fan of planes,' he said.

She showed him into her neatly furnished lounge, got him settled on the sofa and brought coffee. Nightingale couldn't see any ashtrays, so resigned himself to abstinence for a while.

'How much did Alice tell you?' asked Annette.

'Very little, except that you'd recently lost your father, and there was something pretty odd about it,'

'Alice is a dear friend,' she said, and Nightingale couldn't miss the tears in her eyes, though she quickly blinked them away. 'It's been years since I saw her. In the flesh, anyway.'

'You do that astral plane thing?'

She nodded. 'You too?'

'I'm a beginner,' he said. 'She can contact me but I can't really be active, if you see what I mean.'

'It takes practice.' She paused, maybe gathering her courage, then blurted it out quickly. 'Okay, I work here as an attorney, have done ever since I moved back home. I lived in London for a while, had an English husband. He died and afterwards I couldn't face living there alone so I came back. I lived here alone until four years ago, and then I moved my father in. He was getting a little unsteady on his feet. My mother died many years ago, when I was at college. Breast cancer.' She paused and Nightingale realised she was close to tears.

'I'm sorry,' said Nightingale.

She forced a smile. 'She died a long time ago. When I was a teenager. Anyway, having Dad here worked fine until around eighteen months ago, when...when...'

Another pause. Nightingale smiled encouragingly, and finally she spat it out.

'My father started to show signs of dementia, Alzheimer's. It came on quickly and got worse pretty rapidly. Money wasn't a problem, so I scaled back my work so I could look after him better. I didn't want to put him into a home.'

Nightingale nodded. He'd seen enough of care homes to know he didn't want to end his days in one.

She went on. 'I had some help, of course. A nurse slept here two nights a week and I had a day carer who came when I really needed to work. And a friend or two who'd stay with him if anything came up and I needed to go out. By the end he rarely recognized me, talked nonsense and couldn't do anything for himself. Until last Saturday.' She took a deep breath. 'I went to bed around ten, I'm usually quite tired. I'd given my father his sleeping powder, that generally kept him out all night, I woke up around four in the morning, needed to go to the bathroom, and looked in on him on the way back. He was gone. Vanished. His bedding was disturbed but his slippers were still by the side of his bed.'

'Was the window open?'

'No, nor the front door. But he could have pulled that closed after him, if he'd left, obviously.'

'And then? What happened then?'

'I called the police to report him missing but they had already found the body. They hadn't identified it, but after I phoned they put two and two together. They found him six miles away. Down by The Tracks.'

'The Tracks.' repeated Nightingale. 'The railway tracks?'

'Not really. Well, yes, but not any more, if you see what I mean. The railroad used to run just north of here, but they changed the route more than fifty years ago, and tore up most of the tracks. For some reason they left about half a mile of it in place. I think it might have been something to do with the war, or the company going out of business. I know there's actually quite a lot of abandoned railroad all over Utah. Anyway, out there it's pretty isolated and quiet, I think couples park down there sometimes. A sort of lover's lane. And that's where they found him. Dead.' She shuddered, then reached for a box of tissues and dabbed her eyes with one.

'How had he died?' asked Nightingale quietly.

'They still don't know. Almost every bone in his body had been broken. Almost as if he'd been hit by a train, but that's not possible. Hasn't been one around in decades.'

'A car? A truck?'

'Couldn't be, a car couldn't drive along near those tracks. You can't get to within fifty yards of the tracks in a car. You have to walk. And they say he died where they found him.'

'Could he have fallen from a height?'

'Not out there. Not anywhere around here. Scarsdale doesn't do skyscrapers. How did he get there, Mr Nightingale? That's what I don't understand. There's no way he could have walked seven miles in two hours.'

'How was he dressed?'

'When they found him he was dressed the same as when I last saw him. Just pajamas.'

'Nothing on his feet?'

'Nothing. As I said, his slippers were still in the room.'

Nightingale nodded again. 'Did he have any enemies?'

She snorted. 'Not before his illness, as far as I know. And why would a man with advanced dementia have enemies?'

Nightingale exhaled heavily. This one made no sense on any level. 'Do you have a dollar Annette?'

Her eyebrows shot up in surprise.

'Of course, why?'

'If you give me a dollar then officially I'm working for you and I can ask questions on your behalf. Otherwise I'm just a busybody.'

She fumbled in her purse and handed him a dollar bill.

'OK, now I'm working for you, and maybe I can persuade some people to talk to me. I'll get on it and see if I can make some sense of things.'

'Please, Mr Nightingale. I can't stand not knowing what happened to him.' She dabbed at her eyes again.

* * *

It was getting close to six o'clock but Nightingale figured he might as well swing by police headquarters before finding a place to stay. His SatNav took him to the building, a two-storey nondescript cube with two cruisers parked outside. He gave his name and business to the bored-looking desk sergeant and a few minutes later was shown into office of Chief Christine Davis. Nightingale was a little surprised that the chief was a woman but he tried not to show it. She looked to be around forty-five, kept herself in good shape and her hair was an attractive shade of golden blond that looked too even to be natural She was wearing a black pant-suit, the cut of the jacket slightly spoiled by the bulge of the gun under her armpit. She looked at the card and smiled.

'So, Jack Nightingale, PI, what can I do for you?'

'Annette Carson has asked me to help look into the death of her father.'

Chief Davis stopped smiling and tossed his card on the desk.

'Well now,' she said. 'And there was me thinking that was what I was paid to do.'

Nightingale held up his hands. 'I'm not looking to interfere. Maybe I have more free time than your officers, perhaps I could help, that's really all I want to do.'

The smile returned. 'Are you a Brit?'

He nodded. 'But based in the US for the moment. I just want to help Annette. She's a friend of an old friend of mine in London.'

The Chief's smile widened. 'Annette's well thought of in this town. As was her father, Paulie.'

'You knew him?'

'Everyone did, he'd been Mayor here a while back. Before he got sick.'

'But nobody recognizes his body? I heard that it was only when Annette phoned in to report her father missing that the body was identified.'

'Nobody would have known it was him. It was smashed to hell. I've been to my fair share of car crashes, but this was something else. He was mangled.'

'The tracks are in the middle of nowhere, right?'

The Chief nodded. 'That's right.'

'So who called it in?'

'Didn't give a name.'

'Man or woman?' asked Nightingale.

'Man.'

'And your switchboard didn't get a number? I thought all calls to the cops were recorded these days'

'He didn't call the switchboard, it came to me direct.'

'Is that normal?'

The Chief shrugged. 'To be honest it's not normal to find bodies in Scarsdale. Lots of people here would know my number. Whoever called me withheld theirs.'

Nightingale had the impression there was something she was holding back, but decided to change tack. 'So what do you think was the cause of death?'

'The ME says his injuries would be consistent with a train, a fall from a great height, being caught in heavy machinery, maybe hit by a bus, or a truck. None of which are possible, unless he was killed elsewhere and brought there. And that didn't happen. His injuries would have killed him instantly, but there was plenty of blood where he lay.'

'So what's your best guess?' asked Nightingale.

The Chief shrugged. 'I don't have one. It just makes no sense at all.'

'Are you treating it as a murder investigation?'

The Chief grimaced. 'The problem is, we don't know what caused Mr Carson's death. It was definitely abnormal in that it most certainly wasn't natural causes, but it's not as if he was shot or strangled or poisoned.'

'What about an animal attack? A bear or something?'

'We don't have bears here. But there were no teeth marks or claw marks or anything that suggests it was an animal. The thing is, until we know for sure what the cause of death is, we can't treat it as a murder. Or anything else for that matter.' She threw up her hands. 'It's a mystery, Mr Nightingale. A real mystery.'

Nightingale got up. 'Do you mind if I talk to the ME?'

'Sure, I don't see why not. We don't run to a full-time ME here, so we use Doctor McKenzie. She works out of a clinic on the other side of town. I'll call her and tell her to expect you.' She looked at her watch. 'Probably best if you swing by tomorrow, she'll probably have left her office by now.'

* * *

Nightingale booked himself into the Paradise Motel, about a mile down the road from the police station. It was far from paradise, but it was clean and comfortable and they served a half-decent breakfast in the diner by the main entrance. The next morning he had eggs and toast and two cups of coffee before driving around to Dr McKenzie's clinic. He identified himself at reception and within minutes he was in the presence of Veronica J. McKenzie MD, a fact that was confirmed by the wooden plaque on her desk. Dr McKenzie was tall and slim, wearing a tight olive tee-shirt under a gray jacket. Her black hair was cut short and her brown eyes shone with a fierce intelligence. Nightingale felt himself being weighed up as he sat down opposite her. She was wearing a wedding ring and there was a framed photograph behind her of a husband and two young boys. 'Chris says you're investigating the death of Mr Carson?'

'I've been hired by Mr Carson's daughter. She just wants to know what happened to her father.'

'We'd all like to know that,' said the doctor. 'It's a real mystery. I've never seen anything like it before.'

'The cause of death is still unknown?'

'Not at all. Cause of death is very obvious. Extreme trauma. Smashed all the major bones, ruptured almost every organ he had. Trouble is there's nothing that could have caused it. No fall, no train, no truck, no steam hammer. The only time I ever saw anything like it was when I worked in Chicago, years ago in a hospital. A guy jumped in front of a train. But of course that's not possible here.'

'So do you have a theory?'

The doctor shrugged. 'It's not my job to theorize, I just give the medical facts. The facts are clear. But I have absolutely no idea what caused his injuries.'

'Did you know Paulie Carson?'

'Of course. He was my patient. Has been for five years or so. I was trying to help him with his dementia, but there's not much that can be done.'

'Could he have walked out there on his own?'

She shook her head. 'I would say absolutely not, he wasn't in great physical shape, certainly not up to hiking seven miles in bare feet. And he had severe Alzheimer's, he had no idea who people were, maybe not even himself.'

'So someone must have taken him.'

'It would seem so. But nobody has any idea why. Why go to all that trouble to kill a harmless old man with advanced dementia? If someone wanted to kill him, there would have been much easier ways. And if it was murder, how was it done?' She shook her head. 'As I said, it's a mystery.'

* * *

Nightingale drove back to Annette Carson's house. She showed him back into the sitting room and made him a mug of coffee before sitting down on the sofa next to him. He brought her up to speed on what he'd achieved so far, which frankly wasn't much. 'Nobody seems to have the first idea about any of it. I'm guessing the unexplained death of an old man probably isn't that much of a priority, but there are a lot of questions that need to be answered, and the police chief doesn't seem to be thinking too hard.'

'What kind of questions?'

'For example, why he got up and left the house in the middle of the night, who drove him out to the tracks? It's over six miles and there's no way he could have walked that barefoot in under two hours without being seen. And then there's the question of who found the body and called it in. An anonymous call, said Chief Davis, but again she doesn't seem to be pushing it, and whoever called is the obvious suspect. What would anyone be doing out there at that time of night?' He shrugged. 'I honestly don't know where to go with this, Annette. Nobody seems to have seen anything. I've got nobody to ask.'

The doorbell rang and she got up to answer it, returning a minute later with Chief Davis. The Chief nodded at Nightingale. 'I just dropped by with Paulie's personal effects.' She handed the bag to Annette.

'It's good of you to do it personally, Chris,' said Annette. 'Stay a while? Coffee?'

The Chief shook her head. 'No, I have to be getting along. We're going to take another pass along The Tracks, see if we missed something, maybe some tire marks, I don't know. But I'll see you at the church tomorrow.'

'Do you mind if I tag along?' asked Nightingale.

'Tag along?' repeated the Chief.

'I wouldn't mind seeing where it happened, and I'd probably have trouble finding it myself.'

'I don't see why not,' said the Chief.

Nightingale had picked up the bag and was examining the contents. There were the man's pajamas, torn and bloodstained, a wedding ring, and a white towel robe that was also stained and ripped. 'Church, you said? Tomorrow isn't Sunday.'

'It's the funeral,' said Annette.

'Would you mind if I came?'

'Of course you can come. It's at Saint Mark's, just down the road.'

She sat down on the sofa and winced as she looked at the bloodstained clothing.

Nightingale saw something in the folds of the robe and he pulled it out. It looked like embroidered canvas. About six inches long and two inches wide. Nightingale looked closer and saw that it wasn't embroidered, it was beaded and among the beads were small white shells.

'Any idea what this is?' he asked, holding it up.

'No idea,' she replied. 'Never seen it before, maybe it got mixed up from someone else's belongings.'

She looked up at the Chief. Chris shrugged. 'According to the ME it was in the pocket of your dad's robe.'

Annette took it from Nightingale and looked at it, frowning. 'That's so strange.'

'What is?'

'It looks Indian to me. Native American is what we're supposed to say these days but Dad always called them Indians. Dad was a good man, but he never had much time for Native Americans. He used to be quite vocal about it in years gone by, though he'd mellowed lately. Maybe age brought tolerance. Still. I've never known him to have anything like this in the house. I had a dream-catcher above my bed but he made me throw it out after he moved in.'

Nightingale took it from her. 'Do you mind if I borrow it.'

'Keep it,' she said. 'It didn't belong to my father, I'm sure of that.'

The Chief looked at her watch. 'We need to get going,' she said.

* * *

They drove out to The Tracks in the Chief's cruiser. 'Can I play with the siren?' asked Nightingale. The Chief was just about to say no when she realised he was joking and smiled.

'That'll be the famous English sense of humour I've heard about,' she said.

'Just trying to lighten the moment.'

'Yeah, there's not much to smile about in this case,' she said.

The Chief stopped the cruiser about two hundred yards from The Tracks, next to another cruiser and a people carrier. They walked the rest of the way, picking their way carefully over rocks, round bushes and up and down the undulating overgrown terrain. Annette had put on a pair of boots she kept in the trunk of her car, while Nightingale was hoping his brown suede Hush Puppies would provide enough protection against snakes, scorpions or whatever else might be around.

Finally they came to the slight rise where the abandoned railroad tracks lay on top of their gravel bed. In the distance two uniformed officers and half a dozen young men in blue overalls were slowly working their way along the tracks, eyes on the ground. 'We've drafted in some cadets,' explained Chris. 'Though I'm not sure what we expect to find.'

The tracks stretched out around five hundred yards in front of Nightingale, then came to a sudden end, as the undergrowth took over. There was barely enough track to park a decent-sized train, and certainly nowhere for it to run.

'The body was over there,' said Chris.

She led him a short distance down the tracks and showed him a place where the wooden sleepers were stained with what must have been blood. The rails nearby were burnt black. 'That's strange, right?' said Nightingale, bending down.

'Probably nothing,' said Chris. 'It looks as if something very hot charred this part of the rail. But it could have happened anytime. Lightning, maybe?'

'Was there a storm the night Mr Carson died?'

'No, it was a clear night. But this could have happened at any time. Besides, Mr Carson was smashed to pieces, not electrocuted.'

Nightingale shivered. He could feel the hairs prickle on the back of his neck. The sun was high in the sky but he couldn't feel any warmth from its rays and there was a chill wind running down the tracks.

'I'm going to talk to the guys, do you want to wait here?'

Nightingale shivered again. 'If it's all the same to you, I'll stick with you,' he said.

'You feel it, too?'

Nightingale nodded. 'There's something not right here.'

'You're telling me.'

* * *

Paulie Carson's funeral was a closed casket affair. The old man had clearly been pretty popular because there was a good turnout. Inevitably most of those there were much younger than Carson had been, but there were at least three old men who looked as if they'd probably been at school with him. They arrived together in a black people-carrier driven by a much younger woman, probably a daughter, or so Nightingale thought. Between them they mustered one walker and three sticks as they made their way slowly into the church and up to the front pew. Annette helped settle them beside her, then turned to Nightingale who'd followed them in.

'Dad's oldest friends,' she said. 'Hank Rogers, Jed Boone and Dave Reid. Back in the day they were pretty much inseparable. Called themselves the Four Aces, apparently, though lately he didn't see much of them, and they didn't get out much. Dave's in a care facility now.'

The service wasn't a long one, and featured a short eulogy from Annette, before the coffin was taken out into the graveyard. When the burial was over, Nightingale waited while Annette spoke to the majority of the mourners. The remaining Three Aces had quite a lot to say, but Nightingale wasn't listening. He was trying to decide whether Utah anti-smoking laws could possibly apply in the grounds of a church, and was relieved when he saw a few other people lighting up. By the time he'd finished his cigarette, the majority of the mourners had drifted away, and Annette was talking to a tall woman in her thirties, with high cheekbones, a copper complexion and long dark hair flowing over her shoulders. Nightingale figured she was probably a Native American, or an Indian as Paulie Carson would probably have said. She was elegantly dressed in a black jacket and knee-length black pencil skirt. Annette caught Nightingale's eye and beckoned him over.

'Jack Nightingale, this is an old friend of mine, Nascha Begay.'

The woman nodded at Nightingale, but said nothing.

'Nascha was a great help with dad towards the end. She sat with him sometimes when I needed to work.'

'I was pleased to help, Annette,' said the woman. Her voice was soft and deep, she spoke slowly and carefully, as if English wasn't her first language. 'I trained as a nurse, Mr Nightingale, though I sell real estate now. I still do a shift to help at a care facility occasionally.'

'Jack, show that thing we found to Nascha. The strip of cloth. I was telling her about it. Nascha's Navajo.'

Nightingale fumbled in his jacket pocket and brought out the blackened strip of beaded canvas.

Nascha took it from him, frowning. 'It was in dad's pocket. Do you have any idea what it is?'

'It looks like Navajo work,' Nascha said. 'I've not seen anything like it before, just a little decorative patch, maybe from something larger. I'm surprised Mr Carson had it, he never showed much interest in Navajo art. I think I was the only Navajo he ever talked to. Not that he knew who I was.' She smiled at Nightingale and gave him back the strip of canvas. 'He was very ill when I met him and got steadily worse.'

'But he recognised you,' said Annette. 'I know he kept getting your name wrong, but he was always happy to see you.'

'He was a lovely old man,' said Nascha. 'I am sorry for your loss, Annette. I hope he is at peace now. It would be good to think so.' She kissed Annette on the cheek and left.

Nightingale walked with Annette back to her house. 'Tell me about Nascha,' he said.

'I've known her a long time, her family moved here from the Navajo Nation a long time ago. She's been through a lot. When she was six her father was killed in a mining accident. Couple of years after that, her mother disappeared too. There was a rumor she'd gone off to Salt Lake City with some salesman, but whatever, she just abandoned Nascha. She ended up being raised by her grandmother, who's a bit of an old witch.' She grimaced. 'Listen to me, talking like my father now. I mean she was a medicine woman, I guess that's the politically correct term. She was good with herbs, plants and potions. Personally I prefer pharmacists.'

'Did Nascha inherit the magic?' he asked.

'Not that I ever heard. She's never been that big on her Native heritage, at least rarely mentioned it to me. Never shown any sign of heading back to the Navajo Nation. She was so helpful with my father. I offered to pay her but she seemed happy to sit and listen to him talk.'

'He talked a lot?'

'Babbled mostly, in recent years.'

'What about?' asked Nightingale.

'His friends, nights out, old girlfriends, cars he'd owned, places he'd been. Childhood memories, I guess. He talked about swimming in creeks in summer, railroads, baseball, shooting ducks, buried treasure...it was all disjointed, and got all mixed up. Mostly he made no sense. It was sad.'

'Buried treasure? Anything in that you think?'

She forced a smile.

'Oh no, he'd probably played at pirates when he was little. I think that happens when you get really old. You lose the memories of stuff that has just happened, but what happened fifty years ago becomes totally vivid. I read that on the internet, I'm not sure if it's true or not.' She took a handkerchief from her pocket and dabbed her eyes. 'What are you going to do, Jack?'

'I'm still on the case,' he said. 'I just don't have any leads yet. Maybe I should talk to his friends, his old friends.'

'Not sure how much use that would be, they stopped visiting when he stopped recognizing him, and I don't think Dave Reid's any too good mentally now. He's in a care home. For sure none of them killed him. They were as tight as tight can be, before they got old.'

* * *

The moon was in its last quarter, but still spread a little light over the street at midnight, though even with the help of the low powered street lamps it was hard to see the outline of the figure sitting in the driver's seat of the dark car outside the single story house. The shaded flashlight shone on the small wax figure that sat on the passenger seat, a lock of gray hair pressed into the crude representation of the head, and red painted markings covering the body. The gloved hands picked up the little manikin, held it up to the mouth and frosty breath covered it. Four words were pronounced in an ancient language, and then the whispered instructions. 'Come to me, Jed. I am waiting for you. Come with me. You know where we must go. It is time. You need not wake. Just come.'

It was two minutes later that the front door opened and the old man, clad only in pajamas, started to totter out towards the car. He stared straight ahead of him and walked hesitatingly forward, but never stumbled. He reached the car, and the passenger door was opened for him. He got in without a sound. The whispering continued.

'No need to wake. No need at all. Not yet, there will be time for that soon. We need to go now, Jed. Sit back, it's very nearly time.'

The gloved hand reached inside the old man's pajama pocket and left what needed to be there. Then the car moved forward and headed south, towards The Tracks.

* * *

Nightingale's cellphone dragged him from a dream he almost instantly forgot. He looked at the display, seven twenty-two a.m. and a call from Annette Carson. He pressed the green button. 'Yeah.'

'Jack, it's Annette, I just heard from Chief Davis. They found Jed Boone's body, down by The Tracks. Dead. His body was smashed to pieces. Just like he'd been hit by a train.'

'Nightingale sat up and ran a hand through his hair. 'When did this happen?'

'They found the body late last night. Jack what's happening here? Two harmless old men dead in a week, out in the middle of nowhere? Who can be doing this?'

'I really don't know, Annette. Look, I need to try to talk to Chief Davis again.'

Nightingale shaved and showered then grabbed a cup of coffee to go from the diner and drove to the Police Department. There he learned that Chief Davis was out at The Tracks so he drove there. There were three cruisers and an ambulance parked where she'd taken him last time, and there was a white van with a satellite dish on the roof and the name of a local cable news show on the side.

Nightingale found the chief being interviewed on camera, some distance away from the abandoned railway line. When she'd finished she walked over. She looked like a woman who hadn't slept in two days, black bags under her eyes, her hair a mess, the sleeves of her cream blouse rolled up and a coffee stain over the left breast. She nodded. 'Annette called you?'

Nightingale nodded. 'Jed Boone?'

'Same deal as Paulie Carson. Miles away from home, dressed only in pajamas, body smashed to pieces, and nothing to show how it happened, much less why.'

'Anything in his pockets?' asked Nightingale.

'Yeah, you got it. A burned piece of canvas. Badly burned this time, whatever had been on it was completely gone. But a little strip of canvas didn't kill him.'

'I suppose not,' said Nightingale. 'Can I see it?'

'Why do you want to see it?'

'Actually I want to photograph it. It has to be significant, right? Same thing found on both bodies.'

Davis sighed. 'I'm thinking I should call the Feds. Looks like we have a serial killer out there.' In the distance two crime scene investigators in white overalls and shoe covers were bending over something. One of them had a camera. Nightingale took out his pack of Marlboro. Immediately he saw the look in the Chief's eyes and realised he was in the presence of a fellow smoker. He smiled and offered her the pack, then lit cigarettes for both of them. They both blew smoke before she spoke. 'You know Jed Boone and Paulie Carson were friends?'

Nightingale nodded. 'Annette said. Hank Rogers, Jed Boone and Dave Reid and her dad called themselves the Four Aces. Now two of them are dead. I can't see that's a coincidence.'

The Chief nodded. 'I'll start looking at connections. See if there's a reason anyone would want to hurt them. But hell, Jack, they're all old men.'

'Do you think it might be worth putting a guard on Rogers and Reid?'

The Chief shrugged. 'Neither of them get out much. Dave Reid is in a secure care home and I've already spoken to the administrator there. Hank Rogers lives with his son and isn't really mobile. I can't see him leaving the house under his own steam. I phoned the son and suggested he keeps a closer eye on Hank, but I think that's probably enough for the time being.'

She blew smoke before continuing. 'You were a cop before you were a PI.' It was a statement rather than a question.

'How can you tell?'

'You got cop eyes.'

'It's been said before. Yeah, a firearms officer and negotiator in London. In another life.'

'I figured.' She sighed. 'Look, there's something I need to tell you. I get the feeling you're going to dig and dig so it's better I tell you this now. I was there for the first killing, down at The Tracks.'

Nightingale certainly hadn't expected that, and his poker face failed him completely. 'What? You saw what happened?'

'No. Not really, not exactly. Look, I was down there with someone, doesn't matter who. It's a quiet place, and I'm married with kids, so is...the other person. We'd...we'd finished, just getting ready to go, when we heard...we heard what sounded like a train. Well, anyways, a hell of a noise and a whole load of flashing lights. Felt like it was coming straight through us, then it stopped. That's when we heard the scream. We went out, found the body. Nobody called it in, I made that up. I called for backup and a CSI team and waited for them to arrive.'

Nightingale raised his eyebrows, drew on his cigarette, but still kept silent.

'Puts me in a mess. I...well and the other person...we're the only ones who saw and heard what happened. If I tell anyone, it blows two marriages. If I keep it quiet, maybe it blows the case.'

'How was this one called in?'

'Couple of teenagers. They were walking along the tracks at night. For a dare, I think. They found the body.'

'But they didn't see what happened?'

'The body was cold. What was left of it.'

Nightingale blew smoke. 'What do you think you saw, that night?'

The Chief shuddered. 'I wish I knew.'

'I really could do with a photograph of the thing you found.'

'Why?'

'I showed it to a friend of Annette's. She said it was Navajo decorative art. Thought I might show her this latest one.'

The Chief looked at him for several seconds and then nodded. 'Okay, wait here. I don't want you trampling over my crime scene.' She put out her cigarette and slipped the butt into her pocket before heading over to the crime scene investigators.

Nightingale smoked his cigarette until she returned, carrying a see-through evidence bag. She held it out so that he could look at it but wouldn't let him touch it. He took out the one he had in his pocket and compared the two. They were similar but not identical. 'That can't be a coincidence,' said Nightingale.

'Maybe,' said the Chief.

Nightingale took out his cellphone and took a couple of pictures of the evidence bag.

'I'm thinking I should take that back,' said the Chief, nodding at the strip of beaded canvas he was holding.

'Let me hang on to it for a day or two,' he said.

'It's evidence.'

'It might be evidence. Let me see if I can confirm that.' He nodded goodbye and headed back to his car.

* * *

Nightingale waited until he was back in his car before phoning Annette. He asked her for Nascha Begay's number and he arranged to meet her in a local diner. She gave him the address and he keyed it into the car's SatNav and thirty minutes later he was walking into a family restaurant called Bob's bar. A waitress showed him to a booth and he was halfway through a mug of quite decent coffee when Nascha arrived. She was wearing a tan fringed jacket and matching short skirt that showed off her elegant long legs to perfection. Nightingale thought she might be a few years older than his initial guess of thirty-five, but she was definitely wearing well.

'Nice to see you again, Mr Nightingale,' she said, easing herself into the booth.

'Jack,' he said.

She smiled, then ordered a coffee.

'Nascha, that's a Native American name?'

She nodded. 'Specifically, a Navajo name.'

'Like Natasha, I guess.'

'I think my name was around long before Natasha,' she said. 'Nascha means 'Owl' and Begay is pretty much the Navajo equivalent of Smith or Jones. So fairly ordinary, really. Not like Nightingale. Now that's an unusual name.'

Her coffee arrived and she sipped it.

'There's been another death out at the Tracks,' he said. 'Jed Boone. He died the same way as Mr Carson and this was found on his body.' He held out his camera and showed her the photograph of the evidence bag. She took the phone from him and squinted at the screen. 'What do you think?'

'It's Navajo art,' she said. 'You think it means something?'

'I was hoping you'd be able to tell me.'

'I've seen bigger pieces hanging on walls,' she said. 'They're the sort of things tourists would buy. Those and dreamcatchers.' She gave him the phone back.

'Do they work? Dreamcatchers?'

She laughed. 'I don't know,' she said.

'I thought you were up to speed about traditional Navajo magic.'

She laughed again. 'Be serious, Jack. This is the twenty-first century. I respect the traditions, but if I get sick, I'll be heading for a doctor and a hospital. I think my grandmother still believes in that stuff, maybe even in The Great Spirit, but even she heads to the pharmacy for her aspirin.'

'Could I talk to your grandmother? She might know something.'

'She's not good with strangers,' said Nascha. 'To be honest, she barely speaks any English these days.'

Nightingale put the phone away. 'Did you know Jed Boone?'

She shook her head. 'First time I saw him was at Mr Carson's funeral. I'm told he was a nice guy. What do you think, Jack? You think that a Navajo souvenir is connected to the deaths? That makes no sense. The Navajo religion is peaceful, meant to let men and nature live in harmony, There's nothing in it that I know of about smashing old men to pieces.'

She finished her coffee and stood up. 'I have to go,' she said. 'But if you need anything else, you have my number.' He started to get up but she put up her hand. 'You finish your coffee,' she said.

Nightingale watched her go, then phoned the Chief. 'Hi. You getting anywhere?'

'Not too far,' he said. 'You?'

'Not much, Ronnie McKenzie says the cause of death is identical to the way that Paulie Carson died. Massive trauma to all parts of the body, consistent with being hit by a train, a truck or a fall from a very high building. None of which are an option given the place we found the body, which, once again, was where he died. What about you? What's your plan?'

'I'm going to head up to the Navajo Nation Reservation. I need to talk to a medicine man.'

* * *

The Navajo Nation reservation was a huge territory occupying large parts of Utah, Arizona and New Mexico. Nightingale's SatNav took him south to the Utah portion and it took him several hours of driving around before he managed to find what he wanted. Tahoma was old, maybe eighty, dressed in a Utah Jazz sweatshirt and a pair of shorts that looked older than Nightingale. His hair started halfway back on his scalp, then hung downwards in two long gray braids over his shoulders. Nightingale had paid an old woman in a tourist gift-shop fifty dollars for Tahoma's name and address, explaining that he had a problem that only a powerful medicine man could solve. When his SatNav took him to a down-at-heel trailer park populated by old people and scabby dogs he wondered if he'd been sent on a wild goose chase but the man who responded to his tentative knock looked to be almost eighty-years-old and nodded when Nightingale asked him if he was Tahoma. 'You are Nightingale,' said the man.

'How do you know that?' asked Nightingale. He hadn't told the woman in the gift shop his name so she couldn't have called ahead and given him the information.

'It is a good name, Nightingale,' said the old man, ignoring the question and ushering him inside. 'Almost an Indian name. Bird names are always powerful.' He showed Nightingale into the living room of his trailer and gave him a bottle of Budweiser. Selling alcohol was banned in the Navajo Nation, but drinking it seemed to be permissible. The old man took a swig from his own bottle and waved it at him 'You want something, I know. What is it you want?'

'Two men have died in a place called Scarsdale. Have you heard about it?'

The old man shook his head. 'I don't hear about anything outside my trailer these days. Tell me.'

Nightingale told him, and the old man listened in silence, his eyes closed, his face as immobile as stone. He grunted once when Nightingale described the injuries to the bodies, then relapsed into silence until Nightingale told him about the two pieces of beaded canvas. He opened his eyes and leaned over to grip Nightingale's wrist tightly.

'The wampums were on the bodies?' he asked.

'Wampums?'

'What you have just described.'

Nightingale pulled his wrist away and reached into his pocket. He pulled out the strip of canvas and gave it to Tahoma. The old man stood up as if an electric current had shot though his body, his jaw dropped and he stared at the beaded canvas in horror,

'You bring this here?' He thrust it at Nightingale. 'Take it and go, Go now. Go.'

'Wait, Tahoma, please. You have to tell me what this is. Please.'

The old man was frantic with fear now. 'You go, now.'

'Just tell me what it is and I'll take it away.'

The old man emptied his beer bottle in one long pull. This is strong medicine, the strongest. A wampum to summon Otshee Monetoo, the evil spirit. The spirit of death. Take this from my house now.'

'I showed this to a Navajo woman, she said it was nothing, maybe a souvenir,' said Nightingale.

'So she might,' said the old man. 'Why would she ever see this, few are those who would recognize it. Take it from my house, now. And do not return.'

The old man bundled Nightingale out of the trailer and slammed the door shut.

It began to rain as Nightingale turned out of Tahoma's trailer park and onto the road back to Scarsdale. Whatever the canvas represented, it had terrified the old medicine man, but had no effect at all on Nascha. The medicine man had talked about 'Otshee Monetoo, the evil spirit. The spirit of death' and she had dismissed it as tourist tat.

The rain was getting heavier, and the clouds darker, so he was glad he only had another forty miles to go. He heard the sound of a heavy truck approaching, and saw its headlights in his mirror. The lights were blinding and he narrowed his eyes. He frowned as the lights changed to red to blue, to green and then back again to red. The engine noise grew ever louder, much louder than any truck he'd ever heard. He looked in his mirror again, the lights were charging at him and the noise was almost unbearable. Like a train.

He twisted the wheel and pulled the car over onto the shoulder. The thing, whatever it was, followed him. Nightingale accelerated, hard, and the car leapt forward. The lights and the noise followed him. Intuitively he knew how it had found him. He plunged his hand into his pocket, snatched out the canvas and frantically shoved it into the door pocket. Then he hit the brakes hard and as soon as the car had screeched to a halt he threw the door open and leaped out. He sprinted across the shoulder, rolled down the verge and kept running across the field.

The noise reached a horrendous crescendo, then there was a deafening explosion. A shock wave hit him in the back and he fell forward and hit the ground hard. Pieces of metal started to fall around him and he protected the back of his head with his hands. When the metal stopped falling he lifted his head and looked back at the road. Almost nothing remained of his SUV and flames were licking what was left of the chassis.

Nightingale stood up and lit a cigarette as he wondered what he should do next.

* * *

It took Nightingale much less time than anticipated to get back to the Paradise Motel, since it seemed that standing next to a burnt-out pile of metal brought out the sympathy in the citizens of Utah, or at least in the farmer who'd stopped his pick-up three minutes later and driven him all the way to the Paradise Hotel where he had no problem fixing up a replacement rental from a local company who within an hour had an almost new Ford Escape for him, including a brand spanking new SatNav. Nightingale figured he'd wait until he got back to Denver before explaining to Avis what had happened to their car.

He grabbed a steak and chips in the motel's diner and then drove out to Annette Carson's house to bring her up to speed, getting there just after six.

She made him coffee and then sat down on the sofa next to him. 'Before you say anything, I've got news for you,' she said. 'Dave Reid died this afternoon.'

Nightingale almost dropped his mug of coffee. 'What happened? Was it at The Tracks?'

She shook her head. 'He killed himself, at least that's what the Chief told me. He was on a lot of medication and he swallowed the lot, along with half a bottle of Jack Daniels.'

'Did he leave a note?'

She shook her head again. 'Apparently he'd been really down since my dad died. Then when Jed Boone died, he just went downhill. He wasn't in the best of health anyway.' She shrugged. 'It's sad, isn't it?'

Nightingale nodded. 'It was definitely suicide?'

'Check with Chief Davis. But she seemed certain.'

'So that's three of the Four Aces dead,' said Nightingale. 'That can't be a coincidence.' He sipped his coffee. 'Where did that name come from? The Four Aces?'

'They went through a phase of driving motorcycles. Harleys. They had leather jackets made with four aces on the back. Like a hand of cards. They stopped riding years ago but they kept the name. They were tight, Jack. Had been since they were at High School. They all played on the football team together, they dated the same girls, they did the bike thing together, they hunted together. As they got older they played cards together most weeks.' She forced a smile. 'Now they're dying together.'

'They dated the same girls, did you say?'

She laughed. 'That's what I heard from my mum. Before they married they tended to pass girls around. Not in a bad way. But my dad would go out with a girl and then they'd break up and Jed would date her and then a few months later it would be Hank's turn. They were all good-looking guys and played High School football, they pretty much had their pick of girls.' She laughed again. 'That was before they all married and settled down.'

She sipped her coffee as he told her about his meeting with the medicine man on the reservation. 'Here's what I don't get,' he said. 'The medicine man knew exactly what that strip of beaded cloth was. So why didn't Nascha?'

'Maybe she didn't know?'

'Her grandmother knows all about the Navajo ways. I asked if I could talk to her but Nascha fobbed me off.'

'To be fair her grandmother is in her eighties and pretty much housebound these days,' said Annette.

'What about Nascha's mother? You never said what happened to her.'

'No one knows for sure. It must have been thirty years ago. More, I guess. Like I told you, there was talk of Kai having a boyfriend in Salt Lake City, but there were some people who thought something bad had happened to her. From what I remember, Johona reported her missing, but I'm not sure the cops looked too hard. Maybe back then a missing Indian woman wasn't a high priority.' She shrugged. 'It was a different world.'

'Nascha would have been pretty young at the time?'

'Yes, I doubt she'd remember her mother all that well, she grew up with her grandmother.'

'Do you think I could see her? The grandmother?'

'I don't know if she sees anyone now. You could ask Nascha.'

'I did. She didn't seem keen on my talking to her.'

She turned her head to look at him directly. 'Jack, what is all this? You can't think Johona had anything to do with Dad's death, or Jed's. She's an old woman. She doesn't leave the house.'

'I don't know what to think,' said Nightingale. 'Are you any good with computers?'

She laughed. 'I get by,' she said. 'Why?'

'I wouldn't mind seeing what was reported in the press at the time Kai went missing.'

'Let me get my laptop,' she said. She left the room for a minute or so and then returned with an Apple MacBook. She opened it and switched it on and tapped away on the keyboard for a while before sitting back and shaking her head. 'I guess the papers for that long ago haven't been digitized,' she said. 'I've searched for her name and there's nothing.'

'What about similar deaths at The Tracks.'

Annette leaned over her laptop and tapped away for several minutes. 'No, nothing,' she said eventually.

Nightingale was about to make a joke about it being a dead end but as Annette's father had died there he figured she wouldn't find it funny. 'Where does Hank live?'

'With his son. They have a house on the edge of town. Hank's son runs a courier company. He's done quite well for himself.'

'I'll need the address,' said Nightingale.

* * *

Nightingale parked a short distance away from the Rogers house. It was a large, spreading single story ranch house. To the left was a parking lot with half a dozen courier vans parked in a neat line, and beyond them a large billboard advertising the company's services. Nightingale had picked up a Subway ham salad sandwich and a coffee, and he ate and drank as he watched the house. Most of the lights went out at about ten o'clock. One, which he figured was the son's bedroom, stayed on until half ten then it went out and there was a flickering light on the curtains which was almost certainly a TV. It finally went off at just before eleven.

Nightingale reclined the seat to make himself as comfortable as possible, and tuned the radio to a talk show so that he had something to keep himself awake.

It was almost two-o'clock in the morning when the front door opened and Hank Rogers shuffled out, wearing only his red and white striped pajamas. As he tottered down the drive a dark sedan drew up, the passenger door opened and the old man bent to step inside.

Following the car was a breeze because Nightingale knew where it was going. The Tracks. He let the sedan get well ahead and kept his headlights off. By the time he reached the parking place near The Tracks, the sedan was empty. There was enough of a moon to see by and the fact that his headlights had been off meant that his night vision had kicked in, so he picked his way across the rough ground towards the abandoned railway line.

He saw the two figures about a hundred yards ahead of him, one supporting the other. He reached the twin steel rails and was able to quicken his pace now that he had the level ground of the rail bed and sleepers under his feet.

The others had their backs to him and he was only twenty yards behind them when they stopped, just about where Nightingale had noticed the burnt rails the day before. The taller figure lowered the smaller one to the ground, and words floated back to Nightingale. 'Sit here, Hank. It is nearly time for you. It's nearly over.'

Nightingale moved a few yards nearer before he spoke. 'It's over now, Nascha. You're done.'

She turned to look at him and he realised she was holding a gun, a small automatic. Small, but definitely powerful enough to blow a decent-sized hole in his chest if she pulled the trigger.

'Stay where you are Mr Nightingale. This is nothing to do with you. What are you doing here?'

'I followed you. I know everything, so you might as well call it a day.'

She gestured at his chest with the gun. 'Go back to your car, or I will shoot you.' Behind her, Hank had started shuffling down the track, his hands loose at his sides.

'Put the gun down, Nascha,' he said. 'Put it down and let's all go home.'

'I'm serious. I've come too far not to finish this.'

'Your mother's buried out here isn't she?'

Her jaw dropped. 'How do you know?'

'I didn't, not for sure. I guessed. Revenge is the only motive that makes any sense and they're too old to have done you any harm.'

'They raped and murdered her, then buried her, somewhere near the tracks. I don't know where. And they've all forgotten.' She shuddered. 'I thought my mother had left me,' she said. 'I spent my whole life thinking I'd been abandoned.'

Hank was still moving down the tracks, his head down, muttering to himself.

'Have you given him the wampum?' asked Nightingale.

'It's what he deserves,' she said.

'Are you sure, Nascha? Are you sure you have the right men?'

Her eyes burned as she nodded. 'I'm sure. It was Reid who told me. I was by his bed, and he was rambling. Except I knew what he was talking about. Willow, he said. That was my mum's name. Kai is Navajo for willow. That's what they called her. The weeping willow. It was a joke. After they'd raped her, they joked.'

'Why did they do it?'

'They were drunk. They'd been hunting and were in Carson's truck. My mum was walking home and they offered her a lift. She refused but they grabbed her and drove her to The Tracks. They raped her in the back of the truck, then one of them killed her.'

'Who?'

'I don't know. Reid said it was Carson, Carson said it was Rogers. I was talking to Rogers in the car and he says he doesn't remember. That might be right. It was so long ago.'

'Why did they do it? Did any of them say?'

She shrugged. 'Drink. They weren't bad men, they were drunk. But that doesn't make what happened any the less wrong. My mum was an Indian so in their minds she was less than human. She didn't matter. Well she did. She did matter.'

'Why didn't you go to the police? Chief Davies would have been sympathetic.'

'To who? To me, the daughter of an Indian? Or to four old men, pillars of the community? And I have no proof. No proof at all.' She shook her head. 'No, this way is better. This is justice. Navajo justice. We decided that the old way was the best, innocent blood calls for guilty blood in vengeance.'

'We?'

'My grandmother and I. It is she who summons the avenging spirit, though each summoning weakens her gravely. I don't think she will survive this final one. It takes a lot out of her.'

'What is that thing? The thing that kills them?'

'Otshee Monetoo, an avenging spirit, it feeds on the evil in men and destroys them. It is an old secret known to very few. My grandmother may be the last to know how to summon it. My work is to get them alone and to guide the spirit.'

'How do you get them to do what you want?'

'With the old ways, my grandmother showed me. A manikin. little clay figure, a lock of hair, some words of power and I can summon them to me, while they still sleep. Then I mark them to guide the avenging spirit.'

'With the wampum?'

She nodded. 'My grandmother knows the secret of the wampum.'

'You know it tried to kill me?'

'My grandmother knew you had been to see a medicine man on the reservation.'

'How? How did she know?'

'She has her ways. Old ways. She never leaves her home now but she knows everything that happens. She sent Otshee Monetoo to harm you. She was trying to protect me. For what it's worth, I am glad you weren't hurt.'

'Me too, but I'm not going to stand here and watch another man die. Put down the gun, we're all going home.'

'Not until it is finished. Reid has cheated us of our full vengeance, but he will answer for his crime in another place. But Rogers has to die.'

'No, Nascha. It's over.'

They both flinched as they heard the roar off in the distance. Nascha smiled. 'Soon it will be over,' she said.

Away in the distance Nightingale saw a small red light, which changed to blue then green, back to red and seemed to multiply into hundreds of flashing lights in all three colors as it raced down the tracks toward them. His ears filled with a crescendo of roaring, for all the world as if an express train were bearing down on him. Closer, brighter, louder.

Nascha walked towards him. He tried to move but discovered that his feet were rooted to the spot. She reached him, put her arms around him and held him tightly, She put her lips to his ear, and he heard her urgent whisper even above the awful roar. 'Keep still, you will be safe with me.'

Nightingale looked over her shoulder as the lights and the unbearable noise bore down on the sitting figure of the old man. The lights seemed to disappear inside his body, which was lifted into the air, fifty feet or more and then slammed down onto the ground with frightening force at sickening speed. The old man gave one agonized cry, and The Tracks were plunged into darkness and silence.

Nascha released her hold on him and stepped back. 'Now it's over,' she said, her voice soft and almost devoid of expression. 'The guilty blood has been shed, the innocent blood is avenged, and my grandmother's mission is complete.' She shuddered. 'She has passed.'

'How do you know?' Nightingale asked.

'I know, that is enough. It is time for us to leave this place.'

'And go where?'

'I shall go home and grieve for my mother and grandmother. You will go where you are needed.'

'Was I needed here?'

'Perhaps not,' she said. 'But still you were sent, and still you came. Maybe it was fated that someone else should know the truth.'

'And what am I going to do with what I know?' asked Nightingale.

'That is for you to decide. You could tell Carson's daughter. Maybe tell the police. I don't care. Those men needed killing and now they are dead.'

Despite himself, Nightingale laughed. 'You know, somehow I can't see me telling Chief Davis this story. Maybe some secrets are best left buried.'

He pulled his raincoat tighter against the sudden chill in the air, turned and walked away from her, back to his car. What was he going to tell Annette Carson? He didn't know. But he'd have a clearer idea of what to say after he'd spoken to Mrs Steadman.

THE UNDEAD

It was getting dark in the Great Smoky Mountains of North Carolina. The four hikers, Dave, Aaron, Laura and Stephanie walked silently on pine needles towards Grant's Peak, an overlook with sweeping views of the forested valley. They were exhausted; they'd been hiking since sunrise thirteen hours ago. Since then they had covered some twenty miles, beginning just after Fontana Dam – they now had another 51 miles to go until the Davenport Gap, the end of the Smokies.

It had been slow going for them on the Appalachian Trail. They'd been averaging ten miles a day, but nearing mid-summer already and wanting to hike up to Maine before the cold weather set in, they were quickening their pace, which meant short nights and thin gruel suppers. But Dave promised that if they reached the hiking lodge before sundown he'd make them a good old-fashioned camp stew. In his backpack he had the onions, beef stock, carrots, and cans of Spam he needed. It wouldn't be Gordon Ramsay standard, but it would fill them up.

Dave kept looking at the map with concern. At twenty-three he was the oldest of the group, a tall, thin redhead wearing a North Face waterproof jacket. He looked up from the map, frowning. Already the woods were dark and silent. 'Hell,' he said. 'I could've sworn it was right around the bend here. That's what it says.'

Aaron snatched the map from him. Aaron had just turned twenty but his hairline was already starting to recede and he studied the map through thick-lensed spectacles. 'Let me see that,' he said, biting his lip and running his finger along the trail. 'Where did you say we were?'

Dave pointed at the map. 'Right here. Supposedly.'

Aaron squinted at where he was pointing. 'Right here?'

'Yeah.'

'And when was the last white blaze? At the stream?' The trail was marked with splashes of white paint, but they could be easily missed.

Dave paused. 'No…' he said slowly. 'I saw one about two miles ago.'

Aaron gaped at him. 'You what?'

'I saw one,' Dave repeated.

'But you didn't care to inform us about it.'

'Shit man, I'm tired, I don't know.'

'You don't know whether you saw one or you don't know what the hell you're talking about?' He glared at Dave and punctuated his words with a jabbing finger.

'No, I saw one,' said Dave. 'I told you. I was just tired and forgot to mention it. What's the big deal? We're not lost.'

Aaron slapped the map against Dave's chest. 'Actually, we are lost, dumbass. Because you didn't mention the white blaze. That was the marker leading up the path to the lodge. Two miles ago. Now I don't know where the hell we are. But it's not the Appalachian Trail.' Aaron let out a deep sigh.

'So what?' said Dave, trying to sound calm. 'We backtrack the two miles and go to the lodge. It's downhill anyway.'

Stephanie groaned. 'No way, seriously? I'm not going back there.' She had just turned nineteen and had a crush on Aaron which was the only reason she had agreed to go on the trip in the first place.

'Why not?' said Dave.

'Because I'm tired!'

'It's two miles to the white blaze,' said Aaron, 'another two and a half to the lodge. So fuck that.'

The three of them started to argue. Off to the side, Laura watched with folded arms. She was wearing tinted glasses that barely hid the look of contempt in her eyes. She shook her head, set down her backpack on the trail and walked into the woods. The harsh voices diminished behind her.

The sun was setting and she took off her glasses and slid them into the breast pocket of her khaki shirt. The woods were dark and gloomy. Laura couldn't see more than five feet in front of her. The surrounding forest was almost completely silent, except for the nighttime birds and the call of a barred owl somewhere close by. A safe distance from the path now, Laura turned her back to the woods, facing the path, and pulled down her shorts to pee. She wondered what they were going to do for the night. She wouldn't mind sleeping around here in their tents – she was totally spent and really didn't want to walk any more. Then again, they were four miles off-course; maybe it would be best to head back so they could sleep in a shelter for once and be all ready for the trail first thing. There would be other hikers in the lodge. Some human interaction other than Dave, Aaron and Stephanie would make a nice change. She realised she hadn't seen anybody on the trail for the past six hours. It is getting late in the season, she thought. We had better start hauling ass if we want to finish the trail before winter. She had no problem with covering more distance, it was Steph who couldn't handle the long days. In fact, Steph had no business being on the trail in the first place. Her idea of a vacation was lazing on the beach in Miami, drinking cocktails and flirting with the boys. It was a shame they had ever brought her along, because now she was holding everybody up. Secretly, Laura wished she'd just go home.

Laura looked around at the imposing woods. Who knew where they were now, or who owned the land they were in. Was it the conservancy, or was it private? Laura hoped they weren't trespassing on anybody's property. That was the last thing she needed. It would be a hefty fine, and Laura had already spent all her savings on this trip. Come to think of it, she didn't know what she was going to do when it was all over…

A rustling in the bushes interrupted her thoughts.

Something was moving behind her.

She turned around quickly and almost fell over. Darkness. She saw nothing. But she felt a cold presence, as if someone was standing five feet away, watching her from the darkness. Goosebumps crawled on her skin, on her naked thighs. She hurriedly pulled up her shorts and backed away. In the darkness was the faint outline of a man. He was standing perfectly still.

'All right Aaron,' she said. 'I know it's you, you perv. You can come out now.'

The figure remained still.

Laura's heart was racing. She stepped back, against a tree, and started. 'Dammit!' she said, and moved around the tree. Heavy footsteps approached her. The figure was moving now, following her, breathing heavily.

'This isn't funny anymore,' said Laura. 'Cut it out. I mean it.'

Twigs snapped underfoot. Whatever was coming towards her was picking up the pace. The figure loomed close, reached out an arm. The arm was colorless. A white hunk of flesh, the nails caked with dirt and blood.

Laura screamed, turned and ran.

Branches slapped her face and arms. She flew through them, panting and yelling. Suddenly she crashed into something fleshy and hard.

It was Aaron. He yelped as she crashed into him. 'Laura? What's the matter with you? Why were you shouting?'

Laura was gasping uncontrollably. She looked wildly at Aaron, Dave, Steph. All of them were right there in the path. They hadn't moved. She spun around and faced the forest, preparing to face her pursuer head-on. But the movement had stopped. There was nothing there.

'Something's out there,' she said breathlessly. 'In the woods. It chased me!'

'What chased you?' said Aaron.

'Fleshy arms... pale arms...' she panted. 'They reached for me.'

'Oh, please,' said Steph, rolling her eyes.

'I'm not joking!' shouted Laura. Everybody fell silent. They stared at her. 'Something came after me,' she said, composing herself. 'I don't know what... We should go back to the trail. Now.'

'We can't go back,' whined Steph. 'That's like five miles. No way.'

'We need to go back!' She was close to panicking.

Aaron put his hand on Laura's shoulder. 'Whoa, Laura, take it easy. What happened exactly?'

'I told you already, there was something in the woods and it... it chased me. It looked like a man... I don't know. It had hands, pale ugly hands with... with blood.' She covered her face.

'Blood?' said Aaron.

'Maybe it was a bear?' suggested Dave.

'It wasn't a fucking bear, Dave,' said Aaron. 'If it was a bear, it would've got her. Everyone knows bears can outrun humans.'

'Is that supposed to help the situation?' said Dave.

Laura had her face in her hands. She was panting and on the verge of a panic attack.

'You're very tired, Laura,' said Aaron. 'We all are. Your mind's playing tricks on you. It's dark, you're exhausted...'

Laura picked up her backpack and began walking in the opposite direction.

'What are you doing?' shouted Dave.

'I'm going back to the trail.'

'Hey, wait,' said Aaron, catching up with her. 'We've been checking out the map. It looks like this path takes a loop around the mountain a few miles and then comes back just past Grant's Peak. I say we follow it. No use backtracking. We'll waste time. Plus, it's late. If we go back now we won't get to the lodge until midnight, or later. Why don't we go ahead a little longer and make camp somewhere? We'll put a safe distance between you and this place. How's that sound?'

Laura was silent for a while. She looked into the dark woods, waiting. Nothing moved. Finally she looked at Aaron.

'Fine,' she said.

***

Another mile down the trail they came upon a shack in the woods. It was to the right of the path overlooking the valley. There was a chimney on the roof and smoke poured out of it. In the yard in large piles were cords of firewood. Faint firelight came through the windows of the shack.

They stopped on the trail, talking in hushed tones.

'What do you think, guys?' asked Dave. 'Should we go ask if we can bed down?'

'Sounds like a good plan to me,' said Aaron, throwing him a withering look. 'For once.'

Laura shook her head. 'We should keep going.' She hadn't spoken during the walk there. She'd felt like someone, or something, was following them. Watching them from the tree line. 'We're too close,' she said.

'Not that again,' said Steph, crossing her arms. 'Don't be such a pussy. It was probably just a porcupine or something.'

Laura stepped toward her. 'Just shut up, Steph, or I'll make you shut up.'

'Whoa, whoa!' said Aaron. 'Why don't we all just calm down? Look. Whatever you saw, that shack is probably a hell of a lot safer than sleeping out in the open. Don't you think?'

Laura said nothing.

'I think we'd better go check it out,' said Aaron. 'Besides, I don't know about you guys but I'd like to get some sleep tonight. Somewhere warm and out of the elements sounds pretty damn good right about now.'

They all nodded. It was decided.

They walked up to the house, navigating piles of wood. An owl hooted in the darkness of the forest, and the moon shone bright and full. Aaron knocked on the door. No one answered. 'Hello?' he said. 'Anybody home?' He knocked again.

Dave peered through the windows. 'Doesn't look like anyone's home, man.'

Aaron shrugged. 'Let's go inside. Maybe he went out to take a dump or something.'

Laura clutched his arm. 'That's someone's house, Aaron. We can't just break in.'

Aaron tried the knob: it turned freely. 'Jesus, you're such a stick in the mud. It's not breaking in if it's open. There's nice people all along the trail offering food and board. I'm sure this one's no different.' No one argued with him so he pushed the door wide.

A flood of firelight fell on them as the door opened. They went inside. A fire was crackling in the hearth, sending up sparks. The room was small and cramped. Open wood beams stretched the length of it and various herbs hung from them. There were a few old dressers collecting dust, some books on local flora and fauna, a water jug, a sink full of dirty dishes. Best of all was a pot of savory-smelling stew hanging over the fire, filling their noses with scents of roasted chicken, butter and herbs. Their mouths watered.

'Excellent,' said Dave, 'I want some of that! I could eat a horse.'

In the corner of the room was a bed covered with animal skins. Hanging above it was a dream catcher made of bones.

Steph went over to it and twirled it around her fingers. 'Gross,' she said. 'What is it?'

'Some weird decoration or something,' muttered Dave.

'It's a dream catcher,' said Laura. 'It's supposed to protect you from nightmares, and give you good dreams.'

'Hello?' said Aaron, pacing around the small room. 'Anybody home? We're hikers from the trail just passing through. Hello?'

'No one's here,' said Dave, looking sadly at the stew. 'Maybe we should go. It wouldn't be right to stick around, you know, if he's not here...'

'No,' said Aaron. 'We're staying. Once the guy gets back we'll give him some money. Got any cash on you? We could leave the owner a few bucks for the food.'

Dave nodded vigorously and took out his wallet. He slid out a five dollar bill.

'Cool, that should do it,' said Aaron. 'Now let's check out that stew.'

'All right!' said Dave, putting the bill under a salt cellar.

Aaron rummaged in the cabinets for bowls. Laura walked slowly around the room, peering at knickknacks and books. There weren't any photographs or mementos. Just weird things made of animal bones: dream catchers, animal carvings, even a small lamp.

Aaron, Dave and Steph helped themselves to the stew and sat around the fire, eating noisily and chatting. Laura didn't like being there, eating the owner's stew. It was disrespectful. Whoever he was, he probably wouldn't appreciate it. And a lot of people who lived in the wilderness had guns.

Laura was going through the books by the bed when she found a very old volume bound in soft leather, patched in places. It was very heavy, and when she opened it there were hundreds of pages of neat script. It looked like a sort of diary, except there were sketches... anatomical sketches of bodies, human and animal, depicting their bones, flesh, tendons and muscle tissue. It looked like an ancient copy of Grey's Anatomy. How old was this book? It felt ancient.

Laura peered closely at it, trying to read the copperplate handwriting, but the words were in German. She had taken half a semester of German in college before dropping out; she hadn't paid much attention in that class. The language was so guttural, so primitive, not romantic like French. But she recognized a few words...

'Tot' meant Dead, she knew. Creepy.

'Fleish'... flesh.

Laura passed over several sentences she didn't understand and squinted at a word.

Opfern... opfern. Wait a second. Didn't that mean 'sacrifice?'

She heard footsteps on the porch outside and the sound of heavy breathing. Everyone stopped eating and froze. The blood drained from Laura's face. Slowly, the front door swung open.

A man stepped inside, haggard-looking, middle-aged, wearing suspenders to hold up his baggy jeans and a flannel shirt. His face was pockmarked with scars.

He was carrying a rifle.

'Huh,' said the man, looking skeptically at the hikers. 'I wasn't expecting no visitors.'

'Sorry sir.' Dave trembled, gaping at the gun. 'We just assumed you'd be right back.'

'You helped yourselves to my stew, meantime.'

No one spoke. The man held his gun. He watched them, expressionless.

'Dave,' Aaron stammered, annoyed. 'Give him the money.'

'Oh, right.' Dave pulled the five dollar bill from underneath the salt cellar and thrust it at the man. The man peered down at it as though it was a strange artifact from a foreign land.

'Money? No, no. You keep that.' Suddenly his demeanor changed. He became friendly. 'Don't be silly, I was only fooling. I host hikers all the time. That's what you are, right, hikers?'

The group nodded. Dave gulped.

The man smiled at them. 'Well good! Chow down. My name's Earl. How are y'all?'

He grabbed a bowl, filled it with stew, and joined them at the table. One by one they introduced themselves, though Laura stayed by the bed, still holding the book. Sacrifice, she thought. Why was that word in there? Earl turned to her and smiled, pointing. 'I see you got my granddad's old sketchbook there. Damn sight, ain't it?'

Laura swallowed. 'Sketchbook, you say?'

'Yes ma'am.'

What's with the sketches of human bodies?'

'Laura!' Steph hissed.

Earl waved her to sit down with his big meaty hands. 'No, it's all right. She's got a fine point. My granddad has pitchers of dead bodies in there.'

'Eew,' said Steph, looking uncertainly at her bowl of stew.

'Don't I know it,' said Earl. 'Nah, those are just copies of pitchers from old books he was into. He wasn't no doctor, my granddad, but by God he sure wished he was.'

Laura didn't seem convinced. Earl thrust his hand forward. 'What's your name, young lady?'

His scarred face, his dark eyes, his broad shoulders – everything about the man made her uncomfortable. Was he the figure watching her in the woods? Did he follow them back here? 'Where were you just now?' said Laura.

'Me?' Earl smiled at her and pointed at the gun. 'Just out back hunting 'coons.'

'Coons?'

'Raccoons,' said Earl. 'Them bastards been making a mess of my compost bin. I need those food scraps for my vegetables, but try telling that to them fellas.' He shrugged. 'I get one or two every now and then. They got dens in a clearing out back. I like to hang around and wait for 'em to come out. They're nocturnal, you know. But I suppose they caught on to me and built another den, or at least a different exit, because I ain't seen tell of them lately. Not for some time.'

Earl looked nervously at the book, then smiled at Laura again. 'Say, why don't you come over here Laura, make yourself comfortable. Have some stew. It's rabbit.' Earl winked.

Reluctantly Laura set the book back and joined them at the table. Earl did the honors of ladling her stew. She ate quietly while the hikers talked with their host. She noticed Earl smiled a lot, but it wasn't a happy smile, it was more of a nervous smile, as if he had something to hide and the smile was his way of hiding it.

For the next hour the group traded campfire stories. Earl was once attacked by a black bear, he said. He shot it with his rifle, which only seemed to make it angrier. He shot it eleven times before it died, stuck up in a tree with the rifle pointed down at its head. The bear crashed through several branches before hitting the ground. Earl laughed while he told the story, everybody else laughed, too. Except for Laura. It seemed to her that Earl had a pretty grim sense of humor, and she had to wonder what was the purpose of all those bone artifacts around the shack.

Soon they were unrolling their sleeping bags near the fire and getting ready for bed. Earl warned, 'Now don't sleep too close to that fireplace, now. One time a fella got too near it and a cinder fell on his bag. Made of, what is it... polyester? Anyhow, the whole thing caught on fire, him in it, and damn near set him afire too! Just saying. Best be careful.'

Those were the last words of the night: Be careful.

* * *

Sometime in the middle of the night Laura woke. Heavy rain drummed on the roof and pattered the windowpanes. For a moment she thought she woke up from the rain, but there was another sound: someone was muttering in the darkness.

Slowly, she sat up. By the sparse light of the dying embers Laura saw Earl seated in a chair beside the sleeping hikers. He was reading from a book in a foreign language. At first, Laura suspected she was dreaming, but then she saw the book: it was the soft leather volume with strange writing in it. Earl was reading it aloud, in guttural German.

'What are you doing?' said Laura.

Earl didn't notice her. He kept reading in German, his voice intensifying, filling the shack. His pockmarked face was different than before, focused and dispassionate; it looked as though a dark veil had fallen over it. Fear washed over Laura. He kept saying, 'Ein Opfer... Ein Opfer.'

A sacrifice.

Without thinking Laura got up and went for the door, but something stopped her.

Outside, three nude figures were running swiftly across the lawn in the rain. Two men and a woman, their pale skin gleaming. They looked like corpses. And they were coming towards the shack.

The breath caught in Laura's throat. She rushed over to Aaron and shook him. 'Guys wake up! Wake up!'

Her friends stirred and moaned. Aaron opened one eye. 'What now?'

'Get up! They're coming! Hurry!'

'Who's coming? What are you talking about?'

Aaron sat up and saw Earl reading from the book. Earl was now chanting a single phrase repeatedly: 'Wecke sie auf! Wecke sie auf!'

Awaken them! Awaken them!

'Earl?' said Aaron in a daze. The door burst open. The first of the dead things came in, and suddenly the room stank of rotting flesh. The dead man's eyes were empty. He reached for Laura, but she screeched and darted away, picking up a chair and throwing it through the window.

The dead woman came in next. She ran forward and clutched Steph's throat, lifting her up in the air and squeezing until Steph's eyes bulged, her legs kicking frantically. Steph's skin turned pale and her eyes clouded. There was a loud Crack! and she fell motionless to the floor.

The dead men were grabbing Dave and Aaron, still stuck in their sleeping bags. Aaron yelled and tried to fend off his attacker. The dead man snatched at his tongue, and Aaron watched helplessly as his tongue was ripped from his mouth, spraying blood on the shack's floor. Aaron shrieked and choked, drowning on his own blood, while the dead man went about systematically breaking his limbs.

Earl had stopped reading from the book and was now running across the room after Laura. Without thinking she jumped through the broken window, slicing her shoulder on a piece of glass. She hit the ground heavily and cried out in pain: one of her ribs cracked. Groaning, she got up and stumbled into a run towards the woods. Behind her were only screams and growls.

* * *

Sirens woke Jack Nightingale from a dreamless sleep as they did most mornings. New York might well be the city that never sleeps, but the emergency services carried the philosophy to the extreme. Fire engines, cop cars, ambulances, even though his room was on the fifteenth floor one or another would wake him several times a night. Nightingale wasn't a fan of New York City, but his benefactor Joshua Wainwright had insisted that he go there, though he'd yet to tell Nightingale why. The Texas billionaire and secretive Satanist used Nightingale as his eyes and ears and sometimes muscle but he had gone quiet not long after he'd told Nightingale to relocate to the Big Apple.

Nightingale rolled over and squinted at the display on the clock radio on his bedside table. It was just before eight. He got out of bed, shaved, showered and pulled on a suit and tie and went down to the street for his first cigarette of the day followed by breakfast. Smoking was prohibited pretty much everywhere in New York, but he could still smoke a cigarette as he strolled around the streets. Not that he didn't get hostile stares and mutterings from the health Nazis, especially the ones out for an early-morning jog.

He took his pack of Marlboro out and lit one with his battered Zippo, inhaled deeply and kept the smoke in his lungs for as long as he could before blowing a fairly decent smoke ring up at the sky. There was little wind and the ring travelled a good two feet before dissipating, giving him a warm feeling of satisfaction.

'Hey, mister, can you spare a cigarette?' It was a little girl's voice. Nightingale turned and his eyes widened when he saw the girl sitting cross-legged in a shop doorway, a black and white collie at her side. She could have been in her late teens or early twenties, white-faced with heavy mascara and a black t-shirt with a red pentagram on it, a black leather skirt and black boots and she had a studded collar around her neck. The dog wore a matching collar. Nightingale knew she was much older than she looked. Proserpine was a demon from Hell and was eternal. She smiled up at him. 'I'm gasping for a fag, mister,' she said in a very fair imitation of a Cockney accent.

'What do you want, Proserpine?' he asked. Normally he had to summon her, a process that she hated and which put him at risk. But she had the ability to appear before him whenever she wanted. And that was usually when she needed something from him.

'I told you twice, Nightingale,' she said, her voice deeper and more masculine this time.

He took out his cigarettes and tapped one out for her. She took it. He reached for his lighter but before he could get it out her cigarette began to burn. She took a long drag at it and blew out a thin plume of smoke that formed a perfect pentangle before dispersing. 'Rings are so passé, aren't they?' she laughed.

'Other than the cigarette, what do you want, Proserpine?'

The dog growled at him and Proserpine stroked it behind the ear. 'Easy, boy,' she said. 'It's just Nightingale's way.' She smiled up at Nightingale. 'He doesn't like it when people are disrespectful,' she said.

'I'm sorry about that.'

'He's ripped off people's heads for less.'

'I don't doubt it. So how can I help you, Princess of the Lower Realm.'

'See, you just made that up,' she said. 'But I like it.'

'My stomach is rumbling,' said Nightingale. 'I need to eat.'

'I could join you for breakfast,' she said. She nodded down the road. 'Have you tried the waffles in Eddie's? They're to die for.' She smiled. 'Not literally, obviously.'

'I'll give it a go,' he said.

'I'll join you.' She stood up and walked with him to the diner. The greeter, a blonde girl just out of High School – wrinkled her nose at the dog. 'You can't bring dogs in here,' she said.

'I don't have a dog,' said Proserpine, looking into the girl's eyes.

'Okay,' said the girl brightly, turning on her heel and leading them to a booth by the window. The dog went under the table and curled itself into a ball while Nightingale and Proserpine sat opposite each other. The girl gave them menus and walked away.

'That's a nice trick,' said Nightingale.

'People see what they want to see,' said Proserpine. 'It doesn't take much to make them see what I want them to see.'

'These aren't the droids you are looking for?'

Proserpine frowned. 'What?'

'The Jedi mind trick? Star Wars?' He smiled at the look of incomprehension on her face. 'Forget it.'

A middle-aged waitress with too much make-up handed them menus and poured coffee into white mugs. 'I know what I want,' said Proserpine. 'A waffle with chocolate ice cream and that cream you squirt from a can, and maple syrup and bacon.'

The waitress frowned. 'Are you sure about that, honey?'

'I'm sure.'

'It's your stomach, honey,' she said. She looked at Nightingale.

'Can I have a bacon sandwich?'

'That's not on the menu, honey.'

'Okay. Do you have a BLT?'

'Sure we do, honey. Best BLT in the city, so they say.'

'Terrific. I'll have a BLT, but hold the lettuce and hold the tomato. And don't toast the bread.'

'Coming right up,' she said, and hurried away with the menus.

Nightingale looked at Proserpine over the top of his mug as he sipped his coffee. She stared back at him with black, featureless eyes, and he could see his own reflection in them. 'So how can I help you?' he asked as he put his mug down on the table.

'I've got a job for you,' she said.

'I don't work for you.'

'Then I need a favour.'

'Favours are for friends, and we're not friends, Proserpine. You stole my soul, remember?'

'Your soul was given to me, and I gave it back to you. You should be grateful you're not burning in the fires of Hell as we speak.'

'I am. Very grateful. But you didn't give it back to me, remember. We negotiated a deal.'

'I'm not here to quibble, Nightingale. I need you to do something for me. You have to go to North Carolina. Some hikers were murdered at the hands of a Satanist and his little friends. I need you to put an end to it.'

'You're Proserpine, a Princess of Hell. Why don't you do it yourself?'

Proserpine ran her finger across the table; as she did she seemed to burn the wood, carving a smoking black line in the shape of a pentagram.

'The waitress isn't going to like that,' he said.

'She won't see it,' said Proserpine. 'To answer your question, Nightingale, I can't.' She tapped the pentagram. 'I'm a demon. I don't have the power to stop them. They're Wights.'

Nightingale shifted in his seat. 'Wights? You mean like in the Tolkien books? I thought that was an old German folk tale.'

'It is. But like you humans say, every story has an element of truth. The Wights are soulless. They don't possess self-awareness. Their only purpose is to serve the Satanist who summoned them, Earl Haverford. You must stop him. He has an old book of spells in his cabin. That's your key to killing the Wights.'

'And if I say no?' asked Nightingale.

'Don't play games with me, Nightingale. This is important. For me, and for your kind.'

'My kind?'

'Humans.'

Their food arrived. The waitress put Nightingale's sandwich down with a smile but tutted at Proserpine when she put the waffle, ice cream and bacon on the table.

As the waitress walked away, Proserpine leaned across the table. 'I need you to go to Bulger, North Carolina. There's a survivor called Laura – find her and she'll lead you to the book.'

'Then what?'

'You'll know when the time comes. But let's just say the Wights have an aversion to fire. The best way of killing them is to chop off their heads.'

'That pretty much works for anything, doesn't it?'

'You'd be surprised, Nightingale.'

'I have a question. Well, a few actually.'

Proserpine sighed. 'Just go to Bulger and stop Haverford.'

'Why me?'

'Because you've got the skills to do what has to be done.'

'Right, but why can't you just stop him yourself?'

'He has protection.'

'Protection?'

'He has sold his soul to a devil. That's where he gets his power from. So I cannot interfere.'

'But you are interfering.'

'Don't try my patience, Nightingale. I cannot interfere directly. But I can get you to do what is necessary.'

Nightingale nodded. 'So you're attacking another devil's minion, is that it? There's some sort of power play going on?'

'Enough questions, Nightingale,' she said. 'I don't have to justify myself to you.'

'But you'll owe me a favour, right? If I help you out on this.' Proserpine pointed a warning finger at him. The black glossy nail flickered with flame. Nightingale held up his hands in surrender. 'Okay. I'll do it.'

'I know you will,' she said.

There was a crash from the far side of the restaurant. A waitress had dropped a pile of plates and they had smashed into dozens of pieces. When Nightingale looked back across the booth, Proserpine and her dog had vanished and her plate had been licked clean.

He picked up his sandwich. 'Always a pleasure, Proserpine,' he muttered, before taking a bite.

* * *

Nightingale walked out of the Raleigh-Durham International Airport shaken and tense. The flight was overlong and there had been turbulence most of the way. Having left the terminal he spent three hours on a bus headed to a small town called Bulger, population 997, and checked into a cheap hotel outside of town. As he paced up and down the threadbare carpet listening to the dripping tap in the bathroom, he realized that other than a couple of names he had basically nothing to go on – he didn't know where to find Laura or Earl Haverford. He needed intel and he needed it quickly. He went on a stroll to the gas station and bought the local paper. Sure enough, a 'Laura Reynolds' was mentioned alongside the names of the deceased in what had become a murder mystery straight from the pages of a Dean Kootz or Stephen King novel - three hikers had been found dead in the woods a few miles outside of town, their limbs broken, tongues ripped out, skulls smashed. The bodies had large holes in the stomach area and were missing vital organs, presumably eaten. Traumatized survivor Ms Laura Reynolds claimed a local recluse called Earl Haverford committed the killings. Haverford was currently in police custody but would soon be released if evidence was not established. According to the article in the paper, Earl Haverford was going to be released in twenty-four hours. The paper had been printed that morning and it was now late afternoon, making it eighteen hours until Haverford's release. He had to find that book before Haverford was back on the streets.

Nightingale paid for the paper and a cup of coffee. He held up the paper for the clerk to see, showing a picture of Laura Reynolds. 'See this?' he asked.

The man behind the counter nodded. 'Sure. The Reynolds girl. I hear she killed all them kids, made it look like good old Mr Haverford did it.'

'Know where I can find her?'

The clerk shrugged. 'Heard she's in town at the motel with her gram. Her gram came up once she found out what happened. Don't suppose she'll be there very long.'

'And why's that?'

The clerk looked at him seriously. 'She killed all those kids. She's gonna get arrested, ain't she?'

Nightingale left, following the sidewalk into town. Huge trees shadowed the road, blocking out the summer sun. He smelled baked pine needles and hot dirt, and the fresh scent of a nearby stream. Birds sang in the forest around him as he walked.

He reached the town a half hour later, the woods opening up before him to reveal a wide clearing of green hills and small, stout buildings. It wasn't much of a town. He saw a post office, a bank, a grocery store, a fire station and a police station. There were a lot of houses, and as he walked on main street he noticed several pubs and churches of different denominations. He counted three pubs. Why would they have three pubs in a town with less than a thousand people?

It was late afternoon and people were just getting out of work and filling up the pub parking lots and buying groceries. Nightingale passed several of them and asked where he could find the motel Laura Reynolds was staying at. A few of them frowned at him, probably taking note of his foreign accent.

'Why do you want to know?' asked a middle-aged man wearing a black and red checked coat with a fur collar.

'I'm a journalist,' lied Nightingale.

Suddenly everybody wanted to talk to him.

'Oh, sure, I know where Laura's staying!' said a little old lady. 'You're a journalist? Why didn't you say so! My name is Madeleine Barker. You go ahead and write that down, dear, so's you don't forget. If you want my opinion, I'll tell you right now. That girl did it. No question. She killed her friends because she was good and jealous of that other girl. She was head over heels for that Carter boy, the way the Herald tells it.'

'Which boy?'

'The Carter boy. Aaron his name is – or was. Gosh I have got to remember he's passed on. Such a shame, it is. He and that Stephanie gal were seeing each other and Laura was good and jealous. Gosh, everybody knows it, dear. Where you been?'

'I'm from out of town,' said Nightingale. 'You think Laura murdered three of her friends because she was jealous? Doesn't add up to me.'

'Well, gosh, I wouldn't put it in such plain terms as that. But if you want my opinion, yes, dear. She sure did. It's only a matter of time 'til she's the one in prison, and not that kind Mr Haverford.'

'Mr Haverford, right. Who is he, Mrs Barker?'

She smiled wide and clutched his arm. 'Oh, call me Maddie, dear.'

'What's he like then, Maddie?'

'Why, Mr Haverford is a nice fella. It's a darn shame the horrible lies that little girl is spreading about him. Mr Haverford wouldn't hurt a fly. Honest. He's a noble breed; his granddaddy was one of the founders of this town, mind you. All he does is stay in his camp and pay no mind to anything else. He's got some crops he tends, and he goes on walks, and if anybody around town needs a fixer, he's our man.'

'His grandfather was one of the town founders?'

'Oh sure. Elton Haverford Sr, he was. A fine man. We used to play on his farm when we was kids.'

'And why do you think Laura's making all this up?'

The old woman scowled, clutching Nightingale's arm tighter and pulling him close. She whispered, 'It ain't no rumor she's been smoking the Devil's lettuce.'

Nightingale frowned. 'The Devil's lettuce?'

Maddie eyed him seriously. 'Smoking drugs, she was. And that's the God's honest truth. I wouldn't lie.'

Nightingale had to work hard to keep from laughing.

'Where can I find her, Maddie?'

'Who? Laura?'

'Yeah.'

'What do you want with her? I told you, she's guilty as sin!'

'Oh sure, that's what I want to speak with her about.' Nightingale smiled a crooked smile. 'I am a reporter, after all.'

Maddie smiled wide and told him where he could find Laura, but not without first making him write down her address so he could drop in for a cup of tea. She touched his arm tenderly. 'And maybe something a little stronger.' Maddie winked.

* * *

Laura was staying in a nondescript motel with her grandmother in the center of town, across the street from the post office. Nightingale got her room number from the front desk and knocked on the door. A few minutes later an old woman answered it. She was wearing a flower-embroidered dress and her hair was long and gray. 'May I help you?' she said. She seemed distracted.

'Yes. I'm looking for Laura. My name's Nightingale. Jack Nightingale.'

'I'm sorry, we're through with reporters.' She went to close the door.

'But I'm a private investigator.'

The door cracked open again. 'Really?'

Nightingale nodded.

'From England? What are you doing here?'

'I'm here to solve the case for a... client.'

'What's your client's name?'

'She's, uh... she's very private...'

'Okay. Well, does your client think my granddaughter is just another crackpot or does she believe her story?'

'She believes Laura's story. We're on the same side here, I assure you. We just want to find out who, or what, did those awful things to her friends.'

The old woman seemed to be thinking to herself a minute. Finally she opened the door and let him in. She seemed upset about something. 'You'll have to excuse us. Laura thinks she's going on a trip. You can find her down the hall on the left. Tea?'

'Yes, please.'

Mrs Reynolds nodded with pursed lips and went to a small coffeemaker on the dresser. Nightingale sensed a disagreement. He went down a short hall and stopped at the open door to the bathroom, where a young woman with brown hair was stuffing toiletries into a bag. She was small, and very pretty. She had moles on her face and arms, and she was wearing a black rock band T-shirt and dark jeans. She had headphones on and Nightingale could hear music pouring from them. She looked angry about something.

'Laura,' Nightingale said loudly.

Laura jumped backwards and ripped off her headphones. 'Who are you? What are you doing here?'

'My name's Jack Nightingale. I'm a private detective. Your grandmother let me in.'

She put her head on one side as she stared at him. 'You're British? Or English?'

'Both.'

'So it's the same?'

'The same?' he repeated.

'British and English. It's the same?'

'No, not really. You can be both, but Scots and Welsh are also British. And some of the Irish.'

'The Irish are English?'

'No. But the Irish in the north of Ireland are British.'

'It sounds complicated.'

'It is,' agreed Nightingale.

'And what are you doing here?'

'I look into paranormal disturbances.'

Laura shuddered. 'Then you've come to the right place.'

'I'm glad to hear that – I think.'

Nightingale saw a padded spot on her shoulder where there was probably a bandage, and he noticed the way she hunched a little, as though the wind was knocked out of her. He gestured to the bag. 'Going somewhere?'

'Yeah. Away.'

'Your grandmother doesn't seem too thrilled about that.'

'She's not, but it's not her choice, it's mine.'

'Actually, it might be the choice of the district court. I'm betting the police asked you to stick around for a while. Right?'

'So?'

'I'm just saying, it wouldn't be wise to run now. You'll look guilty. People in this town already think you're guilty.'

'Screw them. This whole town is certifiably insane, and I'm getting out of it.'

'Agreed. But you still need to stick around, at least until a suspect is finalized. Trust me, I know all about it, which is why I'm here.' Laura looked at him. 'You said Earl Haverford killed your friends?'

'No, I said Earl Haverford summoned some creatures that killed my friends.'

'And how did he do that, exactly?'

'He read some German stuff from a book he had. Why are you here?'

'I want to catch the killers.'

Laura leaned against the wall and had a good laugh. It was a mocking sort of laugh, and Nightingale didn't like it. 'You're going to catch the killers? Do you realize how ridiculous that sounds? Look, Mr Nightingale, you can't catch the killers because they're monsters. They're strong enough to lift a grown woman four feet off the ground and snap her neck like a twig. They're strong enough to break every bone in your body with their bare hands. How are you going to catch them? And if you do catch them, what then?'

'How did you get away, Laura?'

'I ran. While they were killing my friends, I ran.'

Nightingale nodded. 'You did the right thing.'

'By being a coward, you mean?'

'If you'd stayed you would have died and then no one would have known what happened.'

'Except no one believes me,' she said. 'By the time I'd reached the town and called the cops and we'd gone back, the monsters had gone. Then Haverford turned up and denied he'd been there all night. Said I was there with my friends and that I must have killed them. They didn't believe him so they took him in for questioning but now I hear they're going to release him and maybe arrest me.' A few tears ran down her cheek and she brushed them away.

Nightingale took a tentative step forward. He wanted to reach out, but he didn't. 'Laura, if you run now you'll be running all your life. Trust me on this. You can't run from evil, it finds a way; you've got to stomp it out whenever it comes up. Listen, you don't have to do this, but I do. All I'm asking for is your help. I just need to know a few things, that's all. Then go or stay, it's up to you, but I strongly suggest you stay.'

Laura sniffed, wiped her eyes, then dabbed at them with a corner of her shirt. She looked up at Nightingale. 'You know what I want?' she said.

Nightingale shook his head. 'No. What do you want?'

Laura gritted her teeth and glared at him. Nightingale stepped back, suddenly aware that this was someone who shouldn't be underestimated.

'I want to kill him,' she said. 'The bastard that killed my friends, I want him dead.'

* * *

They drove Laura's grandmother's car to the police station. Mrs Reynolds seemed happy that Nightingale had convinced her granddaughter to stay on in Bulger. If she knew the real reason, thought Nightingale, she'd probably have a heart attack. In the car Laura recounted the full story of what happened when she was out hiking. Nightingale listened without comment. 'So what do you think they were?' she asked him when she had finished. 'Those things that attacked us?'

'Wights,' said Nightingale. 'Ever heard of them?'

Laura shook her head. Nightingale continued. 'Wights, from Old High German 'Wiht,' meaning, "an incorporeal undead being that drains the essence of living beings to stay alive," to quote the Internet. Wights are usually controlled by a higher power such as a necromancer. In this case, Earl Haverford.'

Laura sat back in her seat, staring at him. 'That's not good, is it?' she asked.

'Tell me about it. That old book you read probably was a journal of sorts. But it was also a book of spells, chief among them the conjuring spell, or something like it. I've never dealt with this kind of thing before but I've dealt with something similar. What I'm wondering is, why? Why would Haverford summon these things to kill a couple of hikers on his own land? There's no better way to draw attention to yourself.'

'He probably didn't think anyone would live to tell the tale,' she said.

'How much do you know about him?'

'Only what I heard after I got to town. He's like a local hero. Seems like the whole town loves him. You're loved like that, you're above the law.'

'Yeah, why is this guy so popular, anyway?' asked Nightingale. 'He sounds like a pretty weird recluse. Usually townspeople make fun of someone like that.'

'Apparently his grandfather built this town. I did some digging online. Pretty much everything in Bulger belonged to the Haverfords at one time or another, until they sold it off to the people here. It was a big deal. They sold houses, land, stores, the banks, all for a very good price, too. Now the townspeople own everything and they're self-sufficient. The economy isn't great, but it pretty much stays the same and everybody has a job. The Haverfords did that, so now everyone thinks they're holy or something.'

'I wonder why the Haverfords did that? Out of the goodness of their hearts?'

'Why do most people make nice gestures? To look good. Plus, people with that much money can afford it.'

Nightingale nodded. 'Maybe,' he said. He pulled into the police station and parked. 'You stay here while I go in for a chat,' he said.

'Don't tell them I'm here,' she said. 'I'm sure they're going to arrest me.'

'I think if they were going to arrest you they'd have done it already,' said Nightingale. He went inside and gave his name at the front desk and asked for the detective in charge of the hiker killings. He had to wait five minutes before the detective appeared – a tall black man with a shaved head. He nodded briskly at Nightingale. 'Detective Rice. You looking for me?'

'Yes, I have a few questions about the Reynolds case. The name's Jack Nightingale.'

Rice raised his eyebrows. 'You a journalist?'

'No. I used to be a cop, back in England. Now I'm just an interested party. But I might have some insight that could help the case. '

Rice seemed unconvinced. 'Do you now? You're not one of those psychics, are you? They always come out of the woodwork in a case like this.'

'No, I'm not psychic. But I might be able to give you some guidance. If you want it.'

'The way things are going I'll take any help that's offered,' said the detective. Come on through.' Detective Rice led Nightingale to his office and offered him coffee. Nightingale declined. 'So what sort of special insight do you have for me, Mr Nightingale?'

'Well, the man you're going to release tomorrow is guilty, for starters.'

'Guilty? I don't think so. And I'm not releasing him tomorrow, I'm releasing him today.'

'Today?' said Nightingale. 'Why?'

'Because we've found no evidence that Mr Haverford had anything whatsoever to do with the murders. I don't know how they do things in England but here in the US we can't hold an innocent man.'

'You have sworn testimony from a witness placing him at the crime scene.'

'So?'

'So you're letting a guilty man walk free.'

'And what do you have in the way of evidence?'

'He was there when it happened. He was the only one who wasn't attacked.'

'So you admit he wasn't the attacker?' The detective leaned back in his chair. 'Look, I don't know who you are or where you come from, but this is my case, and I sure as hell won't risk a lawsuit. We have twenty-four hours to hold Haverford without evidence and after that it's time's up; he's got to go.'

Nightingale was exasperated. 'But you're letting him leave before the time is up. At least keep him behind bars for the full twenty-four hours.'

'Listen, Mr Nightingale. Haverford's family is a respectable one. They've done a lot for this town. There probably wouldn't be a town if not for him and his family.'

'What if he's guilty?'

'He's not guilty. But if he is there must be some evidence out there to prove it. In which case we'll bring him back here and have him tried. But as things stand...' He shrugged and didn't finish the sentence,

Nightingale shook his head. 'You interviewed Laura Reynolds?'

'We did, yes.'

'And what did you think about what she had to say?'

Rice frowned at him. 'About a mysterious book and corpses running around? Mr Nightingale, please. Those are fantasies brought on by shock. She saw something, sure, but not that. She's suffering from post-traumatic stress. Nothing more.'

'She says Haverford was there, in the cabin.'

'And Mr Haverford denies it. He said, she said.'

'So is she now a suspect?'

Rice shook his head. 'You haven't been to the crime scene, have you?'

Nightingale shook his head.

Rice opened a blue file with a police crest on the front and passed over half a dozen photographs. Nightingale grimaced. The bodies had been torn apart and savaged. Bites had been taken out of arms and legs and throats ripped open. 'It looks like wild animals have done this,' said Nightingale.

'The bite marks are human,' said Rice. 'And there are plenty of bloody footprints.'

Nightingale looked at the photographs again. The detective was right. There were footprints everywhere where the killers had trampled over the blood.

'There were three killers, clearly,' said Rice. 'And they'd have to be a lot stronger than Laura Reynolds to do that sort of damage.'

'Could Earl Haverford have been one of the killers?'

'There was no blood on his clothing. So, no.'

'Then why have you been holding him?'

'Because the two stories don't match up. Laura says Earl was there, Earl says he wasn't. One of them has to be lying.'

'And now you think it's Laura who isn't telling the truth. But why would she lie?'

'Like I said, post-traumatic stress. Maybe she's just confused. Anyway, we've dusted for prints and checked for DNA. All the blood and tissue we found is from the victims but there were several prints around the cabin that didn't belong to Haverford or the victims so we're having them checked now. Haverford says that he does have guests at the cabin from time to time so I'm not sure how useful the prints will be.' The phone on the detective's desk started ringing. He picked it up. 'Rice,' he said.

Nightingale stood up and began pacing the office, wondering what to do next. He had hoped to find proof of Haverford's involvement before he was released. Now Haverford was bound to run... or worse. Would he go after Laura, the only witness?

'Is that a joke?' said the detective into the phone. Nightingale's attention perked up. He sat back down and leaned forward, listening. 'That's not possible, Tom. Run them again... So? Run them again then, dammit! Well I don't care how many times you checked, that's simply not possible.' Detective Rice took a deep breath and massaged his temples. 'But it just doesn't make any goddamn sense, Tom. How do you explain it? No? Well I can't either. Where are the bodies now? Fine, Tom. Thanks.' He put the phone down, frowning.

'What is it?' said Nightingale. 'What's happened?'

Detective Rice shook his head. 'It can't be... there has to be some mistake.'

'What mistake?' demanded Nightingale.

'The prints in the cabin. They're from three different people. Drug dealers.'

'Okay, so it's a drug-related killing. Maybe the kids stumbled on some sort of drug operation out in the wilderness.'

Rice shook his head. 'These guys were active in the Sixties, then they went missing. If it was them, they'd be in their nineties now.' He gestured at the photographs. 'I don't see old timers doing that now, do you?'

The phone rang again and Rice answered it. He frowned as he listened to what was being said. 'I'll be right there,' he said. He put the phone down. 'I've got to go,' he said. 'There's a problem down at the mortuary.'

'What sort of problem?'

'Haverford's not guilty. I'm releasing him.'

Rice stood up and headed for the door without answering Nightingale's question. He stopped at the secretary's desk and told her to have an officer release Earl Haverford right away. Nightingale followed him out of the station, confused. Rice got into the passenger seat of a police cruiser and Nightingale rushed over to Laura's car. 'What's happening?' she asked.

He pointed after the cruiser pulling away from the kerb. 'Follow that car,' he said.

'Are you serious?'

'Just do it!'

'Okay, okay,' said Laura. She started the engine and gave chase. The cruiser wasn't using its lights or sirens and traffic was light so she was easily able to keep it in sight. 'They're going to the mortuary,' said Nightingale.

'Why?'

'I don't know, but something has happened.'

It was just a ten-minute drive to the mortuary, a sprawling three-story colonial with green siding. The sky was darkening as they arrived, and there were thick clouds overhead. There was a parking lot to the side and Laura pulled up next to the cruiser. Rice was on the radio and his jaw dropped when he saw Nightingale get out of the car. Rice climbed out. 'Who invited you?' asked the detective. He caught sight of Laura in the driving seat. 'And what's she doing here?'

A uniformed cop got out of the driver's seat, his hand on his gun. 'It's all right Officer Howzer,' said Rice. He gestured at Nightingale. 'Mr Nightingale says he knows what's going on, which is more than I do.'

Officer Howzer was a short bulky man with a blonde mustache. His uniform seemed one size too small for him. He nodded and took his hand off his gun.

'What's happening?' asked Nightingale.

'There's been a death in the mortuary. No details yet.'

Laura got out of the car. 'Is this where they took my friends?'

'Your friends?' said Rice. 'Yes. This is where they check for cause of death and store bodies while investigations are on-going.'

'Detective Rice, there's something you need to know,' said Nightingale.

'Spit it out, then,' said Rice.

Nightingale took a deep breath, then explained about the book and the Wights. He also mentioned something he had forgotten until that moment: as legend had it, when a man was killed by a Wight he would come back as one himself, sometimes immediately, sometimes after a few hours or even days.

Laura looked at him in amazement. 'You think my friends have come back to life?'

'Not back to life, no. They're undead.'

'You've got to be fucking kidding me,' said Rice. 'Like a fucking zombie? Is that what this is? The walking fucking dead? That's a joke, right? Some sick attempt at humour?'

'I'm not joking,' said Nightingale. 'You don't believe me, fine. You'll know soon enough.'

Howzer and Rice exchanged worried glances. Rice cursed under his breath, then turned back to Nightingale. 'Now listen, I'm not saying I believe you or that I agree with you, but for argument's sake let's just say you are right. How do we kill the damn things if they're already dead?'

'Fire. Or you can chop off their heads. But shooting them won't do any good. Because they're dead already.'

'Bullshit,' sneered Howzer.

That was when they heard screams from inside the building.

'Go, go, go!' said Rice. They ran into the building. Rice and Howzer unholstered their guns. Nightingale found an emergency axe in a glass case. He took off his coat, wrapped it around his fist and punched the glass. Then he grabbed the axe. 'You should wait outside,' he told Laura.

'No,' she said. 'I'm coming with you.'

The screams were louder now, from the other side of the building. Rice flicked his head in that direction and Howzer, trembling, went to find the source. Nightingale followed Rice silently, gripping his axe until his knuckles were blanched white.

Rounding the corner they saw a naked man with Y-stitching across his torso. His skin was so pale it seemed translucent, purple veins encircling his flesh. His eyes were cloudy and lifeless and he had deep gouges all over his body as if he'd been eaten.

Laura screamed. 'That's Dave!' she shouted.

'Your friend?' asked Nightingale.

Laura nodded fearfully.

Dave was bent over a woman and punching her in the chest. She was unconscious, but she grunted each time he hit her. Then he opened his mouth, preparing to bite her.

'Hey!' hollered Rice, raising his gun. The Wight stopped, stared at Rice, and started running towards him. Rice fired four rounds into the Wight's head, neck and shoulders, but the Wight was unfazed. Rice fired two more rounds before the Wight grabbed his head with both hands and raised him in the air, preparing to snap his neck. Nightingale's axe came soaring in the air and lodged in the back of the creature's neck. It paused for a moment and Rice fell gasping to the ground. Nightingale pressed his shoulder against the Wight's back, heaved against it and wrenched the axe free. Before it could turn around Nightingale swung the blade like a baseball bat and cut deeper into the neck. The Wight groaned. Nightingale pulled it out and swung again, this time cutting through the tendons and bone and severing the head. The body fell on the ground, twitched for a few moments, and went still.

'Holy shit,' said Rice. 'They're real.'

'I told you!' said Laura.

'You better believe it,' said Nightingale. 'Remember, you can't kill them by shooting them. Burn them or cut off their heads. Your guns are useless. Where's your backup?'

'They'll be here any minute.'

'All right. Let's find Howzer and regroup.'

Nightingale knelt to check the mortician's assistant. She was still unconscious and appeared to have a concussion. A quick glance at her bruised stomach revealed several broken ribs.

Rice was gasping. 'Is she ok?'

'She'll hurt for a while, but she'll be fine.' Nightingale eyed a broom closet a few paces down the hall. With Rice's help, he took the woman under her arms and dragged her to it. They opened the closet and set her in. 'She'll be safe for now.'

Several gunshots rang out in the hall. Howzer was screaming.

'Howzer!' Rice called. 'Hold on!'

They ran down the hall towards the mortician's room. They found Howzer on the ground, his body twisted at an impossible angle. His skull had been caved in. Rice swore aloud. 'My God,' he said. 'They got him! They fucking got him!'

Something was scraping in the next room. Nightingale opened the door and peered in at a few stainless steel dissecting tables, bloody rags and several knives laid neatly out – scalpels, fishhook-shaped rib knives, thin organ knives, a bone saw and two large cleavers. There was another room leading off from the dissecting area where something was chewing and slurping behind the swing door. Nightingale held up a finger, picked up the two cleavers and handed them to Laura and Rice. Then he motioned forwards and they crept silently to the plastic swing door at the end of the hall, holding their weapons high. Police sirens screeched outside, and blue and red lights flashed intermittently in the room behind them. 'They're here,' whispered Rice.

'No shit,' whispered Nightingale. 'How many?'

'Eight men, maybe. Four cars, two from my precinct and two from Salsbury... I hope.'

'I hope that's enough,' said Nightingale. 'You need to warn them that their guns will be useless.'

Just as Rice reached for his radio, they heard a loud grunt from the next room. Then something began sniffing roughly. Nightingale kicked open the door. Stephanie, nude, was bent over the mortician, his throat ripped out, and sniffing the air. Her pale dead face remained impassive as she growled, hopped to her feet, and charged them. Nightingale went to hit her with the axe but she was quick – much quicker than he'd anticipated – and she head-butted him in the stomach, knocking the wind out of him. The axe clanged to the floor.

Laura and Rice began hacking at her with their cleavers but she showed no sign of pain. She simply turned, grabbed Rice's hand as he swung, and snapped his wrist. He cried out and dropped his cleaver. Laura struck Stephanie's head, getting the cleaver stuck as Stephanie shook her head violently and sank her teeth in Laura's shoulder. Laura howled and flew back against the wall, trying to fight Stephanie off.

Nightingale stood up and chopped Stephanie's leg at the knee with the axe, sending her tottering to one side. He brought the axe down on her neck again and again until her head came off. He was breathless and covered in blood. 'You okay?' he asked, nodding at Laura's wound. She was pressing it with her hand.

'Yeah, I think so...' Her face suddenly turned pale. 'Wait, will I turn into one of those things?'

'No,' he said. 'Their bites aren't infectious, they only reanimate after they've been killed.' Rice was wheezing on the ground, his wrist bent. 'And you, detective? Are you okay?'

'I'll be fine,' said Rice. 'I just have to learn how to swing a cleaver with my left—' A barrage of gunshots filled the mortuary. The police had burst in. 'Wait a second,' he said. 'They don't know, I didn't warn them!'

'Shit,' said Nightingale. 'Call them. Now.'

As Rice reached for his radio, Nightingale bounded down the corridor, ripped open the door and stepped into the hallway. Gunshots echoed down the hall. Someone was screaming. Then there was a loud crunch and the screaming stopped. Rapid footsteps thumped on the floor above him like children rushing from room to room playing tag. He heard hissing up there, then more gunshots followed by screams. Nightingale slipped, only managing to stay up by pressing the axe handle on the floor like a cane. He looked down and realised the floor was covered in blood.

Rounding a corner, Nightingale glimpsed the woman he'd saved earlier, but she was no longer a woman. She was bent over a police officer, her face covered in blood, gnawing at the man's open stomach. Chewing on something wet, she looked slowly up at Nightingale, bared her teeth and lunged at him. Nightingale slammed the axe onto her head and it got stuck. She crashed forward, flailing, the axe embedded in her skull. Nightingale pulled it out with a sickly sucking sound and cut off her head with two violent blows. He stood there breathless, wiping the blood from his face. He didn't notice the dead officer rising silently behind him until he sank his teeth into Nightingale's shoulder. Nightingale hit the Wight's head with the axe until it let go. Then he wheeled around and kicked it in the chest. An arm reached out and he chopped at it.

There was movement behind him. In the corner of his eye he saw two more Wights running full speed towards him, their jaws snapping like sharks. He cursed and ducked around the Wight in front of him and ran, finding a door leading upstairs. He took the stairs three at a time, hearing the door rip open behind him.

At the top of the stairs he came face to face with Aaron, tall, nude and pale, huge chunks missing from his body. Aaron's mouth was a mess of blood and gore, and Nightingale glimpsed two police officers down with their brain matter peppering the floor. Aaron hissed at him and reached out, his fingers curved into talons.

Nightingale turned a corner and ran down a hall with official portraits covering the walls. He stopped briefly at a room where another police officer was slowly rising to his feet in spite of a gaping wound on his neck. Nightingale kept running. Several Wights were chasing him now. He wheeled around a corner, saw a tiled bathroom and crashed into it, falling over a claw foot tub. He got to his feet and hit the first Wight over the head with the axe, then kicked them out. He slammed the door and locked it. The door shook. They were ramming it. He clutched the axe to his chest and scanned the room. No exits. It was a dead end. There was a window leading outside but he was two stories up. He opened the window and looked out, hoping to see a fire escape, but there wasn't one. To the left was a drainpipe. He grabbed at it. It was metal, so hopefully it would bear his weight.

As he tucked his axe into his belt, the door began to splinter inwards.

***

Rice took his radio away from his mouth. He'd told the back-up not to bother using their guns but their had been no response. Through the walls they could hear screams and furniture smashing. It was total chaos. Grown men were wailing like grief-stricken widows. Wights were growling. Someone in the next room was weeping. A man. They listened to him for a few moments but then a door burst open and the man began to scream. 'No! Wait! Wait! N—!'

'What do we do?' asked Laura.

'I don't know,' said the detective. 'Maybe we stay here. Wait for help.'

'What if help doesn't come?'

Something grabbed Rice's leg and he flinched. The mortician sat straight up, his face blue, his jaw hanging loose. His black hair was matted with blood. The mortician hissed at Rice. Rice grabbed the cleaver with his left hand and chopped off the mortician's arm with two savage blows

He raised his cleaver again but then a voice shouted 'Stop!'

Rice turned to look at the doorway. Earl Haverford was standing there holding a large book. He pointed at Rice. 'Leave my property alone!' he shouted.

Rice stared at him in amazement. The mortician seized his chance and leapt forward, biting at Rice's throat and ripping it open. Blood spurted and

Laura screamed. She rushed to help the detective, slashing at the Wight with her cleaver but two powerful hands grabbed her and picked her up. It was the female Wight that had killed her friends out in the cabin. The other two stood motionless behind Haverford. Laura struggled for a moment but Haverford backhanded her hard across the face and the cleaver fell from her hand.

Haverford's face darkened. 'You dumb bitch,' he said. 'You ruined everything. I don't know how I'm going to clean up this mess, but a sacrifice ought to help.' He nodded at the Wights. 'Come on. Bring her to the cellar.'

***

Nightingale slowly inched his way onto the sloped roof in the dark, his Hush Puppies barely gripping the asphalt shingles. Moving right, he slipped, but he regained his footing by clutching the side again. Mineral granules dislodged from the asphalt and went rolling down the rooftop, dropping thirty feet to the ground below.

While the Wights surged into the bathroom, growling and hissing, Nightingale slowly crawled up the roof, clutching the side with his left hand and keeping his right palm flat against the shingles for balance. He slipped a few times but he was able to stay on, thanks to his left hand holding most of his weight. In a few moments he reached the top. There were two chimneys. One had a plume of fresh smoke pouring from it. There was an incinerator, he thought. Down in the cellar.

He could see the lights of the town a few miles away. The moon reflected off the windshields of four police cars down below. On the other side of the roof there was a maple tree with big bushy branches, one of which came close to the roof. He walked across and inspected the branch. Deciding it was sturdy enough, he took two deep breaths and jumped, grabbing it. The limb bowed twenty feet in an arc, then snapped in half. Nightingale fell the remaining ten feet and hit the ground hard. The wind was knocked out of him but as he got to his feet he realised he had been lucky and hadn't broken any bones. Nor had he impaled himself with the axe in his belt.

He couldn't hear anything from the house, aside from muffled thumps as the Wights hurried from room to room, searching for prey. He knew Laura and Rice were still in there. He hoped they were still alive.

There was a window at the back of the house leading into what looked like a kitchen. Nightingale smashed it and climbed inside, ducking into the pantry. Two Wights immediately raced into the room. The tops of their heads were missing and their brains were exposed, but they didn't seem to notice. Nightingale watched them from behind the pantry's shuttered door and held up his axe, ready to strike. The creatures moved about aimlessly, first looking out the window and then picking up cracker tins and pots on the stove and knocking them to the ground for no apparent reason. They stopped and listened. Then one of them picked up a glass decanter and smashed it on the cupboards. Again they stopped and waited. It was as if they were trying to scare Nightingale out into the open.

As quietly as he could, Nightingale felt around the pantry shelves, running his fingers over jars of preserves and packets of instant rice. He touched plastic bottles of cleaner and dish soap. Then he found what he was looking for. A can of WD40. He was pretty sure it was flammable. Not a hundred per cent sure, admittedly, but it was better than nothing.

Snorting like a pig, one of the Wights lumbered towards the pantry. It pressed its face against the slats of the door, making a dark shadow on Nightingale's chest, and began to sniff. Nightingale gripped the axe tightly. A tongue came out and began licking the inside of the slats, then the Wight growled and seized the door handle. Nightingale stepped back and smashed the axe through the door, into the creature's head. He struck it twice more, pushing through the door and taking off down the hall just as the other Wight caught on.

Nightingale heard them running behind him. He took out the can of WD40 he'd found in the pantry, fished in his pocket for his lighter and whirled around. As the Wights reached him, he held the lighter flame over the nozzle, and sprayed. A cloud of fire engulfed them; they went up in flames. For a few moments they screeched like banshees and hurled themselves against the walls, then they shrank down and stopped moving, still burning. Footsteps bounded down the stairs. Nightingale trained the bottle on another Wight and set it on fire. Then he heard it: a loud voice in the cellar was chanting in German. It could only be Haverford.

Nightingale found a door leading to the cellar. A Wight lurched for him just as he opened it. He extinguished the last of the WD40 on the Wight, setting it on fire and kicking it down the stairs, where it tumbled and fell to the bottom, twitching. The chanting stopped. Nightingale unsheathed the axe from his belt and hurried down the stairs. Laura was tied to a post. Her mouth had been gagged. Earl Haverford stood next to her, holding an old book in one hand and gripping a long curved knife in the other. Three nude Wights stood beside him. 'Kill him,' ordered Haverford, and continued reading aloud from the book.

Nightingale spied the live incinerator against the wall behind Laura and Haverford. Wights were coming down the stairs behind him. Three were advancing from the front. He waited until the last moment, and jumped, soaring over the three Wights and landing heavily on the concrete floor. Haverford's jaw dropped in surprise and he turned and ran. Nightingale embedded the axe in Haverford's back and the man screamed in agony. Nightingale let go of the axe, wrenched the book from Haverford's hand, opened the incinerator door and threw it into the open flames.

All at once the Wights in the cellar caught on fire. They ran wildly around, banging into the walls and into each other. Nightingale could hear more of them howling and smashing into the walls upstairs, but after a minute or so all was quiet. The ones in the cellar were on the ground, their fat sizzling and sputtering in the silence of the night.

Nightingale removed the gag from Laura's mouth and untied her. Haverford groaned on the ground, a pool of blood forming around him.

'How did you know that would work?' asked Laura.

'I didn't.'

'You were lucky.'

'Yeah, sometimes I am,' said Nightingale.

***

Twenty-four hours later Nightingale was on the train back to New York. His wounds were superficial – some scratches and a few bruised ribs, a mild concussion – and he didn't want to hang around for the investigation into what had happened in Bulger. An hour outside the Big Apple, his cellphone rang. It was Joshua Wainwright. 'Where are you?'

His tone suggested that he already knew.

'I'm on a train,' said Nightingale.

'Going where?'

'Back to New York.'

'From where?'

Nightingale swallowed. He knew there was no point in lying to Wainwright. 'Bulger.'

'I thought that was you. What the hell were you doing there?'

'Doing the Wight thing, I guess.'

'Is that supposed to be funny? English humour?'

'Just trying to lighten the moment. Anyway, it's all done now.'

'To be honest with you, you did me a favour. Earl Haverford has been a pain in my butt for more years than I care to remember. One of those Satanists who give us all a bad name. We're better of without him.'

'So all's well that ends well?'

'Just get back to New York. I've a job for you.'

'I'm on my way.'

Wainwright ended the call. Nightingale put his phone back in his pocket and looked out of the window. When he looked back, Proserpine was sitting next to him. He flinched. 'Would you not sneak up on me like that?' he said.

Her dog was at her feet, ears pricked. She patted it on the neck. 'My, you're jumpy,' she said.

'After what I've been through, it's hardly surprising.'

'That's why I popped by. To thank you.'

'A demon from Hell saying thank you, that has to be a first.'

'I needed that taken care of and you came through. So yes, it's only right that I should acknowledge what you did.'

'So you owe me one, right? A quid pro quo.'

Her jet black eyes hardened. 'I owe you nothing, Nightingale.'

There was a flash of lightning outside and Nightingale looked through the window as a peal of thunder made the window rattle. When he looked back at the seat next to him, Proserpine had gone. Nightingale smiled to himself. Despite what she had said, he knew that she owed him a favour, and at some point he would claim it.

20920253R00205

Printed in Great Britain
by Amazon